A Game

By Mark Milne

Acknowledgements

The people who have read this book over the years and given me their advice and comments are at the top of my list. I stand ready to read your own works, so please, keep writing! I must give a very special thanks to my dear friend Patrick Spurling, musical genius, who wrote for me a wonderful text for the musical chapter which I then adapted. Pat's Bar. Thanks, my friend. The philosophical works of the late Richard Rorty, and especially of Peter Kingsley, have been invaluable for me and for this book. Is anybody reading? Well, thanks to you, too.

For Sebastian, Sophia, Emma and Arista

"Attend to yourself: turn your attention away from everything that surrounds you and toward your inner life – this is the first demand that philosophy makes of its disciple."

- Johann Gottlieb Fichte (1762 – 1814)

"...contemporary study of the Presocratics has reached a crisis point. The crisis revolves around two words: authority, and tradition. On the one hand, post-'Enlightenment' scholarship over the past two centuries has persistently viewed the history of early Greek philosophy as a progressive evolution towards some extremely vague, but numinously seductive, ideal of rationality; and in doing so it has almost unquestioningly decided to embrace Aristotle's arrogant assessment of Presocratic philosophy as no more than a stammering attempt to say what only he, at last, was able to articulate with any fluency. . . On the other hand, since the publication of Cherniss's work on Aristotle and the Presocratics in 1935 there has been a deeper awareness not only of the fact that Aristotle and his school were frequently capable of misinterpreting the Presocratics at a very fundamental level, but also of the fact that he and his followers systematically used deliberate misunderstanding and 'shameless' misrepresentation as a way of silencing their predecessors."

- Peter Kingsley, *Ancient Philosophy, Mystery, and Magic – Empedocles and Pythagorean Tradition*

1

The morning sun shone across the bay through the twenty story window into the interviewer's spacious office, creeping over the unused oval meeting table in the corner, across the dull grey carpet and across the tips of Richard Peel's shoes. The interviewer, Mr. Kinkaid – call me Jim – stood next to his desk gazing through the massive wall of glass covering most of the east wall of his office at the view of the bay and the city in the foreground as he paused in mid-sentence, rubbing his chin thoughtfully. He still hadn't said anything about the job, whatever it was. Strange. Upon entering the office, Richard was initially put on the defensive as the man had announced "So, you studied philosophy." It hadn't been put as a question. Richard hadn't been meant to clarify the point. He wasn't being asked to confirm this fact, which could have simply been the beginning of a review of his qualifications. It was just left to hang there, like bait thrown in the water. In any case, he had been conditioned to respond to such statements as though they were challenges. He had been about to simply fess up to it. To admit it with a simple "Yes," when the man jumped in again. "That's great."

Richard hadn't had a clue what to say. Then the man repeated himself. "That's great. I studied marketing. Never took a philosophy course. Wanted to, but..."

And there they were. Richard seated before the desk, Jim staring out the window over the bay. Richard watched the man for a moment, silently willing him to find his way and continue. When it was clear that he would not, he joined him in considering the view from way up there. Watching the cars heading east over the Bay Bridge from the City he realized how badly he wanted to make this man his ally in his search for work. That realization brought the story to mind of the young man who traveled from a distant place to find the Zen master, announcing to him as he finally approached that he had come to learn the meaning of life. 'Is that so?' the Master asked him. 'Yes,' he replied. No sooner had he spoken than the Master had grasped him about the neck and with great strength brought him over to the water trough, forcing his head into the water and holding him there while the man struggled madly. After a few moments the Master released him. When the young man had finished coughing and shaking the water from his long black hair, the Master asked, 'Tell me, what was it that you wanted more than anything just now?' The man stared at him with wide eyes, barely able to stifle his urge to knock the Master a good blow. 'I - I wanted air, of course.' The Zen master nodded, and turned to leave. 'When the meaning of life is what you seek even when drowning, then you will be ready.'

Richard frowned. It wasn't a fair comparison. Everyone needed to work. To earn a living. That fact had been brought home in what would come to be called the Subprime Financial Crisis of 2007. Suddenly, people were shown once again the value of simply being employed and able to provide for oneself, or for one's family. One felt lucky again to have a job. To live without feeling as though being held at the gunpoint of insolvency. It wasn't as though people had been drunk on feelings of wealth and superiority. There hadn't been any new economic era, or new paradigm announced by those who somehow manage to find a voice to say such foolish things. This was not another dotcom bubble, where the very sense of value in business had somehow simply vanished, as if money grew on trees planted by this new electronic force called the Internet. Strangely enough, many had foreseen a tidal wave coming this time, as more and more money went into property, financed by middle-class America, financed even by the unemployed, financed even by the homeless. It was the shoe-shine boy giving stock tips all over again for some, when news of the (later decried as insanely) irresponsible lending practices of packaged debt producers crept into the media news waves. But the vision of those few did not gain momentum and bring a rush for the exits. Instead, it went challenged by those who were paid to know. By the professionals in finance and investment who, naturally, knew better. It was ignored, but with one eye kept upon it. Oddly enough, people everywhere sensed that something may have gone wrong, but the majority were content to look the other way. Many investors came eventually to shun speculative investments in packaged debt, and felt safe in that very asset that had melted down so famously and repeatedly in the past. They kept their money in stocks.

With the collapse that began as a tumbling in 2007 and developed into a full-blown crash by 2008, people once again showed their ability to consider their own time and experience as so utterly unique as to already begin comparing their woes to that other great catastrophe of financial ruin, the Great Depression. When times are good, we feel that our good time is better than, and somehow different from other good times of the past. When times are bad, our vanity compels us to claim a prize for being the worst. What will it take? Perhaps the next manned space flight to the moon should involve the installation of some great statue to our stupidity for it to ever begin to set in. But then again, the moon would always just look pretty at night, wouldn't it?

A faint waft of air brought his attention back to Jim, who began waging his finger as he turned toward him. "You see," he started, only halfway into his train of thought, "I never... well it wasn't like I didn't have the time, naturally, but, well, what I mean is, it just wasn't important to me. Not then, anyway."

Richard sat up straight. Help him. Say something. But the man nodded, and kept nodding. Mulling it over. "I just – I sit here now, and I wonder. I've been so busy for the last – how long? Years, anyway.' He sighed and looked at the floor. "So... so damned *busy*. In a hurry to get ahead. I think I took a holiday only once. I mean, a holiday where I actually *went* somewhere. In the last five years, I did it only once. I went for a two week trip to Hawaii. My boss more or less forced me to go. Said I needed it. And you know what?"

When the man turned to hold him in his gaze, Richard realized he was meant to answer. "What?"

The man smiled. "After a week, I came back."

"You mean..."

"Yes, I came back a week early. I'd had enough of the beach, and the waves, and the lush green forests. I *quit* my vacation! Can you believe it?" He looked out the window again. When his forehead finally rested on the glass he stood up straight and returned to where he had been sitting, across from Richard.

"I guess your boss should have let you take your vacation when you were ready for it, not when he thought you were ready."

But the man hadn't listened.

"What I'd like to know is, what am I *doing*?" He looked at Richard as if it were the easiest question of all to answer, an encouraging smile hanging on his lips. After a prolonged silence, he spoke again. "What are we all *doing* here? What is the *point*? We've been building this big tower of sand and now it's come crashing down. What were we doing?"

Richard was having difficulty with the idea that he had merely been summoned to be milked for some kind of ancient wisdom that he didn't possess. He hesitated. Jim wanted an answer. Richard decided to ease the pain by joining the man in his error. "We were living in the here and now," he began. "That's what we were doing. And we got caught up in it. Now, we see that there's more. We always knew it, but we didn't care until now." The man listened carefully, and nodded slowly. "It's human nature, I suppose," Richard finally said raising his eyebrows to signal the end of a train of thought. This discussion was so deadly serious that Richard felt it was an impossibility for a job offer to emerge from the atmosphere that was being created. He didn't need to be anyone's mirror. Didn't need to make people feel guilty. He needed to change the subject. To chase the gloom away. He took a deep breath first. "Don't it always seem to go, that you don't know what you've got 'till it's gone?"

Mr. Kinkaid tilted his head. His eyes narrowed as his brain worked that thought over, trying to find its wisdom. "Did Plato say that?"

In the elevator he felt defeat dancing around him, laughing its silly head off at him. He looked up and was surprised at his own face in the mirrored wall. He watched the floors ticking by.

4

There were no jobs at Axon Corporation.

They had let ten percent of their people go, and were getting ready for the next round of cuts. Mr. Kinkaid, Jim, had himself been informed that he would be out by the end of the month. Hence the 'interview.' Richard could not find any humor in the knowledge that it had been his first interview arranged solely because of his educational background. He glanced at his watch. "An hour!" he cried out loud. "For what?" He looked down at the useless, empty black case that he gripped in his hand, staring at it over the neck tie that would soon go back into the darkness of his closet. He gripped the knot and loosened the tie, unbuttoning the top button of his shirt as he did. "Fuck!" He walked a small circle in the gently falling box and stopped when he faced the double doors, his lips pursed, his jaw set.

When the doors hissed open he nearly lunged out into the brightly lit lobby that echoed with the sound of an army of feet and the birdlike chatter of the happily employed that surrounded him. He headed straight for the revolving doors and felt a scream rising within him but not yet able to emerge, as if he needed to break the surface of the outdoors before he could fill his lungs with air and issue the cry. Pushing on the smooth steel bar in the middle of the revolving door seemed to make it turn a bit more slowly, like a mule with a mind of its own, rebelling at the indignity of being rushed. The sunlight struck him in the face as he exited and felt the concrete stairway that led down to Market Street under his feet. He stopped and clenched his fists once, and then again. His rent was overdue. He had lost his job, as so many others had. But for him the timing was rotten. He had just finished school and had planned to replace his student's job at the liquor store with something "real." But by now, any job was real. He contemplated hurling his briefcase into the street. Why not? Why the hell not?

As he descended the steps and headed off at a speed induced and fed by his rancor, without really knowing where it was that he was going he thought to himself that what he really needed right then, immediately, was a drink. With that desire to satisfy he reoriented himself and soon found his way to the bar in the lobby of the St. Francis Hotel.

It was unusual for him to be in a bar like that one, with tourists and the people in suits who worked downtown. Not really his kind of people, or so he told himself. But now, in his suit, he fit right in. He decided right away to make the best of it. With a little luck, he might even be able to amuse himself. He, the imposter.

The bartender, moving with a natural efficiency, did not seem to notice him. He was busy washing and then filling glasses in the crowded bar. Most of the people were drinking beer. Anchor Steam, the favorite local beer, was finished.

"Can I get another Steam out here please?" the bartender turned and shouted behind him into a room behind the bar. It was only a brief interruption and he was soon chatting away with the regular at his post at the end of the bar, taking orders and filling glasses all at the same time, effortlessly. As Richard eyed the other eager patrons and did his best to exude an air that would convey his proper place in the struggle, the bartender asked him with his eyebrows what it was that he wanted.

"A beer please, Anchor Steam."

"Sorry, I'm fresh out, but I should have a new keg in a minute," he said, his eyes nearly abandoning Richard for another customer.

"Tell you what, until that comes, I'll have a whisky. Jack Daniels on ice, please."

"Sure," the bartender said, taking another order while starting on Richard's. Richard turned to find a place to sit, but there were no empty spots to be seen. Was that proof of the mess they were in? It was only eleven but the place was packed. He made a face and muttered something to himself and then looked down at a man who was seated at a small table alone right in front of him. He had apparently seen Richard's expression of futility, for when Richard looked at him he motioned to him with his hand to take a seat at his table. Richard hesitated, then nodded his agreement. He wouldn't have to talk with the man if he didn't feel like it. Just then the bartender turned to him and spoke.

"Eight bucks. The beer is coming in a minute," he said, setting a whiskey on a cardboard coaster on the bar and putting a small bowl of nuts down nearby. Richard put some money on the bar, took the nuts and the whiskey and went for his seat, looking again at his tablemate briefly. He was middle-aged, handsome, and very well dressed. In fact, Richard saw immediately that there was something unusual in the way he was dressed. It was as if he were too well dressed. Then it occurred to him that the man might not be American. Richard took a seat and thanked him, then turned his chair out a bit to face the room and to discourage conversation, holding his drink in his lap. When the man first opened his mouth to speak Richard felt a wave of dread sweep over him as he envisioned himself trying not to be rude.

"Let me guess," the man said.

Richard took a deep breath and looked over at him.

"Job interview. Didn't go especially well."

"That's an awfully lucky guess."

The man sat back in his chair, satisfied. "Guessing has been given a bad rap. What's wrong with guessing? Certainty isn't everything it's cracked up to be. Besides, it's not luck. It's called 'listening to your intuitions.' Let your mind be still, stop grasping, and just watch what walks in the door."

"Sounds very Zen."

"Zen? Maybe. Or maybe it's a gambler's instinct. You know the expression 'poker face?' Well, you haven't got a poker face. Besides, you don't look comfortable in that suit. It's a cheap suit – no offense – it's hardly been worn, it's still early, and you look like you've been, well, run over," he said, tossing down the last of his drink. He called a waitress over and ordered another.

"Okay, you win. Next time I'll wear my poker face."

"Oh, why bother? Let people know who you are. It makes life easier." The man introduced himself and the two shook hands. He asked Richard what he did. Richard told him about school, and about the job at the wine shop that he had recently lost. "Wine sales," the man repeated approvingly, nodding his head. "I want to say that I cannot imagine a better job for a philosopher," the man told him, "but I'm sure you are destined for something better." Richard just smiled and nodded. The man continued. "But really, philosophy. That's great. We need some people in this world to carry on the tradition of thinking. We have enough manipulators, marketers, and spin doctors in the world these days. And we are all painfully aware, at least now, anyway, that we have far too many bankers. Here's to you, Richard."

Richard raised his glass to meet the one held out to him. "To me. Thanks." He took a sip and then pursed his lips as he remembered the interview. "Yes," he said, "selling wine wasn't bad, although I haven't always felt that way."

"What happened? The economy killing off the business?" the man asked.

"Yep," Richard said, shaking his head. "There was nothing she could do, my boss. I don't blame her. She's been trying to make it work for a lot of years. It's always been tough. The little guy just doesn't stand a chance. And now it's gotten tougher."

The man nodded and shrugged his shoulders in apology. "What'll you do?"

"Well, I'm looking. As you've already figured out." Richard told the man about his interview, happy now to have someone to help him release that event from his thoughts.

They talked about what the man did, how he was "responsible" for some businesses of some kind or another, and then got onto the subject of poker, or rather his regular poker game that was coming up. That was when the man asked Richard if he would like to join the game. "Just for fun," he promised. When Richard finally agreed, the man seemed very happy. He ordered another round of drinks, and then a bit later insisted on yet another round. He would not let Richard pay for anything. To be in the position to be so generous always impressed Richard and made him promise to himself that one day he too would be able to buy the drinks or pick up the bill at a restaurant where he had just eaten with a group of friends. It was not that he had a desire to be wealthy, but he wanted to be comfortable enough that to treat friends would not hurt.

They sat there and spoke for quite a while as the man's tone became more intimate. He seemed to have cast off a layer. Richard felt like he really knew him then.

The man kept asking Richard questions about what he thought about this or that subject. He was very interested in knowing about what it was that he wanted out of life. He asked him if he was happy. Finally Richard took over and asked him some questions. He asked him about the game

8

and about his favorite techniques for reading his opponents. He found himself taking mental notes. The man was obviously quite fond of the game but Richard could not help but notice a sense of resentment coming through. For what, he could not know.

"How do you feel about God?" the man asked quite seriously, his accent showing for the first time.

"I've never met him," Richard replied coolly.

"Ha! You may! You may." he said, with a smile that said he had appreciated Richard's answer even if he had not agreed with it.

Richard shifted in his chair a bit and leaned in close. When he spoke he was surprised by the smell of whiskey on his breath. "You know," he began, "it sounds like you're talking about a game of Russian roulette."

The man inhaled deeply on his cigarette and blew smoke into the air. The conversation had come to a close, and it was time for them to go their separate ways.

"But you're exactly right!" he said. "This is the first thing you will learn. Every game is a form of Russian roulette. You play your chances, you win, you win again, you lose. Yes, the game you play with a pistol has some rather unhappy, permanent consequences if you lose, to say nothing of winning."

Richard thought about that. Would it perhaps be even worse to be the winner in such a game? The man continued.

"But the other game is no less permanent when you've got more money on the table than you can afford to lose. Some," he said, making sure Richard was paying attention, "*wished* they were dead." The man sat and stared down at the table, fingering his half-empty glass. "Do you read Dostoyevsky?" he asked suddenly, almost urgently, as if this might be the secret to all things.

"No. I prefer Chekhov." Richard did not particularly read either of them. He surprised himself, talking like that. It was the other man's style that was somehow making Richard like this. A cool liar. Richard was trying to have fun at the other's expense. He could tell he had had enough to drink, and in a way Richard did not really believe any of it, at least in so much as it was supposed to involve him.

The man put out his cigarette slowly. How could this person appear so destitute? Clearly, he was not in need of money. One could see that. But he twisted his cigarette into the ashtray so slowly. So carefully. He was desperate for something, but Richard could not imagine what it was.

The man looked up slowly and spoke in a mere whisper. "Yes, well...perhaps that's for the better in this case." He then tossed down the rest of his drink and sat up straight, looking ready to leave.

"Mind if I ask you something?" Richard asked. "Are *you* happy?"

For a moment, the man did not speak. He only smiled. Then he got up from his seat. He stood there, smiling heavily, and then extended his hand. "I am feeling quite happy right now, at this moment."

As Richard stood to shake the man's hand, the man's attention was suddenly caught by something across the room. Looking behind Richard, he straightened up and smiled gaily, as though his eyes had just fallen on his one true love.

"Toshika!" he said grandly, stepping out in front of his chair, hands clasped together in anticipation, "What a splendid surprise!"

Richard turned to see who the man was speaking to, and saw her. She was young, perhaps his age, fair-skinned, dark, full hair, large, nearly round dark eyes, and a very fit body. She was tall for a woman – about his height – and, he thought, exceptionally beautiful. She wore a chocolate brown summer dress and sandals. Even her feet were beautiful. Being young, Richard probably fell in love at first sight with a dozen women every year. He thought it was normal. But when it happened, he forgot about the last one, and could not imagine there would ever be another. Not like this one. Not like her. When she approached, Richard was simply stunned. She did not take any notice of him as she approached the man and kissed his cheek. He stood holding her hand firmly for a few moments before he suddenly remembered Richard and introduced him.

"Toshika, I'd like you to meet a very nice young man, Richard Peel. Richard, this is Toshika Tamura."

"Toshika?" Richard asked as they shook hands. "That sounds, I don't know...Russian," he said, confused since she did not look at all like what he imagined a Russian should look like.

"It's spelled T-o-s-h-i-k-a but you swallow the 'i.' *Toshka*," she said. It's Japanese, actually."

"Well, I figured as much from your last name, but you just don't look very Japanese, I suppose."

As they shook hands, Richard felt the way she looked at him was nice. Something special. But it was very fleeting and then her attention was back to the man.

"Richard is a philosopher," the man told her. She raised her eyebrows and considered Richard once again.

"Oh really? Since when do philosophers wear suits?" she asked, playfully.

"I'm between jobs right now," Richard told her. "And anyway, the philosophy thing is just, it's what I studied is all."

The man felt bad for having put Richard on the spot. "And what brings you here, Toshika?" he asked her, as he motioned for her to sit in the chair next to Richard. The three of them sat down.

"I've just come to say hello to Steven and to check on the drinks and food for tomorrow," she said, looking towards the bar. The man just sat and smiled at her, not really hearing what she said.

"Uh huh," he said, "Great. How are you feeling? Not mad at me anymore, are you?" he asked her.

She glanced at Richard and shifted her weight in her chair. "No, I'm fine."

"I've invited Mr. Peel to play with us tomorrow."

Richard's gaze habitually shifted from the other man to Toshika as he awaited a reaction or reply from her. She was looking at neither of them, however. Seeing the distant but contemplative and serene expression on her face, at first Richard thought she may not have been paying attention to what the man had said. Then she focused on Richard and he realized she had spent that instant pondering the news. Considering what it might mean for her. She smiled at Richard. "Really?" she asked him, a tone of something that bordered on disbelief in her voice, as if he had just insisted that he would soon be spreading his wings and departing for the moon. "Going to join our little poker game are you?"

"Well, Hans has invited me," Richard said, motioning to the man with his hand. "I don't suppose I should turn him down."

It was a good moment while she looked at him, almost searching for something in his face before answering. "Oh no! Please come, we need some new blood!"

Richard shot the man a quick glance and struggled to find something to say.

"We're not *vampires*, for God's sake," the man reassured him.

"Oh you," Toshika said, slapping him playfully on the knee. "And you explained the game to him?" she asked.

"I was just about to," he said, shaking a finger resolutely, frowning in mock seriousness. Then he looked at Richard and winked. Toshika laughed and tried to grab his finger. They all sat quietly for a few moments. "Yeah, yeah," the man said, clearing the air. Toshika stood up and bent to kiss him.

"I'm really in a bit of a rush, please don't be offended," she said to him. "You drove, did you?"

The man rose to his feet. Richard joined him. The man looked at Toshika for a moment before answering. "Yes, of course. You don't think I'd take the bus do you, dear?"

"But I mean, you're okay to drive now I hope? I can smell that Scotch," she said as she leaned closer to him.

"I don't drink Scotch, my dear," he said, rolling his eyes and then giving Richard a wink "I'm fine! I'm a grown boy, you know."

She smiled but was not entirely convinced. She remained there, looking at him, knowing she had best leave it at that. She took his hand. "Oh Hans," she sighed. She kissed his cheek again gently. Turning to Richard, Toshika took his hand and a deep breath and shook his hand up and down, just once. A perfect interview handshake. Or a promise. Still holding his hand, she looked directly into his eyes.

"Richard, it was a pleasure to meet you. See you tomorrow night."

"Yes, see you." Richard replied. With the alcohol emboldening him, he squeezed her hand just a bit when he spoke.

12

"Well," she said, "you two finish your drinks. Enjoy yourselves."

The two men sat down and watched her as she strode up to and then behind the bar and threw her arms around the bartender. Turning to Richard, the man smiled. "She worked for the hotel some time ago for a few months one summer. For fun. She still uses her connections here to supply our little game with food and drinks. Gets a good discount on the booze and catering," he said. He watched Richard as he stared after her, her laughter dancing across the room. "She is a beautiful girl, isn't she?" Richard hesitated before agreeing. Although the man had been ready to leave only moments before, he stayed and the two of them spoke for another few minutes. Finally they said good-bye and the man left Richard to finish his whiskey. Richard looked down into his glass. The color was quite nice. A provocative brown. Immediately he thought of Toshika and looked towards the bar, but she was gone.

He thought about the way the man had looked at her, and what he had said. They knew each other well. Was there something between them, or did he simply lust after her? He certainly seemed quite affected by her sudden unexpected appearance. Richard found it a bit hard to believe that such a young and lovely woman would be interested in him, a man so much older than she. He took a sip of whiskey from his glass, but after three of them the pleasure had long gone. He looked out in the direction the man had gone and saw that he had apparently run into someone else and stood near the entrance of the hotel talking to another very well dressed man. Richard tried to figure out whether or not he was lucky to have met him. For someone like him, this extravagant game might prove to be very interesting, if it did not make him sick to his stomach first. But then he thought of Toshika and realized that anything that would allow him to see her again would be worth it.

He sat and looked around the room, not ready to leave just yet. The alcohol had made him feel slightly heavy. He sat very still, as if in a trance, and gazed into the bunch of flowers on the table in front of him until they became a mass of blurred and shifting colors. The chattering of the people in the crowded bar was like a crackling fire.

Snapping out of it, he took another look around the bar. The man was on the move again. He watched him wave good-bye to the bartender and tip the parking lot attendant who brought him the keys to his Jaguar. The two of them stood there next to the car chatting. Richard began to wonder if perhaps the man owned the hotel. He seemed to know everyone. In a good-humored way, Richard thought aloud. "Oh, how common. He drives his own car." Then, sensing that he was not alone, he turned to see that the bartender, who had come over to remove the man's empty glass, was standing right next to him and leaning over the table looking to see where he had been looking. Then he looked at Richard with a stern expression on his face. "I'd be careful, if I were you," he said, and continued to look at Richard, at his clothes, almost glaring, for several moments before walking away.

What's wrong with my suit? First that man, and now the bartender! With the annoying stare he had gotten from the bartender on his mind and the foul taste of whiskey in his mouth he felt like leaving. He looked at the people in the bar. There were four young men in suits sitting together, their faces drawn and sour, but they were very slick looking, like bankers or young lawyers, getting fairly plastered. There was a table with some well-to-do older women drinking champagne and stealing glances at the noisy yuppies. There was a woman sitting in the corner, very pretty, wearing movie star sunglasses and staring out the window. There were quite a few of these actually, the lone drinkers. Richard was now one of them. Next to her was a table full of mid-westerners looking around with mixtures of delight and disgust on their faces. San Francisco. Near the door and almost behind a large potted plant sat a young couple engaged in a heated discussion, glancing up from time to time as if trying to make sure they were not being heard. And there were others. It was a normal group of people for a nice hotel bar in the City. There were good people there, and, as the law of averages would have it, some not-so-good people. But who could know who was who?

His attention was interrupted by someone passing by directly in front of him. It was the pretty young woman from the corner, and as she passed by she gave him a look over.

Impulsively, he got up and followed her outside and watched her get into a waiting taxi. As it pulled away he thrust his hands into his pockets and looked up into the bright sunshine. Having cast off the gloom his spirits were high, and even though the woman and the job had both gotten away, he felt good again. Better. He began walking slowly towards the corner, soaking up the hustle and bustle of Union Square. At the corner he paused, waiting for his intuition to guide him. It was a beautiful downtown day and he did not get down there that often. Then he felt his stomach rumbling and went off in search of a slice of pizza.

His name was Hans Kienle. He said that the poker game was a game between friends who had been playing together regularly "for ages," with a few minor changes in the players now and then. The stakes were high, but he did not say just how high. All he said was that a bet of less than one thousand dollars was not acceptable. When he was invited, Richard told him frankly that he could not afford to play. Although Richard was serious, he spoke with a smile because he knew that Hans must have known that he could not afford such high stakes, and because he also must have known that this was obvious and that he should not have asked Richard to participate unless... Unless he had something in mind. "Don't worry," the man had said, "You'll be taken care of. It'll be our little secret." Richard had not taken it any further because he had had the feeling that he was being taken for a ride. He hadn't wanted to get too excited in front of the man. Hadn't wanted to give him the pleasure. The whole thing was unbelievable anyway; not that this kind of poker game could not exist, but that someone would simply invite a stranger they had met in a bar along to play who obviously had no real money to speak of was very odd. In Richard's case, he simply had no money at all. It had begun to make him a bit uncomfortable so he had decided not to show enthusiasm and had hoped that this suave drunk would leave him alone. And then Toshika came. Somehow, she validated Hans for Richard.

Riding home on the bus later that afternoon he looked steadily out the window and thought about his increasingly desperate situation. Having graduated with a degree in philosophy he was happy that he had followed his instincts and had dropped out of business school to study what really pleased him instead of just choosing something safe but uninspiring. But as the world around him crumbled he doubted his decision. He felt some comfort knowing that even well-qualified people were being dumped like old garbage every day, but he knew that his odds would be much better had he done the normal thing.

The bus stopped and Richard got out. His apartment was just around the corner at the end of the block. It was a fairly typical Victorian flat on the inside, but on the outside, it bore none of the festive, graceful façade so common to the style. His was one of those that had, for some reason or other, long ago been stripped bare, made to look purposeful instead of inviting. The building had two floors. He and his roommates, Tony and Matt, both of whom had also graduated recently, were on the bottom, above the garage. Above them lived an ever-changing body of university students who helped them stay up late and wake up early. But they at least provided them with a never-ending party to attend free of charge, as almost any night would find a gathering there. As icing on the cake, by some mysterious stroke of luck the female tenants upstairs always outnumbered the male tenants.

Nobody was home when Richard trudged up the two small flights of stairs and went inside. He took a beer out of the refrigerator and tried to find some kind of music to play that would not annoy him too much. Finally he gave up and just opened one of his big windows that looked out over the Richmond district, from where he could see the ocean just a bit. A small triangle of blue. He sat on the sill, legs dangling against the gunship gray aluminum siding, sipping his beer in the relative calm of the late summer afternoon. The light was his favorite kind, the end of the day's sunlight that brought all the color out, with everything holding a golden shine. It was the kind of light that would allow his imagination to wander and he would feel that perhaps the year was 1967, or 1945, or some other distant time that for some reason or other held a certain glamorous appeal to him. He heard keys jingling and saw Tony shuffling down the sidewalk. Tony was the most casual person he had ever known, so he naturally could not walk, he could only shuffle.

"Don't jump!" Tony cried as he looked up and spotted Richard perched on the window sill. "It's not that bad, I promise!" Richard managed to smile and took another sip of beer. "How did the interview go? Did you get the job?" Tony asked, leaning against the wall at the top of the steps.

"You won't believe it," Richard told him, picking a piece of gravel off the window sill and tossing it into the street below. "There wasn't any job."

Tony folded his arms across his chest. "No job?"

"This was the first time, I'm sure of it, that I have ever been called into a job interview because I studied philosophy." Tony cocked his head, confused. "The guy just wanted to talk!"

"About what?"

"About the shit situation we're in. As if I'm supposed to be uniquely qualified here to explain why or how we got here."

Tony walked up the stairs, shaking his head. He stopped on the landing and turned to look at the ocean. "And that was it? Really?"

Richard nodded. "What's in the bag?"

"Garlic and some other stuff. I got a new recipe. You're going to be here, aren't you?" Tony was always on the phone with his mother and she loved giving him recipes to try out. He liked cooking.

"Yes. I'm in."

"Good. Listen, why isn't there any music on? Why don't you put some music on and then run down and pick up a bottle of wine. Here." He threw Richard his wallet. Tony still had a job. He made decent money and always offered to pay for everything, which normally got on Richard's nerves because it reminded him that he had to find a real job. Now he was grateful for it. Tony was in the film business, in editing, primarily. But in the small local film industry one had to be able to do just about anything.

"I'll get it," Richard objected, preparing to throw Tony his wallet back to him.

"No, really. I want a *good* bottle." Tony looked at the sun as it lowered itself beyond the horizon, and then went into the house.

"I'll buy a good bottle, but keep your money!" Richard shouted. "I'm going to be a millionaire tomorrow anyway."

Sitting in his bedroom at the window the next day, at work on finding a job, Richard thought about what Tony had said about the invitation to the poker game the night before. "Yeah, sure it sounds crazy, but there are a lot of people who still have money and like throwing it around. I'd go if I were you, just to see what it's all about."

"But what if I lose? What if they expect me to repay what I lose?"

"First of all, if it's his money, then they don't lose anything, *he* does. And besides, why would this guy invite you to a game of poker so that he could get you into debt – a guy who he knows can't repay him – for some huge amount of money? He's got better things to do, I'm sure. He's just inviting you because it's probably getting boring for him. This'll be some fun for him, that's all. Besides, you want to see that girl again, don't you?"

"Of course. She was incredible."

Richard knew it without asking him, but he needed to ask anyway. It was comforting to hear it from him. Richard had already decided to go, anyway. There was no question about that. He looked at the screen of his notebook computer at the miserable job advertisements. It was hard to stay focused. Richard looked out the window at the people passing by and dreamed. He thought about what he would do if he won ten thousand dollars. He felt a wave of excitement at that. But then he realized he would need a lot more than that to be really free. Ten thousand became a hundred thousand, and then a million, and then he just felt stupid. The whole thing was stupid.

2

When he arrived at the address he had been given he was a bit disappointed. He had imagined they would be playing this game in someone's multi-million-dollar home, but it was just a law office in what was just another nice Victorian. He walked up the long flight of stairs slowly, self-consciously eyeing his clothing. He had tried to dress the way he imagined the others would be dressed, which is to say he wanted to look as though he might have money. Before he left Tony was trying to get him to wear a captain's sailing hat – one of many movie props he kept in odd places around their flat. Richard refused. When he rang at the door, a voice came out over the intercom.

"Yes?"

"Hi, Hans?"

"No." came the reply. "Who is this, please?" Richard could not be sure, with it coming through the speaker, but the voice sounded English.

"My name's Richard Peel, I'm a guest of Mr. Kienle's."

"A guest?" came the reply, the voice sounding almost annoyed. Richard wondered if he should leave.

"Yes."

"Just a moment, please." Richard waited for at least two minutes. Finally there was a hiss from the box at the door. "Please come in," the voice said. Then there was a buzzing noise at the door. Richard pushed it and it opened. He entered a small room with a coat and hat rack, and a light that shone down onto him from above. There was a thick glass door in front of him that was frosted except for one small area at about head height. A pair of eyes looked at him through this spot and then the door opened. A nice enough looking man stood in the doorway, very neatly dressed. He was vaguely familiar.

"Hello, I'm Jeffries. Well, my Christian name is Arnold but everyone calls me Jeffries. Hans isn't here yet. Typical of him. But I've just rung him up and he confirmed your participation. We're about ready to start. You may leave your coat here, if you wish, or you can bring it with you," he said. He was definitely English.

"My name's Richard."

"Right," came the reply. The two of them shook hands.

"I'll just keep my coat, thanks." It was cold in the tiny room, but Richard was sweating.

"Mr. Peel?"

"Right."

"What do you do?"

Richard hesitated, then tried for some humor to help relieve some of the awkwardness of this situation that he found simply very weird. "I've recently been in the philosophy business."

"Well, not much money in philosophy, is there?" Richard went blank. "Just kidding!" Jeffries said. "You're walking on dead men's legs – to quote one of your better writers – aren't you?" he joked. Jeffries leaned in close and whispered, "Most of us are. But really, who cares?"

"Right." Richard tried to laugh, but coughed instead.

"May I have your card, please?"

"Excuse me?"

"Your card? Have you got one with you?"

"As a matter of fact, I've left them in my briefcase with my other...things."

"No problem at all," he said, "Does anyone here know you? Aside from Hans?"

"I don't think so, no. Is Toshika here?"

"You know Toshika?"

"Yes, we met once."

"Splendid! Yes, she's here this evening. But, I'm terribly sorry," he said, clearly a bit embarrassed, "may I see some kind of identification? Driver's license or something?"

"Sure," Richard replied. He took out his wallet and gave Jeffries his license. "Oh, I also have this," he said and handed him Hans' business card with the address of the law office

20

written on the back of it. He looked at it, and then at Richard's license. Then he gave them back to him. He stepped back through the glass doorway.

"All right, now if you could just slowly pass through here." Richard looked up and around at this passageway skeptically. "Not to worry," Jeffries assured him, "It's just a metal detector."

Richard followed Jeffries through a kind of lounge, furnished like a living room minus the television set, on into the main room. There he saw six people seated at a round table. The entire space was L-shaped, with wood paneling and a full bar in the corner near the playing table. Doors at the rear of the house were closed. Toshika was sitting behind the bar smiling at him. He was relieved to see someone he knew, and smiled back. She was even more beautiful than he had remembered. Just then, Jeffries addressed the group.

"Everyone, this is Richard Peel." Richard nodded to those seated before him. The others looked at him in return, expectantly. Jeffries waited a moment before turning to Richard. "Richard, let me introduce you to everyone. Starting here is Sylvia Reed, to her right is Jean LaCroix, Art Peters, Frank Baldwin, David Norton, and Dr. Larry Xang. Richard is Hans' guest this evening, if there are no objections,"

Richard was surprised at the last remark as it was apparently said in seriousness, for the six looked at each other and seemed to be asking with their eyes if anyone did object. One man, Art Peters, an older man of about sixty, asked Jeffries, "And where *is* Hans? We're ready to begin."

"He's on his way," Jeffries told him.

Frank Baldwin, a young-looking man of about forty spoke for the group. "All right, give him Hans' seat and credit and let's begin. When Hans shows up we'll take it from there."

The group began mumbling at the round table and once again Richard wanted nothing more than to leave. But Mr. Baldwin's suggestion was apparently acceptable to everyone and Richard was given a seat next to the woman, Sylvia Reed. Toshika came and said hello, shaking Richard's hand.

"Good to see you, Richard. Can I get you a drink?"

"Have you got any beer?" he asked her as privately as he could without whispering.

"I've got everything," she said. "What kind of beer would you like?"

"Oh, whatever's cold is fine."

"Certainly."

Richard watched her as she returned to the bar. Before she got there he realized that he had been staring and looked at Miss Reed, who had been watching him watching Toshika. She smiled like a cat does with its eyes, then blinked and it was finished. Richard's attention shifted to Jeffries, who sat with boxes of chips in front of him.

"All right everyone, according to the vote from the last game, tonight's game will be five card draw poker. The ante is one thousand dollars as is the minimum bet, but please, let's not be stingy. Let's try to have a little fun, shall we? As usual, there will be an intermission only when agreed upon by the group and there are to be no rest room or any other absences until that mutually agreed upon intermission, right? Okay, you've heard it all before – that is, except you, Richard." Suddenly the players all looked at Richard expectantly. "I assume," Jeffries asked him, "that you've played poker before?"

Richard was unsure if the question was simply a joke, or if it was an attempt to discover just how well Richard might play. He decided to offer the least assuming answer that he could.

"Yes."

Miss Reed let out a loud yawn. "Come on, people, let's just play!" she complained. "I'm bushed! I don't know how long I'll last at this rate."

At that moment a thump sounded behind Richard and he turned to see Hans walking in through the double doors.

"Speak of the bloody devil! Hans, you're late!" Mr. Peters said.

"Well, I'm here now. What's wrong? Did you miss me?" he asked the group, his voice filled with sarcasm. He had that weary look on his face again. Richard was beginning to think that maybe that was just his permanent state of mind. A tired man.

"You've got something we want, Hans, or have you forgotten?" Mr. Baldwin said. Hans pulled up a chair and squeezed in beside Richard.

22

"You've all met my friend Richard, then?" He looked at Richard with a smile that was oddly welcoming. Richard was grateful to be treated so warmly, but at the same time he found it a bit strange. He felt he had known Hans for much longer than he actually had. Hans clapped him on the shoulder and whispered, so that everyone could hear. "Glad you could make it," he said.

Hans turned to see a bottle of sparkling wine hovering in front of his face, with David Norton on the other side of it.

"Hans," Mr. Norton began, "This is yours. Courtesy of my weekend in Napa. Everybody got one."

Hans took the bottle and looked at the label briefly. "Oh, well thanks, David, very thoughtful of you. Looks nice." He turned to put the bottle down and only then noticed the bottles on the floor near the other players. Just then Mr. Norton looked at Richard and shrugged.

"Sorry Richard, didn't know you were coming."

"Sure, that's okay," Richard told him, but he could see that Mr. Norton was not at all sorry that he hadn't a bottle for him.

"Right, well, I've just presented the game, Hans. Don't think I need to repeat it, do I?" Jeffries asked him.

"If it's the same as last time, which was the same as the last time, then no, I don't think so."

Jeffries laughed. "All right then, let's begin," he said. Toshika came to his side. She handed him an unopened deck of cards. He handed them to the man on his right, Mr. Norton. He inspected them, nodded, and gave them back. The pack was opened and the cards were taken out. Jeffries began to shuffle. The cards were cut, then dealt. Richard looked at the five cards sitting on the table before him, picked them up, and felt lucky. He had two queens.

"Where's your wife tonight, Baldwin?" Jeffries asked the younger man. He looked at Jeffries in a rather hostile way. The other players seemed also to bristle a bit.

"*She*, is at *home*," he replied.

The conversation began in this way. The people were starting to show their character. The process of Richard's getting to know them, one by one, had begun. It seemed an odd group. Richard wondered whether or not it was just his being in the presence of a group of people who obviously knew each other well and were not saving anything for his benefit. Toshika came around and gave everyone one of the small wooden boxes that Jeffries had in front of him. Inside were rows of white, blue, and red chips. The white chips had a value of one thousand dollars, the blue chips five thousand, and the red ten thousand. It did not mean anything to Richard. He started counting and saw that he had a quarter of a million dollars in chips in his box. Everyone else's box looked the same.

"Well, I don't know why you bring her here anyway, Frank," said Mr. Peters, the older man who spoke before. Richard tried to figure out what each of them did, but of course did not have much to go on. Mr. Peters looked as though he could be a retired actor, very suave and sophisticated looking, with perfect, silver hair.

"Who brings who? That's the question," said Mr. LaCroix. He looked about forty-five and looked like some kind of artist with his little mustache, his colorful clothing, and fingers that looked like they were probably permanently dirty.

"Please, everyone, let's show our guest we aren't completely uncivilized," Hans said, eyeing everyone for an instant before looking at his cards.

"He's *your* guest," said Mr. LaCroix over his cards.

"Yeah, yeah, let's just play the game," said Mr. Norton, who was the least impressive-looking one there and could have been a construction worker or a mechanic as far as Richard was concerned.

"I happen to *enjoy* Valerie," said Miss Reed. Richard guessed she was in her early thirties. Very graceful and elegant, and rather pretty. He had only seen her as she sat at the table, he realized, and yet he was aware of his impression that she was graceful. He began to consider that oddity when she spoke again. "I think all you men are just jealous of Frank because she doesn't sleep with any of *you.*"

"Thank you, Sylvia," said Mr. Baldwin with a bow and a gracious smile. Richard watched the expression on his face and in his eyes linger. He guessed that there was something between them.

"After all," Miss Reed continued, "She *is* very sexy." She looked at Richard. "You like sexy women, don't you Richard?" Everyone looked at him, but only very briefly, as though her comment had simply reminded them of his presence. Miss Reed looked at him with a completely dry expression on her face. Immediately, he did not like her. He was in an uncomfortable position as the newcomer and she was just making it worse.

"I've never met any sexy women," Richard answered, looking her right in the eye with the same dead expression.

"There you go," said Mr. Norton with a laugh. Hans nodded in approval, his eyes fixed on his cards.

Richard noticed that one person had not yet spoken. Mr. Norton must have read his mind.

"Aren't you talking tonight, Hank?" asked Mr. Norton.

"Shut up! I'm looking at my cards! This is a card game, you know?" answered Dr. Xang. He also looked to be in his mid-forties.

"That's what I mean! Let's play." said Mr. Norton. "Darlin', I'd like to buy Hank a drink please. He hasn't got anything yet," he said over his shoulder to Toshika.

"Don't want a drink," Dr. Xang told him.

"Of course you do!" Mr. Norton looked at Toshika. "Of course he does! Darlin', do your thing, will you?"

"I don't know who you're talking to," Toshika answered as she flipped through a magazine and paid him no attention.

"Excuse me, *Toshika*, would you please bring Hank a bourbon, rocks?"

"Certainly," she said and placed an empty glass on the bar.

"Richard," said Jeffries, "As you probably noticed, you've been given credit of two hundred and fifty-thousand dollars. Hans, what's the story on Richard? Any limit on his credit?"

"No."

Richard felt like asking right then and there about paying for his losses, but knew that that question might cause trouble.

The playing began. With everyone examining their cards, Mr. Norton started the betting. "I bet five thousand," he said, placing one blue chip on the table. The betting went around just once and everyone stayed in the game. The pot reached forty-nine thousand dollars. Everyone was dealt a second round of cards, some taking only one, others more. "Call," Mr. Norton said. He placed his cards face up on the table. He had a three tens. His was the best hand until it was Richard's turn to lay down his cards. Mr. Norton looked hard at them, and then at Richard. "Beginner's luck," he said.

Hans was apparently very pleased with Richard's success and ordered a couple of drinks for the two of them that they promptly tossed down – Richard following Hans's lead – before resuming play.

"Don't assume that Richard's shiny young face indicates a lack of poker playing skill," Hans warned the group with a waving finger. The others traded glances and even a few playful grins.

"You're bluffing Hans," Mr. Norton said without taking his eyes off his cards. Hans arranged his new hand.

"Am I? A bluff can still wipe you out."

"Not in the long run."

Richard kept winning. Everyone won some and lost some, but Mr. Norton and Richard were definitely coming out on top. Mr. Baldwin quickly lost everything and signed for another box. Miss Reed was doing fairly well, and the others, including Hans, were losing somewhat badly. Richard's two hundred and fifty thousand dollars had grown to about four hundred thousand, but it still did not really mean anything to him. It seemed an impossible thing, that he would actually take home a sum of money this great.

Soon an hour had gone by. After a particularly long and drawn out hand in which Richard won eighty thousand dollars, Jeffries collected the cards and spoke to him.

"Well, Richard, you're certainly doing quite well. I'm sure that makes Hans happy," he said, giving Hans a look that was not returned.

What did that mean? Exactly why would Hans be happy about this? Was Richard merely winning money for him? Did Jeffries mean that at least he was not losing Hans' money? Or did he simply mean that, as Hans' guest, he must be happy that Richard was winning? For some reason, that possibility was something Richard did not accept. He really wanted to know what the hell was going on. He looked at Hans. When he noticed Richard's stare he merely smiled and then returned to his cards. The whole evening was like that. Hans rarely looked up from his cards, rarely said anything. At times Richard almost forgot he was there.

They played for another forty-five minutes. Mr. Norton's luck had changed. He was down to about a hundred thousand dollars. Miss Reed and Richard were both doing well. Mr. Baldwin had lost again and had signed for another box as did Dr. Xang and Mr. LaCroix. Mr. Peters had about what he came in with. Hans appeared to be maintaining a stock of chips worth about a hundred thousand. Richard had nearly a million dollars in those little plastic chips.

"Well," Jeffries said after looking at his watch, gathering the cards into a pile and setting them aside, "I, for one, think it's about time for a break. How does that sound to everyone?" They were all in agreement. Everyone got up and headed in different directions. Hans went with Toshika into the corner where they spoke quietly. Richard watched him, envious. Wanting to get a moment of peace to take a deep breath and clear his mind, he went into the lounge and sat down on a sofa, closing his eyes and yawning. It was fairly dark in the room and he quickly began slipping into a warm, comfortable state.

"Well, I guess Hans invited you to clean us all out." It was Miss Reed. She stood in front of Richard and slowly got out of her shoes, her hands on her hips. Richard looked at the shoes as she stepped away from them and came toward the couch, stopping in front of it at the other end. She wore a leather skirt and a white blouse. Her bare legs were tanned and long.

"I haven't cleaned *you* out yet," Richard said.

"Do you like them?"

Richard looked at her shoes again. They were black leather high-heeled sandals. "Yes, but they don't look very comfortable."

"I mean my feet," she said. She sat down at the other end of the couch, pulling one foot into her lap and rubbing it. Then she lay down and tapped her toes against Richard's thigh.

"Oh, well yes, they're very nice feet."

She smiled. "But you're right. The shoes are still new. Would you be a gentleman and massage my feet a little?" she asked, gently lifting them onto his lap and closing her eyes.

This doesn't happen every day, Richard thought. He began to think that, as he had seen countless times on television, this type of behavior was to be expected from wealthy people. But he liked feet, and hers were very nice. His thought that she may have been a dancer seemed to be challenged. He began to rub them gently.

"Well, they're very nice feet," he told her again.

"Really," she said without opening her eyes.

"Yes. Very sexy," he said, keeping an eye on her expression. She smiled, but just barely. "Am I doing this because I'm winning, or because you're trying to apologize?" he asked her. She seemed half asleep.

"Apologize? For what?"

"Well, you were a little weird earlier."

"You don't know me very well."

"No, but your naked feet are in my hands," he said. She smiled.

"First of all, I don't apologize. I'm too much of a bitch. Secondly, I may seem like a bitch sometimes, but it's just me."

"So you mean sometimes you're a bitch, and sometimes you just seem like one, but you aren't?"

"It's not as strange as it sounds."

"No," Richard said, "I guess not. This whole thing is just a little strange."

She opened her eyes for a moment, looking at him before letting them close again. "I *wish* it were strange. It *used* to be strange. Now it's just a game. And we're getting a bit tired of it. As a matter of fact we're sick of it! You can tell Hans I said that." Richard had no idea what she was talking about.

"Okay," he said. "How well do you know Hans?" He stopped massaging her feet and just held them.

"Well, I thought I knew him pretty well up until he got stingy," she said, then looked at him. "The question is, how well do *you* know him? And Toshika? That's what we're all wondering."

"We're drinking buddies. I just met Toshika the other day."

"Really. Hans never mentioned you."

"Funny, he never mentioned you either."

They remained quiet for a while. Miss Reed lay still with her eyes closed. Richard held her feet in his hands and looked at them, thinking about what she had said. After a moment she got up and put her shoes back on.

"There's food if you're hungry. Better get it now before we start again. Oh, if you want to wash your hands the bathroom is right there," she said, pointing to a door near the corner of the room. She turned and left the room, closing the door carefully behind her. Richard got up and went over to the hallway and peered through the glass at the large front door. It was very quiet there. Standing in that small space he felt very content. He remained there for a few moments until the thought of missing out on food forced him to join the others. He entered the bathroom and washed his hands quickly.

In the next room, they were all there. Some standing and some sitting at another large, round table around the corner with an array of cheese, wine, bread, cold meats and fresh fruit.

"When are you gonna get some hot-dogs in here, Toshika?" complained Mr. Norton as he sat, slicing a baguette and then trying to spread Brie over it to make a sandwich. "And some cheddar...or something,"

"Actually I tried to get bratwurst today but they didn't have any and I was pressed for time. Are you finding everything all right, Richard?" No one else paid any attention to him. Even Toshika seemed preoccupied as she spoke to him.

"Yes, everything is just fine."

"We'll try to change that in a few minutes," said Mr. Baldwin who sat at the far side of the table. "How do you know Hans?" he asked, putting his glass of wine on the table and lacing his fingers together on it.

"They're drinking buddies," said Miss Reed. Mr. Baldwin looked at her in mild surprise.

"Hans! You don't drink! What's he talking about?" Mr. Nelson hollered.

"And how long have you known Richard?" Mr. Baldwin asked Miss Reed, skeptically.

"He massaged my feet," she said. Richard shot a glance at Toshika, who looked as though she had not heard a thing. He had hoped that would not have been mentioned this evening and did his best to divert attention away from himself by concentrating on the food, as if that would make a difference. Mr. Baldwin and Mr. Peters both stared at him.

"There you go," said Mr. Norton. He began working on another sandwich. Finally Richard felt compelled to speak up for himself. A few minutes later, after he explained most everything to the satisfaction of the others, but without giving away very much at all, the group began working its way back to the table. Only Hans and Toshika remained. They were quietly discussing something. It looked like Hans was not really interested in talking about it, whatever it was. For some reason, Richard imagined they were talking about him. Although he strained to listen to what they were saying, the only thing he could catch came when they were nearly finished.

"Will you promise me now?"

"Oh Toshika, please!"

"I'm not a child, you know."

"Oh, I know. Twenty-four and all grown up, like the rest of them."

Just then Hans looked over at the group and, finishing his drink, came to sit down. Toshika brought a stool over from the bar and sat just behind him to watch the game.

They played for a long time without stopping. Hans was not doing well. Finally the time came when there was yet another large pot of chips in the balance. The bet was called, and Hans had run out of chips. He could no longer keep up. He sat and stared into the pile of chips in the center of the table with glazed eyes.

"You have one more chip," Mr. Norton said, gazing steadily at Hans. On the table next to his box of chips lay a black chip that Richard had not noticed until that very instant. After some moments, Hans turned to look at Richard. His face bore no expression as he searched Richard's eyes. Richard, whose hand was not strong, had been trying his best not to give away his position to the others, including Hans. But Hans had been playing the game for many years and he was not easy to fool. Finally, he turned his cards face down and placed them on the table.

"I fold," he declared.

Sighs and gasps went around the room, with several players tossing in their cards face down, indicating that they, too, were finished. Everyone began breathing once more.

Richard thought he heard Mr. Norton curse under his breath.

"Well then, I call," Mr. Baldwin said. He lay his cards down for everyone to see. Three aces. Richard showed his hand as well. A pair of tens and a pair of sevens. Not bad, but not good enough. Only Mr. Norton remained holding his cards, which he slowly placed face up on the table.

"Bugger!" Mr. Baldwin said, pounding his fist on the table. Mr. Norton had lain down four Jacks. He reached out and drew the pile of chips in.

"You're broke, Hans," Mr. Norton said flatly.

Everyone in the room fell silent.

All eyes were on Hans, but no one moved or spoke. Richard looked at Toshika. Her expression told him that this was the most exciting moment of the evening, but for what reason? They all wanted to see Hans fail? Why? Hans sat with his head slightly bowed, a smile on his lips that was just barely perceptible. Everyone watched with great interest as Jeffries spoke to Hans.

"Well, Hans, what'll it be?" As he left his question hanging he glanced at Toshika, who sat now looking down into her lap. It seemed that her eyes were closed.

"Yeah, Hans, what's it gonna be?" asked Mr. Norton.

When he spoke, he looked only at Jeffries, whose face betrayed no opinion as he heard the request. "Give me another box, Jeffries."

Like air rushing out of a balloon, everyone gasped. The entire group seemed stunned and angry by Hans' response. Richard was fascinated by it, and wore a faint smile of wonder at the scene until Toshika interrupted him, rising suddenly and storming out of the room. Mr. Norton got up and went after her.

"What the hell is wrong with you, Hans?" Mr. Baldwin cried. Jeffries stepped in to Hans' defense.

"Listen everyone, you all know the rules! The bet belongs to Hans and he is free to use it or not. He certainly isn't the only one to have held back on it, now is he?"

At this, the others seemed to give a little ground.

"But it's been four games!" Mr. Baldwin spat.

Hans sat silently for some moments. He contemplated diffusing the situation by advising them all that he had decided that this would be his last game. But then, as he looked at their sour, contemptuous faces, he changed his mind. Screw it. Let them stew in it a bit longer. With a final look at Norton, he took a drink and addressed them. "Well, are we playing? Or aren't we?"

Just then, Jeffries considered Richard and cocked his head to one side. Soon the others were looking at him as well. Sensing another inquiry, Hans lied, assuring the group that he had discussed this situation with Richard. The others seemed satisfied, and Jeffries began shuffling the cards as Toshika returned, followed by Mr. Norton. The playing resumed as if nothing had happened.

Some time later, Richard's luck had faltered, leaving him with slightly less than before but still comfortably ahead of where he began. Miss Reed had lost most of what she had. Mr. Peters came back strongly and had well over a million dollars. Mr. Norton and Dr. Xang were in possession of over half a million each. Mr. LaCroix had signed for another box of chips. Mr. Baldwin was still losing and had signed for yet another box, his fourth. Hans' luck had not improved; he had less than one hundred thousand dollars left. Through it all, Richard was impressed with the lack of emotion most of the players displayed. Did the money mean nothing to them? Were they so wealthy that it just did not matter?

It was after midnight. A few of the players began to show signs of fatigue, including Richard. He had just asked Toshika for a cola to help keep awake when Dr. Xang received a phone call. The reaction at the table was swift, sparking surprise in Richard.

"Dr. Xang," he answered, standing slowly and moving towards the table covered with the remains of the night's appetizers. "Yes, are you sure? Dammit! Yes, okay." Dr. Xang hung up and hung his head. Cries erupted from the group and several players threw their cards down on the table in disgust.

"Goddammit Xang!" Mr. Norton hollered. "You're not leaving here yet, understand?"

Dr. Xang regarded him with an expression that said that he should have known better.

"Not again!" complained Miss Reed, who, with a toss of her head threw her hair back behind her shoulders and then emptied her wine glass.

"I have to go to the hospital. Heart transplant. The team needs me," he remarked apologetically.

"Well," Jeffries began, "we shall have to postpone the game. I suggest that we continue tomorrow night at the same time. Any objections?"

"Goddammit!" Mr. Norton said again.

"Let him go if he has to go, but I think we should continue without him," said Mr. Peters.

"That's fine for you," Mr. LaCroix interrupted, "but I'd like to win some of what I've lost back from him."

"I agree with Jean," Mr. Baldwin said.

"Why must we always do this?" Jeffries said. "Okay, let's vote shall we? Those in favor of postponing the game raise a hand please."

Mr. Norton and Mr. Peters were the only ones out. With that, each player's chips were counted, Dr. Xang's being counted first so that he could leave, while the others milled about. Richard's chips were counted last. When he stood up from the table, Jeffries took Richard aside. "Richard, I'm sure we'll be finishing the game tomorrow. Tonight you have done very well for yourself. Congratulations."

"I knew he had it in him," a voice called from behind them. It was Hans, returning from the rest room. He stood behind Richard and placed a hand on his shoulder. "Sorry about that Richard, but doctors have to be doctors! Let's hit the road, Jack," he said, grinning jovially. The two of them headed for the door.

"And Hans, be on time, will you?" Jeffries called out after them.

Hans turned and smiled, raising a hand in a feeble wave. As they were collecting their things in the foyer, Hans asked Richard if he would like to go and have a quick drink.

"Sure, what have you got in mind?"

Hans paused for a moment before answering. Richard thought he saw him smile to himself as he looked down at the space between them.

"Let's go to your part of town. Where do you normally go?"

By the way he said that it was clear that he had not thought that the bar at the St. Francis, where they met, was Richard's everyday bar.

"Well," Richard began with some degree of uncertainty, "I usually go south of Market, or the Haight. I've got it, you know the Noc Noc?"

"No, shall we go there?"

"Yes, let me take you there. I think you'll like it."

Just as it had been decided, Toshika entered from the game room followed by Mr. Norton and a couple of the others. She stopped in front of Richard and Hans.

"What are your plans?" she asked. Her lack of emotion surprised and disappointed Richard. He had been looking forward to more contact with her and had even hoped that she might want to join him and Hans.

"We're going to the Noc Noc," Richard said, trying his best to sound inviting. He glanced at Hans, who was fumbling with the zipper on his jacket.

"Oh. Well, enjoy yourselves." Toshika turned to Mr. Norton. "Can you give me a lift?"

"I don't see a problem there," he answered.

Grabbing a leather Jacket, Toshika spoke to Richard and Hans over her shoulder as she walked out the door. "See you all tomorrow," she said. Finished with his jacket, Hans turned to speak but the door was already closed. He looked back at Richard and made a futile gesture.

"Hey, forgot your champagne," Richard said. He quickly went back through the lounge and retrieved the heavy dark green bottle. "Careful with that," he told Hans as he handed it over. "It's a heavy one."

The two of them said good-bye to the others and went outside. Richard watched as Toshika got into Mr. Norton's car.

"Don't worry," Hans said, "you'll have another chance tomorrow."

The comment caught Richard off guard. "Oh, yeah." Richard said, trying not to sound too interested. Save for the cars jammed in along the roadside wherever space could be found, the long street was empty in both directions, and strangely quiet. It was agreed that Hans would follow Richard in his car.

"Don't lose me now," Hans told Richard, as he climbed into his Jaguar. Richard smiled and laughed once.

"Yeah, right."

3

The Noc Noc was in the lower Haight, the area east of Divisadero. Not a very smooth part of town, but that's the way Richard liked it. A bit more real than other places. The bar was small. Upon entering, Hans felt as though he had entered a dimly lit cave. The walls, curved and bulging like stone, were fashioned from cement and painted a muddy brown color. Odd items were encased in the cement here and there: a television that always displayed a black and white test pattern, spotlights, vague elements of machinery, a compass from an old ship, pieces of broken mirror. The floor consisted of alternating plates of rusted steel and old Persian carpets, giving rise to either plate steel tables and stools or large, comfortable throw pillows. The effect was very cozy, oddly enough.

Richard and Hans went to the bar and ordered a couple of beers. They found a place on the floor and sat on pillows on one of the old rugs in a corner near a window that looked out onto the street. Candles lined the windowsill. Neither of them spoke for the first minute or so, both perfectly happy to slow down and absorb the life of the place, watching the others around them. It was like an intimate party where the guests did not know each other. Richard watched as Hans' eyes roamed the bar, a smile building on his face until he looked at Richard, nodding his head.

"Great place," he told him.

"Yeah, I like it," Richard replied, watching the bar for another instant before taking a long drink from his glass. He stretched his arms above his head and shook off the evening's stress. "That was some game, Hans. And some group of people."

Hans smiled. "Like them?" he asked. Richard chuckled.

"Oh, I don't know about that. Who is that guy, Mr. Norton, anyway? I mean, he sure was mad at you about something."

"Yes, David Norton. He is a retired police officer, believe it or not. Actually, I'm sure that from observing him tonight you won't be surprised to hear that, but what should surprise you is that he has enough money to participate."

"You're right on both counts."

"Well, the doctor – Dr. Xang, that is – brought him along originally a couple of years back. Thought it would be good for us to have some 'protection' as he called it."

"And how can a cop afford to play in your game?"

"Yes. It seems that he was injured – and treated by Dr. Xang – forcing him to retire. He received some kind of financial award in a lawsuit. His pension keeps rolling in, but like many others he's made quite a bundle on the stock market."

Richard let out a short laugh. "Yeah, and now he's lost it again." He looked at Hans for confirmation. Hans looked at him very seriously.

"David is very shrewd," he said. His sudden contemptful tone surprised Richard. "Whether it was just luck or not, I have no way of knowing. But David made sure everyone knew, months ago, that he had sold all of his investments in the stock market before the crash."

Richard nodded, then shook his head. "He sure was upset about something tonight," he offered, hoping that Hans would supply some explanation of those events. But he remained quiet. Pensive. Sipping his beer as he became drawn into private thoughts that Richard held little hope in discovering.

"Yes," Hans began slowly. Richard waited for an explanation, but Hans ventured no further.

"So tell me, what's your story? I mean, your English is perfect but sometimes I can detect a slight accent. Where are you from?"

"What's my story? Well, I originally come from Switzerland. From Zurich, the largest city in Switzerland. I came here about 20 years ago. At first I lived in New York, but then moved here and I've been here ever since."

"I've never been to Switzerland. Or Europe, for that matter. Which country do you like better?"

Hans laughed and took a sip from his beer. "That's typical for an American. 'Which country is better?' That's like asking me which of my children I love more."

"Do you have children?" Richard asked, glad to change the subject.

"I was merely making a point. You recognize their strengths and weaknesses but you love them all. It's the same with different countries." Hans took a deep breath and sighed, rubbing the back of his neck. "Americans think that everything is a competition. Too much in life is a competition, unfortunately. It gives many people a headache, but Americans seem to thrive on it."

Richard nodded, trying to overrule the defenses that had begun to set up, but failing. "So why do you stay here if you don't like it?"

Hans rearranged himself on his cushion. He was not as flexible at his age any more. He gave Richard a consenting nod before speaking. "I never said I didn't like it here. Richard, you know, it's hard to leave a place once you have been there long enough. I stay now because I'm here. Most of my friends are here. It's become home to me," he said. "I go back to Switzerland quite regularly, of course. I'm still a Swiss citizen, and I have family there, and a house on the lake." He eyed Richard quietly for a moment, and then looked into his beer as he spoke. "Many Swiss think I'm living some kind of 'California Dream,' but most of them know that going for a holiday somewhere is one thing. Settling down, raising a family, for example, that's a different story." Richard was silent. "I don't want to make a big speech, but America is not all it's cracked up to be. This mess we're all in now, the so-called financial crisis. Well, it really is one, it was born here, and it couldn't have happened anywhere else."

Richard felt as if he were on a stage without a spotlight, groping for material with which to claim his rightful place. "Yeah, whatever," he said, waving his hand and looking out over the heads of the crowd.

Hans sipped his beer, keeping his eye on Richard. "Come on, Richard. Don't take it personally." Richard allowed himself a quick glance at Hans and forced a smile before turning his attention to his beer. "I've been here twenty years!" Hans said. "Jesus, how time flies."

"What is it that you do again?" Richard asked. "When we first met you said you own a business?"

Hans nodded. "Yes, I have a few businesses here. A few restaurants, an art gallery. Rich kid stuff, you know. My family was wealthy, so it was always pretty easy for me. I originally came here to be with an American woman I met back home. She was away on a skiing holiday and we met at a ski resort. I followed her here. But that was a long time ago."

"Were you married?" Richard asked.

"Yes, for a time. She wasn't happy with me. Back then I was too involved with my businesses. Even though I didn't need the money. Stupid."

"Did you have any children?"

Hans took a long drink, nearly finishing his beer. He tapped the glass against the table. He spoke slowly. "I have a wonderful daughter."

He spoke as if confronting a distant memory. Richard felt this was not a good subject for Hans and searched for something new. "Wow, great. How are your businesses doing, now that the economy is so bad?" he asked him.

"Oh, I'm doing okay. Things are slowing down but I'm okay. And I'm not letting staff go unless things get really bad."

"You're lucky," Richard told him. "Your whole life, never any financial worries."

"Hey, listen," Hans began, "it's not like that at all. Don't get me wrong. It's a convenience that can be very oppressive, because in the end you always seem to desire more. You get used to it and then all you see are those who've got it better than you. And suddenly you don't feel so lucky anymore. It's like the Beatles when they sang, 'Money can't buy me love,' and you'd better believe it." He finished his drink and did not look up from the floor. Richard could see a struggle in him. "Money isn't everything."

"That's easy for you to say. I just... I just want freedom."

" 'Freedom'? From what? Hell, you're a young man, you've got everything ahead of you. All kinds of possibilities. Freedom from what?"

Richard searched for an answer. "From uncertainty."

"Sometimes, my good man, uncertainty is one of the best things a man can have going for him. Try to imagine knowing all the answers. Try to imagine: no surprises..." he whispered, waving his hands in the air like a magician dazzling his audience. He saw the serious look on Richard's face and gave him a gentle pat on the shoulder, coaxing a smile out of him. Richard began reconsidering. "Keep your feet on the ground," Hans told him, as if reading his mind. Richard picked up his glass and took a long drink. He was tired. He looked out the window and saw a police car going slowly by. Then he heard Hans snapping his fingers. " 'I don't care too / Much for money / Money can't buy me love' "

The two sat in silence for a moment. The noise in the bar seemed to rise. Richard and Hans took a moment to look about them again and take in the scene. Richard's eyes unconsciously roamed the bar looking for attractive women until he was reminded of Toshika.

"What about Toshika?" he said, before he had any idea of what he meant to ask. Hans questioned him with his eyebrows. "I mean, she seems like a nice girl."

"Oh, yes! Very nice. Do you like her?" Hans asked him.

"Well, I don't really know her," Richard offered, not willing to meet the question head on.

"Yes, Toshika is very special," Hans sighed, tapping his now empty glass against the table again. "She just needs some... stability. A nice young man, perhaps."

"Another beer?" Richard asked. He hopped up and went to the bar. After he ordered another round he stood waiting, thinking about what Hans had just said. It seemed Toshika was indeed single. He said she needed a nice young man. That must mean she was single. Unless Hans only meant that now she had a man who was not so nice. Or so young. Paying the bartender, Richard returned to his cushion with the beers.

"Ah, that's better. Thank you, Richard."

"Sure. So, Toshika is single then?" Richard asked, trying his best to sound uninterested.

Hans smiled at Richard's efforts, but only briefly, as his expression darkened. "She sees a few people, now and then, but it's not right."

"What do you mean?"

"Oh, it's complicated, like I said. The others are too old, and... It's just not good for her. She needs a normal relationship with a good, bright young man like you, Richard, as a matter of fact. Yes. That would make me happy."

"But would it make her happy?" Richard tried to joke.

"I don't think she knows what she wants," Hans said in a distant voice. "So. Tell me what attracted you to philosophy." he commanded.

Richard was surprised and disappointed at the sudden change in subject. Thinking of Toshika had him nearly spellbound. "What?" he asked Hans.

"I said, tell me what attracted you to philosophy."

This was a question that seemed simple enough, but which gave Richard trouble every time nonetheless. But before beginning to even try to answer, he had to ask a standard question.

"Have you studied philosophy?" he asked Hans.

"In Europe, everyone studies philosophy," he said. "Of course, it was a long time ago, but yes."

Richard nodded, unaware of the fact. Having to face the question now, his shoulders sagged. He was not sure why he chose philosophy. It was simply a subject that appealed to him intuitively after his initial exposure to it in school. Why does anyone like anything? He knew it was a perfectly acceptable answer, but he felt that he had to have something to match the grandeur of the task of philosophy itself: an understanding of life. He pondered for a moment and then gave up.

"I know it doesn't sound impressive, but in the beginning, after I learned about argumentation and logic, I just enjoyed being able to smash up other people's arguments. Philosophizing with a hammer, so to speak. After that initial phase, philosophy was for me simply something that I looked forward to doing. So I kept doing it."

Hans smiled wistfully, rubbing his hands together. "Ah, yes. Learning is wonderful, isn't it? You know what's nice about getting older? You realize you have more time to learn. You aren't as interested as you once were in running around, doing *everything*. You really have time, if you play your cards right, to relax and explore. If you're interested, of course."

"I suppose that's true."

"Yes. Tell me, who are your favorite philosophers?"

"My favorites?" Richard asked. "I liked Plato's dialogues. So readable. Like reading a novel, almost. And I liked Nietzsche because he was so daring. He could be everything. A dry, analytic philosopher, a poet, or a wild upstart out picking a fight," he said, his eyes shining.

"And what is your own philosophy? How do you see the world?"

Richard shrugged. "Well, you know I have been concentrating more on learning the history of philosophy more than I have been developing my own ideas. It's natural, I guess. But I would have to say from an ontological point of view I'm a realist."

Hans considered Richard's words a moment. He did not seem to approve. "Yes, realism," he said. "It is a sensible position to take. Everything is as it seems. Everything is simple. But nothing is simple, and nothing is as it seems. Or if it is, how do we know?"

"But why assume that anything might be different than the way it seems to be?" Richard asked. "Why make things more complicated? Just because one can formulate the question 'What is the meaning of life?' doesn't mean it makes sense, any more than 'What color is your soul?' "

"So maybe life has no meaning?"

"Exactly."

They sat in the dim light of the bar, nursing their beer, considering life's meaninglessness.

"You know what?" Hans finally asked. "I think that's just the easy way out." Richard stared at him and shrugged. "Well, let's shove off, shall we?" Hans said, both hands slapping his knees.

Richard looked at his watch. "Yes, okay."

They stood up and each took a deep breath. As he began to make his way to the door Richard felt the alcohol pushing his body in directions he had not commanded it to go. His first thought was to the drive home. Gauging his ability as he walked, it was not so bad, but he did not feel extremely confident and would have taken a cab if Hans had not spoken up just then.

"I say, Richard, I wonder if you wouldn't give me a lift home? I'm not sure if it would be so smart for me to drive just now. That is, if you feel up to it."

Reluctantly, Richard agreed. For some reason the thought never occurred to him that they should just share a cab. Out on the street the air was chilly. They walked a few yards down the sidewalk to Richard's car. As he unlocked the door, Hans said that he had to quickly get something from his car. Richard stood and waited, glancing quickly up and down the street to see if he should be concerned about anything. A few people were walking towards them quite a ways down the street. Someone started a car on the other side of the street a half block down. The coast was clear. Richard looked back to Hans, who was still fishing around inside his car. Finally he got out and with his briefcase in one hand and keys in the other, locked the car and came back.

"Okay," he said, walking around to the passenger side of Richard's car.

"Are you sure your car will be all right here? In this neighborhood?" Richard asked him, realizing now for the first time that it was actually a pretty dumb idea to leave such an expensive car sitting here overnight.

Hans looked at Richard and it seemed to dawn on him, too. "You're absolutely right," he said. "Well, let's do this. Will your car be okay if it sits here tonight?"

"Sure. What have you got in mind?"

"Let's take my car. Drop me off, drive yourself home, and bring my car to the game tomorrow night. I've got another car. It's no problem. I'll get a cab to the game. Then we can return to your car tomorrow night."

"That's fine by me," Richard said, and they walked back to Hans' car. Hans gave Richard the keys to his Jaguar. Richard looked at the car's sumptuous interior as he sunk into the soft leather seat and held the wheel.

"Like it? Take it out for some exercise tomorrow, I don't care. Have a ball."

"Oh, no," Richard began, "I couldn't."

"No, really. Go ahead if you feel like it," Hans told him.

Richard started the engine and carefully pulled away from the curb. From there he drove slowly, with Hans giving directions to his house. It was a large, beautiful home on a hill in Pacific Heights. As Richard slowed to a stop in front of the house he bent forward to get a better look at it.

"Very nice," he told Hans. "These houses up here are great."

"Yes, terrific. And terrifically expensive. I bought this place about fifteen years ago. Could sell it now for three or four times what I paid then. Cash, even. Despite the economic situation, the price of homes here is holding up very well." He looked up at the house through the car window. "Well, would you like to come in? Have a look around?" He did not look at Richard when he asked, but continued to look at his house through the window. He seemed to be studying it with interest, as if the two of them were house hunting.

"No, thanks. Actually, I'm pretty tired, but maybe another time."

"Sure," Hans said, still looking the house up and down.

Richard stared into the center of the steering wheel and, drawing inspiration from the snarling gold Jaguar there, finally asked the question he had been trying to ask all night. "Listen, Hans, about the game. This money,"

"Enjoy it," Hans interrupted. "Buy yourself a little freedom."

Richard looked at Hans and could not believe his ears. Was it right? Had he heard correctly? Did Hans really mean it? What *else* could he mean?

Richard was playing for himself! Overwhelmed, he nodded, and then mumbled a kind of thanks. It was the least he could do. Hans watched Richard's expression. When he got what he wanted, he laughed, and then glanced once more at the house before he swung the door open.

"Wait," cried Richard, leaning over and fetching the bottle of champagne that lay at Hans' feet and holding it up to him."

"Oh, right. Well I think I've had enough for tonight, but this'll go in the fridge."

He rose up out of the car and shrugged, making some remark about the cold before quickly jogging up to the front of the house. He opened the door, waved, and was gone. Richard saw the lights come on inside the house.

As he was about to drive off, a car passed by from behind and stopped a little way ahead of him in the middle of the street. It was a rather shabby car for this neighborhood. Richard pulled out from the curb and drove forward slowly, and then an arm emerged from the driver window of the car in front and waved him on. As he drove by he fought the desire to look into the car and lost, shooting a quick glance to his right as he passed. It was a police officer. He could not really see him, but he saw the uniform. Then he remembered all the beer he had been drinking and immediately became tense, feeling heat on the back of his neck. Gripping the wheel tightly he tried by sheer force of will to throw off the effects of the alcohol. He took a deep breath. "I'm fine," he said aloud. "Fine." When he came to the end of the street he stopped and looked in the rearview mirror. The car was following him. He hit his turn signal, proceeded slowly, and continued. Glancing in the rear-view mirror he saw that the car kept pace with him. "Fuck!" he shouted. "Go find a real problem, you asshole!" he said, whispering this time in some absurd effort to hide. Some two blocks later, he saw the car's left turn signal blinking. "Yeah!" he cried. He held his breath as the car slowed, turned, and was gone. "I'll never drink and drive again!" he cried, turning on the radio.

With that behind him, he realized he was hungry, and turned and headed to one of the best late-night restaurants in the city, Orphan Andy's in the Castro. He had a burger and fries and a big chocolate shake. That was the kind of place it was. When he finished, he just sat there staring out the window. Some kind of wild jazz was playing in the background. Richard was drifting off into the musical landscape, as the sleazy, sweaty, boozy saxophone floated heavily through the air. Noticing his odd stare the waiter came by his table.

"Lose your luck, sailor?"

Richard shifted his stare from outside over to the man. The waiter stood there smiling and looking sorry for him. "No!" he said finally, snapping out of it. "No."

"Well, that's better! Good for you," he said, and taking Richard's plate and glass left him alone again. In a few minutes he rose abruptly, put some money on the table, and left.

Derick sat next to Alan on the bed and watched the small screen as Alan ran Mr. Mario through an avalanche of unending obstacles, bounding, leaping, ducking and flying as he picked up bonus points, grabbed special tools and life points, and, inevitably, was either whacked by the enemy, fell off a cliff or drowned. It was a tough world in there, and Alan was much more expert at working his way through it than Derick was.

"Ahh, man," Alan squealed. He was a goner. "Your turn." He passed the Game Boy into Derick's eager hands.

"Yeah," Derick said, grinning, as he readied himself for his lightening run. "This time, I'm gonna get me some." The machine blinked and bleeped, announcing the advent of the next play. Then, small fingers pressed, buttons clicked, elbows flapped, tongues darted in and out of mouths aiding concentration, breathing proceeded erratically in huffs and puffs. It was a good show, but Derick hadn't racked up nearly as much time or points before his death was announced by the digital fizzling of the toy.

"Ahh, man," he cried, in unison with Alan.

"You doin' it, you gettin' it."

"I know, I mean, that was better than last time, wasn't it?"

"Shhh!" Alan warned, looking over his shoulder toward the closed door of his bedroom. He looked at his friend. "Sure," he said. And he meant it.

The two ten-year-old boys sat on the edge of Alan Porter's bed in their pajamas.

"What time is it?" Derick asked, turning to look at the clock on Alan's night table just as Alan did. "Whoa! Almost two-thirty!" he whispered. "You sure your folks can't hear us in here?"

"As long as we whisper, it's okay. But they're really light sleepers."

A shadow crossed before the window just in front of them that was covered by the faded red blinds that had hung from them since Alan was a baby. They were nearly pink now. Not a color he was thrilled to have in his room. The two boys had barely noticed it when they heard a plastic metallic clatter just outside the window. Something had just hit the ground outside. Derick shot Alan a look and the next moment the boys were on their knees at the blinds. Alan grabbed the blinds where they met in the center of the window and opened them just enough to get one eyeful of whatever it was outside his window. "Ahh! I can't see!" Derick hissed from behind him. He quickly hobbled over to the edge of the window and peaked. The boys saw a man walking away from a small pile of electronic gear that lay on the sidewalk in the beam of a streetlamp, balling up a plastic garbage bag as he did. He stuffed the bag into a trash can that hung on a pole in the sidewalk and then turned to get into his car which sat idling right there just at the edge of the bright beam of light. He glanced up and around as he swung the door open and got into his car and drove away. With the man gone, the boys both stared at the goods that had hit the concrete just moments ago. They couldn't believe their eyes: a notebook computer, a camera, a cell phone, a man's wallet. All of it just sitting there for the taking. The boys pulled back from the blinds and stared at one another open-mouthed.

"Whoa!" they hissed, simultaneously.

"Let's go get it!" Alan said. "But really quiet, okay?" Derick nodded. The two boys walked quietly out of Alan's bedroom, down the hallway, past his brother Leon's room on the right, door open, lights out, empty. They passed his parents' closed door on the left. They stood at the front door while Alan looked at Derick and raised a silencing finger to his lips. Alan stood up on his toes to take down the chain lock, then unlocked the bolt that was just above the door handle, and then slowly turned the door handle as he looked back down the hallway. The two of them stepped outside and closed the door quietly.

Derick was first to step down the three steps to the street. It was quiet in the darkness. No cars passed. No one was in sight. He paused at the corner and peered around the brick wall of his friend's house. "Wait!" Alan cried, bumping into him as he tried to peer around the corner from behind Derick.

"Coast is clear!" Derick said.

All at once the two boys clamored for the small pile of goods that lay under the streetlight. In a moment they were back inside, looking at each other with wide eyes as they reverted to their silent mode. Alan carefully closed the door and began locking it. In their bare feet the boys padded slowly down the hallway as quickly as they could, finally turning right at the last door. Once inside with the door closed, they lay down their prize on the bed, climbed onto it, and broke out into wide grins as they began to take inventory.

4

He slept poorly again. At one time, early in the morning, he awoke with a start and looked at his alarm clock before remembering that he did not have a job any more, and before remembering the game. He lay in bed for some time, rolling things over and over in his mind, struggling to get a firm hold on reality. What is happening? What is happening to me? Am I finally getting lucky after all these years?

He had never done well in school. Never shined in anything. Not academically, not in sports. His father, a penny pinching, unpleasant man who placed unnecessary and painful burdens on Richard and his brothers, had not instilled in him a drop of self-confidence. Growing up, Richard did not know of his father's own frustrations. Would not have cared either, had he known of them. They would not have been a good enough excuse. There is never a good enough excuse. No, it was not possible for him to know what burdened his father's mind and heart. A certain relationship must exist between people before they open up to each other. "I'm not your friend," his father had told him. "That doesn't fit in with my philosophy of fatherhood. I'm your dictator." Richard had only been fourteen, but he knew enough to know that his father should never have told him that. Regardless of how he felt about parenting. Saying it changed everything.

Somehow, he always knew he would be all right. Finding friends was not a problem. Never had been. He would be fine as soon as he left home. He knew it. But the nagging sense of having to do without, of financial worries, would follow him. He felt that someday, somehow, he would be all right in that way too. How, he did not know. He had not prepared himself for a lucrative career. Philosophy. What was philosophy? Many had tried to tell him that this was not the age for philosophy. There was "little momentum to capitalize on." Teaching? For years he had been told by those who only had his best interests at heart to look around himself at the exploding technological revolution that was gaining speed every day. He was advised to grab a meal ticket. He was told that no job that paid well was particularly enjoyable. He was told to tone down his expectations and to focus on money and the good life. In this way, they said, he would be happy.

He had listened to them, until it was just not possible for him to go any further. Then he chose philosophy. Having finished his undergraduate studies, he was at the juncture where most sought a career. He wanted a break from school. Wanted to work for a time, and think about going back to prepare for a career teaching if he felt the pull. But now, wanting or not wanting to work was not the problem. Employers firing scores of people by the day was the problem. How would he manage? Would he have to move back home, with his parents? He had resigned himself to that probability only days before. And now, with the game appearing to be something real, things were different. All these years, he knew he would be all right, but was this the way it was going to happen? To simply fall into fortune? Things like this do happen, he told himself. Yes, but they happen to other people. Always to other people. So, what – am I going to turn it away? Am I going to refuse this gift? This opportunity? There was no question about it. The excitement at these thoughts made it clear that he wouldn't be able to get back to sleep. He lay awake and stared at the blackness above him.

When he awoke again it was nearly lunch time. His head was clear. He was amazed at how good he felt. The events from the night before seemed far away, even insignificant in his fresh state of mind. He went into the sunny front room and pulled the shades open. There he stood in one of his favorite spots, in front of the bay windows, naked, looking at that small bit of ocean that he could see beyond the rooftops. A little, shimmering blue triangle. It was so small, really, but to Richard it could have filled the entire landscape.

It was a beautiful day. Looking out his window onto the world he had the idea to spend the day at the beach. He put on some clothes, had something to eat, and set off for his favorite piece of coastline across the Golden Gate Bridge. The view from the bridge on a sunny day for him elicited a feeling of joy and freedom that he would otherwise only associate with being far away from home on some exotic holiday. The kind of holiday he had never taken.

The drive took him into the Marin County Headlands to the highest point along the coast and the beginning of a one-way road that snaked through the chaparral with dramatic, teeth-sucking views to the water. Lying just opposite the tip of the peninsula of San Francisco, the Headlands contrasted completely with the pretend metropolis that lay across the water. A vast area of protected coastland, it offered a few of the most spectacular beaches in the area. Hans' Jaguar hugged the road, tempting Richard to explore its ability.

After parking in the large dirt lot at the top of the trail, he made his way down to the beach. The trail ended on a rocky outcropping in the middle of the beach. He stood on it and looked left and right before heading off to his usual spot. He went to the west end and found a place amongst automobile-sized boulders. Removing all of his clothing, as was the practice at this beach, he lay down on his towel and closed his eyes, feeling the heat sink in to his body, drawing him into a state of deep relaxation, and then once again into sleep.

He awoke to the sound of a wave dashing itself into the sand. He wiped his eyes and sat up, removing his sun block from his bag and rubbing it all over his body. The tide was high and the waves were bigger than they normally were. To help shake off the sleep he got up and went off further west toward the rocky cliff wall that jutted out into the ocean from the beach just a stone's throw from where he lay. It was an enjoyable place to climb around and watch the crabs doing their crabwalk. Where the beach ended and the cliff's steep slopes came to meet the beach, a rocky platform began and extended about a hundred feet into the water. It was an easy climb up onto it from the sand. Richard thought he would go along the left edge where the rock sits only a couple of feet above the water, and then dive in. The rock was very sharp, forcing Richard to carefully watch where he put his bare feet. As he made his way out to where the water was deep, he sensed danger and looked up to see a large wave coming. It was going to break right over the rock. He had no time to do anything except crouch a bit and brace himself. The wave hit him and knocked him flat on his back onto the sharp rock.

The cold water of the Pacific Ocean instantly shocked him into action. He quickly got up and shook his head, throwing water off his face and eyes, feeling grateful that he had not hit his head. He stood on the rock and wiped his face. He was so shaken by this violent act of nature that he forgot to look out for the next wave until the sound of it breaking against the rock in front of him interrupted his stupor. This wave was even bigger than the last one. He looked back to the beach but he was too far out to make it back to safety. In a panic he stepped to the right and crouched behind a lump of rock that came up as high as his knees, grabbing the knobby top of the rock. In this position he felt secure, but as the wave broke against the rock and shot over the top of it, its force broke his grip and sent him backward. Landing once again on his back, he felt a sharp pain in his shoulder blade. The water quickly escaped into the cracks and holes in the rock and left him dazed. This time it was the salt water in his mouth that brought him to his senses as he turned his head and spat. He rose quickly and checked the water. The waves were smaller now. He made it to the edge of the rock and dove into the water, turning immediately and swimming towards the shore. Shaken as he was, he had to laugh when the thought of being mauled by one of the great white sharks that roam the bay entered his mind.

As he pulled himself from the water he looked at the few people scattered amongst the rocks, expecting someone to come rushing up to him to comment or offer help, but to his surprise it seemed that nobody had been aware of his ordeal. Wiping his forehead he headed back to his spot. He was full of adrenaline and wanted to talk to somebody. On his way back he noticed a woman sitting up and looking out at the ocean. He approached her and waved a hello as he neared.

"Did you see what just happened to me?"

She looked up at him and put her hand over her eyes to shield the sun. "No, what happened?"

Presented with the opportunity, he knew right away that he did not feel like going into it. He was sure it would be anticlimactic, so he just told her that he had gotten knocked over by a wave and that she should be careful if she went up on the rocks. She thanked him.

When he got back to his place he sat down and started looking himself over. He had two cuts on his back and one on his buttocks, but they were not serious. He lay down on his towel and dried in the sun, trying to forget about it. After lying there for a few minutes he felt the pain in one spot on his back getting worse. He sat up tried to check it, but having no mirror it was not possible. Resigning himself to this pain he looked out over the water. Then, thinking that the sun might help his wounds somehow he rolled over onto his stomach. He looked at the Golden Gate and watched a tanker coasting in under it. He watched it as it moved, nearly imperceptibly at that distance, until he heard voices off to his left. His eyes followed the sound. Two women were approaching, barefoot and in shorts with bags slung over their shoulders. They were young and attractive. He raised himself onto his elbows for a better look. They passed by and then stopped near the end of the beach and began to get undressed. One was blond and had very obvious tan lines – the initiate – and the other had none at all. When they were finished they ran to the water and plunged in. It was a lovely sight. They shrieked at the cold, but pressed on until their feet could touch the sand no more, and they swam out into the blue. Richard watched anxiously, hoping they would not venture up onto his rocky platform. They swam in the opposite direction, back towards him. After a minute or so they headed to shore directly in front of where he lay. As they entered the shallow water they laughed and played, splashing and pushing each other as they headed out. The dark haired woman came first. Richard watched how the muscles moved in her legs as she stomped clear of the water, and the way her wet body shone in the sun. Then he looked at her face.

It was Toshika. He gasped. This beach had always been a fantasy world where he would strip and become a different person. Now, in the presence of someone whose face had a name, it was very real. He quickly grabbed his sunglasses and pretended to look off into another direction, hoping she had not noticed him. His heart raced. Now he had been able to see everything long before he had ever hoped. He kept his eye on her and before he knew it she looked directly at him. Her expression changed and he felt sure that she had recognized him.

"Hey!" she called out, breathing heavily. Richard paid no attention. "Hi!" she said, stopping just a few yards in front of him as she turned toward her friend who stood in the surf, wringing out her hair. Richard tried to sound as natural as possible.

"Oh, hey! I didn't recognize you."

"After just one day? You've got a bad eye for faces."

Now what? He looked down into the sand, then down the beach. Anywhere but here. The silence rushed him into saying something stupid. "Well, I guess I didn't look at your face until now." Nice. Way to go.

Toshika issued him a testing smile. "Should I take that as a compliment?"

Feeling foolish, Richard waved his own comment away. "Forget it, I didn't mean it."

Toshika turned toward her friend as she arrived. In a moment they stood side by side. "Richard, this is my friend Page. Page, Richard," Toshika exclaimed, as though she were introducing her fiancé.

"Hi," Richard said, taking off his sunglasses. Toshika's friend waved without enthusiasm. Realizing that without his sunglasses on his gaze would be transparent, he put them back on. Under the circumstances, the brief de-masking had served its purpose as a polite gesture.

"Richard is the new gambler," Toshika informed Page.

"Oh, right," Page said, "The new guy from last night. Pretty young compared to those other guys," she remarked. She waited for Richard to answer.

"Well, yes..." It was all he could say. He still felt like an impostor and did not like talking about the whole gambling affair. Suddenly, both of the women sank to their knees directly in front of him.

"Just lucky, I guess," Page said. "How did you make your money?" This kind of talk was just what he was afraid of. He did not want to get involved in it at all. "You don't look like a wealthy person," she added.

"Well..." he struggled lamely.

"It's all right," Toshika said, "you can keep it a secret."

"Right," he said, "it's really the best policy not to talk about those things. It's so boring anyway, really."

Page looked at Toshika. "The way rich people talk about money is just, I just can't get over it," she said in disbelief.

Toshika smiled and looked at Richard. "Well, anyway, you were doing quite well last night from what I could see."

"Yes, it wasn't bad."

Page brushed some sand from her breast and looked at Richard harshly. "Why don't you sit up and be polite?" She looked at Toshika. "He's probably as hard as a rock!" she said, smirking. Then she raised her arms above her head and shook her breasts, taunting Richard.

"Page!" Toshika cried, then looked at Richard. "Excuse her, please."

Page got up and waved to Richard, smiling in apology. "I'm going back and dry off. Don't be long," she said, and then began jogging back to the place where they had left their things.

"No, she's right, I'm just lazy," Richard said. Neither of them spoke for a moment.

"So what did you do last night? You and Hans?"

"We just had a drink. Didn't stay out late."

"Yeah? What time did you get home?"

"About two."

"Two? That late?"

"Yes, well, after I dropped him off – he didn't feel like driving – I went and got a bite to eat."

"Oh," Toshika said, eager to change the subject. "You know, about this whole gambling thing. I have the feeling that you aren't like the others. I mean, you aren't really wealthy, are you? Hans was... I mean, he... you're playing with *his* money, aren't you?" Richard held his breath. "Don't worry," she continued, "I mean, I don't care since I'm not playing. But the others might not like it so much if you end up losing a lot and can't pay them. But if Hans is fronting you then it's no problem. I was just curious, that's all. Am I right?"

"I think it's best if we don't go into it right now," Richard said, trying his best to avoid trouble. How had she known? Had Hans done that sort of thing before? Toshika looked down the beach in the direction of her friend.

"Well, I should go dry off before I get too salty," she said. She reached back and gathered her hair in her hands, pulling it to her chest and playing with the ends. "We have some wine and something to eat if you want to join us."

"Well thanks, but I think I'll be leaving soon." As soon as the words came out of his mouth he cursed himself. He was not planning on leaving, so why had he said that? Was he crazy? What kind of opportunity did he just excuse himself from?

"Oh," she said softly. Dropping her hair she grabbed a handful of the black, flaky sand and then let it slowly slip through her fingers. She looked at him, and he watched as her eyes roamed over his backside.

"Hey!" she said, "What's this? What happened?"

She was instantly up on all fours, leaning over his back. He felt a painful touch as she examined the cut on his shoulder.

"I fell on the rocks," he said weakly, "A wave came."

"You didn't even clean it off."

"Well, I can't see it. Is it bad?"

"No, but still, it must hurt."

"A little."

Toshika leaned so close over him that he could feel the coolness emanating from her still wet body as she brushed some sand off of him gently with the tips of her fingers, her wet hair brushing his back. "Oh! You've got one here, too," she said, moving even closer on her knees until they were just touching his shoulder. He felt another twinge as she examined the cut on his buttocks, again brushing away the sand. The feel of her fingers gave him goose bumps and he found himself laying his head down on his towel, looking at the skin of her thigh in front of his face. "It's not so bad," she said. "Should I kiss it and make it better?" Her hand, resting on Richard's lower back just above the cut, burned a hole right through him.

"Yeah," he said, waiting. He held his breath. There was no sound except for that of the waves as he waited for that kiss. He could feel that she was bending closer and closer. He imagined her lips together before they pressed against him. He stared ahead at the flesh of her leg, not daring to close his eyes. Then he felt the gentle touch of her lips as they came down upon his wound, sending a hot flash through him. Just before she retreated he felt the faint brush of her nipples against his back and was suddenly overcome by the image of her crouching naked over him. He felt a wave of energy course through him lasting just an instant and leaving the skin all over his body fresh with a sensitivity that he was sure she could see, giving him away to her.

"Oops," he heard her say to herself quietly as she moved back away from him. "There you go," she said, "All better."

"Thank you."

She stood up. "Well, see you tonight." She turned and walked away.

His heart was beating powerfully as he felt himself nearly out of breath. He was glad she was gone. He had never been very smooth with women. He found it hard to have a normal conversation when confronted by a woman he was attracted to. He could tell that this thing with Toshika was one of those that comes along rarely, so powerful was her effect on him. He lay there a while longer and then got dressed. With his pack over his shoulder he walked over to Toshika and her friend, who sat on their towels sipping white wine and eating cheese and bread. After he had wished them a nice afternoon and shook Page's hand, he stood there, unable to break away.

"Are you forgetting something?" Page taunted.

"What?" he replied.

"Page! Don't be a jerk!" Toshika cried, before jumping up and sending Richard off with a gentle push. "Take care of that butt," she said.

"Will do."

He drove home, showered, and in the fading hours of the afternoon he walked down to Haight Street and into Henry's bar. Before taking a seat he dug out Hans' business card from his wallet and took out his cell phone. For some reason he was feeling again like this thing was just a fantasy. He wanted a few words with Hans to restore his confidence. As the phone rang he quickly thought of what he would say. After ringing several times, someone finally answered.

"Hello?" came the cautious greeting. It was not Hans.

"Hello, may I speak with Mr. Kienle?"

A long silence followed. "He is not here now. Who is this?"

For some reason the tone of voice on the other end annoyed him. Since he would not be able to get the reassurance he was looking for, he immediately felt uncooperative.

"Do you expect him back soon?"

"Yes, very soon, but who is this?"

"Please tell him Richard called and that I'll try him later."

"Richard?"

"Thanks."

He stared at the phone for a moment before telling himself to forget it. He took a seat at the bar and ordered a beer, watching the bartender carefully but for no particular reason. After placing his beer in front of him the bartender returned to the sink and began washing glasses with a fluid efficiency. Richard watched him mechanically washing them and speaking to someone who sat there looking quite comfortable. A regular. They spoke casually, neither one paying too much attention to the other, and as he watched them he realized that being a bartender was probably all this man would ever be. It was him. He fit. And it was not a bad thing at all. He was a bartender. He was completely essential to the proper operation of the place. It was his domain. Richard realized he could not have put him down in the least. As a matter of fact, he realized then that it was nice to see someone who really belonged to their job. Someone who was perfect right where they were. He gulped from his glass and turned, resting his back against the bar.

Having been on the beach, in the sun, and having not had anything to eat besides a bagel and an apple, his beer was having an unusually strong effect. The departure from common sense was welcome. He smiled and anticipated another winning night at poker as his mind began to buzz. Hearing a commotion to his right, he turned and watched as half a dozen Hare Krishnas trouped into the bar from the street in full song, with finger cymbals clinking and voices chanting. The patrons of the bar watched wide-eyed but with good humor as the whole group of them made their way once past the bar to the back of the room, once around the pool table, and then back, all the while singing the only tune they seem to know. As they neared him once more, Richard held up his glass in a toast to their cheerful delirium. Recognizing his gesture as one of genuine camaraderie, a girl no older than seventeen or eighteen stopped in front of Richard and, grabbing his knees, leaned forward and licked his face from his chin right up over his lips and the tip of his nose up to his forehead. He felt something hard in her tongue. As a sort of finale she stuck out her tongue with a big smile and opened her eyes wide, revealing a small silver stud in the center of her pierced tongue. Something to spoil for him whatever was erotic or sexy about it. Before dashing out the door her hand came flashing up to Richard's face and he felt the tip of her finger against his forehead right between his eyes.

In a moment all was as it was before. As Richard sat, dazed in his beer mind, the smell of the girl's saliva drying on his face seized him and he quickly looked out the window hoping to catch another glimpse of his priestess. He licked his lips and felt an urge to run out the door after them. Turning around on his stool he found the bartender standing opposite him pointing at his forehead with his hand over his mouth as he laughed. "What?" Richard asked, as he lifted his beer and glanced at his reflection in the mirror behind the bar. A pasty yellow fingerprint between his eyes looked back at him. He looked at the bartender and smiled triumphantly in his elevated status.

5

Without really being aware of why, Richard parked down the road about thirty yards from the law office, as if this would shield his identity or connection with the goings on inside. Standing next to Hans' Jaguar, he hesitated and took a deep breath to steady his nerves. Looking in the direction of the office he noticed Dr. Xang and Mr. Norton climbing the steps to the door. As he watched them, Dr. Xang looked in his direction. He stopped suddenly and looked directly at Richard for a moment as Mr. Norton stopped behind him and looked at him as well. Richard hesitated. Something was not right. Mr. Norton nudged Dr. Xang and they resumed their climb, standing a moment at the door until they were buzzed in. As the door closed, echoing down the lonely street, Richard locked the car door and crossed the street. He arrived at the door and rang the bell only moments after Dr. Xang and Mr. Norton had entered, but waited more than a minute before he heard a reply.

"Yes," came a familiar voice over the speaker.

"Hello, it's Richard."

A faint hiss issued from the speaker as Jeffries held the button down in silence. "Just a moment," he finally said. It did not sound good. But just then the buzzing from the door forced him to enter, and, standing in the doorway in the dark, was Jeffries.

"Hello, Jeffries," Richard said, extending his hand and looking Jeffries in the eye. Jeffries hesitated, an unnerving forcefulness in his gaze. He shook Richard's hand. Something was wrong. Richard could see it in his face. Jeffries was burdened with something that he was at odds to contain. Jeffries took several steps backwards through the metal detector, then halted and called Richard forward with his eyes. Richard stepped through the glass doorway and then waited to be invited further. Jeffries stood waiting for Richard but seemed to be keeping a rather safe distance. With a gesture of his hand he beckoned Richard to enter the room first, ahead of him. Entering the room Richard saw that the others were all present and seated at the round table. They watched him steadily. Toshika sat behind the bar with her fingers laced together on it, her expression keenly distant.

No one made a sound. Looking for some comfort, Richard's eyes searched among the faces for Hans, but he was not there yet.

"Please have a seat, Richard," Mr. Peters said.

Richard went to the table reluctantly and took his seat, trying not to make eye contact and fussing with his chair a moment in an attempt to remove the attention that had been so squarely placed upon him.

Jeffries cleared his throat. "Richard, Hans has been murdered."

Richard turned in his chair to face Jeffries, who had not moved from his position in the doorway. "What?" he asked. The words he had heard were so ridiculous there was no need for genuine alarm.

"He was found this morning at home by his housekeeper. Apparently he surprised a burglar who hit him on the head, and that was it." He looked at Richard steadily, waiting for him to speak. But Richard found no words. He had never been informed of someone's murder. Someone that he knew. Someone who had been killed soon after he had been with them. He brought up images of Hans, remembered things he had said. He saw him getting out of the car and walking to his front door, then turning to wave. He remembered meeting him, and how he seemed so at ease with himself. Just like the bartender, he belonged. Richard looked at Toshika, hoping to find some support. But she merely sat quietly. Her expression was now meaningful to Richard, and seemed to be not merely a distant thoughtfulness, but more the result of having been made aware of something shocking. Something emotionally devastating. Something indeed like the death of a friend.

The others seemed to have been alerted to this news some time ago, judging from their expressionless faces.

Richard was stunned. His mind was fighting some kind of noise that seemed to crowd out every rational thought he could put together. Murdered. The word rang in his ears, and turned his stomach. He kept seeing Hans' face in the bar in the soft light. He was just a nice man, he thought. Just a nice man.

He felt the eyes of the group upon him. They were waiting for an answer to their question. The obvious question. The one he couldn't answer.

"Shit."

"Yes." said Jeffries.

"Do they know who did it?" he asked, barely able to put words together.

"The police are still questioning people. No one has been arrested. I spoke with them today, and I gave them your name," Jeffries said, and he walked into the room and took a seat at the table. A few moments later Richard was struck by the last thing he heard.

"What?" he asked.

Jeffries gave him a puzzled look. "I didn't say anything. I said I spoke to the police and gave them your name."

Did Jeffries give the police his name out of routine, or did he think that Richard had something to do with his murder?

"You left with Hans last night, didn't you?" Mr. Peters asked him, his face betraying the shock that he felt.

Richard nodded. "Yes, we went out for a drink in the Haight, and then I took him home."

"What time did you drop him off?" Mr. Peters asked him.

"About two," Richard told him. He looked at Jeffries. "Should I call the police?"

"Why would you do that?"

"Well, I may have been the last person to see him alive."

"Then you would be the killer," said Dr. Xang.

Richard had had enough. "Look," he began, but was interrupted.

"Oh come on, look at him!" Miss Reed scoffed, "He doesn't know anything!" She looked at Richard. "Did you have anything to do with this?" she asked as a sort of formality for one who knew already what the answer was.

"No, did you?"

At this, all eyes turned to Miss Reed. The tables were turned as quickly as if everybody secretly considered everyone else suspect. The light above the table shone down on them all as though the whole lot of them were being interrogated.

"Me?" she gasped. And then, throwing up her hands with a short laugh, "And what about you, Toshika?"

"What *about* me?" she asked flatly. Mr. Norton stared at Miss Reed.

"She just serves the drinks," he said to her. She looked back at him, and then spoke in an exaggerated, apologetic tone.

"Oh, of *course* David. Pardon me!"

"All right, all right, let's remember what the police are for shall we? There's no need for us to behave like junior investigators," said Mr. Peters. He looked around the table at the hostile group and finally spoke to Jeffries. "Well, Jeffries, what shall we do?"

"What else can we do?" Mr. Norton asked them all.

"You're the expert here, David," Miss Reed said.

"I think our friend was talking about the game," Mr. Norton said.

There was a long silence. Mr. Peters got up and headed for the rest room, excusing himself. Richard suddenly realized that the game was over. Over for him, in any case. Under the circumstances, the thought of it all evaporating had little effect on him.

"I'm sorry to have to say this," Mr. LaCroix said to Richard before addressing the group, "But we still don't know anything about Richard, do we?"

Richard stared into the deep green of the felt covered card table. He no longer cared about the game. As much as he told himself that it was a silly thought, he felt responsible for Hans' death. The game just did not matter any more. Before he knew it, he was standing, looking at the group.

"I'm out. I'm finished."

Everyone stared at him open-mouthed.

"Wait a minute Richard," Jeffries began, "Just wait. Sit, please." Richard sat down on the edge of his chair, one arm on the table. Jeffries addressed the group. "At the moment,

Richard is up nearly a million dollars. He owes no one anything." Then, looking at Richard, he continued. "You have won a considerable amount of these people's money and I think they would like to have a chance to win it back. We agreed to postpone the game until today. It is not finished for anyone. We might prefer it if you would stay and play out the game."

Richard put his hands on the table and searched Jeffries' face for a sign of what he was up to but he was unreadable. They all waited for him to speak. "I don't suppose," Richard began bitterly, "that in light of this terrible news you would rather forget about the game?"

No one spoke. Mr. Baldwin shifted in his chair and examined his fingernails. The others involved themselves in similar preoccupations. Then Mr. Peters returned and took his seat.

"Did I hear you say 'Forget about the game'?" he asked Richard. "I should say not, young man. We never forget the game."

Richard shook his head in disbelief. Jeffries continued. "The money that Richard opened with belongs to Hans. It doesn't belong to Richard. What to do with it is another question entirely. But the issue remains: should Richard be allowed to play?"

"Hans is gone. Now we have a young man here whom we don't know. What if he loses and ends up owing us money?" Mr. Baldwin asked the group.

"Richard, do you have money?" Mr. Peters asked him. "What is it that you do?"

"Yes, are you one of those 'dotcom' millionaires or something?" Mr. Baldwin suggested, assuming that at such a young age, it was fairly likely.

Although he was tempted to just refuse to play and leave the place, Richard found that he could not. Something inside of him was clinging to having a shot at this money. He forced himself to set aside Hans and face the situation at hand. He felt certain he would be out if the others had thought he could not cover his losses. They were right to be concerned, he knew that. He felt close to caving in, to admitting that he was simply an invited guest of Hans and that he had no money of his own to play with. But then something happened that took the situation out of his hands.

"Yes, that's right," Toshika said to the group.

Richard turned and stared at Toshika, sizing her up. She gave him nothing, just returned his gaze for a moment before looking down into her lap and then standing and moving about behind the bar. The clinking sound of glasses followed.

The group became quiet. Richard caught his breath. "I started a company a couple of years ago called Paradigm Shift."

"Yes!" cried Dr. Xang. "My broker told me about them." He looked at the others and spoke with enthusiasm. "Sounds like a great company. You're going public soon, aren't you?"

Richard hesitated. He hadn't counted on anyone being at all familiar with the company that Tony had mentioned recently, which was in fact started by a friend of his. Richard had to steer this subject away. Fast. "That's right. So now you know."

"My broker was pretty impressed." Dr. Xang continued, to Richard's dismay. "I'm going to subscribe to your IPO. We can talk about that later, okay?"

Richard nodded. Mr. Peters snorted and pointed at the others with his whiskey glass. "Internet companies. Really!"

"Well it seems we can trust that Richard will be able to cover any losses he may end up with. If not now, then later. When does your company go public?" Mr. Baldwin asked.

Richard looked at the table. "Soon."

"In the fall, right?" Dr. Xang asked him.

"If everything goes as planned," Richard said.

Jeffries surveyed the others quickly and rose from the table. "Well then, should Richard remain in the game?"

It took only a moment for everyone to assent.

"What about Hans' chip?" Mr. Norton asked.

"Yes, what about that?" Jeffries asked wearily, drawing a deep breath.

"I think it should revert to the previous party."

"Ah, yes, and who would that be, exactly? Oh, that would be you, wouldn't it David? I think we know why you feel that way then, don't we?" Jeffries said with an over-enthusiastic smile that quickly disappeared when he spoke again. "Listen, all of you are biased. The only sensible thing to do here is for us to draw straws."

The others looked satisfied with the decision, but Mr. Norton stood up suddenly, sending his chair flying back and falling over behind him in a loud clatter. Everyone jumped at the violence of his movement. Miss Reed cried out, startled. Mr. Norton was livid.

"Now wait a minute, Jeffries," he said in a low, dangerous tone, "I don't think you can speak for the group on this! You certainly don't speak for me."

"Just a moment, David," cried Jeffries, looking quite surprised, his obsequious air now gone, "Remember, this is a bet. It can change hands at any game! It's not permanent!"

"It changes when the holder decides to place it, you know that! How many games had Hans, even when he was losing, held it back?" Mr. Norton asked, looking round the table at everyone. "It's been four games! A year! So don't tell me about 'any game,' all right?"

"Fine," Jeffries conceded. "I stand corrected. But without simply giving the chip back to you, how else shall we go about it? What do you want to do, David? Vote?"

"He's right. Sorry David, but come on. We draw straws," Dr. Xang said.

After a few assenting noises from different members of the group all nodded except Mr. Norton, who looked at the group with wide eyes and seemed to be trembling. He looked at Toshika, then back at Jeffries.

"Well then, are we agreed?" asked Jeffries.

All around, the players nodded, again with the exception of Mr. Norton. "No, I don't agree!" he cried, his fingers gripping the edge of the table. "And what about Toshika?" he pleaded. "Doesn't she have any say in this?"

"Toshika? Why should *she* have any say?" Mr. LaCroix asked, his hands leaping to his aid. "She's not a player!"

"Don't you feel you have some say in this?" Mr. Norton asked Toshika, turning in his chair to look at her when he spoke. She made no eye contact with him. She stood rigidly and spoke without any emotion. No sadness at Hans' murder, no anger, no determination.

"Jean is right. This is something for the players to decide, not me."

With a flick of his hand David Norton sent his whiskey glass flying in her direction, standing up as he did, but remaining rooted in place at the table. Toshika jumped as the glass broke against the base of the bar beneath her. Richard was on his feet instantly.

"What the fuck?" he shouted at Mr. Norton. "What the hell is wrong with you?"

Mr. Norton ignored Richard as his hard eyes confronted everyone desperately, like someone who had been wrongly convicted of a crime and was about to be dragged off and put away.

"David!" Jeffries cried.

Slowly, Mr. Norton sat down. With a supreme effort, he calmed down and indicated that he would be all right. Jeffries shuffled the cards. Richard left the table to help Toshika clean the broken glass and whiskey from the floor.

"Thanks," she whispered to Richard. "Go. Just sit down." She then made sure everyone had a drink. When she brought Mr. Norton another whiskey all eyes were on him.

"I'm sorry, Toshika," he apologized, "I don't know what came over me."

She considered his apology and carefully set his drink on a coaster in front of him. "That's all right," she told him, lingering for a moment at his side before taking her place once more behind the bar.

Jeffries held the cards in his hand as if they were a bomb about to go off. "Listen, everyone," he began, "with Hans now gone, I think you should find yourself a new dealer. After tonight, I won't be involved in the game any more."

With no objections forthcoming, Jeffries began shuffling the cards. He dealt them. Then he placed a black chip at the center of the table. "It will go to the winner of the first hand," he said.

The players eyed each other, some nervously, others confidently, and still others wore their poker faces. David Norton, among them. The hand proceeded in a pronounced silence. Picking up his cards, Richard thought only of Hans. Sitting there hoping to win money felt wrong. He arranged the cards with wooden fingers as he tried to legitimize the game for himself. His hand was very good from the start. He would only draw one new card. Waiting for his turn, he looked at Mr. Norton. He did not at all like the way that he had treated Toshika. He never liked him from the start, and now even less. And so, he found his new purpose. Play the game to beat Mr. Norton. Beat him for Hans. He would do his best to win this first hand and take the black chip, whatever it was, to spite Mr. Norton.

The players held their breath as each fought to take control of the black chip. Soon Richard was looking at his final hand. He could see Mr. Peters was no threat to him. Neither was Miss Reed nor Mr. LaCroix. Mr. Baldwin was harder to read. Dr. Xang held a good hand. Mr. Norton, as usual, was not giving anything away. Richard knew he would have to bet hard to drive out at least one of his adversaries. Mr. Norton started off with a heavy fifty thousand dollar bet. Mr. Baldwin stayed in, followed by Dr. Xang. Mr. LaCroix hesitated, but put his own fifty thousand up. When it came to Richard, he quickly placed fifty thousand in and then reached back for more chips.

"Raise you twenty-five," he said.

"I'm out," said Mr. LaCroix, slapping his cards down in front of him and finishing his glass of wine in one gulp.

"Fuck me," Mr. Baldwin said as he joined Mr. LaCroix in backing down.

Dr. Xang and Mr. Norton stayed in. Then Mr. Norton called the hand. "All right boy, let's see 'em."

When he placed his cards down for all to see, Richard knew that he had won. The faces of Mr. Norton and Dr. Xang confirmed it. As he drew in the chips Mr. Norton excused himself and quickly left the room. Everyone became slightly uneasy at this.

"I'll go talk to him," Dr. Xang told the others as he rose and followed Mr. Norton. After he closed the door firmly behind him, the others breathed a collective sigh of relief.

"Are you all right, Toshika?" Mr. Peters asked. Before she could answer, he cleared his throat and spoke again. "At this point I think we all should consider whether or not we want to continue playing with the likes of him," he said, his eyes searching the faces of the others for support.

"What can we do?" Miss Reed asked.

"He's protection, you know," said Mr. LaCroix.

Mr. Norton came back into the room looking fresh and in good humor and took his seat before the conversation had time to develop. The game resumed.

After about an hour Richard had lost all he won on the first large hand and then some. He was down over one hundred thousand dollars. He was having trouble concentrating, and it was affecting his game. Mr. Norton had assumed his leading position and was obviously intent on beating Richard. Throughout the game he behaved in a hostile way towards him. He was especially pleased when he won larger hands that Richard had remained in to the end. This, of course, was noticeable only to the better players. Richard felt he knew this about Mr. Norton because he had noticed that when he won one of the larger hands, one in which he had stayed and then lost a sizeable sum, Mr. Norton closed his eyes – just for an instant – and hesitated before drawing in the chips. It was as if he were saying something to himself. A mantra or prayer, perhaps. Wasn't it supposed to be a game? Just a game?

But Richard knew now that it was not just a game. It was not about the money. It could have been a game, even with triple the stakes. A game is in the attitude of the players. Richard wondered to himself if Hans had been killed because of this game. Had he won too much money from these people? Was he too successful? In the previous night's game Hans had not displayed any special winning ability, but Richard was certain that he had been the strong player. He knew it, somehow.

"All right, everyone, let's pause now for a rest," said Jeffries, who was up immediately and disappeared into the room at the rear of the playing area.

When everyone got up from the table, Richard remained seated. He had not yet had any contact with Toshika, and it bothered him. He was hoping that Toshika would come over so they could talk. The others went across the room to where the food had been laid out and busied themselves with it. Only Mr. Norton and Dr. Xang stayed out of it, going instead into the next room. Richard had the feeling that Mr. Norton did not know that Dr. Xang was following him as they left the room. With them gone conversation began to get back to normal. Richard watched everyone pile food onto their plates as Toshika came to him from behind the bar. She picked up a couple of empty glasses from the table, and then took his. Before she left, she placed her hand on his arm. It was almost a caress. Richard looked up at her and felt heat rushing through her hand into him. He gave in to what he had been feeling for her since the first time he saw her. Unable to control himself, he began to speak, but Toshika placed a finger on her lips and then was gone.

Vowing to follow up what had been started later, Richard got up and went to the food table. The others grew quiet. Miss Reed moved aside to make room for him.

"Here, Richard, have a plate and help yourself. There's meat, fish, cheese over here, everything you need," said Mr. Peters. Richard appreciated him trying to make him feel welcome, but wondered if the others felt as he did. His appetite had not returned, but he filled his plate in any case and took a seat in one of the large leather chairs arranged around the table against the wall.

Mr. LaCroix watched Richard for some time. Then, after taking a sip of wine and a deep breath, spoke in a very solemn tone. "I want you to know," he began, "that nothing like this has ever happened here. We are normally very civilized, and generally have an enjoyable time. I'm sorry that the playing is not so pleasant."

"Pardon my asking, but when did all of you first hear about Hans?"

"Jeffries called all of us as soon as he heard from the police about it this morning," said Mr. Peters. "Terrible. Hans was a wonderful man. I just can't imagine who would do such a thing."

"Well, surprising a burglar is dangerous. Even if they didn't intend to hurt anyone." said Miss Reed. Mr. Peters put his fork and knife down abruptly and looked at her.

"Now I hope you're not suggesting that this was Hans' fault?"

"No!" Miss Reed cried, "Of course not. If I heard something in my house in the middle of the night I would also get up and investigate. I just mean that, well it's risky, for one. And we don't know if the burglar-"

"We don't know if the burglar was a good burglar or a bad one? Is that what you want to say?" Mr. Peters asked again, this time less forcefully.

Miss Reed reached over and patted Mr. Peters on the arm. "Art, I'm sorry. I'm not expressing myself very well right now. I liked Hans too."

Mr. Peters avoided her gaze. He looked at his plate of food and slowly pushed it away.

Richard watched Toshika, who sat behind the bar, reading, oblivious to his attention. When the others had finished and had returned to the table, Miss Reed, who had taken a seat next to Richard, turned towards him and leaned very close. The musky smell of her perfume was not exactly feminine, but Richard liked it all the same.

"I guess you've gotten more than you bargained for," she said with a jealous look. "Let me give you some advice. Don't get attached. Try to remember that it's all just part of the game. And," she said as she looked in the direction of the others for a moment before leaning so close that Richard could feel her breath. With an alluring smile, she continued, "If you're the kind who likes to share, let me know." With that she produced a card and held it out. Richard took it and looked it over. 'Sylvia Reed Investment Services.'

"I understand," Richard lied, then stood up. He placed his empty plate on the table and returned to the others. After all were seated Jeffries appeared and came to the table. Before he sat, he looked toward the entrance.

"Is Mr. Norton all right?" he asked no one in particular. Without waiting for an answer, he went to the door and opened it. Richard had turned in his chair and could see Dr. Xang and Mr. Norton sitting in the room. Neither one spoke or looked at Jeffries. After a brief moment they got up and followed Jeffries to the table, and the game resumed.

As the cards were being shuffled and the players made themselves comfortable and examined their chips, Mr. Norton spoke. "Well, Mr. Peel, let's see if I can't whittle you down to nothin'," he said, looking at Richard only after he had finished speaking. His expression was blank for a moment, and when he saw that he had gotten to Richard, he smiled. Richard was glad to see that he was still calm and looked forward to playing a normal game. "Deal them cards, Jeffries," Mr. Norton said, giving Dr. Xang a wink.

For the next hour Richard was locked in a furious battle with Mr. Norton. Mr. Norton was trying to rile him by sarcastically admiring his skill every time he beat Richard. "Damn," he would say, flashing a big grin, "You're pretty good." The others were suffering. Some were forced to draw more credit. Richard and Mr. Norton were on top. After another hour, only four of them remained in the game. Mr. Baldwin, Mr. Peters, and Mr. LaCroix dropped out after losing everything. Of the three of them, only Mr. Baldwin seemed especially affected by it. Mr. Norton was setting his sights on Richard and was determined to take him out. He had grown more serious now, and rarely spoke, preferring to try to wear Richard down psychologically with a constant, steady gaze. Instead of playing this game with him, Richard tried not to look at him at all, concentrating only on each hand, alone, without giving a thought to winning.

After another forty-five minutes Dr. Xang dropped out as well.

"Well," he said, throwing his cards down in defeat after an especially long hand that had seen a pile of ninety-three thousand dollars in chips in the center of the table – a hand that Miss Reed had finally won, "I've had enough. Toshika, my chips please."

As Richard watched him sink back in his chair, he realized that Dr. Xang still had what must have been about a hundred thousand dollars left in chips. Richard was struck by the idea that perhaps he could quit at any time, if the same rules held for him as for everyone else. He did not have to try to win. He could be a winner whenever he felt like it. Unfortunately, he did not feel he could broach the subject, and ask if he really could in fact quit and walk away with his winnings. Somehow, it seemed unlikely. He had not put up his own money. He should not have the right to quit. He sat in a daze, reeling over this thought, a blank expression on his face.

"Richard," Jeffries said, "is there a problem?"

Mr. Norton chuckled lightly. "What's wrong, Richard? Losing your balls?" he jeered.

They all watched him, including Toshika. Richard felt his face grow hot and wanted to stick his foot right through Mr. Norton's smiling, sweaty face.

The next hand was dealt. Richard did not have much, two tens, seven of clubs, king of hearts, and a three of spades. The way Miss Reed was breathing, very slowly and deeply, he could tell she was disappointed with her hand. Mr. Norton was very calm. Richard could not read him at all – until he started to bet. He began with forty thousand, hoping to intimidate the others into dropping out, which was normally a signal that he was bluffing. But he could not be sure. Miss Reed sat for some time before placing her forty thousand into the pile. Richard looked at Mr. Norton and placed his bet as well. "Raise you another forty," he said, and reached for four red chips.

Miss Reed dropped her cards. "Fold."

Mr. Norton chewed on his lips for a moment before reaching for his chips. "I'll see your forty and raise another forty," he said, plunking down eight red chips with a hard whack on the table.

Richard placed his chips. "Call."

Mr. Norton lay down his cards and looked into the pile of chips in the center of the table before turning a blank face to Richard. Richard looked down at his cards, and then at Mr. Norton. Mr. Norton had nothing.

"Read 'em and weep?" Richard teased, a smile creeping over his lips. Mr. Norton waited until he could not stand it any longer.

"Let's see your cards, Peel!"

Richard placed his cards face up on the table, and without looking at Mr. Norton reached for the pile of chips, looking at him only as he pulled them in. Richard could not believe it, but Mr. Norton managed a smile. He was not beaten yet.

From then on, for the next half hour, Mr. Norton and Richard forced Miss Reed out. She had played down to nothing. They continued playing much higher stakes, each of them trying to hit the other harder and harder with bigger and bigger losses. But Mr. Norton was not able to keep his composure as he had before.

The amounts did not really mean anything to Richard anymore. He could not appreciate how much money was sloshing around on the table. It had become just chips. Just numbers. He did not even think of taking something home with him. It was just a brawl between him and Mr. Norton. He no longer wanted to win, he merely wanted Mr. Norton to lose. And he was getting exactly what he wanted. Mr. Norton's situation was getting more and more desperate until it looked like he had something in the neighborhood of a million dollars left.

The cards were dealt. After a brief inspection Richard took two fresh cards and Mr. Norton only one. Having made a rough assessment of Mr. Norton's chips, Richard realized he had no idea of his own winnings. Looking at the stacks of red, white, and blue, he was shocked. He had more than twice that of Mr. Norton. Once again the idea that these chips would translate into cash was nearly incomprehensible to him. It just could not be that he was possibly about to become a millionaire. Last week he could not afford to go out and eat a nice dinner with his friends. He was unsure of his future and concerned about how to make ends meet. And now he might be given enough money so that work could be the farthest thing from his mind if he chose it. He began to count more carefully when Mr. Norton spoke.

"Well Richard, I'll tell you what. It's after midnight. I'm getting a bit tired, so here it is," he said, and started putting stacks of chips – first the reds, then the blues, and finally the white chips – into the center of the table until he had none left. Taking a last look at them, he set his cards face down on the table. "A million, plus five," he said. "I'll bet the game right now! The whole thing. If I lose, I'm out. And all you have to do is put in that little black chip."

Richard looked at the pile of chips and then at his black chip. It was no joke. Mr. Norton's grim expression made it clear. Richard looked around the room at the surprised faces of the others. Toshika got up and stepped out from behind the bar, stopping in front of it and crossing her arms over her chest. What in hell did this black chip mean? Richard had to know.

"Sorry, I don't understand," he told them.

"That chip is worth a million bucks right now!" Mr. Norton said.

"So, it's that simple?"

"It is for me," Mr. Norton declared, leaning back in his chair and folding his arms over his chest. Richard was tired too. If he won the bet the game was over and he might take a lot of money with him. If he lost, the game would be over and he would still have all his chips, which were worth plenty. Either way, if it was not just a joke or a horrible misunderstanding, he would win more money than he could believe. It was a simple decision to make, but before making it he looked at Toshika, hoping that she would signal him if she thought something was wrong. She did nothing. He thought he could see the very faintest smile on her lips. He picked up the black chip and held it out in front of him. He looked at it for a moment, then carefully set it down on the smooth felt surface of the playing table. Mr. Norton sat up straight in his chair and picked up his cards.

"Call."

Mr. Norton looked at his cards apprehensively. He seemed now to be having second thoughts. He picked up his glass of bourbon and tossed the rest of it down. Then he quickly put his cards down and waited. His hand was good. A full house. But Richard had four queens. He put his cards on the table and waited. Mr. Norton gasped as though he had been shot, and then stood up. Fumbling behind his back he grabbed his chair and moved it away, turning as he walked toward the door to the waiting room. He walked as stiffly as if he was expecting a bomb to go off under his feet. Richard was expecting him to fly into a rage at any moment. Opening the door with a sharp yank, Mr. Norton turned around and looked at Richard with wild eyes.

"Who the fuck *are* you, anyway?" he cried. The door closed behind him, leaving the others in a heavy silence. Richard turned and looked at the faces of the gamblers. He felt he had robbed them.

"Nice going, Richard," Mr. Peters said, coming forward to shake Richard's hand. Richard was surprised. Maybe he was just pleased that Richard had frustrated Mr. Norton? In any case, his comment made Richard feel a bit better.

"Don't worry about David," Jeffries said, "He's always a sore loser."

All the other players rose and left the table. Mr. Peters, Mr. Baldwin, and Mr. LaCroix drifted over to the bar where

78

Toshika waited. Miss Reed and Dr. Xang followed Mr. Norton into the waiting room. Unsure what to do, Richard remained seated at the table.

"Sorry Richard, but would you mind giving me some room to concentrate here while I count the chips? We want to make sure you get all you deserve, don't we?" Jeffries asked.

"Oh, sure. Sorry," Richard said. He got up and sat alone near the food table on a large leather sofa. He was exhausted. As he sat holding his head in his hands, his eyes closed, a voice pierced through the fog and fatigue.

"You okay?"

Richard looked up. Toshika stood next to him. She placed her hand on his shoulder.

"Oh, I don't know. I'm glad the game is over. But I don't know what to think, either. How about you? I still just can't believe it about Hans."

Toshika sat next to him. "I know how you feel, but I've had some time now to deal with it. You haven't." She leaned in close and spoke softly. "Don't feel bad about Hans. And about the game, remember that he wanted you to be here. He wanted you to win. And you did. It's okay."

Richard was not convinced. He knew she meant well, but Toshika's comments did little to change things for him.

"Who could have done this?" he asked her. "Did he have enemies? I mean, who on earth would want to kill him? It just seems crazy. It's TV stuff."

Toshika had nothing to offer. She stayed with Richard in silence, the two of them allowing their attention to drift around the room, falling on one object after the other.

With the counting done, Jeffries called to everyone. "Okay everybody, let's go," he announced. "Richard, why don't we start with you." He walked into a small office at the rear of the house. Richard saw how, removed from the group and the game, Jeffries sagged, stopping for a moment at a mahogany desk and resting his fingertips on it, as if steadying himself. He brought his hands to his eyes and rubbed at them. It was more than fatigue that Richard saw in that gesture. Richard sat, frozen. Toshika nudged his shoulder with her own.

"What are you waiting for?" she asked him. Richard got up and followed Jeffries into the room, closing the door behind him at Jeffries' request.

It was a small office with nothing in it other than the desk, some near empty bookshelves, and a chair that sat opposite the desk in the middle of the room. On a coat hanger hung a black coat and tall black hat. Jeffries took a seat at the desk and motioned for Richard to sit. Richard sat down and folded his hands together in his lap. Jeffries looked horrible. He had managed to hide it until now. Richard began to search for comforting words for the man who had lost a friend, but he was out of his depth. "I'm very sorry about Hans," he ventured, knowing that this most simple expression of consolation was nearly impossible to improve upon. Jeffries reacted with a fleeting effort to compose himself. A faint smile crossed his face but just as quickly was gone.

"Thank you, Richard. It is," he started, pausing at his own loss for words, "such a shock." He said nothing more for a few moments. Then, he gathered himself and glanced at his watch. "Okay, this is how it works," he began, slowly. "We all have private offshore accounts plus our main account, which holds a million dollars for each player, you see?"

"Right."

Jeffries studied Richard's face for a minute. "Richard, I know that the police will speak to you soon, but I must ask. Do you know anything…" he stopped, trying to formulate his question. "You were one of the last people to see Hans." Jeffries sat quietly for a few moments, his fingers laced together on the desk. He looked like he was about the same age as Hans, tall, thin, distinguished. Looking again at the coat and hat on the rack across the room, Richard realized that it was Jeffries whom he had seen talking to Hans at the St. Francis where they first met.

Richard stared into the grain of the desk in front of him as he answered. "We had some drinks last night at a bar and then I drove him home. I dropped him off, he went inside, and that was that, really. I wish I could say more."

Jeffries considered his answer only briefly. "I don't believe, Richard, that you had anything to do with his murder. I can tell a decent man when I see one. I also know that Hans was very fond of you, even though you had only just met. He and

80

I were good friends, you see. Friends as well as business partners. And I know," he said, leaning in over the desk ever so slightly, "that you are not involved in any Internet business." Richard felt the blood run to his face. "But I don't care. I know why you fed us that story. You wanted to stay in the game. You wouldn't have had to do so had Hans been here. I understand," he told Richard reassuringly. "You managed to beat some pretty good card players. I'm impressed. You obviously aren't new to the game," he suggested. Richard did not offer any explanation but instead simply sat still, awaiting the verdict. "Not everyone plays well, to be sure. Mr. LaCroix, for example. Hopeless. Always loses." He sighed and closed his eyes as his shoulders slumped against the aging evening. He yawned and sat up straight again. "Yes, if it weren't for Toshika I daresay half of them would have buggered off by now." Richard leaned forward, unsure that he had heard correctly. He was about to enquire but Jeffries spoke again. "So I don't care if you have money or not because Hans would have wanted you to have the money you won. He invited you to this game for one reason and one reason only. You are half way there. I wish you luck, Richard." Jeffries then read from the sheet of paper in front of him that he had used to tally the game results. "Four million, one hundred fifty-five thousand dollars."

The words sunk into Richard until he actually felt pressure on his head and shoulders. Richard felt as though there was nothing half way about winning four million dollars. He repeated the number to himself. He blinked, feeling strangely disconnected from his surroundings. Floating in a silent world. He looked at Jeffries for what seemed a long time, neither of them saying a word. Something he had always dreamed about seemed to be coming true. Confronted with it, he was numb. He hit himself with it over and over in an effort to be brought to an appropriate response.

"It's a lot, isn't it?" Jeffries asked him. The sound of his voice shook Richard free. He nodded, feeling a thrill at his new prospects. "Now, a question for you. If I transfer this money into your bank, you'll have to pay taxes on it. Something around forty percent." Jeffries raised his eyebrows in agreement as Richard's mouth dropped open at this number. "I'm sure you have no safe offshore account, have you?" Richard shook his head. Jeffries smiled, and continued. "No, of course not. If you'd like to pay the taxes, then so be it. I'll transfer the entire amount to your bank here. If you'd rather avoid those taxes, I can help."

Richard sat up straight but found the weight on his shoulders was more than he could manage. "I don't want to be one of those tax cheats," he said to himself, trying it on. Then he thought of the ones who could really make a difference. That one percent of the population who possessed ninety percent of the country's wealth. Those who brought the world to a standstill just months before, claimed ignorance, and who received no punishment, no censure. They were not barred from working in finance for the rest of their lives. They were not even asked to give the money back. Most were taking a short holiday and networking in preparation for their next victim. Richard looked at Jeffries. Four million dollars was a lot. But it couldn't even buy a three-bedroom house in Pacific Heights, just a half a mile from where he sat. "Okay, so what's the alternative?"

"Well, let's at least get you started," Jeffries suggested, standing up and then having a seat on the corner of the desk. "I'll transfer something into your bank here, then wait for you to set up an account elsewhere and wire the rest when you're ready. Sound good?"

"Sure."

"How much do you want to start?"

Richard hesitated as various scenarios occurred to him at once. He hardly knew any of these people. "A quarter million," he said.

Jeffries stood up. "Fine," he said, as he returned to his seat behind the desk and scribbled something in his notebook. "I would get a good accountant if I were you. In the meantime just ask Toshika. She's got all of this mastered." Jeffries had Richard write his bank account information down for him. "As I mentioned before, the police will be in touch with you over the matter with Hans. It would be best for us, and wise for you, if you would mention to them nothing whatsoever of this game. Tell them that you were invited to a dinner party, held here, you later went to a bar, et cetera. As for the game, you know we play the first Friday night of every quarter. The others will expect that you play the next game as well so that they might try to win some of their money back, at the very least."

Richard nodded his head in approval. It seemed done and dusted. "Is there anything else?" he asked.

Jeffries managed a smile. "You're welcome," he replied holding out his hand.

"Oh," Richard gasped, smiling an apology. "Thank you very much, Jeffries," Richard said, shaking his hand gratefully.

Richard left the office with Jeffries close behind, and walked back to the playing table, placing his hands on it. Toshika stood behind the bar washing glasses. The moment had arrived for him to test the bond that he thought had grown between them. He wondered how in the world to proceed. He looked at Toshika and raised his eyebrows, trying to figure out what to say to her. He thought he would offer her a ride home and was about to ask when she began to speak.

"I'll be finished in just a second," she said, indicating that she would be going with him. Richard was not prepared for that, but could not have been happier. Picking up a small overnight bag from behind the bar she showed him she was ready. "I'll take care of this other stuff tomorrow, Jeffries," she said.

"Certainly. Who is coming next?" he asked. Mr. Baldwin quickly jumped off his bar stool and went toward the office.

"Might as well get it over with," he said, sourly.

Toshika came from behind the bar and stopped in front of Richard. "Ready?" she asked him. He thought all along that he was very much ready, but now he was not so sure. It was all too easy. First the money, and now Toshika. He could not believe his luck.

"Sure," he answered casually. The two of them went through the doors into the waiting room. There sat Mr. Norton with Dr. Xang and Miss Reed. Toshika told them all good-bye over her shoulder. At the door to the foyer, Richard stopped and turned, choosing to make eye contact only with Miss Reed. "Bye," he said to her.

Once in the foyer they put their coats on and stepped outside into the cool early morning. There was a heavy mist blowing through the air, almost like it does in winter. They stood at the top of the stairs looking into the sky before looking at each other. Toshika was beautiful in the darkness. Richard could not believe she was with him. He wondered what she saw in him, then wondered if she even saw anything at all. Nothing had happened yet. He looked at her feet in her small black leather mules. He loved those shoes. Looking into the air at the mist Toshika gathered her coat together around her neck.

"Where are we going?" Richard asked her.

"Where do you want to go? You're the boss."

"It doesn't feel like a great thing at all, you know?"

"I know." Toshika reached down and took his hand. "Let's get a big room in the St. Francis or the Portman and just disappear for a while."

Richard saw that she was not kidding. There was a kind of strain showing in her eyes that he was immediately sorry to see, and at that moment he wished only to please her. The hotel idea sounded like a good one.

"Sure, okay. But I don't have anything with me. No change of clothes, no nothing."

"It's okay, we can order an overnight kit no problem. It's just room service."

"Okay, well...which one should we go to?" he asked her. "I haven't stayed in any of them so I don't know which is better."

"Where's your car? Let's drive."

They slowly went down the steps and walked to the car. Toshika stopped short. "That's Hans' car," she said, her voice tight with apprehension. Richard explained what had happened at the bar the previous night. Toshika was unmoved. "I don't want to go anywhere in his car," she said, turning and walking to the sidewalk. In an instant her phone was in her hand. Richard stood, helpless. He looked at Hans' car, then at the key in his hand. He placed it back into his pocket as Toshika began to speak.

"Hello, taxi please to number 49, 28th Street."

Richard gave Hans' car sympathetic looks as they waited for the taxi. Then he noticed Toshika's bag. "Do you always carry an overnight bag?" he asked her, drawing from her the first smile of the evening that he could recall.

84

"No, not always."

When the cab came, Richard opened the door for Toshika and helped her inside. As they drove off, he saw that she was not wearing her seat belt. He reached across her lap and fastened it for her. As soon as it clicked into place she pulled his face to hers and kissed him. The first kiss. He would never forget it. Her face shined from the mist. He looked into her eyes just then. They were sparkling. Like her face.

6

The cab stopped in the driveway of the Mark Hopkins Hotel, which sat grandly on the corner of a hilltop overlooking the financial district and Chinatown. Toshika had suggested the St. Francis, at first. Richard had immediately thought of how he had met Hans there, and suggested that they think of another place. The two of them got out of the cab. Richard retrieved his wallet from his coat pocket and stood at the driver's door.

"Sixteen-forty, please," the cabbie told him, his hand sitting palm up on the window frame waiting to receive the money. Richard winced at the thought of paying good money for a ride when he could have driven there himself, and then he remembered. He rolled his eyes and gave the driver a twenty.

"Here. Keep it."

"Thank you, sir!"

They went quietly to the front desk where Richard asked for a big room as high up as possible.

"Please send up a toothbrush, toothpaste, and anything a man might need for overnight," Toshika told the clerk.

The clerk eyed Richard. "Will you need pajamas?"

"No," Toshika told the woman, who nodded and handed her the room key. They were shown to the elevator. A porter followed them inside, empty-handed save for their room key. Richard glanced at Toshika as he felt gravity tugging gently at them from below. This suddenly did not feel like a good idea. The stress of the charade of the poker game, and now this? What was happening? Richard hadn't noticed before that Toshika was particularly fond of him, and now she was with him in a hotel? Richard's mind was racing. There was the firm handshake and the pleasure she showed at discovering that Hans had invited Richard to the game, back when they first met. That was something. But then, after the first game, she just left, with David Norton of all people, and had no interest in coming along with Richard and Hans.

He felt lost. He finally remembered a mantra that he had repeated to himself in similar situations since he first started dating. You will never understand a woman. Never.

He looked at Toshika. She returned his glance and reached for his hand as her eyes returned to the floor and a smile curled the corner of her mouth.

Never.

The elevator chimed and they followed the porter.

"Hmm, not bad," Richard said as he stepped inside the room. The porter was immediately in front of them, going through his routine of explaining the room's amenities, drawing back the blinds that covered the balcony, and returning to the door. He paused just long enough to set Richard's hand in search of some money to give him. Richard handed him a dollar from his wallet. The porter accepted it without removing his gaze from Richard's face, thanked him, and then was gone.

It was indeed a large room. Straight ahead in the corner was a sitting area and desk on the right, with the bed and bathroom around the corner next to large glass doors giving access to what looked like a generous balcony. Deep carpeting, high ceilings, warm tones and expensive-looking paintings lining the walls gave it a luxurious feel beyond any hotel room Richard had experienced on family holidays.

Toshika set her bag on the bed and went straight to the windows. Opening the blinds, she inspected the view for a moment before opening the door to the balcony. Stepping out onto it she went to the railing and rested her elbows on the cold metal, looking over her shoulder for Richard. "Come on out," she called to him, stepping out of her shoes and taking a deep breath.

Richard followed and placed his hands on the cold iron. "Well, that's quite a drop." He looked down to the streets below where the dim sounds from the cars barely managed to reach them. The fog moved through the air all around them with surprising speed. "It's like flying through the clouds."

"Nothing can touch us here," Toshika whispered.

"I need a drink. Can I get you something?" Richard asked her.

"I'll have a glass of champagne with you. To cheer us up. But don't take the bottle in the mini-bar. Call up for something really good."

Richard went into the room and got on the telephone. A moment later he was beside Toshika again. "Should be here in a minute," he said. Staring out over the city lights, Toshika did not respond. Richard joined her in her quiet reflection, knowing it must still be a shock for her. He had only just met Hans, but Toshika had known him for some time.

"Sorry about Hans," he told her, after waiting as long as he could. She said nothing. Finally he figured that maybe it was best just to leave it. He could not do much more than he had done, anyway. She would need time, that was all. He returned his attention to the view and tried to think of something he might say to change the subject, or... No, he thought, stop thinking of yourself. Just let her have some peace.

"I've known him for years," Toshika said. "He knew my mother. He asked me to come along to the game once. Long time ago. I think he thought I was lonely. I served them their drinks just to keep busy. Poker isn't my thing, and sitting there watching a game for hours is deadly boring. So I served the drinks. I don't know why, but I started going regularly. This was back when they played every month. I brought some magazines or books, served the drinks, and – I don't know. It was kind of fun. Something to do. I was halfway through school. Sometimes I studied while they played."

"Did you tell your mother? About Hans, I mean."

Toshika shook her head slowly. When Richard was sure that she wasn't going to speak, he opened his mouth to say something, but he was too late. "No," she said. "Not yet."

"What did you study?" Richard asked, thinking that he was helping Toshika to exit a subject he imagined her to find awkward.

"History."

"Hmm. Interesting."

Toshika stood in silence, obviously thinking of something else. "Hans more or less organized the games with Jeffries. He was a friend of my mother's for a while when I was younger but I actually didn't see him often. He came just to pick her up once in a while when they went out."

"Were they dating?"

Toshika hesitated. "I don't think it was like that, no. But I don't really know. I know it sounds funny, but my mother wasn't very up front with me. I didn't know much about her life. I was normally at school, and she had her business to run. And in the evenings we were both busy. I never felt very close to her. She's in France now. In her summer home."

"France?" Richard asked, his eyebrows raising in mild surprise. "What does she do?"

"She's an artist. She used to run an art gallery."

"What about your father?" Richard asked, realizing she had not mentioned him yet.

"My father," Toshika repeated, looking out through the mist and fog. "I was told that he was a good, kind man. But I never knew him. Not even his name. Another one of my mother's secrets. It's a subject that I don't really enjoy discussing."

Richard did not need to go where he was not welcome, and accepted her silence without pushing further. "Was your mother Japanese?"

"Yes. But born here, in California. Not a 'real' Japanese, she always told me. I don't think she was very... proud, of being Japanese."

"Why not?"

"I don't know. She spent some time there. Went to Kyoto to study art – the capital city before Tokyo became the capital – and I guess they didn't treat her very well. Her Japanese wasn't perfect, you know? I don't think they feel comfortable around people who look like them but are obviously different."

Richard studied Toshika's face as she looked out over the rooftops. He kept reminding himself that he had seen few faces as beautiful as hers. "Yes," he said, resting his elbows once again on the balcony. "I mean, I suppose I could see that." He looked at the lights in the windows of skyscrapers across the horizon, thinking of their first meeting at the St.

Francis. Now it seemed very far away. "Hans seemed very fond of you," he told her, remembering how pleased he was to see her at that first meeting. He waited for some kind of acknowledgement but none came. Then he noticed he was alone. He turned and looked inside the room and saw her disappearing into the bathroom. "Stupid thing to say," he whispered, rapping his knuckles against the iron as he watched the light in the bathroom come on and the door close. He picked up her shoes and brought them into the room. Just then there was a knock at the door. Richard went to the door and looked out of the peephole. Someone in uniform stood outside with a bottle in an ice bucket. Richard opened the door.

"Champagne, sir."

"Yes, thank you," he said. He fished in his pocket for some change but found none. "Sorry, wait." He hurried over to his coat, pulling out his wallet and removing a five-dollar note. It seemed to him then that he was doing nothing but handing people his money. Offering the bill to the young man, he took the champagne and closed the door. He set the bucket on the table in the sitting area. Settling into on one of the couches there, he opened the bottle and quickly poured a glass for himself. He tossed it down and looked at the empty flute, running his fingers through his hair. Relax! As he sat waiting for Toshika he thought of the money. Excitement at the thought of having four million dollars deposited in a bank account for him returned. You did it! He thought about what Jeffries had said and hoped that Toshika would go with him to Switzerland to help him carry out his task. Just then she opened the door and stepped into the room. Her face brightened when she saw his expression.

"Feeling better?" she asked him, approaching and raising her hand for some champagne. He noticed immediately a change in her mood and her expression and wondered if she were simply reacting to his own. He poured them both a glass and held hers out to her.

"Yeah. You too?"

Toshika appeared not to have heard his question. She glanced at the bottle in the bucket and nodded approvingly. "Good choice," she said. "Well, let's make a toast to your newfound wealth, if you can manage to keep it, and to our adventure."

"Our adventure? Sounds great."

Richard sat staring into his glass, watching the bubbles rising to the surface. He felt his conscience losing its grip on him. You just won four million dollars, he told himself. Toshika put her drink on the table and placed a hand on Richard's knee.

"I know it sounds crazy. They didn't used to play for such high stakes. It used to be a hundred dollars was the minimum bet, not a thousand. But the stock market kept going up, and then when I started coming regularly things really got out of hand. Well, not 'out of hand,' but they all just got greedier and greedier. They're letting you keep the money you won because there's nothing else they can do. It's poker. And I know it's hard to believe, but they can afford it, more or less."

Richard eyed her carefully, waiting when she had finished speaking just long enough to allow her to see that he had no reason to doubt her. "Jeffries said I need to open up an offshore bank account. Will you go with me to Switzerland?"

"I'm all yours."

Richard let the words dance around his ears for a moment. "Okay then," he said brightly, raising his glass to hers, "to our little trip."

" 'Little trip'? Forget it. I said we're going on an adventure, and I meant it!" After a long sip from her glass Toshika stood up, raising her arms as if she were balancing on a high wire. "Take off my panties," she said.

Richard nearly choked on his champagne. He was sure he had not heard correctly. "What?"

"Take off my panties! *Slowly.*" Toshika answered, closing her eyes. Richard sat looking at her in disbelief, but there she stood, barefoot in her short summer dress, asking the unthinkable. Although it seemed the perfect fantasy, he was not able to comply. Years of practice in achieving a woman's trust before becoming intimate with her, combined with his inbred lack of self-confidence, forced him to be cautious. Placing his champagne glass on the table he rose before her, placed his arm around her waist, and kissed her. She pulled her head back and opened her eyes in surprise.

"Don't kiss me! What are you doing? I said take off my panties. Do it now!" Sensing his shock, she smiled and repeated her order more gently. "Go on, do it," she teased.

Her already proven boldness struck again. Getting down on his knees before her, he reached up and raised her dress over her hips and, hooking his fingers under her panties, slowly pulled them down, letting them fall to the floor at her feet. She stepped out of them but remained there, standing. Then in a swift motion she unzipped her dress and let if fall, pushing it aside with her foot.

After looking at her beautiful smoothness for a moment, Richard looked up to her for guidance, unsure of what his next move should be. Toshika brought her champagne glass to her lips and took another sip. Then she lowered the glass and poured it gently over her exposed belly, where it ran down between her legs and onto the floor. She stopped. "Let's not make a mess of the carpet, shall we?"

Placing her hand on top of his head and stepping slightly forward she slowly poured once more. This time he caught the drink in his mouth. She stopped again. "Clean me," she said softly. He obliged. She poured again. After a few moments she held his head back, tossed her glass onto the couch, and reached for the bottle. Taking aim once more, she poured slowly. He drank hungrily, and as she poured faster and faster until he could not keep up, he began laughing at their debauchery. Seeing that he had finally let go, she set the bottle on the table and gripped his head tightly with both hands, planting her feet firmly in the deep carpet. Finally, on the edge, she collapsed onto her knees and kissed him, pulling him down onto the floor on top of her. When she had gathered her breath she whispered to him once more. "Take me to the bed."

The sun shone in through the thin fore blinds and spilled across the bed, warming them as they lay sleeping. There was no movement in the room save for the gentle rising and falling of their chests as they breathed in the new day. As time rolled in and around the room, poking its head into every corner, they remained still and untouched, lost in the peace they had created for themselves. They were not far away, for theirs was an existence that needed no escaping. They merely slept a beautiful and relaxing sleep that would not be greatly missed when they awoke. It would only invoke a lightly held but fond memory. He would find in this room a peace that would seem to mark for him the beginning of a new life. A life of everything that he had ever thought he wanted: love, warmth, beauty, and the expectation of great things to come. The affection, if not the love, of a woman he found beautiful and engaging would seem to have been found. That alone was above all other considerations for his happiness, the one thing he thought he could not do without, and which he would strive to find no matter how long he had to search. As if that were not enough, a newfound wealth that would act as a kind of magic potion with the power to erase so many of life's worries would seem to have been granted to him. Time would be his. He would not have to work unless he chose to. He could go anywhere, have anything, and do anything he chose to do. He would be in total command of his life. He would finally have his freedom.

She stirred, and he awoke. In a moment he realized he was not at home, then found himself in his new surroundings. He lifted his head. She was still asleep. She was still there. It was all real! He lifted his head once again and glanced around the room. Smiling, he lowered his head and looked towards the ceiling. Fine particles of dust struck by the sun's rays above him made their way through the air like forgotten thoughts. As he lay there in the morning's quiet beginning, he remembered scenes from the night, and his heart beat faster. Why was he so lucky? He always knew that he was good. He knew that he was deserving of the joy that he had not known, but to find it without effort filled him with a playful suspicion. The more he thought about it, and the more he awakened to the realization that it was indeed happening, the lighter he felt. It was a kind of drunkenness that brought him to the verge of laughter. He felt as if on stage, receiving fanatical applause simply for being there. He could afford to smile back into the audience and pose theatrically, dipping to one knee and sweeping his hand in a wide arc in a comic gesture of thanks. Is this how it is? Is there nothing more to be done?

Suddenly he rose and stepped naked from the bed. Going to the balcony, he quietly unlocked the door and cast a glance back at Toshika. Still asleep. He opened the door and peered outside. Finding no one, he strode out onto the balcony, his skin protesting in the frigid morning air but feeling the heat from the sun as it rose, its strength concentrating on their corner of the sphere. Looking out over the city, he felt triumphant. It occurred to him that winning required a loser. Feeling a pang of guilt at the consequence of his success, he considered the random nature of recent events and declared to himself that it did not matter that there should be losers. The others could afford the loss anyway, so why worry about them?

Daring himself to shout with joy, he hesitated, and, looking round, threw his head back and howled with delight. As his cry left him and he drew in a breath, the sharpness of the silence jolted him into retreat and he quickly turned and stepped lightly back to the door.

Stepping inside he found only an empty bed. He closed the door behind him and noticed the bathroom door was closed. Hearing the flushing of the toilet he quickly jumped back into bed and threw the cover over himself, lying still as he waited. The door opened and once again he was struck with self-doubt. Would she get dressed quickly and be gone? Did she regret what had happened? He lay quietly, barely breathing, as he heard Toshika's footsteps approaching. She quietly slipped under the sheets and found his body, molding herself to his shape with a slight shiver and bringing her lips to the nape of his neck. Feeling her warm breath, he closed his eyes and took the hand that lay now against his stomach.

"Good morning," she said quietly. He hesitated, then turned to face her, adjusting the sheet so as to keep their warmth trapped within. Seeing her face now for the first time since he had awoken, he was shocked by her beauty. Her dark eyes showed signs of a long sleep, but were otherwise just as he had remembered, only lovelier. Her perfect nose, full lips, and faintly dimpled chin caused him to freeze, unable to speak.

"Good morning," she said, speaking for her mute lover. "Did you sleep well? Yes, I did, thank you, and you? Oh, I slept very well thank you." She pinched his leg. "What's wrong with you, handsome?" she said, laughing, slowly pinching up higher and higher on his leg. "Are you deaf? Are you dumb? Are you blind?"

He stopped her hand just before she found what she was looking for and held it tightly. "God, you're beautiful," he said, pulling her forward and kissing her once on the mouth. Pulling back, he looked again closely at her lips. They were perfect for him, and like the rest of her, overpowered him effortlessly. He leaned forward and took her upper lip between his teeth and sucked on it, as if to reassure him that it was indeed real. Letting go, he turned onto his back and stared at the ceiling. "I have died and gone to heaven."

"You have died and gone to a fancy hotel. One with room service. Look at me," she said, placing her hand on his chin and turning his face to her.

"Gladly."

"Oh, you sweet talker. How do you feel?"

The question seemed so absurd that he could not say a thing. He was about to tell the truth, when his instincts took control. "A little sleepy, but... what time is it?"

"I don't know. What time does it seem like?"

"God, I don't know. How late were we up? It seems like we've slept a lifetime."

Toshika made a face. "Well, I wouldn't mind some more sleep. But I can see that you're done. I guess you're pretty excited now. Or should I say, shocked?"

He looked at her. She'd hit the nail on the head with that one. "I have to figure out what I'm going to do now."

"Well, you need to get an offshore account set up right away. We should leave soon. I have some things to do, but then we need to go. And it would be best if we planned to be gone for a while. At least a month."

"A month?" he cried, having never gone anywhere longer than a week. "What will we do for a month?"

"Anything we want to," she said playfully. "Seriously, Richard. This is your new life. Live it up."

"Yes, I guess so. And you're really here with me."

"What?" she asked him, pulling her hair up into a ponytail and yawning.

"Toshika," he said, gathering himself for a final confrontation with the side of him that failed to believe that she could really be interested in him.

"What," she said, dropping her hands into her lap, giving him her full attention. Again, her beauty struck him, and he hesitated as he stared at her. Averting his eyes, he told himself he would have to avoid prolonged eye contact with her unless he wanted to look silly.

"About last night," he began, "First of all, I'm not seeing anyone right now."

"Except me."

"Except you. Right. But," he hesitated, searching for the words. "Listen, when we went to the bar that night, Hans told me you were seeing someone, or some different people, or something."

Toshika laughed and looked at the ceiling. Richard feared he had embarrassed her. "Yeah, well, not for a while now," she said. "Ah, this whole game thing is really..."

"What?"

Toshika looked at Richard before answering. "Nah, it's just... It's getting old," she said, her eyes drawn to the bed sheets once more, her voice nearly a whisper. Suddenly she looked up at him. "But look, I don't have a 'boyfriend.' I am not seeing anyone. Okay? And I haven't been interested in anyone in that way for a long time. But you... you're different," she said, as if she were trying to figure out just what it was that made it so.

Upon hearing this his heart pounded in his chest. He could not hide his pleasure at her confession. He felt the urge to tell her that he loved her, and with that realization wondered how it was that he was once more in this situation. This psychotic emotion called 'love' that filled him with joy and fear at the same time, and installed itself permanently in his mind commanding his total attention, was back. But he knew that he could not possibly love anyone in such a short time and he also knew that in any case, saying such a thing now would run the risk of pushing her away.

"Well, it's nice to hear you say so." Hearing the hesitation in his own voice, he was filled with an almost violent determination not to be once more the one to lose control of his emotions and allow himself to be too easily won; to have no carrot to hang in front of his pursuer. Toshika was a woman, not a girl. He would have to be careful to keep her interested. It simply would not do for him to appear weak or indecisive considering her apparent ease in being with people. Unexpectedly, the opportunity to step from childish relationships to one that he could grow with confronted him. To make this kind of step was exciting. He swore to himself that he would not fail. "So," he began, looking at her in a way that told her he was sizing her up, "You studied history. What do you do now? For a living?"

She rolled her eyes in thought before answering. "For a living. Not very much. I don't work – not for money anyway. I'm independent financially, so I do a lot of traveling, reading – I love to read – and I have a pretty active social life. And," she said, taking deep breath and holding it, as if she were not sure about what to say next. "Other things. You know."

Richard was now used to meeting wealthy people since his involvement in the game, but he was not expecting that one as young as Toshika would belong to that crowd.

"You mean, you don't have a job," he said, trying not to sound too surprised.

"No. The closest thing I have to a job is managing my investments, I guess. But then I don't really do it myself. Most of the work is done by a couple of other people."

"Oh," he said. He was at a loss for words. She lived in a different world than he had known. He knew of no one, young or old, other than retired people, who did not work. He could scarcely believe that this young woman his own age lived such a life.

"Does that sound boring?" she asked him.

"No, I just don't know anyone who doesn't work. Is it a fulfilling life?"

"A fulfilling life? Well, what would you prefer: working ten hours a day in an office doing something that sometimes gives you pleasure, and if you're lucky pays enough so that you can buy a nice watch for yourself once in a while? Instead, imagine waking up every morning at a time you choose knowing that the events of your day are decided by you, meaning that if you feel like staying in bed all day and reading a great book you bought you can, or if you decide to fly to Alaska to go whale watching you do it, or if you want to make some phone calls and begin planning the opening of your new restaurant, or nightclub, or...daycare center – whatever – you can. You can do what you really want to do." Richard was speechless. "Which would you choose, in order to be fulfilled?" Toshika asked him.

"I guess it's an easy choice." Richard stood on the threshold of the realization that this was now his own decision to make, but was as yet unable to make the first step.

"You know it, don't you?" Toshika asked him. "You do. It takes a while, I know. I somehow always knew it would be that way for me, but until I was really on my own it still seemed, I don't know. Undecided."

Richard looked out the window through the thin gauze of the fore blinds, got up, and opened them all the way. Returning to the bed, he took a seat once again against the mass of pillows and, for a lack of anything to say, fixed his gaze once more on the sky, punctured as it was by random skyscrapers. Toshika could see his mind working.

"Hello," Toshika called to him. He smiled uneasily at her and afforded himself a moment of honesty.

"I'm at a loss here. I cannot believe what's happening. This money still means nothing to me. It isn't real."

"But it is."

Richard looked out the window over the balcony. "It isn't right," he told her. "I'm rich and there are people in this city who are starving. Really starving."

The air went out of Toshika. "Oh, please, not that. Come on, Richard. It's not like you've won a billion. This isn't obscene, for Christ's sake." She stared at Richard until he looked away from her. He settled back into the pillows, sliding down as he did like a lump of warm butter.

"I don't know what to do."

"You'll figure it out," she told him, nodding her head once as if it were final. Then she suddenly sat up and stretched, her nakedness bathed in the sharp morning sunlight.

"Listen," she told him. "I'm hungry. What do you say we eat a big breakfast, right here in bed? We can call room service and go crazy."

"Okay."

"You call while I make a list," she said, looking skyward as she mumbled to herself. When he had room service on the line, she dictated her wishes. "Okay, everything enough for two, of course. Cappuccino, croissant, fresh fruit – make that a fruit salad, plain yogurt, bacon, fresh orange juice, butter, jam, honey – and?" she asked, indicating that he should add anything else that he wanted.

"And a bottle of Mumm's, please," he added, much to Toshika's delight. He hung up the phone. "Twenty minutes," he told her.

She raised herself onto her elbow and stretched out her leg, placing her big toe on his lips. "A lot can happen in twenty minutes."

There was a knock at the door. Toshika placed a hand on Richard's shoulder when he swung his feet onto the floor and looked toward the pile of clothes on the couch.

"I'll get it," she said. Throwing back the sheet she stepped from the bed fully nude and walked toward the door. "Coming," she announced. She stopped at the table by the couch and lingered for a moment before bending to pick up her panties from the floor. Placing them on the pile, she turned to look at Richard. With a teasing smile, she watched his wide eyes as she headed off to answer the door. Richard heard a polite exchange of 'Good-mornings' followed by the whine and clatter of the breakfast cart. A young woman, nearly a teenager, came into view and rounded the corner, stopping as she entered the bedroom. Toshika was close behind her.

"Good morning," the woman called to Richard, who sat fully shrouded in white on the bed.

"Richard, take a hundred dollars out of my purse for the lady, will you please?" Toshika commanded. Richard raised his eyebrows and then reached for her purse. The young woman tried not to notice the appallingly generous tip that was being prepared for her as she set about arranging things on the already perfectly arranged tray. Toshika retrieved the money from Richard and then returned to the trolley, stopping directly in front of the pretty girl.

100

"You know, the last time I ordered plain yogurt here, it didn't taste very fresh," she began. "I guess people don't order it very often and I had the misfortune of being served old yogurt." She stuck her finger deep into one of the bowls of yogurt and then withdrew it, holding it out to her. "Would you taste this please?" Looking at the creamy finger held out to her, the girl blushed and shot a glance at Richard, who simply sat on the bed with his mouth half open in disbelief. "Please?" Toshika asked sweetly. The girl laughed once and then leaned forward, licking some of the yogurt from Toshika's finger. "Come on, do it right," Toshika commanded. She held the money out to the girl, who took it and slipped it into her pocket. Toshika then brought her finger closer to the girl's face. The girl opened her mouth and took Toshika's finger inside almost to the knuckle. Toshika grinned and then slowly pulled her finger out of the girl's mouth.

"So is it fresh?"

"Yes, it's good," came the answer.

Toshika put her wet finger into her own mouth and sucked on it a moment. "Mmm, very good," she said. "Thank you, we'll call if we need you again."

With the woman gone, Richard gasped and held his head in his hands. "God, are you *nuts*? You just can't *do* that!"

Toshika looked at him without speaking, her expression defiant. Then she suddenly appeared embarrassed. She shrugged and approached the bed, sitting down and drawing a duvet over her legs. "I know."

Richard waited for her to continue, appalled at what he had seen and hoping to find that she had some kind of excuse that would help repair the damage to her image for him.

"Sometimes I go too far."

"Is that what wealthy people do?" He could have simply accepted her explanation and kept quiet, but something inside him forced him to push.

Looking down into her lap, she finally met his gaze. He found her then without any pretense, without any mask, without defiance or defenses.

"It's just me."

He smiled and brushed a lock of her hair from her face. Looking at the food on the trolley, he raised his eyebrows.

"Let's eat!"

After breakfast they showered, gathered their things, and took the elevator down. Richard thought of the days to come before their trip. Toshika had said she needed a couple of days to prepare. In the meantime he would prepare himself as well. In the elevator, Toshika played with the room key.

"What are you doing tonight?"

"I don't know. Probably go out with my roommates."

"Celebrate?"

Richard shook his head. "No, not yet. Do you live alone?" Toshika nodded. "I'd like to see your place."

She smiled. "You want to see my place? Okay. You have my number and my address, why don't you come over when you're finished with your friends tonight?"

"Sounds good. What if I'm late?"

"Wake me up."

When they reached the lobby, Toshika went to the desk to pay while Richard wandered into the kiosk. He picked up the Chronicle and checked the front page. At the bottom was a small headline that caught his eye and turned his stomach. 'Local business man found dead'. He felt something touch his arm and looked up to see Toshika.

"I think I forgot something in the room. But you go ahead," she told him, and kissed him quickly on the mouth.

"Okay," he called after her as she headed for the elevator. "See you tonight."

She turned around and smiled. "Yeah."

Richard's attention went back to the newspaper. He held it in his hands for a moment, staring but without reading anything, and then turned and placed it on the counter. Fishing through his pocket he paid for the paper and then turned to leave. Standing in front of him were two men. He stopped short, having thought he was alone.

"Excuse me," he said, waiting for them to allow him to pass. They did not move.

"Mr. Peel?" one of the men asked him.

"Yes," he answered, quickly sensing where this was going. The man held up a badge with his photograph on it.

"I'm detective Ryan from the San Francisco Police Department. This is my partner, detective Williams," he said, in smooth, well-rehearsed speech. Both of them looked like police officers, very clean cut and rather bulky. "We'd like you to come with us, answer a few questions."

"This is about Hans," he said, absently. The policemen gave no reply. He felt no real danger, knowing full well that he had nothing to do with Hans' murder. He hesitated to answer, but knew he had no choice. As he spoke, it was with a concern for Hans and a desire to know what happened that made him want to help the police if he could.

"Yes, sure," he told them. The three of them walked across the lobby. Richard looked at the front desk team who stood watching them carefully. "How did you know I was here?" he asked detective Ryan, looking back toward the elevator for a sign of Toshika. Detective Ryan said nothing. He opened the door, holding it open for Richard, and then followed him outside to a plain-looking car that sat waiting in the driveway. Detective Williams showed him into the back seat of the car and got in next to him. As they drove across town and the constant chatter from the police radio reminded him of scenes from television, Richard began to feel less comfortable with the situation. He knew he was innocent, but he did not have any idea what these two men thought about him. The thought that he could be wrongly accused or even found guilty crossed his mind and before he knew it he had visions of a nightmare world unfolding before him.

Toshika retrieved her iPod from the bathroom of their suite and rode the elevator down to the lobby once again. Through the revolving doors, she entered a waiting taxi and settled into the back seat.

"Vallejo and Divisadero, please."

"Yes ma'am," the driver said, eyeing her in his rear view mirror for a moment after he settled into traffic.

Toshika pulled her phone from her bag. It was eleven. For most people it would be much too late for a phone call. She hit the speed dial, then put the phone to her ear and slumped back into the seat. The phone was picked up after five rings.

"Hi mom...Hi...You painting?...Reading?...What are you reading?...Oh, no. Never heard of it...I know...I know, but you aren't asleep, are you? Because I just knew you wouldn't be...I just had a feeling...Yes...No. Nothing's wrong...How are you? Yeah? And your painting? You did? Yes, I know it, in *Le Quartier latin*...Really? How many? Well that's good. Should pay the rent for a while...No...No, I haven't...I don't know, I'm just not ready yet, that's all...I know...Listen, I'm going to be in Switzerland and will probably come by...I'm not sure yet, but soon...No, I'm probably coming with Page. Yes...Well, she's doing well...She's selling a lot right now...No, still in the shop...No, just privately, just in the shop...She's trying, believe me...It's a competitive business, mom, I mean, come on, you know that...As tough as painting, yes. Absolutely...What do you mean? Why does she have to struggle? Look, these are businesses, you know? It's not like I can command people to buy the clothes, or visit the gallery and buy the work...It *is* work, mom...I know I haven't had to suffer! Jesus, mom, what is it with – what do you mean 'suffer' anyway?...Did you suffer?...No, I'm serious...Oh, that's just ridiculous, please...Sure...Sure...Yeah, okay, well for you maybe, but not for me, and – wait a minute – not for most people, really. Yes, I do know...Well in this case I think it does matter what most people think...Anyway, look...Hmmm...Yeah...Okay. Fine. Okay, well I guess you were reading your book, right? So I'll just let you go...Okay...Oh, I almost forgot the reason why I called. Mom, I have some bad news. Hans is dead...Hans...Yes...He was killed the night before last...Are you there? It's not a joke, mom. I wouldn't do that...Right...Okay...Well, of course I knew you would want to know...So, okay...Yes...okay, bye."

Toshika closed her phone and held it in her hand as the cab turned right onto Divisadero and headed toward the hills of Pacific Heights. The driver cruised slowly into the neighborhood, glancing left and right, savoring the advancement into the upper echelons of society. With home prices here beginning at not less than ten times the national average, it was real estate that the driver could never dream of owning. Cresting the hill on Pacific Avenue, the cabbie slowed, looking left and then right before proceeding slowly through the intersection, dropping down and then hanging a left on Vallejo. Finally the cab pulled up in front of a wooden house and halted. Toshika paid the driver, let herself out of the car, and silently went inside. She dropped her bag on the floor just inside the door and walked, mechanically, through the cavernous living room to the large glass door at the back overlooking a view of the bay. Once outside on the patio, she placed her hands on the wooden railing and looked out over the little forest of her backyard, carefully manicured so that the view of the bay would remain unobstructed, her concentration slipping away, melting into the view of the cerulean water. She stood there letting the breeze mingle with her hair, angling strands of it here and there across the soft skin of her face. She raised a hand without thinking to brush a bit of it back and noticed a noise nearby. It was the sound of a big noise emanating from a small source. She realized it was music and that it had indeed been beating in the background since she arrived on the deck. She looked to the right and below, where a house bordering her own was undergoing renovations. She saw a man bobbing his head to the beat of the music, and heard laughter as he and a co-worker or co-workers went about their construction work, their radio, or more likely portable CD player, blaring encouragement nearby them. Then she brought her full attention to the noise. To the scrapping sound of nails on plastic she heard an angry voice shouting "Fuck that shit! Fuck that shit! Fuck that shit! Fuck that shit!"

Her jaw dropped. An angry rapper. Aren't they always angry? She laughed once, at the idiocy of the lyric, at the idea of the inevitable complaints from neighbors, of the poor hammer swinger who hadn't paid much attention to his choice of music on the job. This isn't done in this neighborhood. It just isn't done. And then she was crying. Then sobbing, as she let go of the railing and slumped down onto the deck, remembering the last time Hans had been standing with her on this very spot, trying to offer her advice as gently as possible so as not to ruin a friendship, and she allowing him to be concerned but wishing that it had come not from a father figure, but from a father. Her father. And she finally was hit with the full realization of what had ended just two nights ago. For her and for everyone who knew Hans. He had been such a friend. Always there for her, despite the distance she intentionally kept from him. He had been perfect. Always there. Never pushing too hard. Always respectful, always true to her. She covered her eyes and then pressed on them, wishing for once in her life that he had pushed harder. As hard as was needed. For her own good, and not out of friendship.

Just then she noticed the angry rhythms ending abruptly. A voice called out. "Thank you." Vallejo Street was peaceful once again.

7

It was only a few minutes before they arrived in a secure-looking parking lot behind the main station on Bryant Street, parked the car, and went into the building. Stopping in a small room just inside Richard was asked to remove everything from his pockets. He was then patted down quickly before they proceeded further into the building, up a flight of stairs, and into a large office with desks enough for twenty people. Being Saturday, the place was only at about half capacity and surprisingly quiet. Richard felt at once that he would have been more at ease had the offices been filled with people and the usual noises of an office place. They went into a small room adjacent to this large office. Inside was a table and four chairs. Richard was asked to sit.

"Can I get you anything to drink?" detective Ryan asked him. "Smoke?"

"No, thanks."

"Okay," he said. The two detectives sat down across from each other. Detective Ryan turned on a tape machine that sat on the table and then turned to Richard. "State your name please."

Richard took a deep breath. "Richard Peel."

"Sorry, once more please?"

"My name is Richard Peel," he said, mildly annoyed at having to repeat himself.

"Richard, tell us what you did last Thursday night, July 23rd."

Richard thought for an instant about what Jeffries had told him. "On Thursday night I went to a dinner party with several other people and... and we had dinner."

"Where was this dinner party?" detective Williams asked.

"It was on 28th in Noe Valley."

"Can you tell us the exact address please?" asked detective Ryan, putting a pencil to a pad of paper he had in front of him.

"Number forty-nine. It's a law office."

"Okay. Who did you go with?"

"I went alone. Everyone else was there when I got there."

"Who was there?" he asked, again ready to copy down names on his pad of paper.

Richard told him their names as best as he could remember. He noticed the detectives exchange glances when he mentioned David Norton.

"What time did you get there?"

"I got there at about eight."

"Tell us about the dinner."

"Well, we just ate dinner. It was a party," Richard said, unsure of what the detective wanted to know.

"Okay, and when did you leave?"

"It must have been about midnight."

"Did anything strange happen at this dinner? Anyone exhibit any unusual behavior?"

"No."

"Did you do anything like, I don't know, listen to music, play some cards, you know, party things?"

"Not really," Richard said, shrugging his shoulders.

"Sounds like some party. What about Mr. Kienle? How would you describe his mood that night?"

"His mood? He was in a good mood, I think."

"And everyone else? Also in a good mood?"

"Yes. It was a party. We all had a good time," Richard told him. He was beginning to feel very uneasy about so many direct questions about what they were doing there that night. He did not know what kind of details anyone else had given and did not want to make any mistakes that would force him to discuss the game, and reveal that he had been lying about it.

"Okay. You said you came alone. Did you leave alone?"

"No, I left with Hans."

"How did you get to this party?"

"I drove."

"When you left, did you give Mr. Kienle a ride, or did he have his own car?"

"He had his own car."

"Where did you go then?"

"We went to the Noc Noc, on Haight Street."

"Was it just the two of you?"

"Yes."

"What happened at the bar?"

"We had a few beers, and then left. I think it was about two when we left. I didn't really feel like driving, because of the beer, but Hans asked me if I would give him a ride home."

"Why did he ask for a ride home?"

"Because of the alcohol. I mean, neither of us should have been driving."

"Okay Richard, now...at the bar, what did you two talk about?"

Richard exhaled loudly and held his hands in the air as he recalled the evening. "We talked about a lot of things. I mean, what do you want me to do, tell you everything we said? I can't do that anyway. I wouldn't remember everything."

"Just tell us what you talked about. Baseball? Politics? What?"

"Oh, lots of things. We talked about America. Hans is from Switzerland, and so we talked about what it was like living here, stuff like that."

"Did he like living here?" detective Ryan asked.

Richard thought about exactly how to answer that question. "Yes. Yes, he liked living here. But he also said that, I don't know, America wasn't all that great." He stopped and thought back for a moment. "That it wasn't all it was cracked up to be. That's what it was. "

The two detectives looked at each other. Detective Ryan frowned. It was barely noticeable, but Richard saw it. "He said that?"

"Yes, he did." Richard had the feeling that these policemen were not happy to hear this, giving him a small sense of satisfaction.

"How did that make you feel?" detective Ryan asked.

Richard made a noncommittal face. "I don't know. It wasn't a big deal."

"But it wasn't a compliment either, right?"

"No."

"It couldn't have made you feel good, could it? Did you feel good when he said that?"

"No, of course not."

"So then you didn't like it."

Richard could see where this was leading. The efforts of the detectives were completely transparent. In one of those moments when one can feel danger coming and one feels bizarrely compelled not to turn away from it, Richard chose to flirt with disaster, confident that he could always explain later if he wanted to. Confident that because he knew he was innocent of this crime, nothing else would come of it. A desire to stand on the edge had flared up within him, and he accepted the challenge. "No, I didn't," he said, "Certainly not." Then, feeling that perhaps he had overreached himself, he added one more thing. "But I can say that it seemed perfectly reasonable, after he explained himself."

Richard watched as detective Ryan made some lengthy notes. He exchanged looks with detective Williams and then looked at Richard. "I'm sorry, you said it seemed reasonable?"

"Yes," Richard said evenly.

"Okay, enough of that. How many drinks had you had that night, from eight o'clock until two?"

Richard watched the pencil in detective Ryan's hand start to scribble down his words as he answered. "I think I had two at the party, and three at the bar."

"Would you say that you were drunk when you left the bar?"

Richard took a deep breath and shrugged his shoulders. "No, not drunk. Maybe legally, I don't know."

"Okay, go on."

"What?"

"Where did you go when you left the bar?"

"Oh. I drove Hans home, watched him go into the house, and then I went home."

"You went straight home then?"

"Yes. No! Sorry, I went to Orphan Andy's for something to eat."

"Orphan Andy's? Why there?"

"Because it's one of the only places open that late."

"What did you eat?"

"I had a hamburger, fries, and a milkshake. Chocolate."

"When did you leave?"

"It must have been about a quarter to three. I paid and went straight home."

"Okay. We'll check the restaurant to see if anyone remembers you there. Jim?" detective Ryan said, looking at his partner, who nodded his head and turned again to Richard.

"Richard, when you dropped Mr. Kienle off, did you see anyone or anything at his house? Something that seemed odd to you?"

"No."

"How long had you known Mr. Kienle?"

"Not long. I only met him this week."

"When?"

"Tuesday, at the bar in the St. Francis."

"And you are already having dinner with him Thursday?"

Richard thought for a moment about whether or not it really sounded so strange. "Yes, he invited me when we met," he told him. Then he remembered Toshika, and realized the story made a lot more sense now. "When I met him we ran into Toshika Tamura. I think he invited me to this party so that we could get to know each other."

"You and this Toshika?"

"Yes."

"Well, it seems to have worked, doesn't it?" he asked him, his face completely expressionless.

"Yeah, it did."

"Richard, what do you know about Mr. Kienle?"

Richard shrugged. "Not much. I know that he had been here for about twenty years, that he came from Switzerland, that he owned a restaurant or two and an art gallery, and... That's about it. He seemed like a really nice guy."

"Did you know that he was gay?"

Richard looked at detective Williams, and then at detective Ryan. "No," he said, "I didn't. I don't really believe it, actually," he told them.

"Why not?" detective Ryan asked.

Richard stared at the tape machine, feeling no words come. "I just don't think so. I didn't get that impression at all. He told me he was married, actually. Or he had been. He was divorced."

"And that means he wasn't gay?"

"No, but... I just would not have thought that he was gay, if you asked me. That's all. But if he was, well, okay. I don't care."

"Do you have something against gay men, Richard?"

"No!" he told them, annoyed at the question.

"Are you gay, Richard?" detective Williams asked him.

"No, I am not gay. What the hell is this, anyway?"

"When you drove him home, did he try to kiss you, or touch you?"

"No! Shit! You guys are completely wrong here. I told you, he never did anything to make me believe he was gay, okay?" Richard told them. His heart was racing and his mouth was dry. "Can I have something to drink, please?"

"Sure, are you nervous?" detective Ryan asked him.

Richard tried to gather himself and think before he answered again. "Yes, I am getting nervous because your questions are making me angry, and I feel nervous talking to you here in an angry tone. That's why I'm thirsty."

"Okay. Do you always choose your words so carefully, Richard?"

"No. I don't know, I studied philosophy," he said before he realized how odd it may have sounded to two policemen. Detective Ryan got up and left the room. Moments later he returned with a small paper cup filled with cold water, placing it on the table in from of Richard.

"Thanks." He picked up the cup and drank it all.

"Do you own a gun, Richard?" detective Ryan asked.

"No. I never have."

Detective Ryan looked at his partner and raised his eyebrows. Detective Williams nodded. "Okay, Richard. Thanks very much for your help. Please don't go anywhere, okay? Don't leave town for the next few days. If you need to go somewhere, call me first, or you might get into trouble." He told him, sliding his card across the table to Richard. His tone of voice was suddenly very nice, and Richard felt bad for having begun to start to hate the both of them. They're

112

just trying to do their jobs, he told himself. They all stood up and went downstairs. Stopping in the waiting room, Richard was given back his belongings.

"Can we give you a ride somewhere?" detective Ryan asked him.

Richard nearly told them no, but the station was not convenient for him to take public transportation home. "Can you take me home?"

"Sure, no problem," detective Ryan said. "I'll be back in thirty," he told his partner, and then the two of them went outside. After they had been some minutes on the road, Richard turned to detective Ryan and spoke.

"About Mr. Kienle's death. Do you have any leads? Anything at all?"

"I'm not at liberty to comment on the investigation. Sorry," detective Ryan answered. Richard felt instantly that he should have known better.

"But you don't think I had anything to do with it, do you?"

"All I can say right now, Richard, is don't leave town."

Richard thought about Switzerland and did not ask any more questions. As he sat inside the detective's car, watching familiar scenery go by, telling himself that it was going to be okay, that they were clearly not after him, he remembered something from the game the first night that he almost began to mention to the detective. Luckily, he caught himself. Hans had told the others, while Toshika and Mr. Norton were out of the room, that he would not be playing any more. Richard wondered if that had been a hint to the others of what had come to pass. Perhaps Hans was not murdered at all. Perhaps he had killed himself. His mind began to race. No one had mentioned suicide. Wouldn't they have been able to tell from the evidence, assuming there was any, how it had happened?

"Was it... very messy?" Richard heard himself ask. Are you crazy? What kind of stupid question is that? Detective Ryan shot him a look that he could have expected. A look that told him what an improper question it had been.

"Like I said, Richard, I can't comment on the case," he said, a suitably rough edge on his voice. Richard nodded and bit his lip.

A few minutes later detective Ryan stopped in front of Richard's house. Richard thanked him for the ride and got out of the car. He did not look back as he stepped onto the sidewalk and went to the stairs. Climbing the steps to his flat, he suddenly felt exhausted. His hand found the railing and he half walked, half pulled his way into the apartment. "Tony?" he shouted into the empty apartment. He hung his coat and walked to his bedroom door – the first one in the long hallway. Looking down into the kitchen at the end, a sunny Saturday peace filled the air. Shoes lay scattered in the hallway like so many guard dogs. He entered his room and flung himself on the bed. He felt much better now that he was home, and the fear that had mounted earlier with the police seemed exaggerated. There wasn't a sound in the apartment, but the quiet was the quiet of home. Sleep began weighing in on him, pulling him down. He thought of the money, and the traveling, and of Toshika, and the excitement nearly kept him awake.

8

He was on a landscape of rolling green hills when he began to bounce with big steps like one would on the moon, going higher and higher until he willed himself to move forward through the air, keeping speed and altitude as long as his concentration remained unbroken. The next thing he knew, he was flying. Over buildings, over skyscrapers. As he passed by he would look in through windows at scenes inside. "Toshika's house!" he yelled, and then began heading straight for a tall building that lay directly ahead of him. It was the hotel, and as he neared it he saw Toshika standing on the balcony, nude, her hair wet. She stood leaning with her back against the railing, combing her dark hair back neatly. On their balcony next to her, a young couple sat eating breakfast. Richard landed on the balcony and turned to Toshika. "It's all wet!" he told her. She just smiled. He looked at the couple on the next balcony. The young man suddenly turned to him, looking very annoyed. He gestured to the food on his table. "The food was late! But *she* doesn't care," he cried, pointing to Toshika with his elbow. Richard approached Toshika and stood naked before her. He took hold of her arms and pushed himself into her. As everything went black, he closed his eyes

When he awoke, he looked at his watch and rolled onto his side, looking into the room. By no means as fancy as the hotel room he had woken up in that morning, this room was, nevertheless, more relaxing to be in. It was home. The dream, fading fast from his memory, brought a smile to his face as he stretched.

All things considered, he had enjoyed this space very much. It was a large, sunny room, which had served to win his allegiance to the otherwise unremarkable apartment. Large bay windows overlooking the street filled the room with afternoon sunshine. Propping himself on one elbow he looked at the familiar surroundings. His desk, inherited from tenants long since gone, sat opposite the bed. Piled with books, paper, candles, loose change, pocket knife, assorted tools that were necessary to keep the flat functioning, a baseball tucked into its glove, old bills, and various other articles, it would be impossible to sit and work at that desk. Indeed, most of his studying over the years had been done on the floor, or in the Twilight Café around the corner, or in the university library. Next to the desk was a bookcase, again from an unknown inhabitant, which held his treasured collection of mainly used books. Then came his television, handed down to him from his parents, and his stereo, the one piece of equipment that he had put a lot of money into. More than he could afford, in fact, but it was at least completely paid for. It was a powerful system that he used to its full potential, thanks in part to very uncomplicated neighbors who failed to complain even when he was enjoying his 'concert level' listening experience. Yes, he thought, this place has been good to me.

The days spent in his little piece of relative freedom had been happy ones. Far away from the oppressive shadow of his father, far away from the suburb where his awkward teenage years were spent, this room, and this apartment, may not have looked like much. But to him, it was a home that he was always happy to come back to. Even though it had no proper furniture, no heating. Even though the walls needed painting, and the old wooden floors refinishing. Even though the ancient linoleum in the bathroom and kitchen were a complete disaster. Even though there were holes in the ceiling. Complaints to the landlords were futile, and when acted upon, almost served to make him and his roommates regret having spoken up. After complaining about the state of the paint some time ago, they came home one day from school to find that much of the apartment, but not all of it, had indeed been repainted while they were away. Even though the paint job was very sloppy and obviously not

116

professionally done, they were quite pleased until they tried to open one of the windows and found that it, along with the others, had been painted shut. A hammer and chisel freed the windows, but at a price. They looked as though they had been chiseled open. Such was the life of a poor university student. Looking around him now, he knew that he would be saying good-bye to this place. He had no idea where he would live, or if he would buy or rent. How would he furnish his new place? What style would it be? The possibilities were not endless, but even to have possibilities was beyond him.

He got up and went down the hall to the kitchen where he took a bottle of beer from the refrigerator and went out onto the back porch. The sun beat down on the mostly dead and disorganized plant life that had been someone's garden project years ago. He took a seat on a hot metal chair and tipped back against the house, putting his feet up on the wooden railing that threatened to expire under even this minor weight. Sipping from his beer he put his head back and closed his eyes. The heat began to set into his skin, and his thoughts drifted.

"Hi Richard," a voice called from somewhere in front of him. He opened his eyes and put a hand over them to see. It was the daughter of his neighbor, a student who lived far up in the north and who visited once in a while. She was standing on their deck wearing a bikini, holding a towel and a magazine.

"Oh, hi Kayla," Richard answered, raising his beer to her. "Getting some sun?"

"Yes," she told him. She was a pretty girl. "But I'm heading back inside now. I've had enough. How're you doing?"

"Oh, pretty well, thanks. Are you down for long?"

"A few weeks. Taking it easy for a while. Hey, I heard you went to a big poker game?"

"Oh, has Tony been telling stories again? Experimenting with movie ideas?"

"I don't know, was it just a tall tale?"

Richard shrugged his shoulders. "No, not really. I did play some poker."

"Did you win anything?"

"Yes, as a matter of fact."

"Great! How much?"

"About four million dollars."

The young woman laughed and wished Richard a nice day, waving as she stepped into the house without closing the door behind her. Richard tipped his head back once again and returned to his beer.

The banging of a door somewhere startled him, his body stiffened momentarily. He turned and looked into his apartment through the window near the door.

"Tony?" he hollered in through the open door.

"Nope," came the reply. It was Matt.

"Hey! Come have a beer," Richard called to him. "Bring me another one, too."

In a moment, Matt stood in the doorway, dressed only in his long army shorts, a beer in each hand. "Holy fuck," he said, squinting against the sunlight that reflected off the clean cement of the patio. "Is it as hot as it looks out here?" he asked, stepping down onto the porch. He handed Richard a beer and pulled a chair over.

"It's pretty warm," Richard replied. "You woke me up. I was having a great dream."

"Sex dream?" Matt asked him, a devilish look in his dark eyes.

"That's right, pal. And you ruined it."

"Sorry."

They brought their beer bottles together with a loud clink. "Hey, be careful," Matt warned, "I paid for these, you know."

Richard turned to him and looked at him with one eye. "Don't worry. The beer's on me from now on."

"Oh yeah?" Matt asked him, eyeing him suspiciously through his long black hair. Just then it occurred to Richard that Matt probably did not know about the game. He had been back home in Southern California the last few days for a wedding. "What, did you steal a bunch from work?" he asked him sarcastically.

"No," Richard answered, deciding to keep his secret a bit longer. "I just thought I would pay you back for keeping us in beer."

"And in good coffee. Don't forget about the coffee."

"Right. The coffee too."

Matt tossed his head back and drank half his beer, following with a very loud belch.

"Nice."

Suddenly Matt set his beer down and grabbed Richard by the arm. "Rich, come with me," he told him, with a stern expression. "Come on," he said, standing up and heading inside. Richard followed him into his room. Matt turned and cautioned him with a finger to his lips. "Check this out," he said quietly. Reaching up on top of a large bookcase that he had filled with vinyl LPs, he took a plastic bag down off the top and placed it carefully on his bed. From the bag he pulled out three records. "Check this out," he said again, "Beach Boys. The first three LPs, unopened. Mint. Perfect," he said, arranging them side-by-side on the bed and tilting his head at them in appreciation. He turned and looked proudly at Richard. " 'Goo-hoo-hood! Good vi-bra-shuns' " he sang, swinging his hips and snapping his fingers.

Richard would never have bothered with the Beach Boys, but Matt was something of a connoisseur and had a much wider musical appreciation. "The shrink wrap is all torn up," he complained. Matt's head whipped around and his eyes narrowed on his prize.

"They're over forty years old!" he explained, thumping himself on the forehead with the palm of his hand for emphasis.

"I guess so. Well, that's cool. How much did that cost?"

"Can't tell you," Matt said, picking up the records and placing them carefully back in the bag.

"What are you going to do with them?"

"I'm not going to do *anything* with them. They will simply carry out their lives, and grow old," he said, looking around the room, contemplating their next resting place.

Richard sipped his beer. "Let's play one of them!" he dared Matt, who wheeled around and held once again the same devilish look in his eyes.

"Should we?" he asked, his voice almost inaudible.

"They're dying to get out of there," Richard said. "Set them free." Matt looked doubtful. "Just one."

Matt held his hands together and took a deep breath. "Okay, the first one, because it's been waiting the longest."

The apartment was filled with sound for the next forty minutes as the two of them drained the beer from the refrigerator. When the place was quiet once again, they returned to the patio and dozed in the heat.

When they awoke, they were ravenous. They took Matt's motorcycle down the hill to Haight Street to get a burrito. It was late afternoon, and there had been no sign of Tony. Haight Street was buzzing with activity. Tourists, locals, and the ever-present vagrant youth population were out in force. Richard and Matt sat in the small burrito restaurant taking large bites of burrito and washing them down with fruit juice.

"How was the wedding?" Richard asked.

"Nice. No, it was sad. No, it was nice, but sad."

"How's that?"

Matt set his burrito down and sat with his elbows on the counter, staring out through the large window directly in front of them at the crowds going by on the sidewalk outside. "Yes, it was nice, because it was very well done, and they both looked great. *She* looked *really* good. And their families were there, and their friends, and it was a really beautiful event. And I was there alone, because I don't have a girlfriend, so it was sad." Matt looked at Richard with a weak smile and shrugged his shoulders. "Life," he said to him.

Richard considered his words for a moment. Matt had not found someone he really cared for since he left his high school sweetheart. He had always played the cool womanizer, but in the end he had nothing to show for it.

"Well, we're still young, old boy. If you start getting down about this now, you might doom yourself to a lifetime of solitude."

They resumed eating, speaking with difficulty as they struggled against masses of flour tortilla, beans, rice, cheese, and assorted vegetables.

"Why?"

"Because, who is going to want you?"

"Huh?"

"If you go around with all of that negative energy, who is going to want you?"

"Okay. I see your point."

Their burritos finished, they sat poking at their tortilla chips as they finished their drinks. They spent a few minutes indicating to each other which were the desirable women passing by in front of them.

" 'I'm a girl watcher/I'm a girl watcher/Here comes one now,' " Matt sang, the smile on his face masking the restlessness he felt. "So what about you?" he asked Richard, who had been dying to tell him about Toshika.

"I'm glad you asked," he said coyly. Matt's shoulders dropped.

"No! Tell me."

Richard dusted the salt from the corn chips off of his hands and finished his drink. "Okay," he began.

"Tell me everything."

"Okay, it's like this. I had an interview on Tuesday, right?"

"I remember. You told me that morning when I was heading down south."

"Right. The interview went badly, by the way. Thanks for asking," he said, pausing until Matt made a conciliatory hand gesture. "Well, it doesn't matter anymore. So after the interview I was feeling like hell and I stopped in at the bar at the St. Francis."

"The St. Francis *hotel*?"

"Right."

"Why there?" Matt asked, clearly surprised at this lack of cool on Richard's part.

"It was close. I walked by and went in on a whim. Anyway, I was in my suit, right?"

"Okay."

"I met this man. An older guy. We started talking..." Richard thought of introducing the poker game. "And while we were talking, he sees someone he knows. She comes over to our table, and she is the most beautiful thing."

"But how old was she?"

"No," Richard said, "She's our age. Anyway, she's gorgeous, and he introduced us, and... Now I'm seeing her."

"Wow," Matt said, nodding his head. "But, is that all?"

"I'm not going to tell you everything, okay? You don't need to know that."

"But tell me more about her! Where's she from, what does she do..."

"She – I don't know where she's from, actually. I haven't asked. She's half Japanese, she has long dark hair, but features – eyes, mouth – more Western. Great body, she's smart, she studied history, and... she's rich," Richard said, lacing his fingers on the counter and waiting for a reaction.

"What do you mean, 'rich'?"

"Well, I don't know how much she has, but she doesn't work. Her mother was wealthy, apparently, so that's probably where she got her money. She lives in Pacific Heights and just manages her investments for a living!"

"Jeez, not bad!" Matt said. "Congratulations, man. I want to meet her."

"Yes, well, it'll come. It'll come," Richard said, looking out the window again. "But she's very perfect, I think. Perfect for me." He looked Matt in the eye to show he was serious.

"Well, I wish you luck."

"Thanks," Richard said, measuring in Matt's eyes the friendship they shared. "We went through school together, you know? All those great times." he told Matt. "You're a good friend."

"That I am, Peel-man," Matt replied, his gaze drifting to the action outside once again. He noticed the bookstore across the street, and slapped Richard's arm. "Hey. Let's go check out some books."

They returned their food baskets to the front counter and headed for the door. As they crossed the street, Matt's phone rang. It was Tony. He had been at work all day across the Bay and was calling to arrange for them to meet up later for drinks. With that settled, Richard and Matt spent some time pouring over books before heading down the street on foot, stopping in at one shop after another as they saw fit.

The bar was packed. Richard and Matt stepped inside and stood looking for a familiar face. The place was very simple: the bar at one side, large tables and long benches were arranged in rows on the other. Nothing on the walls, no pool tables, no clutter. Finally Richard realized that the arm waving at the back of the bar was Tony's.

"In the back," he told Matt. The two of them worked their way through the throng of the young alternative clientele towards the back where Tony waited at a large table he shared with several others, picking up a pitcher of beer on the way.

"Hey men! Happy Saturday!" Tony announced, clearing some glasses away to make room for the beer. Richard and Matt sat opposite Tony, who quickly took possession of the pitcher and poured each of them three tall pints.

"Matt tells me you've been in the office all day," Richard said, repeating his longstanding objection to Tony's busy work schedule.

"Yeah. Deadline's coming up and there's still a lot of editing to do," he said, picking up his beer. "Here's to the roommates," he said, as they all raised their glasses in a toast. "So, Mr. Peel," Tony said, desperate to hear the results of the poker game, "What have you got for us?"

Richard said nothing. The look on Tony's face caught Matt's attention. "What's he talking about?" Matt asked.

"Didn't he tell you? The big poker game!" Tony cried.

"Poker game?" Matt realized he was not party to the story and turned to Richard, putting his hand on his shoulder. "Richard, it seems you haven't been completely honest with me about the events of the recent past. Perhaps you'd like to try again, before my Italian Stallion here rearranges your face?"

"You tell him," Richard told Tony.

"Okay," Tony said, "Listen. Richard met some very wealthy guy and was invited to play some high stakes poker. He played two games with them, and now we want to know how much he won!" he cried. "So tell us! What happened?"

"Okay, ready?" This was Richard's moment. The look of anticipation on his friend's faces was perfect. "Well, I *did* win. Guess how much."

"A thousand," Matt blurted out.

"Come on, you think he would make us guess if it was just a thousand?" Tony said, and then looked at Richard and tried to read him. "Five grand," he said.

"More."

"Ten."

"More."

Matt and Tony looked at each other. Matt still did not look convinced. "Fifty-thousand," he said.

"Way more," Richard said, grinning from ear to ear.

"What, a hundred thousand?" Tony asked, his eyes telling Richard that he did not believe it.

"You guys are way off," Richard said. Tony and Matt just sat with their mouths open, unable to accept what they were hearing. "Okay, you'll never get it," Richard said, and then leaned in close and spoke in a hushed voice. "Listen. I won four million bucks!"

Tony and Matt were silent for a moment and then Tony burst out laughing. Matt did not seem to think it was so funny.

"I don't believe this," Matt said, "You won four million dollars playing poker with a bunch of strangers and you had no money of your own to play with?"

Richard just smiled and nodded. "I know how completely ridiculous it sounds, believe me. I've been going out of my mind the last twenty-four hours over this. But it's true. I'm waiting for a starter amount to be deposited in my bank here, and then I'm going with my new girl, Toshika, to Switzerland to open an account. By the way, Tony," Richard said, "*she's* got money too. She said she doesn't work. She just manages her money. Lives in Pacific Heights. Can you believe it?" he said, folding his arms across his chest.

"I will kill you if this is a joke, dude," Tony said, waving a finger. "Are you telling us the truth? On your mother?"

"On my mother?" Richard cried, putting his hand to his head. "What, are we in the mafia now?"

"I don't know, sounds like *you* are," Matt said.

"You swear this is the truth?" Tony asked again, his smile telling Richard that he hoped it was true. Richard raised his hands and told them once more.

"I am not kidding. I will call you in a few days from Switzerland and fly you guys over if you want so we can party," he told them. Tony and Matt still did not know what to make of this story and sat staring at each other. With a fresh idea in his mind, Matt slapped the table and thrust his hand out to Richard.

"Okay, give me that money you just took out of the machine. If you just won four million then it won't hurt you to spread the wealth."

Richard hesitated. It was his first test. The two hundred dollars he withdrew on their way to the bar was still a lot of money to him, and he had not seen the poker money in his account yet. "Okay," he said, obliging Matt and pulling his wallet out. "But remember, I took this out to buy us all drinks with, so now it's up to you." He removed all of the money from his wallet and handed it to Matt. With the money in his hand, Matt looked at Tony.

"I think he's serious," he said. "Wow! Talk about the nick of time. You were going to be moving back in with mom and dad soon, weren't you? What are you going to do now?" he asked Richard, handing him back the money.

"I don't know. I have to figure it out. "

"What are we doing here, celebrating the new millionaire in the lower Haight, drinking beer? Let's go someplace grand and have some champagne!" Matt said, finishing his beer.

"Sounds good to me," Richard said. Tony cleared his throat and raised his glass.

"Laura, Jake, Alex, and Andy are meeting us here. They should be here any minute, so let's wait for them. But listen, man, here's to the millionaire, and I hope you remember who your friends are, okay?"

"Here, here," Matt agreed.

"Hey, listen. Let's not mention the game or the money to the others, okay? I don't have the money yet, and since there still is a possibility that this whole thing flops, I want to keep it between us, okay?" Tony and Matt agreed.

A silence hung in the air. Tony and Matt looked at Richard, but had trouble holding eye contact. In a moment, Richard could feel their unspoken desire pulling at him. They would not ask it, but Richard could feel the question eating away at them. It was impossible for them to broach, just as it was impossible for them to shrug off. Their friend, their brother, had struck it rich. What's in it for me? It would have tortured them for the rest of the evening if he had not mentioned it, but, lucky for them, one aspect of his new wealth that thrilled Richard the most was his ability, and his firm intention, to share with his friends what had so easily come. But first he would savor, just for a moment, their desire against his ability to satisfy it.

"What's on your mind, Tony?" Richard asked casually. The briefest surprise showed on Tony's face before he recovered.

"Nothing. What're you going to buy first?" he answered. Richard looked at Matt.

"Is that what you were wondering too?" he asked him, perhaps a bit too earnestly.

"Yeah, what comes first?"

Richard considered their questions for some time before answering. "I don't know. I'm feeling generous, though," he said, watching their response. They grew still. "Maybe I'll take my mom shopping. Or my brothers! That would be fun. Can you imagine?" he asked them. As soon as he had, he felt like an ogre and decided to end their torture. "Of course, I'll have to take you both out for a colossal spree!"

"Whatever makes you happy," Tony said, trying to combine gratitude with indifference.

"Hey man, I'm ready!" Matt said, "Just say the word!"

Another toast was made, and then Tony and Matt begged for details of the game. They were envious, but Richard's friends seemed happy for him.

Richard found it impossible to ignore the reality of his new life persistently knocking at the back of his consciousness. Like a song that would not go away, his attention was couched in this background noise. At times the thought of what had happened to Hans Kienle and the interrogation at the police department earlier that day threatened to emerge, but Richard couldn't face that now. He was determined not to spoil this evening.

Soon the others arrived. Laura, a former classmate of Richard's and now graduate student in philosophy, Jake and Andy from creative arts, and Alex who, along with Matt, was a graduate student of physics, all stood in the doorway until Tony saw them and waved them over. They all managed to squeeze in at the same table.

"Hey, great to see you all again," Richard said.

"Tony's been calling everyone all day," Laura said. "He said it was about time for a little reunion."

"Where's Danny?" Richard asked Tony. "Did you call him too?"

"Yeah, he couldn't make it. Too much work."

"On Saturday? The guy's a nut," Richard cried. "What are we drinking here? I'm buying," he announced to the group.

"What have you got there?" Laura asked, pointing to the nearly empty pitcher of beer on the table.

"Red Hook," Matt answered.

"Well, let's make it more of the same?" Laura asked the others, who seemed to be in agreement.

"Come with me, Laura," Richard said, taking her by the arm and dragging her with him to the bar. "We have some catching up to do." At the bar Richard made himself noticed and then stood waiting to be served, turning to Laura in the meantime.

"So Laura," he began.

"Tell me."

"No, you tell me. How are things?"

"Good. Pretty good. How about you? How's your love life?" she asked him.

With the secret of Toshika on his mind, Richard was surprised at the coincidence of this question. "Yeah, I've got something going. Something new."

"Sounds exciting!"

"How about you?"

"Nah. Nothing going on there. Nothing serious, anyway."

Richard had always been attracted to Laura, but had felt intimidated by her intellect. With Toshika now on his mind, and romance safely in his grasp, he felt an urge to flirt. "Aha. Still the huntress," he teased. Laura made a face that Richard could not fathom. "What's happening these days in the old halls?" he asked her. "You still enjoying it?"

"Still loving wisdom. How about you?"

"Oh, still missing it all," he said. "Sometimes I'm so close to enrolling in grad school."

"Hey, that would be great! I'd love to have you around again, nipping at my heels," Laura said, giving Richard's cheek a playful pinch.

"I was more than a match for you, you know that," he told her. In fact, Laura was brighter than anyone he had ever known.

"Yeah, you'd like to think so, wouldn't you? Add brains to your good looks?"

Richard made a face and nudged Laura with his shoulder. "No, I'd love to come back but I'm not ready just yet. Plus, I figure it couldn't hurt to work a bit for a while. I mean, something serious. Something that I could build from, if I decided not to teach."

Laura nodded. "Very reasonable of you."

"Come on, give me a break! What's new with students, teachers?"

"You know Tom?"

"You mean, surfer Tom?" he asked. Laura nodded.

"Exactly. You wouldn't believe the transformation he's gone through. I mean, I don't know what you think, but I wouldn't say he was especially brilliant, would you?"

"No. Just average."

"Right. Well, you know he's going for his master's now."

"Yes, I heard."

"After the summer I saw him at a conference down at Stanford. You wouldn't believe it! Long-haired surfer Tom is sitting there in corduroy pants, a tweed coat for God's sake – he's cut his hair of course – and he's wearing this beret. I almost burst out laughing when I saw him except that he saw me right away and so we just chatted for a minute. He was trying to ooze erudition. Didn't work."

"Boy," Richard said, shaking his head and smiling.

"Yeah. I couldn't believe my eyes. I half expected him to pull out a pipe, you know, and a little bag of tobacco."

Just then the barmaid appeared and took their order. Moments later, with three pitchers of beer, they returned to the table. Richard made a space for Laura and sat next to her, noticing as he set himself down that, as always, the group had already become fractured; physicists spoke with physicists, and the artists with the artists. It was just as well, he thought, because more than anyone else, he longed to speak with his former classmate; the only one there who really knew.

Laura, although pretty, looked like a philosophy student; a highly coveted quality that few could so successfully realize. She had a rebellious intellectual air and style about her. Her blond hair was cut short, and her eyes framed by fine steel-rimmed glasses. Richard always had the vague notion that she looked very European. The two raised their glasses, sipped their beer, and returned the glasses to the table without forfeiting eye contact. There they remained, nodding in silence, minds gearing down, building their intellectual energy.

"So, are you still meeting with that guy John at the Café Fleur?"

"Yes. I don't know if I'll make it tomorrow at this rate, but yes, we still meet almost every Sunday. I've been reading what he tells me, but I haven't found it yet. I'm starting to get anxious, to be honest."

"Right. Is it interesting though?"

"Oh, definitely. I'm learning a lot just doing the reading and discussing it with him. He really knows Plato inside and out. Reads him in Greek. I'm still enjoying myself but I haven't seen exactly what he wants me to see yet."

"Do you have any idea?"

"Well, yes. He's trying to show me the spiritual side of Plato. We concentrate on passages that deal with matters of the soul, and of the Forms, and God. But to what end, I don't know yet."

"Why don't you just ask him?"

"I know, but I'll tell you, I really like the process. It's like being in school again. And I know he wants me to find it for myself."

Laura smiled at Richard and thought of a conversation they had had months ago after Richard, in reading various dialogues of Plato at the direction of John, had remarked about discovering a side of Plato that had somehow escaped him until then. "But you're right, you know," she began, "I took another look myself, and the spiritual aspect of Plato's dialogues is very heavy. I don't know how it happened, and I don't want to blame my professors, but you're right, I don't remember him that way at all."

Richard had a drink and looked out over the crowd. A dark-haired woman caught his eye and suddenly he thought of Toshika. He wanted to leap into the air, forgetting all the rest. Instead, he simply smiled and rapped his knuckles against the bench, anticipating the moment when he could see her again. Smiling, he looked at Laura, and with the image of Toshika fresh in his mind, felt guilty at having compared Laura to her. "You know, Laura, you're a pretty girl," he told her. She was amused, but merely stared back at him, raising an eyebrow. "Don't worry, don't worry," he said, raising his hands in reassurance, "I'm not going to try anything. I just wanted you to know."

"Well, thanks Richard, but I don't know how much I care."

He looked at her and allowed their years of familiarity with each other to reestablish themselves. "Sure you care," he told her, lifting his beer. "Hey. Cheers," he said.

After a while they all went outside. Richard, Tony, and Matt allowed the others to believe they were going home, and then went on to the bar at the top of the Grand Hyatt hotel, dressed as they were. There they shared a bottle of champagne before having a late dinner. In the end, Richard's money could not cover the bill, so he furthered his test by settling the remainder with his credit card. Once outside, they hailed a cab. Feeling drunk and happy in the company of his friends, Richard decided not to go to Toshika's house. Instead, he went home with Matt and Tony where they listened to music until they all fell asleep on the couch in Richard's room.

9

David Norton looked once more at her house before turning the key in the ignition, shutting off the engine of his truck. He sat there for five minutes or more, his hands on the wheel, alternating between staring at the hood ornament of his truck through the windshield to staring at some article of her house. The door, a window, one of the chimneys. He had been a policeman for almost fifteen years before being shot and being forced into early retirement. He came from a small, two school city in the Midwest. Grew up on white bread and whole milk. He did all that was expected of him by heartland America, and learned all of the important 'values' that Americans speak so highly of. He was deeply involved in high school sports, honing within him a sense of good versus evil, the priority of action over thought and words, the need to cheer the team on no matter what, plus a fine appreciation for himself and for his side and an equally fine disdain for the other side. This outlook, the seed of which had been planted deep within him long before by all that he saw and heard and felt growing up, formed the background through which he would pattern the world and his existence in it. He managed to pass his other school subjects without having them influence him too heavily. He hunted, fished and drove a powerful car from the age of just sixteen on. Naturally, he also attended his family's church every Sunday. He had believed in God, and although thought that church was boring, felt he ought to go. Felt that it was best for him.

His was a police family. His father, two grandfathers, three uncles and a cousin had also been policemen. His younger brother was planning to join the force as well, but was held up in the Persian Gulf. Blown up by a land mine at the age of nineteen. Donald. Little Donny. He always looked up to his big brother David. Being seven years older, David was always so much bigger, stronger and faster than his little brother that there should have been nothing he couldn't do. But as he got older, and not very much earlier than the end of his brief life, little Donny showed his big brother a thing or two about girls. Although not better looking than his big brother, for whom the term "average looking" would have been a compliment, Donald had no fear of the girls in his high school and was quite a charmer. David was one of those very athletic and rough characters who just didn't know how to behave around that exotic animal that made him feel so pleasurably odd when they looked at him just right. As a teenager, when in the presence of a girl he liked, he was all thumbs. He just couldn't find a way to relax around girls when he was young, or around women as he grew older, the way others did. Unused to being unable to do things that he wanted to do, it made him angry. Brought out the rude boy in him, who grew into a rude man. He was lonely, and starving for affection for most of his adult life. He ended up either with prostitutes – he lost his virginity to a woman who called herself Sunshine – or with the rowdy, crude women he met hanging out at the bars and pizza joints that he frequented. They were never what he was really after. They were not the type that he wanted to show his softer side to. Not women he could let down his guard around.

And then came Toshika. The first woman who was soft, lovely and delicate in the way that he had always wanted. The first one, that is, with whom he thought he was having a "normal" relationship. He knew that he had not been entirely honest with himself about that. It was not entirely normal at all. But she was no prostitute. He had lured himself into the lie that this was just what he had always hoped for. He had thought that he had finally made it. He was happy, there was no denying that. Happier than he could have dreamed.

He looked once more at the house and felt weakness creeping over him. Finally he bit his upper lip for a moment and closed his eyes, and then let go of the wheel. He stepped out of the truck, shut the door, and walked silently over the wide, flat stones leading to her door. He rang the doorbell, and took one step back, lifting his gaze upward, sweeping once over the façade of the house. He heard the thud of bare feet approaching the door inside. A pause as he was scrutinized through the peephole. The door swung open. Toshika stood in the doorway. Uninviting. "David. What are you doing here?" she asked him. Her voice conveyed weariness, not surprise or annoyance.

David didn't speak at first. He put his hand against the house next to the door and leaned forward, shifting his weight onto one foot. With his free hand he brushed his sandy hair back from his face. He sighed, not interested in having to argue or make a scene.

"Mind if I come in?" he asked, the mildest of annoyances creeping into his voice, as if preparing for a refusal. Toshika looked out into the street and then stepped away from the door, leaving him alone on the doorstep as she disappeared into the house. He stepped inside and closed the door behind himself. He was about to allow his keys to join the others on the small iron and tile table that stood inside the doorway, then simply put them into his jeans pocket. He followed Toshika inside to the living room, then out through the sliding door onto the patio. She lay outside under a heat lamp, watching the stars. David pulled up a recliner next to her and sat on its edge, joining Toshika in her appreciation of the night sky.

"You've got your head in the stars, Toshika," he told her before turning to watch her.

"There are a lot of them out tonight," she said, realizing that his comment had not contained the amused tone it should have if he were joking with her. She turned her head to look at him

David breathed deeply. "I mean, with this guy Richard."

Toshika turned back around. "What are you talking about? He won."

"He won?" he asked her, his voice rising. "He won? I won!" He said, thumping his chest with the palm of his hand.

Toshika closed her eyes. "I don't want to do this."

"That's what I mean," David told her, standing up and going to the railing on the balcony before turning to face Toshika. "That's exactly what I mean, Tosh. I thought you didn't want this anymore."

Toshika stood up as well and turned off the heat lamp. She looked at David and folded her arms over her chest. "David, what happened?" When he didn't answer, she went to the sliding door and turned to face him. "What did you do?"

David approached her, his hands pleading. Words of love struggled deep inside him, but were beaten down. "Look, Richard's no different from the rest of them. But I-"

"But you what?" Toshika demanded. "What? You didn't fall into this thing the way the others did? Or you're less possessive? You're - what is it - not thinking only about what *you* want? Don't kid me!"

David stopped, the expression on his face showing his surprise. "You said-"

"I said," Toshika interrupted, "once, okay, *once*, that you were a good guy. And I thought that you were. But I never said that I, that I *wanted* you, okay? Never."

David stood before her, shaking his head slowly from side to side. "After all I've done for you!" he said, whispering as if he were afraid of being overheard.

Toshika stepped inside and beckoned to him. "Come on, it's time to go."

David lingered on the deck and then moved forward so quickly it was if he were making a rush at her. Toshika turned and ran into the house just as the lights came on in the living room and Page emerged from the kitchen, a glass of orange juice in her hand. All three of them froze. Toshika and David stared at Page, who stared back at the two of them, her eyes wide with fright.

"What the hell?" she asked. She looked at David. "It's the middle of the night! What are you doing here?" She saw the look on Toshika's face and knew all she needed to know. "You," she said to David, "out. Get out!"

David eyed the two of them and calmed himself. Then he surprised both Toshika and Page by turning on his heel and heading for the door. Toshika took a few steps closer to the center of the room so she could keep an eye on him. He stopped at the door, opened it, and turned to look at Toshika. She expected some final words. A confession perhaps, or something abusive. But David didn't speak. Everything he communicated to her was accomplished with his stare. As

Toshika began to feel a chill in her bones he turned and left, quietly closing the door behind him. Toshika's shoulders slumped. Page ran over to the door and locked it every way she knew how.

10

The sun was bright and hot. Kicking his sandals off, the cool cement under his feet gave him a bit of relief. Luckily, these meetings took place at a lazy hour, otherwise he would not have made it today. Not after last night's drinking. As it was, he was surprised at how good he felt. Not a twinge of overhang. It would have been unbearable to be trying to discuss philosophy sitting in the hot sun with a headache and an unfriendly stomach. He was lucky to get the only table left, and sat waiting for a sign of a waiter to order something cold. He busied himself by taking the books out of his bag and arranging them on the table in one small stack. With that task finished, he looked to the entrance of the patio at the sidewalk for John. Seeing only his absence, he turned his attention to the books. Turning the stack sideways he looked at the titles on their spines. After considering each he pulled the volume with the *Phaedo* from the stack and placed it on top. Then, wishing to maintain his privacy, as if it mattered to anyone in the world what book lay on his table, he turned the book over. Looking up once more, he managed to catch the attention of a waiter and received a sign that he would be helped sooner or later. Confident with that promise, he allowed his gaze to drift over the faces of the crowd, as the conversations around him provided a kind of background music. There were mostly men in the café, and he soon found himself looking through the thin but leafy bushes that ran along the edge of the patio. He noticed a nondescript car parked on the opposite side of the street, the driver inside at the wheel. Although he wore shades, he seemed to be looking directly at him. Richard continued to look at him, but the man never turned his head. Police.

Forgetting everything was harder now. He knew that he had done nothing wrong, but was still quite bothered by the idea that he was being watched. Not only watched, but followed. He looked again. The man was still there, still staring at something. Was he just being paranoid? How could he know what that man was doing? How could he even know if he was with the police? With that last thought in mind he began to look more carefully at the man and his car. Short hair, clean-shaven, sunglasses. The car was plain looking. It was an American make, with four doors and was painted dark blue. On television, this would be an undercover police car. Just then he remembered the car he had seen at Hans' house the night he had dropped him off. It looked more or less like the one that sat now across the street, but he remembered that inside was a police officer wearing a standard uniform. He had forgotten about this detail when he spoke to the police. Reaching into his bag he pulled out his notebook, tore off a corner of a page and wrote a note to himself to call the detective as soon as he got home.

Tucking the note in his pocket, he looked out over the heads of those around him for a waiter, but saw none. As he settled down into waiting, his thoughts returned to the first time he had met John, at this very same café. He had just begun his final year at university then, his degree in philosophy nearly achieved. Another warm Indian summer was sweeping the city. Feeling it a pity to study in his room on such a nice Sunday, he planned to spend the day studying in the corner of the patio of the café. It was perfect: the din of the crowd was better than the silence or background music that he would have at home, and when he was hungry or thirsty there was plenty to choose from. With a small stack of books and his notebook his world was complete. Having just picked up a large café latte and a scone, he found a table and sat counting his change, wondering aloud how they could charge four dollars for a latte.

"Excuse me."

He looked up and saw an old man whose expression indicated his desire to join him. He was very tan and healthy-looking in his shorts and T-shirt. His weathered appearance gave Richard the impression that he spent a lot of time in the sun, perhaps at the beach. Annoyed at first, not wanting to have any interruption to his plan for learning, he considered the table before him. It was a table for four. What could he say?

"Sure," he replied, moving his books to the other side of the table, keeping his eye on his new guest.

The old man settled himself and placed his own book on the table. Breathing deeply, he closed his eyes for a moment, his head bowed just slightly. Richard watched. What is he going to do? Sit here and meditate? Just then the old man's eyes popped open, his gaze fixed on Richard.

"An old habit," he said, grinning. He then drew his plate of pie toward him and rotated it one way, then the other before cutting into it with his fork.

Richard turned his attention back to his book. The old man looked at his book as well, then looked at the pile of books on the table. When Richard finally lifted his latte to his lips, the old man seized the moment.

"It looks like you're a philosophy student," he said.

Richard groaned at the thought of having a discussion about philosophy with someone who knew nothing about it. He returned the mug to the table and wiped his lip with his finger.

"That's right," he said. He offered a smile and a nod that was meant to close the door on further enquiries, then searched the page for his place in the book.

"It's good to know they still have those," the old man continued. "Today it seems students are only interested in studying business."

Richard looked at him, raised his eyebrows once, and grunted.

"Tell me, what are they teaching you these days in philosophy?"

Richard put a thumb on his place and looked at the old man, taking a moment to study his expression. "What do you mean?" he finally asked him. His feeling of superiority began to fade, turning into one of mild discomfort at the thought that perhaps this man was familiar with his subject. Perhaps very familiar. He certainly had had the time by now, at his age, to have done quite a bit of studying.

"Well, you study western philosophy, I take it."

"Yes."

"So, you're reading the Presocratics, Plato, Aristotle, eventually Descartes, Kant, like that?"

"Yes, exactly." Richard leaned back in his chair. The old man nodded his head and leaned forward, a question forming on his lips.

"What have you read of Plato?"

Richard took a deep breath and thought, trying to remember the list chronologically.

"*The Apology, Mino, Craedo, Phaedo*, and *The Republic*."

"In that order, I presume," the old man said. Richard nodded. "Funny they still don't read the *Timaeus*," he said, more to himself than to Richard.

"Well, there are a lot of dialogues," Richard offered, feeling defensive despite the man's familiarity. Perhaps it was even a challenge.

"Yes. Did you read about Pythagoras at all?"

"Pythagoras? A little."

The old man shook his finger. "You see, they still don't want you to know."

"Don't want us to know what?"

The old man leaned forward and smiled. "They don't want you to know the real deal." He sat back in his chair and shrugged his shoulders. "They don't even know it themselves."

Richard had now had enough and opened his book again as he replied. "The 'real deal,' huh? Okay, well... I guess I won't know the real deal then," he said, and turned his attention back to his reading. The old man said nothing, and continued eating his pie. He cast a glance at Richard now and then, his grin never entirely absent. The din of the tiny crowd around them immediately replaced their conversation, removing any awkwardness that might have normally ensued.

It was sometimes frustrating studying something that so few knew anything about. Unlike many other subjects one might choose to concentrate on in university, philosophy found no general familiarity among people, having never been a leftover from primary or secondary school. Occasionally Richard met people who had some strange opinions about the subject. Most were clearly speaking with no foundation, but the old man seemed not to be.

Richard found himself reading the same paragraph over and over, each time realizing that he hadn't found its meaning and had instead been preoccupied with the old man's words. Something in his relaxed delivery gave him credence, and this went round and round in Richard's head. He noticed him, happily eating his pie, looking content. But he also noticed that the old man held the door open. Finally, Richard looked up and closed his book.

"So what's the 'real deal,' if you don't mind my asking?"

The old man was working on a mouthful and raised a finger. He took a sip from his glass and cleared his throat.

"Sorry about that, but you seem like a good fellow and I really am concerned about the issue," he said, and then sat up straight and placed his hands together in front of his chest and held his breath, gathering thought. "You see, I have spent quite some time studying a lot of this, from different disciplines, and have come to some rather startling realizations. One of those is simply that the truth is being lost. You study philosophy to know the truth, am I right?" Richard nodded. "Well, so did I. I don't want bore you with too many details about myself, but let me just say that I came originally from a very large and powerful institution that, I thought, was devoted to truth. What I found was something else. But this came only after many very difficult years of trying to reconcile what I thought I saw with what I felt at the time must somehow have been my own failing. Eventually, I saw that I was indeed right and I had to make a clean break. I went back to school. Learned some things. Then I began just studying on my own. I didn't trust anyone any more to be my guide. The university professors I had known left me disillusioned. Eventually I arrived at the place I am now."

The old man sat, finished, looking at Richard intently. Richard waited, not sure if the old man would continue, or if he was waiting for him to speak. Finally it became awkward.

"And where is that place?" The old man's shoulders dropped, and he put his hands together in his lap.

"What is your name?" he asked. Richard told him. The old man reached over the table and shook his hand. "Nice to meet you, Richard. I'm John." Then he relaxed in his chair and gazed at Richard. It appeared as though the discussion were finished. At last, John spoke.

"Richard, this would be more interesting for you if you took a good look at something first. Do you have a copy of the *Timaeus*?"

"No, I don't think so."

"Go out and find one. Read it, and then we can talk again. It is one of Plato's most spiritual works. You simply must read it. Then I want you to tell me what your impressions are."

Richard nodded and, always mindful of his student budget, admitted that he could probably find a copy at one of the used bookstores.

"Well, maybe not," John replied. "This dialogue isn't widely read. You may need to buy it new. You may even need to order a copy. Unfortunately, many books that aren't generally read in the university don't often find their way to the shelves of used bookstores," he said, apologetically. "But do read it, and then we should talk."

"Okay, should I call you?"

The old man looked a moment at Richard before letting his eyes wander. Richard had the feeling he had said the wrong thing. Then the man looked at him and smiled. "I'm here at about this time nearly every Sunday. Let's just meet here when you're ready, shall we?"

"Okay, maybe in two weeks?"

The old man seemed pleased, and they agreed to this plan. It was the start of a regular Sunday meeting that both of them grew to look forward to very much. It was also the real beginning of Richard's philosophical education.

"What can I get you?" the waiter asked him. He stood in front of Richard with his checkbook and pen ready. Richard asked him for a latté and an orange juice, not sure if his stomach was ready for food, and not feeling hungry yet anyway. As the waiter made his way back into the café John appeared at the entrance to the patio, his face brightening when he saw Richard waving to him.

"Hey kid, you beat me to it," he said as they shook hands. He took a seat and rested his arms on the table in front of him.

"Yes, and considering that I was out late last night drinking with my friends, I guess you're lucky to see me at all. Or perhaps I should say, I'm lucky to see you." Richard quickly glanced at the man in the car. It appeared that he was still being watched. He wondered if the man was able to see John through the bushes as well. Suddenly he was annoyed at this intrusion, and felt an urge to approach the car and speak to the man, but he knew that it would not be wise. Returning his attention to John, he took a deep breath in an effort to throw off the distraction.

"Is there something bothering you, Richard my boy?"

He felt he could not discuss the game or Hans' murder with John. It would be too embarrassing. For the first time he felt that he should have declined the invitation to the poker game. That he should not have had anything to do with it. Of course, he knew that if he really had a problem, he could turn to John to discuss it. But this was not a problem he could not handle.

"No," he told him, knowing full well how phony it sounded. John continued to examine his expression for a moment, then turned as the waiter approached the table. Having placed Richard's coffee and juice on the table, he turned to John.

"Hi John," the waiter said, "How're you today?"

"Oh, just fine Randy, fine. Another sunny day, right?" he said, smiling at both of them before considering his order. "Yes, would you bring me a cup of coffee and," he paused, a playful look flickering across his face. "How are the blueberry muffins today?"

"They're fat and happy today."

"I'll have one of those then, too." The waiter nodded and disappeared once more.

John considered Richard for a moment before speaking. "How's the job hunt going?" Once more, an invitation for Richard to reveal his newfound luck. "Still tough out there, huh?"

Richard shrugged. "Yes. Still tough."

"Let me guess, Richard," John began, placing his hand atop the pile of books on the table. "These books here. Our discussions. You're wondering where we're going with this – am I right?" he asked him, proving that it was possible to be both right and wrong at the same time. Richard looked at John a moment and wondered at the coincidence of his suggestion and Laura's comments from the night before. Opening a pack of sugar and stirring it into his latté, he was both pleased and anxious at the opportunity to confront this topic head on.

"You know, John, I've really appreciated these talks we've had. When I finished school I felt that I had only just scratched the surface, so I was apprehensive. I worried that my learning would stop. It hasn't, thanks to you, but I also realize now that I can carry this forward myself. I'm more comfortable with that now than I was before. But I admit I'm feeling a bit impatient and can't help wanting to rush off to the end of the book, so to speak."

John laughed easily at Richard's analogy. He was not at all surprised to hear this from him. On the contrary, most people would have wanted to know what they were supposed to learn before they learned it. The fact that Richard did not make this demand of John showed him that he was a good student. John could also see plainly that Richard enjoyed learning.

"In one way it would have made more sense to have begun our discussions with the comments that I'm going to make now. The reason why I didn't begin this way is because I wanted to draw you in first. If I hadn't, I might have scared you off." John drew his gaze inward and prepared himself. Then, leaning forward over the table, his eyes pleading for Richard's complete attention, he spoke. "Philosophy is dying. It has been dying for two thousand years. You know the common complaint one hears about philosophy, that it consists of a few academics discussing issues amongst themselves that interest no one outside their field and that have little to do with daily life, with practical matters? Well, to be fair, this describes many disciplines. All of them, actually. The daily struggles within academic and professional circles of physicists, mathematicians, or in the humanities like history or languages. Even in the arts, academic professionals spend large amounts of time involved in elements of their field that the common person cannot relate to. That's normal. It's one thing to say that philosophy should be written so that any fool can read and understand it off the couch, which is ridiculous. Many seem to feel that nothing that's difficult to understand is worth the effort. You see them now, these children's books on philosophy for adults, 'Plato on How to Win Friends and Influence People,' and things like that. Absurd. I guess I wouldn't have any trouble with them if I thought that they would result in people moving on to real philosophy. Actually reading Plato, reading Kant. What do people think, anyway? They think that because they have a *computer* at home they should be able to *know* everything? Anyway, that's one thing. But the people who complain that philosophers no longer address life issues are more correct than they realize. Philosophy began as a way to understand ourselves, and to know how to live, how to realize who we all are. I am talking about confronting God."

Richard's eyes narrowed as he sat back and held his breath. God? John saw his confusion. He held up his hands in his own defense as he continued.

"Richard, I tell you, the problem with philosophy today is the same as with Christianity. We are all reading these ancient texts as though they were written yesterday. We think they are speaking directly to us, the way we do today. They aren't. They are speaking to us allegorically. This is the way knowledge was passed on back then. They are building a simple story around very complex concepts, because they know that not everyone is ready. But nobody realizes this. They all think that the Bible is trying to tell us about an historical figure named Jesus. That's wrong. And we all think that Plato's *Republic* is just about politics. That's wrong too. The fact is, Western philosophers since the time of even Plato have been turning away from their roots and creating a monster."

At last, Richard thought, as he hung on to John's every word. Just then, the waiter appeared and placed John's order on the table in front of him.

"Thank you," John said. He pointed to his muffin and smiled at Richard. "Now that's a happy muffin." Richard smiled politely and waited patiently for John to continue. "Sorry about the digression into Christianity, but it served a purpose. We are here to talk about philosophy, so let's stick to that."

Richard felt exhilaration as the doors began to open for him. He leaned forward, eagerly awaiting a continuation of the discussion. "Keep going."

John held up a hand to Richard, a polite request for a break, and attended to his food and drink, his eyes concentrated on the space between them. Richard took the opportunity to glance through the bush at the waiting man. Gone. After a minute John straightened up and began to speak.

"This concentration on one side of the coin, on logic and so-called 'rational thinking,' has not only allowed us to stray from philosophy's goal as we begin to feel contempt for our own spiritual strivings, it has also resulted in our inability to think. To really think in the way that philosophy demands."

"What do you mean?"

"We have turned philosophy into a quest to solve certain so-called 'problems' of philosophy. We have turned our attention away from ourselves and onto these impersonal puzzles. We lay them out before us and attempt to carefully dissect them, as though they were only so many laboratory animals, and in so doing, we effectively remove ourselves from philosophy."

"I don't follow you."

"We have lost the spark of wonder that unlocks our minds and makes us open for any possibility of real wisdom. Think of it this way, Richard. Imagine: a building site with many laborers hurrying to pound in a few more nails while there is still daylight. One of them says 'Hey! Look! What a fantastic sunset.' And everyone stops and straightens up to look. It is a gorgeous sunset, the kind that comes only rarely. And they all catch their breath at the sight of it. In that moment, their souls have been awakened, their hearts are filled with longing. For an instant, they find themselves at the center of the world that is represented by that one star in the sky that gives us life. The question breathes in them: who am I? It hangs before their awareness, beckoning. But this stillness of mind is not something they are used to, and no sooner than it appears, it is again gone. Someone moves, raises their hammer, and the whole lot of them are brought back to the task at hand. To their important work.

"Richard, we have been concentrating in our readings here on Plato because I wanted you to see the side of him that goes unnoticed. I chose him because I know you must see him, as he has no doubt been presented to you, as a sort of 'founding father' of Western thought. Like most others, you feel that he and Aristotle are more or less the two figures in Western thought that everyone else merely adds relatively minor adjustments to. Well, by showing you that Plato was nothing like who you thought he was, it makes it easier to appreciate that the same goes for the pre-Socratic philosophers. Plato may even have already been losing touch with what philosophy once was. There has been a tendency among scholars to claim that we have seen an 'evolution' or progression whereby the pre-Socratics are seen as junior philosophers who sort of bumbled along and helped to lay some of the foundation that Plato, in all his greatness, picked up and turned around, showing the ignorance of those before him and creating a diamond from a lump of coal. This is the way the story is told."

John grabbed the waiter as he passed by the table and ordered a mineral water for himself and one for Richard as well. Then the two of them sat quietly for a moment. Richard rolled the ideas over and over again in his mind, startled at what he had heard. Philosophy was about the meaning of life. This is its essential character. People who claim that philosophy is method and not subject really are talking about logic and rational discussion, not philosophy.

"Nietzsche's most famous and perhaps most misunderstood claim was 'God is dead.' He meant that the people of his time no longer believed in God. That they only believed in matter. In cause and effect, and nothing more. This is what has happened to philosophy, as philosophers abandon their own souls. Most of the professional philosophers of today are the result of the death of philosophy that began around the time of Plato. At that time philosophers were still very spiritual, mystical thinkers for whom magic and spirit were real forces in the world. Forces that gave us meaning. If we aren't too embarrassed by it, we see this in Plato, as you've now seen over the last several months."

"Yes," Richard admitted.

"Well, don't think for a second that I am the first to say things like this. As far back as the neo-Platonists we see complaints that philosophy had lost its way in leaning toward the pursuit of pure reason. In deifying reason itself. Or for another, more recent example, take the young Hegel. When he was only about your age he wrote something that not many people know about. It was not even published until over a hundred years after he had written it. Nietzsche didn't know about it, and probably would have been a bit friendlier to Hegel if he had. Anyway, it was just a two-page document, called the 'System Program,' and was a youthful, exuberant challenge to create a 'mythology of reason.' In it he says that the highest act of reason is 'an aesthetic act,' and that poetry would be returned to greatness to become once more what it was. The 'teacher of mankind' as he called it. Imagine that! We can also take Nietzsche himself, who certainly worked very hard toward bringing art and creation back into philosophy and into the spirit of humanity. Or Wittgenstein, who said that philosophy should be designed as 'a poetic composition.' So you see, what I am saying isn't new. Then again, 'new' truths are rare things.

"You probably didn't receive this impression of the ancient Greeks from your studies, and that unfortunately has to do with the prejudices of philosophers – not in your failure to learn. Many philosophers are embarrassed by the reality of ancient Greek philosophy and either ignore or ridicule the aspects of this ancient way of life that don't suit their modern tastes. Philosophers in the analytic tradition, of which you are a product, can be said to have made a conscious decision to exclude discussions of metaphysics. I think you know that," John said.

Richard remembered his conversation with Hans that night in the bar and hesitated before he spoke. He was of such a different mind then. Thinking about it now made him wonder how he had allowed himself to slip back into his earlier, academic way of thinking. "Yes, that's true," Richard said, as the urge to defend the tradition he had learned welled up inside him once more. "But don't you think that there is something to the idea that our ability to create grammatically correct sentences doesn't mean that all of them are meaningful?"

"Oh, certainly that's true," John replied. "But do you really feel that metaphysical questions are meaningless?"

"Well, I don't know. Some of them must be."

"Okay, perhaps, but which ones? Come on now, Richard. You're not going to get off the hook that easily. Let's have some examples."

As quickly as they had come, Richard felt his defenses weakening, turning to dust. "I don't know," he complained. "I feel like I don't even know what philosophy is anymore." The gloom showing on his face gave John pause.

"Well, that's why we're here! Let's talk about it, shall we?" John gave Richard a comforting pat on the shoulder. "If you look at the history of Western thought, remarkably little seems to have been accomplished in twenty-five hundred years. I think it's because of this failure to grasp the journey that the ancients embarked upon. What scholars have done when interpreting the work of ancient philosophers, and again this is perhaps even starting with Aristotle, is to apply their own standards. One of the biggest problems we have here is that scholars have compartmentalised mythology, religion and science when interpreting the ancients, creating barriers or distinctions between them that didn't exist in their own time. The history of philosophy is treated as an evolution from a mythological understanding of the nature of things to a scientific understanding much like our own. We are taught that the pre-Socratics represented the first movement from a mythological/religious understanding of the world to a purely mechanical or scientific understanding of it. But the problem is, there didn't exist a clear division at that time between mythology and science, so what looks to us like a change from something akin to superstition to something like what we see as rational, clear thinking was not at all what it must have been for these ancient thinkers themselves. What is important to see here is that when we look at the pre-Socratics, and even Plato, we see that much of their expression is what we now consider to be of a mythological type. Think about the poetry of Empedocles, or that of Parmenides, and remember also of course Plato's

Phaedo that we discussed. We identify the imagery and the language as belonging to the realm of myth and therefore discount it. It has been placed next to – or beneath to be more accurate – those writings that we identify as being 'pure philosophy' or something such as that. But this is *our* doing! The etymological evidence forces us to consider that this type of expression for ancient thinkers did not imply the kind of polar opposite that we understand. Nowadays 'myth' has become synonymous with 'nonsense.' Even people who should know better have fallen into this ignorance. Karl Popper, for example, referred to myth as 'traditional prejudices, beset with error.'

"When Plato uses the Pythagorean myth of the underworld in the *Phaedo* we are wrong to consider that by doing so he was not attempting to convey knowledge, or that he was merely adding some pretty fluff to his otherwise serious discussion. For these ancient thinkers, *mythos* and *logos* were both accepted ways of communicating what we might want to call 'truth,' but even that is perhaps getting us into dangerous territory, as our notion of truth is again something we have arrived at over time and which did not exist in the same sense at the time of the Greeks. The point is, we have effectively ignored a large quantity of ancient writing by placing some in the category of 'mere myth' and some in the more 'respectable' category of philosophy, or science, or whatever we want to call it.

"Of course, we do this because when we look at myth from our modern, artless perspective, we don't know what it means. It's as simple as that. For heaven's sake, look at the Bible!" John said in exasperation. "People don't know how to *read* it!" John looked as though he might suddenly have nothing more to say as he fought with what was obviously a difficult subject for him. Finally, he leaned forward and spoke softly. "The lucky ones – those of us with keen intellects and open minds – eventually find the next level on which to study that book. But for others, it has to be approached literally, until they're ready. The problem I found was that the church was unwilling to admit to anyone who was not ordained that this other level even existed. And that's when I had to get out."

Richard nodded, hoping that John appreciated that he understood his preference not to convey too much of his own past. John watched the waiter moving from table to table.

"Unfortunately, the university isn't much different from the church. Neither of them reward excellence nearly as much as they reward loyalty. There are scholars, Richard, who have argued my very point. They do exist. But they are overlooked by their peers. Dismissed as second rate. And you won't find them holding posts at the most respected universities. Anyway, those are the special ones. Most scholars didn't, and still don't, know what to make of the more allegorical writing of certain ancient thinkers, especially when it came from someone like Plato who wrote what appeared to us to be both rational, scientific discourse, on the one hand, and myth on the other. It was much easier when dealing with writers like Homer, whose writing might touch on certain historical events and in that way can be of historical importance, but who otherwise is generally considered a writer of mythology. But Plato presents some problems because he incorporates both styles of writing. That in itself should have been evidence enough that something was not right here in our interpretation of things. Someone specialized in the study of myth would come to different conclusions when studying Plato than our academic philosophers have."

"So now, what are we to make of this?" Richard asked.

"Just one simple thing," John said, raising a finger solemnly. "We must realize, by reevaluating and rereading these philosophers, that they were concerned primarily with spiritual knowledge. They viewed a search for meaning as one and the same thing as a search for The Ultimate. The emergence of human beings from ancients to moderns, from believers in superstition to knowers of matter, of stuff, is our own invention, and does not accurately describe the thought and the world of these thinkers. In the beginning, I said that Plato was concerned about politics and social development. Forget it! Plato's *Republic* reads like an analysis of the perfect state, but all that talk is just an analogy for the perfect human! To read Plato as a mere political theorist is to miss his most essential messages.

"Much of early Greek philosophy becomes easier to understand when one considers the religious context of the time, and I'm not talking about the Homeric gods and goddesses – of Zeus and Athena, and the others who represented the politicized religion, the social activities so visible in Greek life. I'm speaking of the religion that involved real dedication from time to time, the so-called 'Mysteries.' Many thousands of people participated in the Mystery religions of the Mediterranean at the time of all of these thinkers. These Mysteries varied widely in style and ideology, but some of the 'higher' versions involved the celebration of and communion with God that began after one had received a certain amount of learning and had passed through a rite of initiation in one of the many places where these initiation ceremonies were held. Have you heard of Eleusis?"

Richard shrugged. "No."

"Eleusis iss on the coast of Greece just outside of Athens and was the site of the most famous of these festivals. The Eleusinian festival was held in a sanctuary comprising a number of buildings surrounded by a wall. Of this sanctuary, all that remains today are ruins. Thousands of people participated in the initiations there every year. As in most of these rituals, initiates were sworn to secrecy concerning the events of the initiation and of their experiences therein. Athenian law held the punishment of death for those guilty of revealing in detail the rites of the Mysteries."

"Death?"

"Yes. They didn't fool around. For some fifteen hundred years the rituals were performed at Eleusis every year in September. The participants came from all walks of life; senators were initiated side by side with slaves, and the event was open to both sexes. Many writers of the time mention the rituals in a manner that would lead us to believe that they were speaking from firsthand experience. Including, I am certain, Plato himself.

"The initiation at Eleusis was said to have changed those who participated forever. Initiates made the journey and underwent the transformation only once in a lifetime. That was to be enough. One thing to consider is just how people, and particularly those who were philosophers, went about their lives after coming back from Eleusis. How does one go about daily living, having seen the light? How does one reconcile the ordinary with the extraordinary? Let's say Plato was one of many at Eleusis one year. Imagine him going home and trying to incorporate his experiences into his daily life, and especially into his philosophical thought. In the *Phaedo* he says 'He who is not newly initiated or who has become corrupted does not easily rise out of this world to the sight of true beauty in the other.' You know what his theory of the Forms sounds like to me? It sounds like an attempt to reconcile this everyday world with the fantastic world he experienced during his initiation. A world even more real than this one. An unchanging, perfect world. Remember the cave? Imagine that Plato's cave allegory is about his own experience. His 'rebirth' upon becoming initiated at Eleusis." John paused for a drink of water. "Consider what he says in the *Phaedrus*: 'If anyone comes to the gates of poetry and expects to become an adequate poet by acquiring expert knowledge of the subject without the Muses' madness, he will fail, and his self-controlled verses will be eclipsed by the poetry of men who have been driven out of their minds. There you have some of the fine achievements – and I could tell you even more – that are due to god-sent madness.' Plato mentions this 'madness' on numerous occasions. What does it mean? Clearly, he wasn't speaking of madness in any ordinary sense.

"When we look at Plato, it seems clear that we are dealing with a man who had *been* there. The Mysteries were related to followers who had not yet been initiated – that is, had not yet taken part in the kind of ritual performed at Eleusis – in a rather roundabout way, through myths. Plato is well known for relating much of his philosophy in the form of familiar Pythagorean and Orphic mythology. The secrecy required of the rites of the Mysteries would not allow adherents, no matter what their profession was, to openly discuss details or to explain God to others, which would anyway defeat the purpose of each individual making their own effort to attain this experience. Again in the *Phaedrus*, as you and I have seen together, Plato discusses the soul's divine origins and of how some people can remember the journey their soul took before their own physical birth,

153

remember? This idea is borrowed from Pythagoras. Plato writes that 'there was a time when, with the rest of the happy band, they saw beauty shining in brightness, and we beheld the beatific vision and were initiated into a Mystery which may be truly called most blessed.' He says 'we were admitted to the sight of apparitions innocent and simple and calm and happy, which we beheld shining in pure light, pure ourselves and not yet enshrined in that living tomb which we carry about.' If he is expressing his own experience here, he has cleverly hidden it in the context of this remembrance that 'some' have of their soul's journey.

"Mainstream philosophers have taken this riveting explanation and have not gone beyond the mundane explanation that it detailed Plato's understanding of the soul. They have not dared to read between the lines. But this is Plato speaking! He even anticipates what has become of this kind of talk, as seen in the eyes of others, when he calls the experience of one who has communed with God a kind of 'madness.' He says that when this person 'sees the beauty of earth, he is transported with the recollection of the true beauty. He would like to fly away, but he cannot. He is like a bird fluttering and looking upward, careless of the world below, and he is therefore thought to be mad.' Beautiful, isn't it?

"We need to view Plato's work in the context of his time, as allegory or myth, in the same way as information of the Mysteries was communicated to followers. Seeing it that way, we can say that today's professional philosophers have failed to really understand Plato. In a way, it is similar to what the famous mythologist Joseph Campbell meant when he said that his favorite definition of religion was that of a misinterpretation of myth. He said the mistake is in attaching historical significance to symbols that are really spiritual and ahistorical. This misinterpretation is the basic problem of Christianity after it became adopted by politicians and those seeking power who took ancient mythology and mythic stories meant to convey a certain truth and grounded them in an invented historical framework. The result is that the original message has been all but lost."

Richard watched as John fell silent for a moment before taking a deep breath and wiping his eyes.

"So there it is, kid. Plato was not some dry intellectual. But philosophy has become dry, almost barren. You said you thought your hopes for philosophy might be naïve. Well, maybe. But you wouldn't be the first one. People have a tendency to expect a little too much from philosophy, just as they often do with psychology. People today want answers, but they don't want to have to work for them. Intellectual progress hasn't kept up with technological progress. The landscape of academic philosophy hasn't changed much from Plato's time. And the question of the good life? You've got to be kidding. What is the meaning of life? Today, that's what everyone who's never studied philosophy imagines philosophers ponder, and what every philosopher only secretly dreams of discovering!

"You said you wanted to know who you were, and what to do. I tell you, Richard, those are two of the only good reasons anyone could ever have for studying philosophy. But you aren't going to find many philosophers trying to help you much on those. We're all a bit self-conscious around other philosophers, aren't we? Remember your apprehension when we first met? We always fear that someone is thinking about us: are you one of those in the audience, hanging around, hoping to have the truth revealed to you? Or are you one of the shining stars who holds the key? We all want to be the next genius. But none of us will be. Not for ourselves, and not for anyone else. Why not? Am I trying to tell you 'the truth is that there is no truth'? Is it because there are no answers? No," John said, raising a finger. "It is because no answer, even the 'right' one, would make anyone stop questioning. We will never be satisfied. If you've got the need, the thirst in you that compels you to step up and ask the questions in the first place, you'll never be satisfied. Never." John waited a moment for his words to sink in. "Unless," he began slowly, "you make the experience yourself. The experience into the heart of your being. This experience will be most powerful, or most true, when you embrace it with all of your being – not just with your intellect, or with your emotions, or through sensation, but through them all. Remember what we said about yin yang, that 'it is never two.' And, remember that this is not something you do, it is something that happens. It is an experience of knowledge.

That experience won't answer all the questions for you, but it will make the old questions old, and you will find a new set of questions. A new stage. You will have finally achieved the confidence to say that your questions are answerable.

"I am not here to simply give you answers, but rather to help you focus on where to look for them, for it will be *your* truth. It will come from you, not from someone else. Not from me. Remember Socrates. He is always telling us that he himself knows nothing! Remember we read in the *Theaetetus* where he says of all those he questioned, 'It is clear they didn't learn anything from me. The fine discoveries they cling to are of their own making.' And this is again what lies at the heart of 'know thyself,' which we see now was not simply about understanding one's self, but was a key to the source of the answers to our most important questions. Know *yourself*. So you see, it is up to you, Richard."

Richard felt as though a stone that kept getting heavier and heavier at those words sat squarely on his chest. The secret had not been revealed. The question had gone unanswered. The realization that the search for such an answer was what had compelled him to meet with John made him feel foolish. He hoped that it would not appear obvious to John, and tried to smile, but a strained grin was all he could manage. He put his hands to his face and feigned exhaustion, rubbing his cheeks and taking a deep breath.

"Talk your ear off, did I?" John asked him. Richard shook his head.

"No, just tired."

"Philosophy these days can be very tiring," John admitted with a sigh.

John's expression made Richard wonder if he knew how disappointed he was. Suddenly he became angry. Angry with himself, angry at his lack of certainty, angry at his *quest* for certainty. His disappointment got the better of him and threatened to completely derail his composure. He would not have that. Not in front of John.

"Well," he said, straightening up and pulling his books toward him, "nobody knows."

"What's that?"

"Nobody knows anything," he said, able to look John in the eye only for an instant before he began stuffing his books into his bag. John remained silent, and then reached across the table to pat Richard on the shoulder.

"You're just frustrated. I understand."

"Yeah? Maybe you're right. Maybe I just need a vacation."

Richard bid John good-bye and left in a hurry. An angry buzz clouded his thoughts and interrupted the world around him as he walked to his bus stop. Stepping into the road the honking of a car horn brought him back for an instant as he stopped and then darted across the road, holding up his hand in apology without looking at the driver. When he reached the curb he continued to run until he stood at the top of Divisadero where he stopped, out of breath.

"Screw it. I don't need this," he said, looking for anyone with which to make eye contact. Any passerby that he could defiantly announce the rejection of himself to. But there was no one.

Once on the bus, he stared out the window, eyes unfocussed, trying to escape his thoughts. When he remembered her name, he smiled, then laughed. Or perhaps he did – he was not sure if he had laughed outwardly or not. He stole a glance around him at the other riders; no one paid him any mind. He let his head rest against the window and closed his eyes.

11

Almost as soon as he arrived in the neighborhood he saw a parking place and gladly took it, hoping it was not too far from her house. Locking the car door behind him, he looked once more at the address on the card in his hand and set off down the tree-lined street, checking house numbers as he went along. The houses in Pacific Heights were beautiful. Each one unique. A Victorian next to a house of brick next to a modern wooden arrangement next to an older stone manor house. Some of the most beautiful homes in the world were here, and this was where she lived. His new girlfriend, if he could call her that. Finally, his eyes fell upon the number he sought. He was surprised at the size of the house; too big for one person. It was very wide and made of wood with what appeared to be stainless steel supporting beams. Like nearly all of the houses here, it was set far forward, close to the sidewalk, reserving more land in the rear for a large and well protected garden. He slipped the card into his pocket and stepped up to the door, reaching for the large metal knocker that hung against it before changing his mind and simply rapping his knuckles against the smooth wood. He heard footsteps, and then the mechanism in the lock. The door swung open.

"Hi," the woman said. It took a moment for Richard to recognize her. It was Toshika's friend Page standing before him, wearing a bikini. Having only seen her once before, he had forgotten how pretty she was.

"Hi."

The unexpected sight of a woman in a bikini left him with nothing to say for the moment. He was surprised. He had been looking forward to a quiet evening with Toshika. But it was still early. There were still several hours of daylight left. Plenty of time for Page to go home.

"Come in," she said, "Toshika's on the phone." He stepped inside. She was no longer the rude woman he met on the beach as she smiled pleasantly at him and showed him inside. Just from the foyer, he could see that Toshika's house was impressive. He looked through both doorways – one to the left, the other to the right – before following Page through the right one into a massive, sunny room with a ceiling twice the standard height. The wall at the back of the room was split horizontally in half, the lower half being solid glass all the way across. In the center was a single wooden door that stood open and led outside onto a large wooden deck. There on the deck he saw Toshika talking on the phone, pacing the wooden planks in her bathing suit. She waved when she saw him standing there.

"Wow." he said, then looked at Page.

"Do you like it?" she asked him.

"So far, it's great. I love it."

She crossed the room and passed through another doorway, calling to him over her shoulder. "Want something to drink? We're having some wine."

"Sure," he called to her. "Anything."

He stepped slowly into the center of the room. Very limited furnishing gave it a powerful feeling of space and peace. With Page in the kitchen, Richard stood looking out over the patio at the view over the bay and the Golden Gate Bridge.

"Great view."

Toshika looked perfect in her bathing suit. Richard watched as she paced the deck, raising a finger to him indicating that her call would be finished soon. Facing him, she blew him a kiss and then laughed, turning to concentrate once more on her phone call. On the deck were two lounge chairs with a small table between them. Two glasses of wine stood on the table.

"Here you go," Page said, appearing at Richard's side holding a glass of white wine. "Come out onto the deck with us. Did you bring a suit?"

"A bathing suit? No," he said, remembering their first meeting at the beach.

160

"No problem. I'll get one for you." She disappeared in the other direction, crossing through the foyer. Richard heard her footsteps echoing lightly down a hallway, then the sound of a drawer being opened and shut, followed by more footsteps. Soon she was at his side, a pair of navy blue swim trunks in her hand. Richard took them and turned them over in his hands, wondering who they belonged to.

"Come on, we're missing the sun," Page said, tugging at his arm. He followed her across the room, past the spacious couch that sat in the middle of the room. Page was taller than Richard. She was less athletic-looking than Toshika, but nevertheless had a nice figure. Richard smiled and wished Tony could see him. After his talk with John, what he found all around him now was just what he needed to help him to forget.

They stepped out onto the deck into the heat. Richard saw that the deck ran the full length of the house. To the right was a long, narrow swimming pool built into the deck. Not more than a couple of yards wide, it looked like it was designed for swimming laps. Beyond the deck was a garden that was obviously professionally cared for. Toshika stepped away from them, making noises of acknowledgement at regular intervals into the telephone.

"You can change there, and there's a chair for you, too." Page said, pointing to a partition that stood off near the pool. There were two more lounge chairs standing against the house next to the pool. Moments later, Richard lay next to Page, and lifted his glass.

"Cheers," he said. Page smiled and raised her glass, which was nearly empty.

"Toshika is consoling a friend who's having boyfriend trouble. I'm not naming names, but this person is constantly having trouble. She's got such bad luck."

Richard was not sure what to say. "Oh, that's too bad."

"Yeah, I'll say. It's one of the reasons why we stay single," she said. Richard eyed her with some alarm before regaining his cool. He looked at Toshika and wished Page was not there.

"What do you mean, 'single'?"

"Well, no serious relationships," she answered matter-of-factly. "Not now, anyway. We're too young for that." She saw the expression on Richard's face. "Don't take it personally. I'm sure you're going to have a great time together," she told him.

Richard studied Page's face. Did he detect a note of jealousy in her voice? "What, you mean in Switzerland?" he asked her. Page did not answer for a moment, giving credence to his suspicion. But soon her concentration gave way to her ready smile.

"Yeah, for a start, anyway," she told him. She leaned in close. "From what I hear, you've already had a pretty good start," she said, raising her eyebrows and winking at him. She was very pretty.

Richard watched Toshika as she paced the deck with the phone to her ear and then gazed out over the garden down to the view on the bay below. "Who am I?" he muttered to himself, wondering what Toshika had told Page about their night at the hotel.

"What?" Page asked him lazily.

"Nothing."

Page looked at him briefly under the shade of her hand and then reached for her wine. Bringing the glass to her lips, she frowned as she saw that it was empty. She placed it on the deck and swung her feet to the floor. "Gotta get some more," she said as she padded barefoot into the house. Richard remained on his chair and yawned, the heat and the wine encouraging inactivity.

"Call me any time, okay? Okay, bye. And remember, you will always have us, right?" Toshika lowered her telephone and crossed the deck. Setting the phone on the table, she bent over Richard and in a moment was lying on top of him. "Oh God, poor Jill," she breathed. "How are you?"

"Fine." Again he wondered how much about their evening in the hotel Toshika had shared with Page, feeling annoyed that details had been given, even though they seemed to have been positive. He had not said anything to Tony or Matt, mainly for Toshika's benefit. Apparently she did not feel the need to be mindful of his privacy. He decided not to get into it at this point. There were more important things first. "She said you don't have any serious relationships."

"Who, Page? Don't worry about Page. The only rules in my life are the rules I make for myself."

Richard felt relieved, and then wondered at how easy it was for a few words to offer such relief. Toshika slid off of him slowly and lay next to him on her chair.

"It's hot," she said. Just then slow, exotic music came on through speakers in the wall. It was loud at first, but then was reduced to a lower level. Richard glanced back toward the door to the living room, which stood open.

"Does she live here?"

"No. I know when you called I forgot to mention that she was here. Do you mind?"

"No, not really."

"Good. We're good friends. She's often here, but don't worry. I don't want any housemates. But you're welcome, of course," she added, giving him a kiss.

"More wine!" Page cried as she bounded onto the deck and came around filling the other's glasses. "Let's make a toast," she said. "To Richard, and to Switzerland."

Toshika raised her glass and then noticed Richard's was absent. She looked to see a surprised look on his face. "Oh, I didn't tell you. Page is coming to Switzerland with us. But don't worry, we'll hardly see her. She knows some people there and she'll be off doing her own thing."

"Oh, that's okay. I just, I was surprised, that's all." It was getting worse. He was not at all happy to hear the news. Toshika looked at Page and offered her an encouraging smile.

"Page is cooking dinner for us tonight," she told Richard, climbing back on top of him and biting his chest. "She's a really good cook."

"Do you like Thai food?" Page asked him.

"Yes, I love it," he said, truthfully, but without conviction.

"Good," she said, getting up from her chair and taking a large sip from her glass. She began to dance to the music, a modern electronic sound with an Indian or some other Far Eastern influence. Her arms slowly waved and wound upwards like snakes while her hips swung gently in a circular motion. Richard watched her self-consciously. "I love this song," she said, moving to a position in front of Richard and Toshika. She danced there for a moment before stretching her arms out to Toshika, inviting her to join in. Toshika raised herself from the chair and stepped over next to Page, mimicking her movements. The two women danced facing each other with a familiarity that was nice to see, but the erotic nature of their dance made Richard uncomfortable. He began to feel like an intruder. Page placed her hands on Toshika's hips and moved with her as her hips swung in a slow and sensuous rhythm. Suddenly Toshika turned and faced Richard as she danced, leaving Page to herself.

Finally, Page ran off and dove into the swimming pool, breaking the spell. As quickly as she was in, she stood next to the pool, dripping on the deck. She gathered her hair in a ponytail and squeezed it out over the edge of the pool. Walking back to her chair she quickly toweled dry, laying her towel out on her chair when she was finished. She then picked up her wine glass and walked into the house.

"I'll start cooking now," she called to them over her shoulder. Making slow, feline movements, Toshika lay down on the chair next to Richard and turned to face him.

"So," she said, looking into his eyes. He felt as if under a spell at the sight of her. His awareness was punctured and set adrift as he fell headlong into her beauty.

"So." He watched as she reached slowly across the space between them, her fingers curious, laying her hand against his face and charging him with energy. Her eyes began to close. When they were nearly shut, he closed his eyes as well, until he could only feel the warmth of her hand and the bright sun against him. He concentrated on her hand, trying to work his way through it back to her center.

It must have been only a few minutes later when he opened his eyes. Nothing had changed. Toshika appeared to be sleeping. He touched her hand, and her eyes came open. She smiled and drew a deep breath, holding it a minute and stretching from head to toe before releasing it.

"Whew!" She sat up and took his hand, pulling Richard off his lounge chair and making the few steps over to the pool.

"Do you swim laps or something?"

"Yes, every day. Keeps me in shape. I'm not a real swimmer or anything, but I always liked swimming." Wrapping her arms around him she fell into the pool, taking him with her.

The pool was deep. They plunged in over their heads, as Richard's feet searched unsuccessfully for the bottom.

Toshika swam a few strokes and then stopped and stood at a place where the water was just at her chin.

"It's deep!" he cried, wiping water from his eyes.

"Yeah, at that end. For diving. Come here," she called to him, but he was already on his way. Soon his feet touched bottom and he moved slowly over to her. "We need to go shopping tomorrow to get you a few things before we go," she told him.

"What do I need? A new wardrobe?"

"Not a whole new wardrobe, but definitely a few things. I don't want you looking too much like an American over there. It's embarrassing." He looked at her and wondered what it was about his clothes that nobody seemed to like. Toshika saw the look on his face and felt she ought to turn things around a bit. "Hey, come on, you have money now, you need to look the part. Get some style, show people who you are." Her tone was reassuring.

"Okay, well, if you help me pick things out, I'll be happy to go shopping with you."

"Good. I've booked our tickets for Thursday night, is that okay?" Richard nodded. "All right. And don't worry about the money for the tickets and everything. We'll settle that later. You do have a passport, don't you?"

"Yes."

"Good. Make sure it isn't expired. Actually, you need to check that and let me know as soon as possible. Tonight, in fact," she said, immediately giving Richard a sinking feeling about his hopes for their evening together. "You've never been to Europe, have you?"

"No."

"We'll stay for a while. Go around, see some sights. Not just Switzerland, but a real tour, you know?"

It was an amazing thought. A long vacation, not spent hanging around the house, but actually flying somewhere far away.

"Okay, why not?"

Toshika looked into the water, and then into the house through the wide expanse of glass before speaking again. "I should say, too, that I do like my space, you know? I know a lot of people in many countries there. You'll meet some of them, too. But sometimes I need to just be by myself, see people, go shopping... whatever." It was not a request of him as much as an instruction. He considered it with ease. It sounded completely reasonable. "You may even spend some nights alone," she added. "Sorry. Part of the deal."

Before answering Richard reminded himself of his promise to maintain an enticing distance between himself and Toshika. "Yeah. Of course. I'll be fine, don't worry."

Toshika looked at the far end of the pool and shot a glance back at him. "Race you," she said, turning into the water and setting off quickly for the end with a very good stroke. Never a good swimmer, he did his best to catch her. They climbed out of the pool and dried off quickly. Toshika produced a couple of bathrobes and tossed one to him.

"So, you like my place?"

"Well I haven't seen that much of it, but so far it's great. Beautiful. Is it yours?"

"Yes, my mother bought it for me a year ago when I moved out."

Taking his hand, she headed inside and gave him a tour of the house. As he walked through it he felt as if he were visiting a house featured in a magazine. Everything was thought out, chosen, totally unlike his own haphazard collection of orphaned furnishings. Finally they came to what would be his favorite room, if it were his.

"This is my office," she said as she stopped at the door and motioned with her hand for him to enter. With a large desk, computer, reading chair, and filled wall to wall with books, it was perfect. He approached one of the bookshelves and looked at the titles on the spines. There were travel books, novels, books on architecture, design, fashion, and a lot of history.

"Right, you studied history," he recalled, pulling out a volume on ancient Middle Eastern history. "Hey, this is great," he said, flipping through it and marveling at the large prints of maps, archaeological digs, ruins, and scrolls written in exotic, unfamiliar script.

"You like history?" she asked him. He nodded.

"But I have to say I haven't read much. I'm fascinated with biblical history though."

She eyed him cautiously. "You aren't a religious person, are you?"

He laughed at her expression. "No, no. It's nothing like that. I was raised Catholic, to some extent, but, no. You?" Toshika shook her head and waited for him to continue. "I'm just fascinated with that place and that time. I don't know why, honestly."

"That's an area I really haven't explored much," Toshika admitted. "My mother is Buddhist, but it was never really apparent."

Putting the book back on the shelf, Richard sat down facing her in a large, comfortable leather reading chair.

"Wow. You could fall asleep in this!" he said.

"What is the most interesting thing you've learned about Biblical history?" she asked him.

"What I've learned is pretty surprising. I'm glad you don't seem to have anything at stake here, otherwise telling you about it could cause trouble. People don't like to find out that there is no tooth fairy, you know?"

Toshika raised her eyebrows. "So, you don't think Jesus even existed?"

"Well, whether or not he did or didn't isn't really even important. 'Jesus' was a common enough name then. 'Jesus Christ' is short for 'Jesus the Christ,' which simply means 'Jesus the holy one.' So you can see that it means nothing more significant than, say, 'Toshika the holy goddess.'"

"Oh, what a charmer," she said, failing to appear unmoved. Then, considering what he had said, she looked at him and thought a moment. "Well, you know, people don't want to know truth."

He opened his mouth to object, but the sudden realization that she was somehow right made him pause. He watched as she shrugged her shoulders in apology. He looked through the window behind her at the Golden Gate Bridge.

"People want reassurance," she continued. "They want love, happiness, pleasure. They want to feel safe. If the truth gets in the way of these things, they'll have no part of it."

"But I want to know the truth."

"I know. The question is, will curiosity kill the cat?" Her expression was so intimate that Richard suddenly no longer cared. Here she is, he thought. I've found her!

She stood up and joined him on the large chair. "You're just like me," she told him, settling onto his lap and resting her head on his shoulder. Richard did not dare to move, but merely closed his eyes, wishing time away.

"Hey you two! Dinner!" Page stood at the foot of the stairs, listening. "Hey, wake up!" she called to them. When she heard movement above she smiled and turned, heading back to the kitchen.

"That was really excellent, Page."

Richard pushed his chair back from the table and put his hands on his stomach. The dinner had been long. Emboldened by alcohol, Richard flirted with Page throughout the meal imagining that his intention and his pleasure had gone unnoticed, seen only as friendly chatter. "Isn't he charming?" was the thought he completed for the women when they traded looks after certain comments he had made. It all seemed to be going his way, and he silently complimented himself, making the mistake all men do in failing to realize that it was a woman's game, and that his efforts were amateurish and transparent.

"What else can you do?" he asked her, placing his napkin on his plate. Toshika and Page shared another of those looks and burst out laughing, unable to control themselves any longer. Richard merely smiled and leaned back further in his chair.

"You know," Page began, "it's just Toshika's house and her marvelous kitchen. It just inspires me to culinary greatness."

"You mean when you're at home you don't cook with such style?" Richard asked her.

"Well, I live in a small flat in the Richmond. It's nice, but... My mother isn't as well off as Toshika's," she said, giving Toshika an apologetic look.

Richard wondered if he had hit a soft spot. "I just realized that I don't know what you do," he told her.

"I design clothes," she told him proudly.

"Oh, that's interesting. Do you work for a designer, or...?"

Page stood up and began clearing the table. Richard was quickly on his feet, helping. "No, just privately. Actually, Toshika is my biggest client," she said.

168

"Oh really?" Richard asked, trying to call to mind things she had worn over the past few days since he had known her.

"She's a genius," Toshika said, "Haven't you noticed?"

"You'd be gorgeous wearing anything," Richard offered, and then turned to Page. "Is she easy to design for?"

"She's pretty picky."

"No I'm not!"

"Yes you are!" Page said as she left the dining room and entered the kitchen with Richard behind her. "We have similar tastes, so it's actually pretty easy. She likes almost everything I make for her. But she's not afraid to let me know when she doesn't. We're going to open a shop soon and I'll finally have a place to exhibit my talent."

"I see. That must be exciting."

Page placed the dishes on the counter and turned towards him. "Yeah."

"Okay, what's going on in there?" Toshika called to them from the table.

Richard and Page returned to the dining room. Richard sat down, but Page remained standing at the foot of the table. Toshika smiled at Page, and the two of them looked at Richard. "So, master. What are we doing now?"

Richard could not say what he was thinking, and his eyes wandered as he searched for an alternative. "Well... we could listen to some music," he offered.

Page rolled her eyes. "Is that what you really want to do?"

Not ready for fantasy to become reality, he hesitated, but then decided to make a stab at it. "Well, you could both take your clothes off and do some nude dancing for me," he said, forcing a laugh for protection. Toshika stood up and tossed her napkin on the table. Richard's grin slipped as he feared that he had gone too far.

"Let's go," she said to Page. The two of them went into the living room, talking to each other in hushed tones. Richard followed, his heart beating madly. Toshika put the same music on they had listened to earlier and then joined Page in the center of the room. "Have a seat," she told Richard, indicating the large sofa in the center of the dark room with an extended finger. The familiar slow groove filled the room. An exotic flute began a hypnotizing melody. Moonlight shining through the glass wall covered the dancing women in a pale brilliance. After a few minutes they began to undress each other, letting pieces of clothing fall to the floor without a sound. For Richard, the discarded clothing crashed to the floor, exploding, sending showers of sparks into the air like fireworks, celebrating a young man's dream. He sat in complete stillness, enthralled by their every move. When the final explosion came they began to twist and writhe about each other.

Eventually he noticed that although paying him no outward attention, they had been making their way over to him.

Finally they stood just before him, nearly within reach. He picked up their delicate scents, carried forward in the air they stirred with their dance. When the time came he raised his hand to take hold of Toshika first, and then Page. Feeling victorious, he pulled them down to him, waiting no more.

12

The next day he awoke alone. He turned his head and opened his eyes. The room was not familiar. But his headache was certainly his own. His mouth was dry. He was surprised at the thought that he must have had a fair amount to drink last night. As he lay there in the bed his memory was not clear. He surveyed the room and then remembered. Toshika's bedroom. Of course. When he realized where he was, he was hit by a hazy memory of the night's events that grew clearer as he was overcome by a feeling of alarm at what had occurred. He sat up and swung his feet out over the edge of the bed onto the floor, his wide eyes staring out the window onto the street in front of the house. His mind raced.

Jesus! Whose idea had *that* been?

He went downstairs and searched the house cautiously, but the women were not to be found. A note stuck to the inside of the front door offered an explanation: "Work to be done, pick you up at your place later in the afternoon for some shopping – T."

So easy. Nothing to be worried about. He smiled, removed the note from the door and folded it neatly in half, its contents hidden. He cleaned up, then went home for a change of clothes and went out for some breakfast. Ravenous, he ate enough for two. With momentum building, he left the café and visited a nearby record shop where he picked up several titles. He had not done that for a while. It felt good. He returned home and listened to his new purchases, tidying up the place as he did in anticipation of Toshika's arrival.

Finally there was a knock at the door. Richard invited Toshika in, confident that his flat was as presentable as could be, but conscious of the serious gap between what she was used to and what he had to offer. But she seemed not to pay much attention to his apartment, immediately finding his closet to see just what he had in the way of clothing before they went shopping.

"Nope, nope, nope," she said, pushing through his collection as he stood with his hand on the doorknob of the closet. "Jeans, T-shirts, awful shirts, wait," she paused, pulling out a T-shirt with the name of an old punk rock band on it. "Good for clubbing," she said, laying it over her arm. The corners of his mouth danced, finally a twinge of pride. Then she took one of many pairs of jeans as well. When she was finished, she held the shirt and jeans out to him. "So, we bring this. Everything else stays. Now, let's go and make a man out of you."

When she had finished, he motioned for her to join him on the couch near the windows. Seeing the odd expression on his face as he sat next to her, some kind of moment having arrived that he could not translate into words, Toshika was impatient.

"What?" she demanded, her smile only barely masking her mild annoyance.

"Last night. I'm sorry, but I just have to ask..."

"Yes, you were fine," she assured him.

"No, that's not what I want to know," he said, laughing.

"Then what?"

"Well, what was that all about? I know it was my idea – or *was* it?"

Toshika smiled. "Yes, it was your idea. Not entirely original, and not shocking to either one of us, but it wasn't like we had planned it."

"But... What next?" he asked, pausing as he looked into her eyes. Toshika merely waited. "Don't get me wrong, I had a *great* time, and I don't have anything against Page, but I'm not after her."

"Oh, I see. And you're 'after' me, is that right?"

Richard caught himself. "I'm not interested in her. That's all."

"Oh. Been there, done that?"

Richard's mouth nearly fell open. He could see that Toshika was not upset with him. It was what she said, not how she said it that was pointed. But why was she doing this? If she wasn't bothered, then why bother? Toshika saw his struggle, and gave in. "I'm sorry. It's okay. I know, she's not part of the deal."

Richard felt relieved. She understands.

"That's good," she continued, "because I know she probably wouldn't have gone for that again. She said something to me about it, actually. I think she's a little possessive of me, anyway. You can have me, but just as long as she doesn't have to be there, you know?" Richard remembered the way Page had acted the day before by the pool. Now it made a little more sense. "Sometimes she's a little scary," Toshika admitted. She held her thought for a moment before tossing it aside with a wave of her hand. "But that's just the way it is with girlfriends, sometimes. I guess you have the same experience sometimes, don't you? When your best friend doesn't want to share you?"

Richard shrugged. He could not recall having ever encountered that situation. "I don't know," he offered. "Maybe guys are different that way."

"Well, in any case, I'm glad we got that out of the way," Toshika announced, standing up and going to the window of Richard's room. "Hey, you can see all the way to the ocean," she said, turning to him and smiling. Richard wished that he had a camera then, as the sun held Toshika in its magnificent spotlight.

Downtown he could not have been happier, spending money and letting everyone see that the beautiful woman was with him. He was feeling very affectionate, touching and kissing her often. She did not resist, but did not respond with quite the same level of enthusiasm, leading him to ask her if she was all right. "Of course I am," she answered, "But we've got a lot to do today, that's all." Her response was reassuring enough, and he soon forgot about it.

They managed to get most of what Toshika felt he needed in one store, but it was quite a lot in the end: two suits – "What if we decide to go to the opera?" – four pairs of trousers, eight shirts, three pairs of shoes, plus coats, blazers, jackets, socks. Even underpants. "Yours are for little boys." And then came luggage. "You're not flying first class with a duffle bag," she told him. She found him something 'suitable' for him. Throughout the event he tried not to look at the prices of anything, but caught glimpses now and then anyway enough to make him feel positively drunk when she finally settled the bill with her debit card. "Never buy anything on credit," she said, as if preparing him for his new life.

Once outside the store they climbed into a cab. "Thank God that's finished," Toshika said. She looked at Richard. "My dear, you needed that. You'll see. People will look twice at you."

Richard looked out the window and smiled, remembering how good he had looked in the store trying on clothes that she had picked that he never would have.

Before he knew it he stood in front of his apartment, five large shopping bags and a set of luggage at his side. With night falling, she had suggested dinner and a nightclub, but he felt he needed an evening alone in familiar surroundings to sort himself out. As he stood on the sidewalk and waved to her in the cab as it pulled away, he felt a chill. He looked up the street at the traffic going by at the corner, and noticed a car stopped there. He tried to get a look at who was driving but at that distance it was just a dark silhouette sitting at the wheel. Police? As the thought occurred to him, the car pulled into the traffic and was gone.

It could have been anybody. Anything. So it was nothing.

He reached for the largest of the parcels he had. It took him two trips to get everything inside.

13

The driver went all the way out to the ocean to Ocean Beach, pulling the car into the nearest spot. He got out and went to the breakwater and rested his elbows on it, removing his sunglasses and rubbing his tired eyes. He took a deep breath and gazed out over the water that had been rolling in for millions of years. New clothes, new luggage. He's going to stash his loot. Pretty obvious. Pretty easy, so far. Before him, a flock of gulls flew by, singing out in their rather pitiable voices which nonetheless brought the beloved image of the sea to the hearts and minds of everyone. "Wonderful," he said aloud, watching the sun's rays glittering over the water. Back home where the weather was so uncooperative, such days were to be treasured. San Francisco's fog was nothing to bother about in comparison. One could still count on the California sunshine to bring innumerable postcard memories to life. At once he stood up and made for the steps down to the sand, sitting at the bottom step and slipping off his shoes as he again shot a glance out over the water. "Diamonds," he said under his breath. As he rose and headed out to the surf, he hummed out a tune.

Arnold Lester Jeffries was born in 1950 at number seven, The Boltons, London, England. As a boy he had delighted in living on a street "the shape of God's watchful eye," as his mother used to put it, "with a church for a pupil." The Church of St. Mary did, in fact, lie in the center. It was as if a bubble had sprung right from the middle of the road, splitting it into two lanes that were joined at either end. In school one day the young Jeffries had flummoxed the entire class as he offered them a riddle when all were assembled on the first day of the third grade when he told them "I can walk on my street all day long and never be more than a stone's throw from home."

Jeffries led a privileged life, with money in the family for as long as anyone could remember. An Oxford education and five years in banking in London found him transferring, along with his wife Rachel, first to New York and then San Francisco, to start the San Francisco office of Ledger Bristol Capital, one of the first foreign hedge fund companies to open in the City. Then one day his conscience got the better of him – he had discovered that the firm was lying about the track record of its flagship fund – and he quit. Since then, he read, wrote, traveled the bay in his kayak and published several well received photographic books focused on West Coast themes. All of this, that is, when he wasn't adoring his six-year-old daughter Penelope. He spent a lot of time with her and was simply fascinated watching the process of his little miracle growing up from a little bean into a bigger little bean. Rachel ran her own interior decorating business with two partners, and was gone about half the week meeting with clients, speaking to suppliers and doing one thing that she loved more than just about anything: turning the Bay Area upside down looking for unique pieces of art, furniture and various odds and ends which helped to make their service stand out. "If you weren't required to go on shopping trips every other day," Jeffries would tell her when he was in a teasing mood, "you'd have given up this business long ago."

He met Hans at a showing of his photographs some eight years ago at a gallery in the Castro. Hans liked his photography very much and in addition to purchasing a few prints and framing them in his home, was able to introduce Jeffries to people in publishing who in turn introduced him to other people in publishing who loved his work enough to commission three books. The two of them had been friends ever since. Until three days ago.

He hadn't been thrilled with the idea of following Richard that day, but he had some time on his hands with Penelope away for the first week in her life in a school summer camp, and he wanted to confirm his suspicions that Richard was innocent. As he ambled down the beach he knew that following him for one day didn't prove anything. There really wasn't any way for him to know what had happened. "Leave it to the professionals," had been his advice to everyone at the game. And here he was, playing cops and robbers. He knew it had been a waste of time but he had never had to deal with the violent loss of a friend like this. He felt helpless, and wanted desperately not to. Then his thoughts shifted to how he really could, possibly, make a difference.

He stopped walking and sat down in the sand, grasping two handfuls of it and letting it run through his fingers as he looked out over the rolling waves.

He had instantly suspected David Norton when he first heard of Hans' death. After all, David was clearly upset with Hans. Everyone could see that. Hans had been holding back on the bet, and David was furious. Assuming an extreme overreaction to this, wouldn't David be a likely suspect? David wasn't exactly a refined gentleman. Very physical, former police officer, guns and ammo...

But then the robbery element stuck out. David wouldn't have robbed Hans. And then it had occurred to Jeffries that the very fact that David had been a policeman for so many years made it seem unlikely that he would commit murder. After all, he knew firsthand how difficult it was to get away with something like that. Technical advancements in criminal forensics had exploded since the advent of the personal computer. It wasn't good enough any more to throw away a murder weapon, wash your hands and run away. As a police officer, it becomes part of your daily routine to preach to people the need to respect the law, settle differences calmly and without resorting to emotional or physical violence. Wouldn't that have made it quite difficult for David to have found it within himself to commit such a crime?

Then again, what if it had been an accident? What if he had gone to Hans's place to talk, an argument ensued, it got out of hand, and then...?

Jeffries recalled that Richard had told him that it was quite late when he had dropped Hans off. Two o'clock or thereabouts. How likely would it be for David to go to Hans's place at two in the morning for a talk? "Jesus," he muttered, disgusted with the whole thing. Just then he felt a pang of love for his little daughter Penelope. He hadn't seen her all week and missed her terribly. Thank God. Thank God for her. It was Saturday. Rachel would be picking her up at the camp in Mill Valley in an hour or so. With a sigh, and a heart that was becoming lighter by the second as he reviewed all the reasons that he felt absolutely lucky to be who he was, he rose and headed back to the car. He imagined a wonderful dinner made especially in honor of the returning princess, and began drawing up a list of ingredients in his head. He had some shopping to do.

Leon Porter was stuck at home on a Saturday afternoon with homework. He stared out the window of his bedroom into their backyard. Sun hit the tops of the houses behind their house. The sky was clear blue. He was nearly finished, but was running out of steam. He took a deep breath and rose up out of his chair and went into the kitchen. He quickly drank half a liter of orange juice and two handfuls of chocolate chip cookies, a banana, an apple, and then he was finished. One more cookie for the road. He headed back to his room. As he turned to enter his room he heard arguing coming from his little brother's room. It sounded like it was getting unfriendly. He turned and swiftly opened the door and popped his head inside.

"Hey!" he cried, hoping to startle the living shit out of the boys. Alan and Derick looked startled indeed. Both jumped from where they sat on Alan's bed, completely taken by surprise. Leon was about to raise one finger for "point scored" and then gloat as he left the room, when his eyes fell upon the object the two boys had been arguing over. Alan had it in his hand now, but when he had surprised them, they had each had a hand on it. It looked like a cell phone.

Alan quickly moved the object behind his back. "Leon!" he screamed, "Don't be doin' that to me!" Seeing Leon's sharp eyes following the device he held in his hands, his anger disappeared as he realized that they had been found out.

"What do you have there, little man?" Leon asked, stuffing the cookie in his mouth and stepping over to the bedside. Derick got off the bed and stood with his hands looking for something to do.

"You get outta my room!" Alan yelled in a last ditch effort to make a stand. Leon put out his hand and waited. Alan knew it was pointless. With both their parents working every day, Leon had to assume the role of man of the house regularly. It was a job he took seriously. He rarely overstepped his bounds, or let the power go to his head.

He called for the device with a twitch of his fingers. "Come on," he said calmly. "Let's see."

Alan handed over a shiny iPhone. Leon took it in his hand, took one look at it, and immediately backed up one step and felt his temper rise. "Okay, what's this all about?"

"Nothing." Alan looked at his closet then and got off the bed. He closed the closet door and then sat down again, hands in his lap. This curious action was not lost on Leon, whose eyes lingered on the closed closet door for a moment after Alan had returned to his seat on the edge of the bed.

"Where'd you get it little man," Leon asked, the rise in his voice clearly communicating that there would be consequences for withholding for more than a few more seconds.

Alan said nothing. Leon was about to speak when Derick's hands went from fluttering at his stomach to straight down at his sides.

"On the street," he said, then looked at Alan.

"Ah, *man!*"

"Alan, be quiet," Leon told him. But Alan was not about to let Derick beat him to telling about what they found.

"Some guy dumped it the other night. White guy. Right there, outside my window on the sidewalk," he told his brother, pointing at the window.

Leon began nodding slowly. "Uh-huh," he answered. "And ah... what else did this guy dump on the sidewalk?"

Neither boy said a word. Alan watched Derick, who glanced at the closet. Leon put one foot in the direction of the closet before Alan bolted over and lodged himself between his big brother and the closet door. With his back pressed up against the door, he pointed a finger at Leon.

"This is *my* room, Leon! *My* room!"

Leon stopped and folded his arms across his chest. Alan relaxed. Then he reached out in a flash and grabbed Alan by the wrist and hoisted him up onto his shoulder at the hip.

Alan squirmed and rained blows on his big brother's behind with his little fists as Leon opened the closet and looked inside. Then he stepped over to the bed and tossed Alan off his shoulder and onto the middle of it. He went back to the closet and looked inside. On a shelf in the back was Alan's blanket he carried around with him wherever he went until a few years ago. He still pulled it out from time to time when he was watching television at night. Especially if it was something scary. It was covering something but was partially folded back, revealing a black case. It looked like a small computer. In his kneeling position Leon turned and looked back at Alan with his eyebrow raised.

"Leave it," Alan told him, but there was no force in his voice. Leon lifted the blanket. When he saw the man's wallet on the computer, he knew it was time. He picked it up and took a seat next to Alan on the bed. He shook it once for emphasis.

"Now, *this* is something *serious*," he told him. Derick came around from behind the bed and stood in front of the two brothers.

"We didn't mean anything," he told Leon.

"We didn't *do* anything," Alan corrected him. "We just picked it up off the *sidewalk*."

Leon opened the wallet. A fair amount of cash. Lots of cards, including several credit cards. A flap with a window, a driver's license. Leon looked at the vaguely smiling face on the license.

"Who is it?" Derick asked him.

Leon closed the wallet and looked at the boys. "Name is Hans." He stood up and gathered the rest of the things. "You know I have to tell Dad about this," he told Alan over his shoulder as he left the room. Alan and Derick looked at each other glumly.

"Yeah," Alan sighed.

14

After cutting tags off of his new things and packing them into the new bags, he sat in the empty house listening to the silence. Matt and Tony would be home soon, he thought, looking forward to their presence. He tried calling them to check their plans for the evening. Matt was not picking up, and Tony said he would be home "later" after meeting some people for dinner downtown. Business. "It could be late, I don't know," he said. Hanging up the phone, Richard felt the air go out of him and he sank deeper into his chair, eyes roaming the room, searching for entertainment. His gaze traveled from the television, to the stereo, to the bookshelf. No luck. Finally, they fell on the window, and what lay outside, waiting.

Feeling hungry, he went into the kitchen and made himself something, returning to his bedroom to eat in front of the television. When he had finished, he switched the television off and looked at his watch before searching the room once more for distractions. Finally, his gaze fell upon the new luggage that sat neatly in the corner. He looked at his watch: only eight o'clock. He would not wait for Tony.

He found himself opening the bags, pulling out the carefully folded items inside and lining them up on the sofa. He was impressed; the fabric, the cut, the colors, the styles. Looking at the new things he had decided in an instant to go out. He quickly took his old clothes off and picked out something from what lay in front of him. Something smooth, trendy, and stylish. Standing in the bathroom in front of the full-length mirror that hung on the inside of the door, he was suddenly unsure of his plans. He felt like he was wearing a uniform of some kind. He knew it looked good, but did it look right? He couldn't tell. "You're just not used to it," Toshika had told him earlier that day, "but you look great. You really look great!"

His mind made up, he grabbed his phone, keys, and his wallet. He called a cab and was told he would have to wait twenty minutes. He thought of driving, but felt it better not to. He did not want to have to watch himself if he felt in the mood to drink. Oh well, he thought, I can wait.

The Thirteen Percent was one of his favorite bars, and tonight, it was jumping. Saturday. No big surprise. He sat near the end of the bar, facing the open room, looking at the faces. Looking around the bar, he was aware that he did not quite fit in. Everyone else looked like he used to look. Like he looked an hour ago. The feeling was validated for him when he tried to have some conversation with a young woman who had taken a seat just next to him. After having returned his "Hello" she glanced at his clothes.

"Where are you from?" she asked him. It was too much. So much for looking great, he told himself. It was not her fault, but it was irritating anyway. And did she say that with a bit of a smile? A kind of a smirk? He was not sure. Looking at her clothes, he felt he would get even.

"I'm from the Parsons Street Palace," he told her, turning back to his beer, finishing it.

"The what?"

"It's exclusive," he said. He knew it was hardly a stinging rebuke, but he was not used to being a jerk.

He stepped down and pushed through the swinging double doors. Outside, he walked the dark street towards Divisadero where he would be sure to catch a cab quickly. He figured he would try a more upscale neighborhood, perhaps somewhere near Toshika's part of town. Once on Divisadero he quickly hailed a cab and was on his way. He took Divisadero straight to Union Street and from there he walked, entering the first bar he found. A friendly, noisy place, but definitely not of the bohemian variety that he was used to. This was more like it. Although there were a variety of people there, he blended in better with the clientele and felt immediately more at ease. He again sat near the far end of the bar and ordered a beer. Halfway through his beer, he was not sure what he had hoped to accomplish. He had a woman now, so he was not especially interested in meeting anyone, although meeting and speaking with a pretty woman was always a pleasure. But he wanted to be out there in the world. He wanted to be seen. A new man. It was a kind of test; a way of trying out his new look. Well, he said to himself, with nothing but an array of different colored bottles behind the bar in front of him, I'm not getting anywhere like this. He turned on his stool and, resting his back against the bar, began surveying the crowd. Among the affluent, confident people spread out before him, his eyes quickly fell on two young women seated at a table not far from the bar. Pretty and dressed for action, they were impossible to miss. They looked to be a few years older than Richard, but not so old that he would have no interest in them. The idea of sitting down with the two of them was slightly intimidating, but he decided it might be a good challenge. The way they looked around the place made it clear that they wanted company. I am alone, and they are two. Perhaps they would feel that one guest was better than nothing? Especially one young millionaire.

Before he knew it, they had spotted him looking at them. They smiled at him, and then one nudged the other. They traded glances and spoke to each other briefly. The one with very short hair suddenly laughed out loud and slapped the other playfully on the shoulder before both of them returned his gaze once again, still smiling. It was clear enough.

"Hi, I'm Richard," he said, sitting down in one of two free chairs at their table. With his beer still in his hand, he hesitated. "Do you mind if I join you?"

"No, not at all," said the one with the short hair. She had very dark features. Richard thought perhaps she was of Italian heritage. "I'm Doris."

"And I'm Jenny," said the other, a blond with shoulder length hair and blue eyes.

"Hi," he said, "Nice to meet you both." Looking at the dark one, he cocked his head. " 'Doris?' " he asked, in a pleasant but inquisitive way. "That's sort of an old-fashioned name, isn't it?"

"You don't like it?" she asked him, not hurt but wanting him to be aware that his comment was slightly off.

Richard smiled in a mild apology and shrugged his shoulders. Be cool... "Maybe I just need to get to know you a bit better," he told her. She smiled sweetly.

"Maybe you won't get a chance."

"Come on now," said Jenny, trying to restore civility. "I'm sure Richard – it is Richard, isn't it – didn't mean anything by it. Besides," she said, looking directly at Doris, "it *is* an old-fashioned name, and you *know* it."

Doris gave Jenny a grim stare and then pinched her cheek playfully. "So, Richard, what do you do?" she asked him, folding her arms over her low-cut blouse revealing a generous amount of cleavage. Richard inhaled to respond and, drawn by the movement of her arms, glanced down from her eyes and could not help but notice her seductive attire. "He's looking at my boobs," she said to Jenny in a tone that Richard now found hard to decipher. "The guy has no manners. First he criticizes my name, and now he's checking me out right in front of my face."

"Doris, you're practically *hanging out* there, give the guy a break!" Jenny scolded. "Richard, were you 'checking her out,' or just having a little look?"

"I was just having a little look, that's all. That's a rather provocative blouse, Doris. Why do you wear something like that to a bar, anyway, if not to attract attention?"

"Yeah, Doris, why?" Jenny chimed in, clearly enjoying putting her friend on the spot. "You trying to get lucky or something?"

Doris' mouth fell open and she leaned back away from Jenny, looking her up and down. "At least I'm wearing a bra!" she cried. "And your blouse is practically transparent!" Instantly, all of them, Jenny included, looked down at Jenny's chest, which she held out, arching her back. She wore a very thin white cotton blouse. Richard tried, but could not see through it. He could only see two small points where her erect nipples pressed against the fabric.

"It's not transparent, and I don't have large breasts. I don't *need* to wear a bra," she said.

They were all silent for a moment as Jenny continued to twist and turn in her chair, trying to find a position in which her blouse might afford a more revealing view of what lay underneath.

"Well," Richard began, raising his beer towards the women. "You're both very entertaining. May I make a toast to... your breasts?" Jenny and Doris conceded and joined Richard's toast. Noticing that their glasses were nearly empty, Richard set his beer on the table and moved his chair back, preparing to stand up. "Can I get you both a refill?"

"Sure," Doris said, eyeing her glass. "I'll have another margarita."

"Me too," said Jenny.

"Strong, weak?" Richard asked them.

"Strong, Richard. We're old enough," Doris replied. Richard took their glasses and went to the bar. In a minute he returned with three margaritas and three shots of tequila. "Hey, that's a good man," Doris said, "He even brings a shot for good luck."

"What a gentleman," Jenny said in a fake whisper to Doris. The three of them sampled their drinks, smiling approvingly.

"Mmm, this place makes the best margaritas," Doris told Richard. "So, back to my original question. Other than checking out women's breasts, what do you do?"

The question was slightly annoying. Did she really care so much about what he did? He realized it was a normal question, but was self-conscious about how important it might be to her. In any case, he relished the opportunity to tell them something that he himself could hardly believe.

"You first," he said. "What do you both do?"

"Right now, we're both between jobs. You know, the collateral damage from major restructuring," Jenny told him, dipping her finger into her drink and then sucking on it. She sounded bitter. Looking at Doris, Richard could see that she had not enjoyed being reminded of their situation.

"Well," he began, drawing a deep breath and auditioning the statement briefly before making it. "I don't really 'do' anything, per se. I manage my investments, and, otherwise, enjoy myself."

Jenny and Doris held their breath for a moment. Then Jenny snickered, unable to contain herself. "You manage your investments?" she teased.

"Don't be shy, Richard, tell us," Doris said, clearly in the same camp as her friend.

"It's true," Richard said very plainly, making it obvious that he was not interested in their opinion. They said nothing, but continued to eye him suspiciously.

"Okay," he said, and stood up. He stepped over to the bar. He had a few words with the bartender, handed him his credit card, and returned to his seat. As he sat down, the bartender leaned out over the bar and called out into the crowd.

"Hello everyone, listen up," the bartender said. Holding his arm outstretched in Richard's direction, he continued. "One round of drinks for everyone, courtesy of this gentleman."

The announcement was met with relative silence, with several people exchanging puzzled looks. Then normal conversation returned, and the bar began to fill up with people coming from their tables to take advantage of Richard's offer, and to get a closer look at this young man who had extended a gesture to everyone reminiscent of the Gold Rush days.

"Well, that was generous of you," Doris said.

"I've never seen anybody do *that* before," Jenny said.

"I've never *done* it before," Richard admitted. "But you have to admit, it does lend some weight to my story, doesn't it? I mean, if I were just kidding, it would be a pretty expensive joke, don't you think?"

"Okay, we believe you. So you have money. It's not like you told us you were James Bond," Doris said. "Sorry we doubted you, Richard."

"So, how did you make your money?" Jenny asked.

This was a question Richard had not anticipated, as obvious as it was. Entertaining possible answers, he found himself stuck. "Gambling," he said, flatly. Jenny and Doris laughed. Then Richard remembered the game, and Mr. Baldwin's guess about how he was able to afford to participate. "Nah," he said. "Just lucky, I guess.

"So what does a young wealthy man like you do in his spare time?" Doris asked.

Richard shrugged. "I'm going to Switzerland in a couple of days."

"Oh, I see," Jenny began, "Going to open a Swiss bank account?" Jenny and Doris laughed again. Richard joined them, struck by the coincidence.

Doris' laughter faded, but her smile remained, drawing Richard in as he surrendered to the captivating charge between people who had only just met. As he held on, gazing into her eyes, her expression became imbued with an animal lust that did not escape him, and made him feel once again that rare triumph when his interest was actually returned.

"So," she said, leaning forward, "Do you need a traveling companion?"

Richard was quietly amazed at his sudden change in luck with women and wondered if all the years of being snubbed or simply ignored were now being compensated. "Well, actually, I'm already going with a couple of girls."

Right away, he knew he had just thrown cold water on the evening and could not believe that he had been so stupid. What was he doing? Was he bragging, or had he just tried to sabotage the fun he had been having for the past five minutes out of some notion of faithfulness to Toshika?

"A couple? How much are you paying them?" Doris asked him.

"What?" Richard felt the room around him begin to become disconnected as Doris' comment cleaved through him like an axe. He looked at Doris and blinked once. "Very funny," he said, his voice distant. Just then the bartender approached and placed Richard's credit card on the table with a bill for him to sign. He reached for the pen and with stiff fingers, signed the bill.

Doris sat back from the table. "Going to the bathroom," she announced. She looked at Jenny. "Coming?"

"Yep," Jenny said. As they stood up and crossed the room, Richard saw Jenny turn to look at him, a conspiratorial smile on her face. In a moment they turned and descended a staircase leading to the restrooms, leaving Richard to be swallowed up by the music and the chatter.

Richard looked at the bar to his left. The bartender stood leaning on the counter behind him, arms folded over his chest. Richard looked once more at the stairs. "Fuck it," he said, and rose quickly, reaching to his hip pocket for his wallet. As his hand slid over the smooth fabric of his new pants, pants that had no such pocket, a panic began to stir in him until he remembered that his wallet was in the breast pocket of the new blazer he wore. He stopped and looked down as he fished his wallet out of the pocket, not recognizing his shoes, or the pants, or the shirt. God, what am I doing? He called the bartender over with his eyes and pulled out some cash.

"How much do I owe you?" he asked, once more looking to the top of the steps at the back of the room.

"You're paid up, guy."

"Okay, thanks. Bye."

Once out on the street, he felt lucky as a cab pulled up in front of the bar. A man and woman got out and paid the driver, who had come around to the curb side of the street. He looked at Richard and raised his eyebrows. "You free?" Richard asked him. The cabbie responded by opening the door for him. "Great." He settled into the cab and waited for the driver to get in. In moments they were heading down the street. "Pacific Heights, please," Richard told him, before being suddenly aware again of his new clothing. "On second thought, make it the park. Corner of Stanyan and Fulton." The driver nodded and turned left at the next corner.

Toshika answered the door and smiled. "Richard!" She stood there for a moment before stepping back so that he could enter. "Come in."

"Hi," Richard said. "Thanks. Sorry, I-"

"No, I'm glad you came. Come in, come in," Toshika said, shutting the door behind him. The warm light inside the house was inviting. He found himself envious of Toshika once again as he took in the surroundings that made him wonder how he could ever have thought that his apartment was a pretty cool place to live. Toshika stood before him barefoot in shorts and a white blouse that looked like it had paint smeared on it. Richard made a face at it.

"Have you been painting or something?"

Toshika looked down at her blouse. "Oh, no. A present from a friend. An artist. He had this idea to market shirts with paint on them so that people could, I don't know, feel like they were artists or something. I think this is the only one in existence." Richard peered down the hallway to his left, listening. "I'm alone," Toshika told him. "I was just reading in bed."

"Well, I know it's late. Sorry."

"Stop apologizing! Come," she told him, taking his hand and heading down the hallway towards her bedroom. "You want to stay?"

As they entered her room Richard knew that if he did not ask her soon, he would never ask her. "Something's on my mind," he told her, more forcefully than he had intended. Toshika stopped and eyed him for a moment before going to her bed.

"Sure," she said, sitting on the edge of her bed. Richard remained standing, then took a seat in a chair nearby, turning it on the hardwood floor to face her. He did not know how to begin.

"I just wanted to know..."

"Yes?"

He closed his eyes. "This is going to sound dumb."

"Don't worry, dumb is good."

"Okay, well, how dumb is this: are you doing it for the money?"

Toshika frowned. " 'It' ?"

"I mean, this whole thing. You and me. It's not about the money, is it?"

"Oh. That's pretty dumb, you're right. Richard, I *have* money. Right? Besides, I'm not getting any money for this, am I?"

"No," Richard told her. He felt relieved.

"No, it's not about the money."

"So," Richard began, not sure what to say now that he had gotten what he wanted.

"So, you mean, what's it about then? Okay, originally, it was just exciting. I didn't have any of that. I was getting tired of what I felt like was a very routine and boring life, so I thought, 'why not?' It seemed like fun."

This was certainly not what Richard had wanted to hear. The feeling of relief that had shown itself began to evaporate. He felt himself getting heavier and moved his hand to get a better grip on the chair.

" 'Fun.' Are you talking about the game?"

"Yeah," Toshika said, giving Richard the feeling that he had just asked another dumb question. "Well anyway, that was a while ago. So then the excitement began to wear off. And then you came along."

"Right."

"And now, things are different," Toshika said. She got up off of the bed and stepped over to Richard. She took his hand and pulled at it until he was on his feet. "Come on," she said, "the book can wait."

Richard hesitated, watching her welcoming expression as he turned their conversation over in his mind and wondered if it was really settled for him. And then, as would happen time and time again, Toshika's gaze made his cares dissolve until he could scarcely remember what the fuss had been about.

"Richard, it's late. Come on, let's go to sleep."

Richard sat down on the bed and pushed his shoes off. "Okay, okay," he told her, "you win."

15

Monday morning. The world was back in action. Richard had spent the previous day at home, reading and doing odds and ends. Toshika had been busy visiting a friend who was in the hospital with a broken shoulder. Mountain biking accident. The evening was a classic, with Richard, Matt and Tony watching an old Clint Eastwood western. "What a genre, what a genre," Tony had kept repeating throughout the film. "I'd love to make a cowboy flick some day." Richard had been keenly aware of the feeling that somehow this was one of the last times they would be doing this, living the old life. Wouldn't he soon be on his own, in a new place, with his new life? But then he hadn't received any of the money he was supposed to have won. Not yet. And until he did, it was too easy to imagine that somehow it would never happen. Some glitch would hang up his millions and he would wake up from the dream.

It was too early yet, he knew it. Nonetheless, there was no harm in checking. The bus rattled and squeaked as it hurtled down Van Ness Avenue. His finger played with the rivet holding the fiberglass seat to its frame as he silently hoped the bank would be open by the time he got there. He had no idea what time it opened, but he figured that by nine it should be open.

Because he wanted the money to be there, wanted it to be real, he felt he would doom himself if he focused his attention on the hope, so his thoughts flicked from one subject to another as fast as they came up. The driver spoke loudly, startling him each time he called the next stop.

"California Street," the driver announced. Richard jumped. He looked ahead and saw the street sign, then the bank. As he stepped off the bus he took a deep breath and told himself he didn't care. He crossed the widest street in the city and approached the bank. He looked at his watch – 9:05 – then noticed a guard standing out front, and someone entering in front of him. The bank was open for business.

"I'd like to check my balance, please," he told the clerk when it was his turn. He gave her his bank card and then entered his code into the keypad on the counter. The woman smiled and began typing into her terminal, eyes dutifully watching the screen.

"Okay," she said pleasantly, having found his account. Then she frowned, squinting as she leaned forward. She looked at him and resumed typing.

"Did I have a deposit recently?" he asked, hearing the words echoing from his mouth.

"Yes, but, I just have to check something. Just a moment, please," she said, before stepping away from her terminal. She walked out from behind the counter and over to a woman sitting at a desk at the other side of the room. She spoke to the woman briefly and nodded toward Richard. He began to sweat, wondering if somehow something had gone terribly wrong. What if the woman's screen read "Call police at once!" What if he had been found out, the winner in an illegal card game? It was preposterous, but so was everything else. The two women came back to the counter, and the new one, clearly one of the managers, greeted Richard before looking into the screen.

"Yes, okay. Print it," the older woman said. The clerk inserted a slip of paper into a machine, and then handed it to the woman who asked Richard if he would like to take a seat, indicating a chair in front of her desk across the room. Richard agreed. Sitting down at her desk, he waited for her to speak. She introduced herself as the assistant manager of the bank.

"Okay, Mr. Peel, you wanted to check your balance, correct?"

"Yes, is there something wrong?" he asked her.

"Oh, no! No, there's nothing wrong," she said, putting a hand out in his direction. "Your current balance," she said,

192

lowering her voice, "is two hundred fifty two thousand one hundred and eighty dollars. And some cents." She pushed the card across the top of her desk over to him. Reading the printout with his name on it, the hair on the back of his neck stood up. He looked at the paper carefully.

"You had a large transfer into your account, Mr. Peel, is it correct? Were you expecting this?"

The sound of the woman's voice startled him. How long had he been staring at the sheet of paper? A minute? Five? He twisted in his chair and rubbed the back of his neck. "Yes, I was," he told her, hoping he would not be asked to explain it.

"Well, you are now one of our Preferred Clients. I'd like to schedule an appointment with you to discuss your account, your investments, and so on," she said pleasantly.

"Well," Richard answered. "That sounds fine. But I'm going to be travelling and... how about if I just stop by when I return and set up an appointment then?"

"Certainly. Come by whenever you're back," the woman said, unable to hide the disappointment of not having secured the appointment on the spot.

Richard went to stand, but stopped himself short. "By the way, is the money available now? I mean, is there any kind of hold on it, or...?"

"Oh, certainly it's *available*," the woman said. "Would you like to make a withdrawal?"

"Oh. Yes, ah... I'd like five hundred dollars, please."

The woman hesitated, nodding her head. "Five hundred dollars," she repeated. "Would you like that in twenties?"

"Yes, please."

The woman rose and stepped away. Richard heard her footsteps across the stone floor behind him and waited. He was losing control and wanted to get out of the bank fast. When the woman returned, she counted out Richard's money and handed it to him along with a balance statement on another small sheet of paper. Then she handed him her card, taking out a pen and underlining her phone number.

"This is my direct line, Mr. Peel."

He accepted the card and read the woman's name carefully to make himself feel legitimate and her feel important. "Yes. Thank you."

Outside, he stood in front of the bank facing the street, unsure where to go.

"Forget something?"

Richard turned. The security guard at the door nodded. "No. Thanks," Richard said. He walked to the corner, turned, and continued on. He had no idea where he was going.

He just roamed, letting his mind wander as he tried to come to grips. At the next corner he turned again and headed towards the Marina. Up ahead, a shop on the right was suddenly familiar. Quality Cars. They sold used cars – mainly exotic sports cars. He stopped in front of the large windows, the sleek machines behind the glass beckoning. Inside were six cars. One stood out: a midnight blue Ferrari 456 GT. Richard opened the door of the shop and stepped inside. A man behind a desk in the corner looked at him and greeted him without enthusiasm. Richard knew how he looked, and that he was young. Too young. He looked at the Ferrari and walked over to it. It was simply stunning. He looked through the window at the beautifully crafted interior and was captivated. He stood up and, running the figure of his bank balance over again in his mind, pointed at the car.

"I'd like to drive this one, please."

The man behind the desk looked up, considered Richard, and smiled. He walked slowly over to him and stopped in front of the car. His skepticism couldn't stop him from smiling and shaking Richard's hand. "Sorry, sir, but you're a pretty young fellow, and that's an expensive car. Are you really interested in buying it?"

"Are you interested in selling it?"

Since the economic meltdown, business at Quality Cars had dried up. Richard was not the first young person to come inside and drive off with a car that was properly for those who had worked long and hard for them, but the man was still not used to it, and was stung with a kind of jealousy each time it occurred.

The man nodded and turned on his heel. "Let me get the keys," he called over his shoulder.

Half an hour later Richard was on his way home with his new toy. Having spent his whole life driving cars that were on the verge of a nervous breakdown, he couldn't get over the experience. The Ferrari was clean, completely functional, in perfect shape, fully registered, beautiful, and sounded like a wild animal lived beneath the hood. Driving up the hills in first gear, he listened to the engine. What a sound. "Unreal," he found himself muttering. He took a detour and went up California Street to Franklin, turned left and had a good look at the Victorian mansion on the corner, then continued on to Vallejo. He had an urge to drive by Toshika's house. He wasn't planning to stop there, just to drive by. Have a look. He slowed a bit as he neared her house, looked at it through the open car window, and then continued on to Baker Street towards home.

16

David Norton watched a dark blue Ferrari drive by from where he sat in his truck, parked a few houses down from Toshika's house on the opposite side of the road, and whistled under his breath at it. He turned up the Journey a notch that was playing on his cd player. He had been sitting there for the better part of three hours. He had to know what she was up to. He just had to. After the game ended in disaster and she began hanging around with that young punk, he became more and more distraught. He couldn't take it any more. It had to end. He was staring directly at her front door when the garage door opened. A red Mercedes coupe slowly backed out of the two-car garage. He sunk down in his seat a bit out of habit. The car continued backing up, and then he caught a glimpse of the driver's profile. Could have been Page, but it wasn't.

Perfect.

David watched the car enter the street backwards. The brake lights lit up and it stopped. Then it drove forward and was gone. He quickly jumped out of his car, his backpack slung over one shoulder. He went to her front door and started to work on the lock. He slipped a pick into the lock and was inside in a minute. When the alarm gave its warning countdown he entered the code, wondering at the odds that she hadn't changed it since his time. Four digits, and the beeping tone was cut. Good. He quickly went to her desk and placed a bug on the phone and fixed a wireless sender to the back of the desk with adhesive. Then he began searching for anything that would give her plans away. Sitting directly in front of her printer was a receipt for a one-way plane ticket to Zurich via New York. Too easy. He picked it up and looked it over. Wednesday. The day after tomorrow. He noted the airline and the flight time and then got out of there as fast as he could. Jeffries' house was next. Then he would be ready.

With one day left before setting off for New York, and with his good fortune bringing him to reflect on his past, Richard drove straight on by his apartment and headed south out of the City towards the Silicon Valley. He went first to visit his old kindergarten and primary school. Like much of the surrounding community, this school had been built not long before his family had moved there. On the outside, the school had not changed much. A new color. He went into the library in search of the books on reptiles and amphibians that he was so fascinated with as a boy. To his amazement the books were still there on the shelves, even though the library itself had been completely renovated and looked nothing like he remembered. He picked up several of the books and flipped through them, feeling a small part of himself transported through time as he recognized every photograph, every illustration. He scanned the checkout registers inside one book, then another. On the cards inside were spaces for perhaps twenty dates, but they remained unfilled. None of them had been checked out in the last half a dozen years. He marveled at the dates that might have been from his own use. He glanced around the room, eager to share with someone what he had found, but of course there was no one there who would care. There was no one there who knew him.

Leaving the school, he drove by the house he grew up in until the age of eight. It was a modest house in a quiet neighborhood near the large and acclaimed community college that was built when he was still a toddler. He stopped in front of the house and got out of the car. In the front of the house was a small lawn. The two walnut trees he used to play on with his brothers were still there. He walked over to one of them and examined its base. Here, at this particular tree, the grass used to grow in small tufts between the roots, which had nearly made their way to the surface. Where the grass was thin, leaving only the bare dirt, he used to sit and, pushing Matchbox cars with his fingers, drive around between the lumps of grass at dangerous speeds, tires squealing, the police not far behind.

Finally he drove into the foothills to visit the second house, where he spent his teenage years, the one where he lived until he left for the university. It was a larger house on a bigger piece of land surrounded by rolling hills and old oak trees. He stopped at the gate – he and his family called it a gate, but it was just a chain attached to two posts his father had strung across the driveway back then. A cheap solution. The new owners had installed a proper gate, which he spent a moment admiring before getting out of the car to have a look up at the house. From the gate he could only just see the house through the trees at the top of the hill. His parents had sold the house some years ago and he had not been back since. He tried to see up to his bedroom, to catch a glimpse of the window he spent countless evenings looking out of, wondering about a better world. But the avocado tree, so many years later now, had grown and he could not see his room.

The day had been humid, with large clouds drifting through the heat of the sunshine. As he stared into his past, a light rain, one of those in which the raindrops seem to vanish before they hit the ground, began to fall all around him. He looked up, but it was still a bright, sunny day, despite the rain that shone silver in the sunlight and fell like beautiful, tiny sparks. Looking up to the old house, his hands on the gate that blocked his path, he thought of the years spent there on the hill that were now gone for good. He felt the rain on his face as the drops fell, courteously distracting him from his own tears, or perhaps helping to draw them out. He looked skyward. Is this some kind of apology?

Moments later a car came up behind him and slowed to a stop just behind his own. Wiping his face quickly, he moved towards his car.

"Sorry," he called out to the other driver, avoiding eye contact as he hurried to get into the car.

But he was too late. The driver had already gotten out and approached his car with a smile on his face. "Well, this is a nice one," he remarked. "It's a Ferrari isn't it?"

"Yes. I'm sorry, I used to live here. Actually, you probably bought this house from my parents."

The man, an Indian who appeared to be about his father's age, nodded and smiled. "Oh, yes, that's right. You're Mr. Peel's son, then."

"Yes, well, one of them," he said, keeping his eyes averted as much as possible so that the man would not see his eyes.

"Well, I'm Ramesh Pandya," the man said, and the two shook hands.

"Hi. I'm Richard."

"I'll bet you want to go up and look around? See your old room?"

Richard fought for a moment with the impulse to be polite and decline the offer. "Well, if you don't mind, it would be nice to have a quick look around."

"It's no problem. I invite you to come and have a look. Just let me unlock the gate and we'll drive up together."

Having parked their cars outside the house, they climbed the brick steps of the front porch and went inside. Richard recognized the structure but none of the things inside as they went straight for the staircase. Seeing so many foreign objects appearing suddenly in his past gave him an odd feeling. When they reached the top of the stairs the man stopped and waited for Richard, then followed him into his old room, which, like the house below, was filled with unauthorized violations of his memory: a new bed, new bookshelves – new things. But somehow, it was still his room, and being there, he became a ghost of the person he once was. He went over to the window and looked out of it onto the landscape that he knew so well. The rolling hills, with the low mountains behind them, were dotted with a sprinkling of houses distant enough from one another to afford a level of privacy not possible in the old neighborhood. His father had wanted it that way. He put his hands on the windowsill and felt an ache in his chest. How many times had he sought solace there, with his view out onto the 'other' world that would, he told himself, someday rescue him from his own?

200

It must have been a full minute later when a barking dog brought him back. He turned, smiled at the man, and headed for the door. As he passed the closet he hesitated. The door was closed. He looked at the man, who did not smile but simply nodded. Richard stepped over to the closet, opened the door, and turned the light on inside. With a hand on the doorframe he leaned in and looked at the inside wall next to the door. Then he looked on the opposite side, high up near the top of the door. There it was. He could not believe it. Why hadn't they covered it? Painted over it or something? He was looking at his own writing, born of helplessness and years of being beaten down, being kept in place. The words, hidden away in the dark, had been a small victory for him, a consolation. 'I will kill my father.'

He switched off the light. "Needs some paint," he said, without looking at the man. Suddenly, the man's expression changed from one of compassion to one of embarrassment.

"This is my son's room now," he said. "He doesn't want it painted."

Richard fought to meet his gaze as the urge surfaced to show this man, this father to someone else, that he was not sorry.

They took a brief tour around the rest of the house and then went outside. Before they reached the bottom of the front porch steps, Richard stopped and sat down, like he had countless times in his youth. The man remained standing and looked out over the property. It was not large for the area, but large by city standards. Unlike the view from his bedroom window, the view from the front of the house contained no reminders of the rest of humanity, no homes, no roads, no telephone lines. Here there was just the hill that rose gradually, whose wild grass was green in the winter and brown in the summer, like it was now, and that was otherwise populated only by a few wizened oaks. Beyond the hill, completing the horizon, was yet another hill, higher and quite distant, goading the onlooker to imagine what might lay beyond and in doing so reinforcing the awareness of solitude.

"It's a nice name, 'Pandya,' " Richard finally told him. "Something very peaceful about it. Gentle. Like a panda."

The man just smiled and nodded. Finally Richard got up, thanked him and left.

He would have called it a day and returned directly to the city, but he was sidetracked. As he left, it occurred to him that, considering what car he was driving, he would be a fool not to take the scenic route home.

From the old house, he drove up further into the hills and headed towards Skyline Boulevard, running along the top of the mountain range dividing the valley floor along the South Bay Peninsula and the ocean. The road up to the top was long and winding. He drove aggressively, easily passing the few cars he found on the otherwise empty road, sending echoes of the Ferrari's twelve-cylinder engine into the canyon below. Reaching the top he headed north along what he always found to be one of the most beautiful roads ever. As he drove he was reminded of a day trip he and some friends made to these mountains last summer. With that trip on his mind he slowed, and was soon near the spot where they had spent a hot afternoon drinking and partying. It had been a very special day, owing mainly to the state of mind they had worked themselves into. With a glance at the clock on the dashboard he pulled over onto the shoulder of the road and parked. Getting out he shut the door and took a few steps back down the road, looking at the hill that rose from the edge of the road. Yes, it was here. He was certain. He bounded across the road and found a faint trail cutting through the trees and heading up through the tall dried grass of an oak-dotted hillside. In a minute he stood on top where there were no trees. Instead, there were several sandstone rock formations, one being wide and flat, like a plate on the hilltop. Hopping onto the rock he was transported back to that day. Looking westward, the Pacific Ocean shone a bright blue in the sunshine some fifteen miles out. Just beyond where he stood, down the slope and towards the coast, a dirt fire road ran parallel to the sea before turning west and disappearing as it worked its way down the slope. After having spent at least a couple of hours on this rock, when the sun had long ago begun to head for the sea, he and his friends had set off down this dirt road to see where it would take them.

He jumped down off the rock and followed the road once more. As it was before, the day was hot and the sun shone down mightily, making the journey more of an effort than it might have been. As he walked, the only sound was the one made by his footsteps in the dirt, and the breeze that combed through the grassy hills and offered a small relief to the sun's heat. He enjoyed walking, content to carry on until he felt it was of no use. After some minutes he found himself looking at a curve in the road ahead and remembered that this was as far as he and his friends had gone before. He continued until he had rounded the curve and the road straightened out again and headed off west, where he stopped. On either side of the road the hillside fell gradually towards the ocean, and now, as then, the tall grass blew in the breeze.

Staring out over the sea, his attention was drawn to his right. He turned and looked to the hillside at the tall grass that waved lazily to him, and then he felt it: a small space just a few steps up into the grass from the dusty road beckoned him to come and surrender himself, called for him to come and sit down forever. "Come here, and everything will be all right," it seemed to say to him. No one would notice, and he would not be unhappy there. He would lapse into another realm of existence. Unable to escape its pull, he walked to the edge of the road and stepped up into the grass, wading into the spot before halting and turning his gaze once more to the sea. Something assured him that peace could be his forever. He need only stay there; to sit down, and belong. To pass into nothingness. But before he could sit down, an acute sense of loss came over him, and for a moment it seemed as though he would be brought to tears once again. Staring at the sea, he could not hear the grass any more. He only felt the blades tapping at his hands that hung loosely at his side. He turned and headed back up the dirt road. He was not ready.

Back in the city the next morning, staring out the window of his bedroom at his new car, the anticipation of the trip he would be taking gave him pause. Tomorrow it would begin. First New York, then Zurich, and then... who knew? He was excited about the idea of taking off with Toshika to go wherever they felt like going, and under such comfortable circumstances. At the same time, it was unnerving. Aside from Toshika and Page, he would be alone in the world out there.

Without being sure exactly what he would say to her, he picked up the phone to call his mother. By the fourth ring, he had a bad feeling that she would not be the one to answer the phone. Why am I even calling? I can't tell them. Not now, anyway. To tell them that I'm going to Europe – okay, but I could do it just as easily from there. Guess where I am? Sure. What difference would it make? When was the last time I spoke to them, anyway? A few months ago?

He was so far into his thoughts that he almost hung up the phone before he realized that it had stopped ringing.

"Hel-*lo*," the voice said, repeating itself, the speaker obviously annoyed.

"Hi. Dad, sorry. I was – I didn't hear you answer."

There was a pause. A part of him still wondered if it were not absolutely too late to just hang up.

"Well, clean out your ears. I think I spoke loud and clear," his father said, his crisp voice too loud as usual.

Richard took the final sip from his beer and rolled his eyes menacingly at the empty bottle. "Where's mom?"

"She's out," his father said, as if there could not have been a more pointless question.

"Oh."

"How are you, anyway?"

"Me? Oh, fine." He could find nothing to say. He could only think of the bad luck of having called when his mother was out.

"I'm fine too. Listen, Richard, you called, right?"

He looked out his window at the fading sunlight and felt the years peel away in an instant. "Yeah dad, right. Sorry. You busy?"

"Busy? No, I'm not *busy*."

"Oh, good." He heard his father exhale loudly.

"Oh, is that good? Is it good not to be busy? That's what *you* think. I'm *bored*, Richard."

What could he say? He quickly brushed away the thoughts of suggesting courses at the local junior college, or of taking up a hobby. He imagined his father seated at a potter's wheel and smiled, just for a moment. He could hear him breathing over the line. "Got some good news," he said before he knew what he was doing. Are you nuts? What were you going to say? Then he thought of Toshika.

"Oh? You get a job?" his father asked hopefully.

"No, not yet."

His father sounded as if he should have known better. "Oh. Well then, what is it? Don't tell me you're going back to school, back to study some more philosophy."

"No, dad."

"You see, you can't find a job, can you?"

"Well, it hasn't been going very well, no. Especially with the economy the way it is now. They say it isn't a good time to be out looking for a job."

"Yeah, well did 'they' tell you to study *philosophy*?" Richard's father paused to allow the question to grow teeth. "You know Richard, I was talking to Frank Steiner the other day – you remember the Steiners – he just hired a kid your age, no experience. For a job programming. Know how much?"

Richard rolled the empty beer bottle across the carpet with his foot. "No."

"Eighty-thousand, Richard. Could have been you. If you'd only taken my advice."

"I don't like computers."

"No, you like philosophy. So where'd it get you? You're a clerk in a wine shop."

It had to end.

"I've got a girlfriend."

"Oh, is *that* it?"

"Yeah."

"Well. Good for you. Don't go and get her *pregnant*. Jesus. That'd be all you need. Kids and no job."

"I'm not stupid, dad."

"Yeah? Well."

"How's mom?"

"Your mother? She's fine. Richard, you've got to make something of yourself, you understand? Your timing may not be the best, but that's no excuse. Other people are out there doing it every day. The only thing holding you back is *you*, know what I mean?"

"She's nice. Her name is Toshika."

Silence.

"Is she black?" Richard's father asked, his voice no longer booming.

"Her hair is black."

"Oh, she's Asian?"

"Japanese," Richard said, standing up to look down onto the street outside. "Only half, don't worry."

"What?" his father asked him. "What was that?"

Richard thought once more of telling his father that he was leaving for New York the next day and would be flying on to Europe after that. "Listen dad, I have to go. Tell mom I said hi, okay? Bye." He hung up the phone quickly and stood up. "To hell with that," he said. He looked out the window once more before grabbing his keys and a sweater and heading outside for a walk.

17

Curtis Porter sat next to his wife Janet on the couch. Across from them, on the other side of the same coffee table that he had split his lip on at the age of two, having found the joy that his feet would give him when they moved fast and swept him along with them, sat their sixteen-year-old son Leon. He had something to tell them. He felt his jaw harden, felt it jut forward under pursed lips. Okay, out with it, Curtis thought. Whatever it is, out with it, and we'll deal with it. Curtis was the fourth son of Marry and Henry Porter. He wasn't the only son to marry, but after seventeen years with Janet, was the only one still married. He was the only one who hadn't ever been arrested, not even for a traffic violation. He was the only son of the four still living with his partner and children. The only one with a family the way his parents had hoped they all would have. His brothers weren't bad, just more hot-tempered. They had all been dealt a difficult hand, and his hadn't been any different. But he had seen their troubles, and had learned from them – perhaps for them, in case they had failed to learn from them themselves. But they were okay now. All of them working, and all of them staying on the better side. It was his primary goal in life to make sure that his own two sons saw his example and followed it. That they stayed away from drugs and from boys with no respect for authority or without enough common sense to know how to help themselves to a better life. He felt he was succeeding. His boys were good. They had, he had always told himself, both been blessed with a generous inheritance from their mother, who was not only one of the smartest people he knew, but also one of the wisest. Be that as it may, he knew the world he lived in and was always prepared for the day when he would hear something that would test his resolve. He was always prepared for the day when one of his boys would get a foot knocked off of that tightrope. When they would falter, and look down into the abyss and struggle to right themselves. He always hoped that in those moments his boys would have the courage and intelligence to come to their parents for help if they needed it. That Leon had told them personally that he had something to tell them already made this a much better situation. It was the late night phone call, with one or both of the boys out, not at home, that both he and Janet dreaded.

Still, he sat and locked his eyes on Leon for any sign that this may be one of those tightrope days.

Leon's face told them that he wished he wasn't in the position he was in. But he said nothing. When he had their attention, he reached out, holding a black leather billfold in his hand. His mother and father frowned and knit their brows together. Curtis reached for the wallet and took it from his son. Both his and his wife's eyes were on the wallet as he opened it and as Leon began to tell the story.

"I found Alan and Derick with it. They say they found it the other night when Derick slept over. Said that in the middle of the night they were playing video games and that they heard something outside the window. A man was dumping this wallet, one of them notebook computers, a camera and an iPhone. Dumped 'em on the sidewalk."

"What, right outside Alan's bedroom?" Leon's mother asked.

"That's right. They said he had his car right there, that he got back in and took off, and they creeped outside and snatched it all up."

Curtis Porter took a deep breath and sighed. "Well, Leon, thanks for telling us. We'll just have to call the police, of course." He was noticeably relieved.

"Yeah, well, thing is," Leon continued, "I remember hearing something, well, reading about something in the paper a few days back. And I went back through the stack of papers in the recycle bin in the laundry room, and found it."

"What did you find?" his mother asked.

"It was an article about a man who had been robbed and killed in his home on the hill," Leon said, his thumb hooking backwards over his shoulder in the direction of Pacific Heights, not far from where they lived.

Leon's father's jaw dropped. "Nah," he said. "Was it – is *this* the man?"

Leon nodded.

"Oh, lord," Janet said, her hand coming to her mouth, and her eyes searching those of her husband.

Curtis placed the wallet on the coffee table as though it had grown hot in his hand and stood up, his hand rubbing his face and then moving back up over the top of his head to the back of his neck where it stayed. "Now, that makes things more complicated. White man killed on that damned hill, white cops looking for who done it, black kids 'find' it..."

"Dad, come on, we have to tell them," Leon said before he looked at his mother for support. Her look revealed something that he wasn't sure how to read. It had looked to him like shame, but that couldn't have been right, could it?

"Leon, you're right honey, but so is your father. In this case, holding up your hand, offering to do what's right, well, it could turn against you, depending."

"What, you mean depending on how bad they want this guy? On how bad they need to pin this on somebody?" Leon could tell from the expression on his parent's faces that he had it right. "But, come on, Alan and Derick?"

"Leon, they might also have a look at me," his father said, his hands on his hips now as he planted his feet firmly. "Or they might have a look at *you*, more likely." He put his hand to his chin and massaged it as an idea came to him. "Did they tell you what time it was when this happened?"

"Yeah, they said it was about two-thirty in the morning. They were watching the clock to see how late they were staying up, you know."

"Mmm, you were out late that night, weren't you? What time you get back home?"

Leon saw his point. It had been after two when he came home.

"And do you have good people who know where you were at that time? People who saw you there?"

Leon thought it over. "Not sure. We were, we were just out, you know. Cruisin'."

"Right, you see, that's a perfect zero for us here. I'm not saying it's going to happen, son, I'm just... you know. I'm livin' in the real world here."

"It's unlikely," Janet told her son. "But honey, when you've seen what we've seen, you think about these things. That's all."

"Hey mom, I've seen it too, you know."

Janet Porter looked up at her husband silently, and he at her.

"Leon," Curtis began, "you have to get on the phone and talk to your friends right now. Tell them they and their parents have to be willing to talk to the police to tell them where they were, even if there's nobody that the police will really want to trust who saw you all there and can vouch for you. You understand me? And I need to speak to their parents too. I want to hear it from them that they are with us on this. And then we can go to the police."

Leon sat still, absorbing the impact of the situation which clearly hadn't dawned on him in these terms until now. His mother rose to her feet and went into the kitchen. She took the cordless phone from its base and came back to the living room, sitting down on the couch again. She held the phone out to her son. "Do it now please, Leon."

Twenty minutes later, walking along the sidewalk aimlessly, his hands stuffed into the pockets of his windbreaker, a bus that roared by him a bit too close brought him out of his stupor. "Geez," Richard gasped, watching the bus as it slowly swerved back toward the center of the lane. But it had been his fault, too. Looking down, he noticed that he had been nearly walking off the edge of the sidewalk. He stopped and looked around, unsure of exactly where he was. He looked at a street sign just ahead of him.

"Broderick," he said, surprised. "What the hell?" His guard suddenly went up. He had wandered into what he would normally think of as not one of the best neighborhoods for him to be in.

He turned around slowly at the sound of children playing. He had not even noticed the small schoolyard he had just passed. Behind the chain-link fence a dozen small children played on a jungle gym made of old tires. A swing set stood nearby, waiting for its turn to amuse and delight. Suddenly, the neighborhood didn't seem so threatening. Richard smiled and though he would head back when he noticed a woman emerging from the small school building and calling out to the children.

"Hey!" she cried. "Who wants to race me on the swings?"

It was Toshika.

The woman ran up to the children and grabbed one of them, a little black girl, her hair filled with colorful bows. Most of the children were black. Some were Asian. One was white. Toshika ran behind the girl to the swings, being sure to lag behind a half a step.

"I win! I win!" the girl squealed.

"Oh," Toshika cried, stomping her feet. "You're so fast! Hey, let's swing," she said, taking one of the swings and slipping down into the seat, watching the girl do the same next to her. "Ready? Go!"

Richard brought his hands to his hips, grinning. What is she doing here? "Great," he said to no one. He went to the gate of the schoolyard and opened it, closing it behind himself as he entered. He ignored the children as he passed by them, heading directly for the swings, his face one big smile as he wondered why it was that he was so glad to see Toshika.

She saw him, but his presence in this world, her private world, required a moment to be real for her.

"Richard," she said. It was neither a welcome, nor a dismissal, but a kind of wall that she erected with that utterance.

Richard's step faltered. He slowed. "What?"

"What are you doing here?"

"What are *you* doing here?" he asked her, reminding himself that he had seen her entering the playground from the school building itself. It was not as if she had just wandered onto the grounds, as he had. Toshika was now racing the little girl on the swings, leaning back and closing her eyes as she shot into the air and laughed with her.

"Who *is* that man, Toshi?" the girl asked.

"He's my friend."

"Come on," Richard said. "I saw you come out of the school. And this girl obviously knows you."

But Toshika ignored him, content to ride the swings and talk to the little girl. Richard was beginning to feel awkward when he felt the burning attention of eyes on him. He looked down and to his left. There stood a boy with his arms crossed over his chest, his small brows bunched together, his mouth in a disapproving frown. What was he, Richard thought, five? Six?

"Hey man," the boy said. "What you *doin'*?"

"Sorry?" Richard asked him.

"You sorry? I'll say you *sorry*." The boy looked at Toshika and hooked a thumb in Richard's direction. "He bothering you, Toshi?"

"You stop it, Brandon," the girl on the swing called out. "He's Toshi's *friend*, that's who he is."

Toshika rode the swing high into the air and then jumped off.

"He your friend?" the little boy asked Toshika, his bravado suddenly gone, replaced by the sweetness that only little children possess.

Just then a woman's voice rang out across the playground. "Okay children, come on in now."

Richard looked to see a tall black woman at the door of the tiny school watching him as she held the door open.

"Yep, he's my friend," Toshika told the boy, turning to the girl and holding out her arms to her. "Come on Keisha, let's go inside."

The boy looked again at Richard. His expression was now friendly but not entirely trusting.

"You got a car?" he asked Richard.

"A car? Sure, I've got a car."

"Mustang?"

"No."

"Lexus? Some day I'm gonna buy me a Lexus. What you drivin'?"

"Well, I just bought-"

"He drives an ugly little Toyota, Brandon. Nothing to get excited about, okay?" Toshika said, fixing Richard's mouth shut with her eyes. With that she wrapped an arm around the boy and hoisted him into the air as he broke out into surprisingly tiny giggles. Setting him down again she slapped him playfully on the behind. "Now, let's see how fast Lexus man can scoot on back inside, okay?"

"Okay, you just watch me!" the boy hollered, as he raced off in a wide arc around the other kids to the door where he stood, jumping up and down, his finger in the air. "Number one! I'm number one!"

Toshika watched as the rest of the children went inside, then waved to the woman at the door who nodded, smiled at her, and mouthed the words to her: Are you coming in? Toshika raised a finger and nodded. "In a minute," she said. She stopped in front of Richard. "Hey, I've gotta go," she said. "This is my place, and my thing, and... I've just gotta go."

He fished after her eyes with his own.

"Okay?" she asked him. She turned and thrust her hands in her pockets. "We'll talk later," she called out to him over her shoulder.

He unlocked the front door and went inside, pushing the door closed behind him. The noise of a television surprised him.

"Tony?" he called down the hallway.

"Yep," came the reply. Richard walked to the end of the hallway and entered Tony's room. Tony sat in the corner, watching the local news on television with a beer in one hand and the remote control in the other which he rapped against his thigh.

"Hey," he said, leaning against the doorframe. "Not working today?"

"No." Tony replied, pointing the remote at the television, cutting the power. "Left early." He studied Richard's face. Richard stood motionless, not speaking. A smile slipped over Tony's face. He couldn't hold back any longer. "That your car out there pal?"

Richard broke into a wide grin. "Oh, you saw it huh?"

"Nah," Tony said, throwing his hands up in the air. "Like I'm not going to notice a *Ferrari* parked right across the street?"

Richard was already out the door heading down the hallway. "Come on!" He waited for Tony at the door, let him pass by, and then followed, watching him as he descended the steps to the street. Tony approached the car as if it were a wild animal that would dart away if he moved too quickly. He stood in the middle of their street and looked the car up and down and then turned suddenly, a comical expression on his face. "It's real! You're *loaded*, right?" he asked Richard, approaching him and then gripping him by his shoulders.

"Well, I didn't *steal* this thing," Richard said, nodding toward the car. Tony jumped into the air and grabbed Richard, lifting him off the ground, laughing hysterically.

"You're *rich*!" he cried. "You're set for life, do you know that, man? For *life*!" As fast as it had appeared, Tony's enthusiasm dried up and, with a quick glance at the new car, he gave Richard a solemn look. "But not if you go around throwing money away, right? I mean, come on, Richard. Don't *blow* it. This car – it must have cost..."

"It was 'a steal,' or so I was told. It was only sixty grand. The fact is, it's fairly well used, eighty thousand miles. That's a lot for a Ferrari, apparently."

"Okay, so sixty thousand gone. Just like that. Hey!" Tony suddenly hissed, guiding Richard off the street and onto the sidewalk as a car approached and rolled by. "So how much did you end up with, really?" Richard told him. He grinned upon hearing the figure and mouthed the words silently. "Okay, so sixty gone," he said once again. "Thing is, if you don't drive this too much it'll probably keep its value, assuming you didn't get ripped off in the first place. But listen, you've got to think now and be cool about this whole thing to make it last."

One thing Richard was not in the mood for right then and there was another long word of advice from Tony. He held the keys in front of Tony's face and shook them, then placed them in Tony's hand, silencing him. "Can you talk and drive at the same time?" he asked, walking around to the passenger side of the car and motioning for Tony to hurry up and get in. Tony got into the car and shut the door behind him and sank into the leather seat as one would into a hot bath. Gripping the steering wheel, he put the key into the

214

ignition and turned, grinning at Richard as the engine roared to life.

"Oh, man... What a *sound*. You can't beat that," he said, and then began examining the dashboard filled with waking gauges. "Where are we headed?" he asked. Richard pointed in the direction of the ocean.

"I'll tell you when we get there."

Soon they were heading south along California Highway One, tracing the ridge of the mountain range that ran all the way to Santa Cruz, about seventy miles down the coast. They didn't talk much on that drive, finding themselves in brief conversations before having their attention pulled into the sheer beauty of the surroundings; the sun setting over the water, bathing the waves of hills to their right in a golden light and casting long shadows across the brilliant road before them, spilling down into the valley on the left whose lights grew brighter as the world turned. In the months of solitude that came later, it would be one of Richard's fondest memories.

18

"Champagne, sir?" the stewardess asked. It was early afternoon. The flight to New York would take about six hours but they would arrive well before dark. Richard looked at the young woman's smile. Frighteningly sincere. But by then he had gotten used to things bizarre. The apprehension he felt upon waking up in the morning at the prospect of a trip overseas, the duration of which was uncertain, accompanied by two beautiful women that he had only recently met, had long since disappeared and he found himself floating through the day, detached and amused. Now he found himself in the front of a jet, in first class. He turned in his seat to get another look at the size of the interior of the plane. He hadn't been on such a large plane in his life. He marveled at how many people it could carry.

"Well," he said, taking two glasses and handing them to Toshika and Page before taking one for himself, "it had better be good."

The smile on the lips of the young woman did not falter. "It's Pommery," she said, turning the bottle to display the label. Richard raised his eyebrows. The stewardess nodded pleasantly before gliding on to the next passenger.

"Lovely," Richard said to his traveling companions as he raised his glass. "To first class," he said.

"Absolutely," Page agreed. "And thank you both for inviting me."

"Always a pleasure," Toshika promised, giving Page's knee a squeeze.

"I'm looking forward to Zurich, but I haven't been to New York for – what's it been? Nearly six months?" Page asked Toshika.

"Yes, when we went together for Todd's opening."

Richard caught Page's eye as she reflected on what Toshika had said. Today was the first time since the evening the three of them had had together that he had seen her. From the time that their limousine had arrived to pick him up at his apartment, he had been unable to notice anything different about her. But he couldn't help but feel like he owed her some kind of explanation. What he would have said had the opportunity arisen, he was not sure.

"That's right! Oh, now I remember," she said. She cringed at a memory shared with Toshika but not with Richard. "Poor Todd, though. What a disaster!"

"Who's Todd?"

"Todd is a spoiled guy who desperately wants to be a famous painter," Toshika said. "His parents are wealthy and they help him out. He doesn't pay any rent because his parents own his apartment, and they pay for his art school, and his private lessons, but they won't go much further than that so he's still under pressure. His first exhibition, in my gallery, was a total disaster. There were people who liked his work, but he had refused to price anything reasonably, so he didn't sell a single piece. And some of the clientele were annoyed with me, even though I had tried to convince Todd to be more realistic. That's what I get for being nice."

"You have an *art gallery*?" Richard asked.

"I'm one of the partners, yes. It's only a small gallery."

"Oh, well... then that's *different*, I guess."

"Hmm." Toshika forgot the comment as soon as it was made. "You'll meet Todd tonight."

"So tell me, what's the plan?" Richard asked enthusiastically.

"The plan is to go to Todd's party and have fun," she explained simply.

"Who's going to be there? I mean, how many people?"

"Oh, everyone will *be* there," Toshika said and looked at Page. "All of Todd's friends, I assume."

"And what happens at these parties?" Richard asked. Toshika stared at him a moment before answering.

"It's just a party! What do you mean?"

"Well, do people behave themselves? I've never been to the East Coast."

Page laughed. "No! Don't worry, it'll be *fun!*"

Richard noticed something wet on his leg and looked to see that he had spilled a few drops of champagne. The plane had begun what would be a long taxi to the runway. The captain's voice was heard over the intercom offering soothing remarks that Richard did not listen to.

"Good. That's what I wanted to hear."

"Oh, Richard, you're such a party animal," Toshika teased.

"You'll see," Richard promised her. Her tone of voice bothered him. There she was again, he thought, being a bit too blunt for his taste. It was as if she were talking to a stranger, and when it happened it made him look again for something to gauge her fondness for him. He hoped it was just because he didn't know her yet that well. He swallowed the last of his champagne and swiveled in his opulent seat as a small television screen emerged from overhead and began playing a short film about safety on board.

The plane had reached its cruising altitude and floated smoothly above the planet, its engines filling the cabin with a low, hypnotic murmur. Their champagne glasses long since collected, Richard, Toshika, and Page all sat quietly, their seats in supine positions. Richard had nearly succeeded in clearing all thought from his attention when he heard the whisper of a deep inhalation next to him.

"What were you doing out there yesterday?" Toshika asked him. "Out at the daycare center."

Richard turned to her. He was glad that she had been the one to bring it up. Perhaps it wouldn't have to be her little secret world to him after all.

"I was just out walking, that's all. I saw the school and saw you in there, so I went in."

"What were you doing walking down *there*?"

"I don't know. I called home and talked to my dad. Pissed me off. So I went walking."

Toshika nodded. "Is everything okay?"

"Yeah. It's nothing. So tell me now, what about you? That place?"

Her expression, devoid of emotion, slowly slipped into a grin. "Keisha," she said, with a look of love and affection normally reserved for mothers of such small wonders. "She's my favorite. They're all great in their own way. But she's my little peanut."

She looked at Richard suddenly as if she'd forgotten that he was there. His look of approval brought her back, but she was now monitoring herself again. "It's mine," she said, proudly. "Rainbow Kids Daycare Center. Free for local families who qualify. It's safe, clean and fun. Most of the parents are single mothers who wouldn't be able to have a normal job without it."

Richard nodded. "But, you said it was yours? You mean-"

"I bought the land and had the center built, with contributions and donations from here and there. About half of it my own. I had to contribute enough to be able to own it, so that I could control it. I wouldn't have wanted to let the city or a government agency have real control over it, you know. Close it down some day because of whatever reason. But I don't have anything to do with the daily operations. I'm there a couple times a week to see the kids and help out. And I keep it funded. "

"When you told me about how you spent your time, you didn't mention it."

Toshika shrugged. "Yeah, I know. It's just so predictable, you know? So comfortable and self-congratulating. People with money talking about their 'work' with charity."

"But, what's wrong with it?"

"Nothing. I just don't like to tell everyone about it. You know, it's not like I just whipped out my checkbook for this place. My name isn't Gates. This was a lot of money for me. Not a lot of risk, really. The land holds its value. But still."

Richard was struck at the idea of having the means to get something like that started. "It's great. You should be proud."

Toshika shrugged, then smiled at him. "I didn't say I wasn't."

As the passengers emerged from the plane and filed into the baggage collection area of JFK, one man, wearing large, dark sunglasses and a wide brimmed hat proceeded straight for the exit and was the object of envy by the few noticing him whose lives and schedules were held up until their bags appeared and could be collected. Richard, Toshika and Page were not among those who noticed him. Once through the double doors he passed by those waiting for loved ones and the men looking bored and holding signs bearing the names of their charges. He did not leave the airport, however, but instead took a seat in a densely populated waiting area adjacent to the exit. He sat with one arm propping the other up at the elbow, his fingers resting on the bridge of his nose and covering most of his face.

When a rotund neighbor of his stood up to fish a phone out of his pocket that had begun to ring, and then stood talking in a loud voice to his caller, blocking the man's view of the arrivals gate, he leaned forward and then backward in order to see around him, but it was no use. He shot the man an annoyed glance. The man lowered the phone.

"Oh, are you waiting for somebody?" he asked.

"Yes, as a matter of fact."

"Well, you won't see 'em so good hiding back here," he told the man.

"Yes, well, it's a surprise," the man told him as he rose to his feet and moved to another chair with a better view.

19

They arrived on schedule, collected their bags, and quickly found a taxi. Driving towards Manhattan, the setting sun turned the downtown skyscrapers into pillars of silver and gold, standing defiantly on the water's edge. Richard was filled with excitement, marveling at the sheer size of the city. Grabbing Toshika's arm, he chattered nonstop. "Where are we now? This is Queens? Hey, I'm in Queens! Where's the Bronx? What a name, *the Bronx*. Sounds so final. Sounds like a prison!"

They checked into their hotel, The Muse, on West Forty-Sixth, and immediately began to get ready for the evening. Toshika had reserved dinner at The Four Seasons days ago. Richard had insisted on eating somewhere "Big, like the Big Apple" and it was the only place she could think of. "We may be the youngest people there," she had warned him on the way over in the taxi. He did not seem to mind. In the end, she was right. Shortly after they had arrived and taken their seats he had felt it would be impossible to enjoy himself after Toshika told him that the place was a magnet for "powerful business people across the country." "So this is like a huge corporate canteen? How boring," he complained. But in no time, the three of them had established their own island, oblivious to their surroundings. Later, Richard had an idea and called the hotel, ordering a stretch limousine to pick them up at the restaurant and bring them to their party. Toshika and Page had said that that was not necessary, that a taxi would do just fine. "Come on, I'm loaded," he told them. "What do we want to take a smelly taxi for, anyway?"

The building did not look like much from the outside. Inside, the hardwood paneling and marble floors told a different story. The dinner had taken longer than they had imagined, making them late for the party. On the way there, seated comfortably in the back seat of the limousine between Toshika and Page, Richard had wondered aloud if they might offend Toshika's friend Todd with their late arrival. She had assured him it would be all right, reminding him that it was much better than arriving early and having to stand around waiting for the others.

As the three of them stood in the hallway outside Todd's apartment door, Richard whispered to Toshika. "Am I going to like it?"

Without looking at him she whispered back. "Yes."

"Is Todd nice? You said he was a spoiled brat."

Toshika corrected him with a sharp look. "I said he was spoiled. He's not a 'brat,' he's very nice."

They stood again in silence. Richard looked at his watch. Reaching in front of Toshika he pushed the bell once more. He looked at Toshika and began to lean in close to her before remembering that Page was there behind him. For the first time since they had left San Francisco he wished she were not there with them.

"Hey," he said softly to Toshika. She looked at him and smiled. He tried to find comfort in her eyes, but could see that she had other things on her mind. Whatever it was – the party, her friends, being back in New York – he could not know, but for a split second he wished that the two of them could abandon everything right there on the spot. That they could simply race out of the building and disappear some place far away. Things were happening too fast.

"Don't ditch me in there, okay?" he asked her.

He thought then that he saw surprise in her eyes, and then heard a thump at the door. He stood up straight as the door swung open. Before them stood a tall and very thin man. "Well finally!" the man exclaimed, hands on his hips in an exaggerated display. "We've all been *waiting!*"

"Todd!" Toshika cried, flinging her arms around his neck, embracing him warmly. He hated himself for it, but Richard could not help wondering if there had been something between them, and was immediately distrustful of Todd. When they separated, Todd looked at Page and smiled.

"Sorry to take so long, but dinner at The Four Seasons is never a small affair, you know," Toshika apologized. "Todd, you remember Page, right?" she asked him.

"Yes, of course I do! She's a wild one! Hi Page," he said, stepping forward to give her a kiss on the cheek. Upon hearing his voice a second time Richard felt at ease: the way he spoke, he just had to be gay. "And you must be Richard," Todd said. The two shook hands as Todd looked at Richard up and down. "Toshika has told me about you. Interesting guy. Maybe we can discuss the philosophy of art later?"

Considering his last talk with John, this conversation was something Richard wanted absolutely no part of. "Sure, why not," he said.

Standing in the foyer they could hear the chatter of many people over the music but could see no one. From the little Richard could see, Todd's apartment looked very posh. He was reminded immediately of Toshika's house as they walked into the kitchen.

"Nice place, Todd," he said, glancing expectantly around the room and then checking his watch.

"Thanks. Toshika recommended the designer. She has excellent taste, don't you think?" Todd said as he poured them all something to drink.

"Well, she chose me, didn't she?" Richard joked. Todd was unimpressed, turning to the refrigerator as he muttered something to the effect of it having been "the other way around." Still smiling, Richard was caught off guard by Todd's attitude and stole a glance at Toshika. Toshika's guarded grin flattened his smile and left him feeling hollow. What is it with her? Whose side is she on, anyway? Richard's sense of frustration turned to one of anger. As the four of them stood in the kitchen Todd began pulling things out of the refrigerator.

"I've got to make just a few more of these," he said, taking a basket of bread already sliced and deftly spreading some kind of cheese over them before placing them on a large tray.

"Oh, Todd, relax, won't you?" Toshika said as she stepped back into the foyer and examined a painting there. Worrying that this was ruining any chance he had of prying into her mood as they waited, and very much wanting to clear it up in his mind before they began mingling with the others, Richard moved to follow her. As he did, a comment from Page made him pause.

"Need some help?" Page asked Todd. Richard felt obliged to remain a moment, lending her offer his support. Todd simply placed one of the finished breads in Page's mouth and raised his eyebrows, awaiting a verdict.

"Mmm, excellent! What is it?"

"Can't tell," Todd said, waving a finger playfully in the air. He passed one to Richard, who dutifully took a bite.

"Very good," he said, watching as Toshika backed up slowly from the painting and then stepped back into the kitchen.

"Come on, I'll introduce you. Toshika, you know a lot of us tonight, I think," Todd said as he pushed through a swinging door that led into a wide hallway that brought them to the living room. Todd stopped at the entrance to the room and picked up a remote control unit from a small table standing against the wall, covered with candles. The volume of the music wound down to nothing, bringing the conversation to a halt. Richard, Toshika, and Page stood facing thirty or forty very young, vibrant people. After a moment the room was filled with the cheers of at least half of the guests as they recognized Toshika.

"Well, of course Toshika needs no introduction," Todd said to everyone. "But she has brought her friend Page, and their friend Richard. Page is a fashion designer, and Richard is a philosopher, so I'm sure we'll all get along just fine." Before he could turn the music back up, the doorbell rang. Todd handed the remote to Richard, as if it could not be taken from the living room, and went to get the door. He reappeared a moment later with a surprised and suspicious smile on his face. "Did anyone order champagne?" he asked, eyeing Toshika expectantly. Toshika's expression was blank.

"Yes, I did," Richard said. "I hope you don't mind. I wanted to contribute something to the party." He snuck a glance at Toshika, eager to catch her response. She seemed surprised, but he could not tell if she was pleased or not.

"Well, a case of Dom Perignon is some contribution! It's even *chilled*! Thank you!" Todd said. "Come help me unpack this stuff, will you?" He quickly took the remote from Richard and turned the music back up before the two of them disappeared back into the kitchen. There they began filling glasses and placing them on trays. Soon they returned to the living room, each carrying a tray.

"Champagne for everyone," Todd announced, as he and Richard began to move through the room. The champagne was distributed quickly and was thankfully received. Few students could afford such an indulgence. His tray empty, Richard looked around the room for Toshika. He spotted her on the balcony surrounded by several people. Page as well had found people that she seemed to know. He felt stranded and was about to approach Toshika and butt into her conversation when he found himself caught in the brown-eyed gaze of what Matt would have called a 'very squishy girl' who rose from a couch across the room and approached him.

"Hello, Richard," she said, placing her hand in his. "Thanks for the champagne."

"Oh, don't mention it," he said, warming up to her.

"I'm Rovna. I'm a 'struggling' artist, like everyone else here. Well, almost everyone. I attend the art school with Todd." She spoke with a noticeable accent that appealed very much to Richard. Her attention was exactly what he needed in the face of Toshika's odd behavior.

"What do you mean, a 'struggling' artist?" he asked, assuming for some reason that everyone who had any contact with Toshika would somehow be well off.

"Well, you know, getting money as an artist isn't easy. It's pretty hard sometimes to get by."

He nodded, then asked the question Rovna knew was coming. "Where are you from?"

"I'm Russian," she said, pronouncing the word with three syllables. "And *not* the daughter of a billionaire. Todd said you are a philosopher? Isn't that a bit strange?"

Richard stumbled on her comment, not knowing what to make of it. " 'Strange?' " he asked, "No, I don't know what you mean."

"Well, I have seen many philosophers, but none as attractive and well dressed as you. Most of them look like half crazy." She looked him up and down. "Does this woman here, the designer," she said, pointing with her nose to Page, "Does she make your clothes?"

"Page? Oh, no! But I have to admit, Toshika helps me sometimes. With clothes, I mean."

Rovna eyed him coyly. "Is she your lover, this Toshika?"

Richard answered with a shrug and a sweep of his hand. "Oh, I think you can see that she's a bit everywhere," he said, realizing at once the foolishness of his comment and then laughing at it in a poor attempt to cover it up.

"So maybe you're just having sex with each other, but nothing serious?" Rovna asked him. Her directness was surprising. He edged closer to her, looking for a hint of her scent.

"Well, you know. We actually met fairly recently, so..." He trailed off, getting lost in his words and urging himself to get it together. He noticed Rovna eyeing Toshika across the room.

"Well, you seem far more interesting than the man I saw her with before," Rovna said, watching Richard's expression carefully.

"Who was that?" Richard asked. It was a natural question, but he was not really sure he wanted to hear about it.

"Oh, I don't remember his name. It was about six months ago. I was pretty new here then so I was, you know, with wide eyes, looking at everything."

Her laughter was lovely, Richard thought, but then willed her to continue.

Rovna hesitated. "This was at Todd's exhibition. He had an exhibition, you know. Not very successful, but,"

"Yes, I heard about that," Richard said, impatiently. "And this guy you saw Toshika with?"

"Oh, yeah, well. Not very smooth, that guy. I think that man was a policeman."

"Really?" Richard could not believe his ears. "But why *him*?" he heard himself ask Rovna, whose shrug and blank expression reminded him who he was talking to. He nearly broke away from Rovna then to go question Toshika about Norton before deciding it better to wait for a better opportunity. Vowing to pick it up later, he smiled weakly at Rovna. "Tell me about you," he said. "Shall we go and sit down somewhere?" He hoped that she would suggest some place away from the others, but she merely turned and went to the same couch and waited for Richard to sit before taking a seat next to him, turning to face him as she did. She sat close enough that their legs were touching. They talked for some ten or fifteen minutes before Todd came by with Toshika and insisted that he give Richard and Page a tour of the apartment. Rovna placed her hand on Richard's leg.

"You had better go," she said.

Richard took her hand in his and stood, promising to return shortly, before rising and stopping directly in front of Toshika. "I met your friend Rovna."

To his delight, Toshika took Richard's hand before turning to follow Todd. "I see. She's Todd's friend, not mine."

The tour amounted to little more than a walk through the place with Todd pointing out and commenting on the artwork that decorated every room, nearly all of it being his own. He asked what Richard and Page thought of his own pieces. Standing in front of an erotic piece featuring a fully nude woman in a Christ-like pose, Todd clasped his hands together and whispered to Richard and Page.

"This one's called 'Love Goddess.' It's one of my favorites. What do you think?"

Richard looked again. The woman was striking, hovering in space with legs together and toes pointed, her arms spread out and upward in an arc above her head as though supporting a huge ball. In place of her head was a brilliant flash of light. Standing behind him, Toshika placed her arms around Richard's waist and nestle her chin on his shoulder.

"Beautiful," Page said, looking at Richard expectantly.

"Yeah, sexy, but... pure," he said, smiling at Todd encouragingly. Todd seemed thrilled.

"Do you recognize her?" he teased. Richard looked again at the painting but said nothing. "It's Toshika!" He said, placing his hand on Richard's shoulder. "She was my *model!*"

"Oh, yes. I see," he said, woodenly. He looked carefully again at the painting, his eyes following the curves created by Todd's brush, seeing easily now how it fit her. "Well, are we finished then?" Without waiting for a reply he pulled away from Toshika. "I'm thirsty," he said as he left them.

The evening dragged on for Richard and he found himself drinking glass after glass of champagne, and then wine when the champagne ran dry, in a doomed attempt to find some light beneath his confusion. Toshika's familiarity with so many of the others made Richard feel like a ghost. Eventually he avoided her altogether, preferring to spend his time meeting new people. He floated from one conversation to another, failing to make any connection. Even Rovna was no longer interested in talking with him. Finally Todd approached him, placing his arm warmly around Richard's shoulders.

"So, Richard, let's discuss your philosophy of art." Richard groaned and neatly slipped out of Todd's embrace, collapsing in a nearby chair. Todd pulled a chair over and sat opposite him. "Come on, now, I need your expertise! I'm having trouble with the concept of 'creation.' I mean, I prepared these hors d'oeuvres myself, but I wouldn't say that I *created* them. I simply put ingredients together from the kitchen and, well, here they are. With my art, I buy the paint, I buy the canvas, you know, but I want to say that I 'create' the painting that comes afterwards. So what's the difference between creating food and creating a painting?"

"Todd, don't waste your time. Forget about philosophy. It's just a bunch of ivory tower nonsense. What difference will it ever make?" Todd stared at Richard, surprised at what he had said. His mouth moved in silence as he tried to summon a protest. "Don't think so much about painting! Why don't you just paint? That's good enough, isn't it?"

Todd's shoulders fell and he fell back into his chair. "Yes, but, oh!... I'm just not making any money with my paintings. By the way, any of my paintings you see here are for sale, if you're interested," he added. Suddenly, he sat up straight and snapped his fingers. "Hey! What about the 'Love Goddess?' Why not buy the object of your obsession, Richard? Think of it: you *own* Toshika!"

Richard remembered the painting and belted the rest of his wine down his throat. "Who says I'm obsessed with Toshika?" Richard waited for an answer but Todd merely let on that perhaps he should have chosen a different expression. Since it was true anyway, Richard decided to let it go. There were other things on his mind. "So you painted Toshika. I mean, she stood there naked for you? How long did that take?"

"Oh, hours! But she didn't have to be there the whole time, of course. Only in the beginning to sketch her basic form," Todd said, sensing a growing interest in Richard and wondering how much he should ask for the painting.

"Where did you do it?" Richard asked.

"In my studio," Todd replied, indicating with a nod of his head the room at the end of the hallway. Richard then remembered having seen it on his tour. It was a large room with tall windows, filled with things one would expect to see in a painter's studio. Richard craned his neck to find Toshika, not having seen her for some time.

"Behind you," Todd said. Richard turned in his chair. Toshika was receiving dance instructions of some kind from a handsome man that Richard remembered having been introduced to. Mack, or Zack, was his name. He stood behind Toshika with his arm around her waist and his hand guiding hers in a delicate gesture. Richard swore at his weakness, at his inability to allow Toshika to be who she was, but was unable to stop himself. He wheeled around and clapped his hands.

"I've got it! I'll commission you to paint Toshika right now. Here, tonight," he cried, pointing his finger in the direction of Todd's studio. Todd's mouth fell open.

"Now? But there's no *time*. It takes far too long," he cried, a wave of his hand confirming the impossibility of the request. "Why don't you just buy the 'Love Goddess'? Don't you *like* it?"

"You can't see her face," Richard said. He refused to budge. "Just do *anything*. A sketch, whatever. How long would it take to make a simple sketch?"

"Oh, I can sketch her in ten, twenty minutes."

Richard leaned forward, pointing his finger at Todd. "I'll pay you five thousand dollars. Is that enough?" Todd was shocked.

"Richard, you're drunk."

"My offer is good!" Richard maintained, folding his arms over his chest.

Todd could not refuse five thousand dollars for twenty minutes' work. He got up and wrested Toshika away from Zack, pulling her over to the corner and holding her firmly by the shoulders. He spoke to her for a moment before giving her a hug and then turning and nodding to Richard. A moment later he followed Toshika over to Richard.

"Okay! She says okay!" he said, beside himself with the thought of a much needed sale. Richard was relieved, and happy to get Toshika away from the other guy, whatever his name was. Todd excused himself and dashed into the kitchen, leaving Toshika and Richard alone. Richard raised his heavy body from the chair and looked toward the kitchen, eager to fill his glass.

"You're drunk, aren't you?" Toshika asked him.

"It's a party, for Christ's sake!" Richard said, stepping backwards automatically and rather clumsily as Toshika leaned into to him and peered into his eyes.

"Don't you think five thousand is a bit extravagant for a sketch?"

Regardless of her comment, Richard could see that she was thrilled with the idea. Suddenly Todd was at his side, remote control in hand, squelching the music. "Okay, everyone! We have a treat," he announced. "Richard has commissioned me for a sketch, right now, of the lovely Toshika. So, come now everyone and watch the master in his element, making a creation far greater than the hors d'oeuvres."

Richard was speechless. Bringing Toshika into the center of attention was not at all what he had in mind. Now it was too late to stop the event without looking like a complete fool. Toshika walked toward the studio, slapping Richard on the behind as she passed him.

Todd put the music back on and followed Toshika. "Okay," he sang, merrily, "Here we go, here we go."

A few of the others followed Todd immediately, until, slowly, nearly everyone began filling the hallway and crowding the door to Todd's studio. Only Rovna and a few others remained. Richard was furious. He approached Rovna and took her hand.

"It's hot, isn't it?" he asked her, rubbing the back of his neck. "Why don't you come out onto the balcony with me?"

"Sorry Richard, but I think I'll watch. Maybe I'll learn something," she said, and joined the others.

Richard went outside anyway and stood in the warm, moist August night. He placed his hands on the railing and yanked on it with all his might. "Shit!" he spat. He turned and went inside again. He strode down the hallway to the studio, excusing himself through the crowd, pressing into the room. He went around behind Todd and stood against the wall. Toshika sat on a stool near a platform that was like a small stage in the center of the room, awaiting Todd's directions. Todd noticed the people crowding at the door and raised his eyebrows. Toshika turned and laughed at the scene at the door.

"Come on, everyone in!" she said. "There's plenty of room inside."

Richard grimaced. As the others filled the room, he found Rovna at his side. Todd was ready, and approached the white platform, asking Toshika to stand. He took the stool and placed it far off to the side before returning to his easel. "Take your shoes off," he called to her. She reached down and slipped her sandals off, standing a couple of inches lower without the aid of the heels. Todd went over to her and placed one of her hands on her hip, then turned her head to one side. He stepped away and looked at her, then returned to his easel. As he lifted the chalk to the paper, Toshika broke the silence in the room.

"Wait a minute, Todd," she said, "shouldn't this be a nude? What will these clothes look like in ten years?"

Richard's mouth fell open, then closed as he silently thumped the wall behind him with his fist. "Yeah," someone in the crowd said, "she's got a point." Others agreed. Todd glanced at Richard, whose eyes were glued to the tops of his shoes as he fought his urge to cry out for the event to be stopped.

"Brilliant," Todd said.

"It makes much more sense," Toshika said as she stepped back and unbuttoned her blouse, tossing it on the floor to the side of the room. She quickly removed her bra and tossed it aside as well, then reached behind her skirt and unbuttoned it. She slowly unzipped and let it fall to the floor, stooping to pick it up and toss it after the other things. In a final swift motion, she stepped out of her panties, pausing to look out over the crowd as she held them loosely in her hand. A young man, standing in the back of the others, hooted and clapped. Toshika's eyes narrowed on him for a moment before she turned and threw her panties out over the heads of the others at him, bringing cheers and applause from the partygoers. Leaning back against the wall for support, Richard groaned.

Toshika held her arms in the air and flexed her muscles triumphantly, stepping off the platform as she did and walking brazenly over to Todd's easel, lifting his wine glass from a table and taking a sip. "Okay, ready." she told him.

She took her place back on the platform, resumed the position Todd had placed her in, and turned to face him. Todd went to work on the paper, his hand moving rapidly in what appeared to Richard to be a haphazard way, as if he were carving Toshika's likeness out of the paper. Richard looked at the faces of the crowd as they watched, some with careful, studied expressions, others with their mouths open and eyes hungry. His eyes fell upon the man Toshika had been dancing with, who stood nearby, watching eagerly. As a wave of anger swept over him, he turned and strode from the room. Feeling trapped in the apartment, he went out once again onto the deck and closed the door behind him. He stood at the railing and looked out at the other buildings on the horizon before his gaze fell to the courtyard below. His body heavy, he slowly sank to the ground, trying to find comfort from the heat as he pressed his forehead against the iron rail.

When he awoke, the first thing he noticed was that his mouth was very dry. Then he noticed his head, or rather, a single point inside from which emanated a fierce, debilitating ache. He put his hand to his head, futilely rubbing his temple. Something was pushing on his shoulder.

"Richard. Richard! Come on, get up."

It was Toshika, her face full from sleep. "Oh, Toshika," Richard said, closing his eyes. "You're beautiful, you know that?"

Toshika shook him. "Richard, let's go!"

As he sat up he was shocked. First to feel the hard surface beneath him, then again when he realized that he was lying on the floor of the balcony. The sun had not yet emerged above the field of brick and metal around him but it illuminated the sky nonetheless in a faint, orange charge. Toshika waited for him at the door to the balcony, pulling her skirt up over her thighs as she did before groping for the zipper behind her. At the sight of Toshika dressing herself, Richard suddenly remembered the evening's events. He looked again to Toshika but she had gone. As he stepped inside the apartment, Richard was struck by the sight of bodies strewn all about the carpeted floor and sofas, most only partially clothed, some completely nude. None of them stirred. Toshika stood waiting for him at the far side of the room near the kitchen and beckoned Richard with her hand as he looked at her. He skirted the fleshy floor and followed Toshika out the front door into the hallway and caught up with her at the elevator.

"What was *that*?" he asked, his arm outstretched, indicating the heavy door of Todd's apartment. "Everyone on the floor naked? What happened? And where's Page?"

"She's asleep on the floor with everyone else. She'll be fine on her own, don't worry."

The elevator chimed and the door opened. Richard followed Toshika inside, his expectant expression unchanging. "What *happened* in there?"

"Well," Toshika began, "When Todd finished, people had become quite worked up, I suppose."

Richard looked at her blankly. "Finished what?"

Toshika shook her head, a smile that bordered on contempt creeping across her lips. "You don't remember, do you?"

He stared into space, searching. "I remember Rovna," he said, speaking as if pulling a distant dream back to life.

Toshika folded her arms across her chest. She began nodding slowly. "Rovna. Nice."

Then Richard's mouth opened as if he were a fish out of water. His hand went to his forehead. "Oh, god! The sketch! Todd drew your picture!" He drew in a sharp breath as the memories finally surfaced. He looked at Toshika then as if discovering a bad smell.

Toshika's head snapped upright and her eyes narrowed on Richard's as she answered him defensively. "I don't know what you were thinking, but your little 'project' for Todd backfired on you. It made everyone else happy, but you missed it. Why did you leave, anyway?"

"Why did I leave? Because I couldn't bear to watch! It wasn't supposed to be done in front of everyone, and it wasn't supposed to have been a *nude*! For Christ's sake, why did you have to *do* that?"

"Why did I have to do that?" Toshika asked. The elevator stopped moving. The door opened. "Why do I do anything? I did it because I felt like it. That's all. I *wanted* to." Richard opened his mouth to speak, but said nothing. "Look, if it makes you feel any better, I didn't do anything with any men up there, okay?"

Richard squinted at her as the door began to close again. Neither of them moved. "No? Well then who were you with?"

Toshika was not able to hide the faintest grin when she answered, and hoped immediately that it would serve to soften Richard and bring them back to peace. "Rovna."

Richard stood quietly for a moment before he watched his hand rise up. He pushed a button in the elevator panel, opening the door. He then motioned for Toshika to exit ahead of him and followed her silently out into the entryway of the building. They stepped outside into the cool morning air and surveyed the street.

"Why did you do that anyway? I mean, the sketch with Todd."

Richard took a deep breath and raised his head. "I felt lost and was jealous of all the people you were with." He looked at Toshika apologetically. "Where's the sketch?" he asked, realizing that for all the misery it caused him, he was leaving empty handed.

"He'll send it to you. Along with his bank details."

His head throbbed and his stomach was threatening him. Toshika could barely hear him as he spoke. "Okay. I'll see if I can get us a cab," he said, his voice merely a whisper. He stepped to the edge of the street and watched for cars. Toshika moved quietly to him and took his hand. "I did it because I wanted you for myself."

"Shhh. There's one, over there," she whispered.

Richard looked at her, then back at the street as he waived his hand to the approaching taxi. He raised his arm up and around Toshika's shoulders, pulling her closer to him. "Thanks."

20

Detective Kevin Ryan was sitting and staring into space above his computer when he finally heard his name being called from across the room. He sat up and turned toward the sound.

"Hey Ryan!"

"Yo!"

"Caller for you on line three, someone with information on your Swiss cheese murder."

The detective nodded, gave the thumbs up and picked up his phone. "This is detective Ryan."

An hour later Alan Porter and Derick Thompson sat in a small room at police headquarters on Bryant Street. Janet and Curtis Porter, as well as Derick's mother Mary, were present along with Detective Ryan and Detective Amy Lindstrom. The boys sat at the table in the middle of the room along with the two police officers while they stood against the wall with Derick's mother. To their great relief, after speaking to the police about what their son Alan had found, the police hadn't mentioned any interest in speaking with their son Leon. They were interested to note that in a short talk with each of the two families independently, both boys had volunteered that they got a very good look at the man who had dumped Hans Kienle's belongings on the sidewalk as he got into his car and drove away. Both boys had also described the events, including the appearance of the man they claimed to have seen, in very similar words and details. It was good news for the police on a case that had so far been difficult.

That talk had occurred about half an hour ago. They now sat together to be briefed on the next step in the investigation.

"Okay now boys," Amy told them, her voice firm but kind. "We have to split you up again. Derick, you and your mom are going to go into that room just through that door there with me, and Alan, you're going to stay here with your parents and Detective Ryan. We're going to see how good you are at recognizing faces, okay?" The two boys nodded. "We've got some pictures to show you, and we want you to tell us if you recognize anyone in those pictures." She stood up. "Okay, so Derick and Mrs. Thompson, please come with me." She carried with her a manila folder as she left the room, crossed the hall and opened the door directly opposite. Mrs. Thompson exchanged a nervous glance with Janet Porter, who took her hand and squeezed it once for support as she smiled and nodded to her.

With the door closed behind them Detective Ryan smiled at the three of them and then spoke directly to Alan.

"Okay Alan, here we go." He opened his own manila folder and took out a strip of film with photographs of six faces on it, each face about the size of a postage stamp. He turned it around to face the boy and placed it on the table in front of him. "Alan, I need you to just look at these people and tell me if you recognize anyone here. It doesn't have to be just about the event you told me about that night. It could be anything, or anyone. Maybe you know one of them from your neighborhood, or from a store nearby. I want you to tell me about anyone that you recognize, okay? Just tell me if anyone looks familiar at all to you."

"Okay," the boy answered. Alan looked at the faces of six men. He immediately felt sorry for them. These didn't look like school pictures. None of them looked happy to be there, wherever they were when these pictures were taken. In fact, they all looked unhappy. Some of them even looked mad. It occurred to Alan that these pictures were probably taken there at the police station. Any anybody who went to the police station to have their picture taken wasn't there for fun.

He didn't recognize any of the faces. He shook his head.

"No, none of these."

"Okay," Detective Ryan said, removing the piece of paper and presenting another one for him to examine. "What about these?"

Again, unhappy faces, but none that looked familiar.

"No, sorry."

"That's okay Alan, that's okay," Detective Ryan told him. "You don't have to know *anyone* here. You might not recognize *anybody*, and that's okay. Try this one."

Alan put his fingers on the corner of the next strip of paper to be placed in front of him and straightened it just slightly. Another set of unhappy faces. And then there was the man. The second one from the right. Alan put his finger on the table just under that man's face.

"That's him."

"That's him what?"

"That's the man who dumped that stuff. That's the guy."

Detective Ryan didn't look at the photos. "Are you sure Alan? It's important to be sure. Take your time."

Alan looked again, but it was easy. It was the guy. "Yeah, it's him."

The detective picked up the strip of pictures and held it to his chest so that the boy couldn't see them. "Okay Alan, now why don't you see if you can tell me if there's anything about that man that makes you so sure it's him? Anything at all you can think of."

Alan put his hands on his face and stared at the wooden surface before him where the photos were just moments ago. He took his lower lip in both hands and pulled down just a little, as he sometimes did when he was working on something hard at school.

"Well, not really. It's real easy to see that it's him, but I guess, you know, it's his eyes."

"His eyes?" Detective Ryan asked.

"Yes. That's what I know most."

Detective Ryan put the photos in his folder.

"Okay folks. I'm happy to tell you that we're finished here. I want to thank you all very, very much. Especially you, Alan. You've done a great job and I think you helped us a whole lot here today to find someone who's maybe not such a good guy." He extended his hand over the table offering it to Alan. Alan hesitated, smiled shyly and shook his hand. "Atta boy.

Great work." The detective stood up and looked at Alan's parents. "I'm sure you'd like to get on home, so let's go and get your coats and we'll say goodbye, okay?"

After seeing the Porters off, Detective Ryan passed Detective Lindstrom in the hallway on his way back to his desk. His eyebrows jumped up. "And?" he asked her.

"Bingo. No mistake about it."

He nodded. "Yep. Looks like we're onto something. I'll go put out the order." He went to his desk and sat down, his phone in his hands before his pants hit the seat. "Gary, hey this is Ken Ryan. We need to get David Norton in here. Yep, *that* David Norton. He's just been positively IDd."

21

It was almost noon. They had drawn the curtains completely. The room was still quite dark, but both of them had slept a good deal. They lay awake, each waiting for the other to speak, each hoping that neither one would break the peace that filled the room. Richard lay still, eyes closed, taking inventory. He was no longer drunk, or so it seemed, lying motionless on his back as he was. But his head hurt. He knew it would. This, at least, was something he could count on. Something he could feel certain of. It was simple. If he drank enough he would have a headache. It struck him then as a comforting thought, which would have been all right had he not had the immediate realization that it was, of course, quite an odd thing to find comfort in a headache. Or was it? Lying in bed with a headache made it quite difficult to be concerned about anything else. He would not fret about any of life's mysteries, nor would he occupy his thoughts with rumors of his own thrills, desires, or great hopes. He certainly would not entertain heartaches, self-doubt, or general worries. For nothing was worse than a headache that gathered so much momentum that it worked its way down, taking hold of his throat, and then his stomach, twisting as it did before shooting back up to his head, like the tail of a whip, wrenching more discomfort from his already suffering gray matter until his stomach took on a life of its own and began rocking back and forth like a boat lashed to the docks, struggling on top of angry waves.

All at once Richard sat up and tossed the cover aside. He leaped into the bathroom and hoped with all his might that it would be over quickly. Flushing the toilet, he got up from the floor and wiped the sweat from his forehead. "Fuck," he said quietly. "God." He looked at his reflection in the mirror before splashing some cold water on his face and brushing his teeth. He took a deep breath and, feeling better again save for his headache, returned to the bed. Toshika had not stirred.

Some time later, Toshika got up and went into the bathroom, pulling Richard from his light sleep. When she came out, Richard could see that she had showered and washed her hair. She wore a robe and slippers from the hotel. Her hair was neatly wrapped in a towel. She crossed the room and opened the blinds before taking a seat on one of the couches and picking up a magazine that lay on the coffee table.

"You drank way too much," she said without looking up, her sarcasm sounding nearly pleasant. Richard sat up in bed, propping himself up on the pillows.

"Yeah. I don't remember very much, other than my great, stupid idea." He looked at Toshika and waited for her to make eye contact with him. Eventually, he gave up. "I also remember being practically ignored the whole night by you," he ventured, anxiously. She lowered the magazine, a surprised look on her face.

"What do you mean? Every time I saw you, you were talking to someone. Most of the time it was a woman, or several women. I thought you were having a ball, until you got drunk and I could see that something was bothering you. And when we toured the apartment early on you seemed irritated with me, or with Todd, I don't know, so I thought maybe you wanted some space," she said, closing the magazine and placing it on the table in front of her. "If you were lonely why didn't you come find me?"

It was just the response that he had hoped for, but it also left him utterly baffled and completely unsure of himself, as well as of his view of the previous night and Toshika's behavior. He asked himself how it could be possible for two people to so totally misunderstand each other. Assuming she was telling the truth, how was it possible for him to get things so wrong? Did he lack some essential ingredient for understanding women? Or was it not about women in general, but about Toshika only? No, he told himself, this

244

was something that always happened, Toshika or no Toshika. He rested his chin on the palm of his hand and looked into her eyes, searching for the sparkle that had convinced him in the beginning that this was going to be special.

Toshika spread herself out on the couch, stretching until she shook. She folded the towel, placed it on the back of the couch, and stood up, removing her bathrobe and crossing the room to the bed, her dark eyes tracking him like gun barrels. She sat at the foot of the bed, her feet tucked under her behind, her hands on her knees. With her eyes, she pried Richard free of himself until he sat, his composure lopsided with half a grin and half a frown. Toshika scooted forward on the bed and laid down on her back, placing her feet neatly into Richard's lap. She reached under her head and spread her hair out behind her. Richard took her feet into his hands. He remembered their first meeting in the hotel bar. Remembered thinking to himself, 'Even her feet are beautiful.' He looked down at them, caressed them, examined the perfect form of her toes, of her nails, bare like they always were.

"I want to paint your toenails," he announced.

"You're going to make a mess."

"No, I won't."

"Have you done it before?"

"No."

"You're going to make a mess."

"Don't worry," he said pleasantly, "I'll pay for it."

"Okay, whatever you want. But call for breakfast before you start. Aren't you hungry?"

"After last night? Not particularly. My stomach feels kind of queasy. What about you?"

"Starving."

Richard reached for the phone. He dialed and then waited. "Hello, I would like to order breakfast for one, but coffee for two and an extra plate. Orange juice for two as well. That's fresh squeezed, isn't it? Good." He hopped off the bed and went into the bathroom. "Where's your nail polish?"

"In the medium-sized bag. What color do you have in mind?"

"I don't know. I have to see what you have." He came out a moment later, looking as pleased as a child with chocolate, a bottle of bright red polish in his hand. Toshika had moved to a chair in the middle of the room next to the coffee table. "Can't we do it on the bed?" Richard asked her.

"See, you don't know what you're doing." Toshika exclaimed, but still willing to allow Richard the pleasure he sought. "You need to be sitting in front of me and looking down onto my feet." Richard shrugged and settled himself down on the floor at her feet.

Breakfast arrived just as Richard had started on Toshika's second foot. He threw a towel over Toshika and held a finger up to her. "Don't you touch that now," he told her. "We aren't having any more displays." He held her under his gaze as he went to the door. Defiant, she poked her tongue out at him, nearly causing him to fall to his knees and confess his love for her. He directed the young man with the trolley to leave it at the glass doors of the terrace. He then asked him to open the blinds. Toshika, unable to get up while Richard worked on her, asked for a croissant. The young man happily obliged, taking the opportunity to imagine what the towel kept hidden. Richard called for him to inspect his handiwork, raising the foot he had already finished so he could get a good look, giving Toshika gooseflesh from head to toe.

"It's my first try. Did I make a mess of her?"

The young man assured him that he had done an excellent job. "Gorgeous."

Richard saw the man to the door, tipped him, and closed the door after him.

After doing her best to sample a bit of everything, but finishing only her coffee, Toshika got dressed and phoned Page, urging her to hurry up and get ready and to meet her in the lobby as soon as possible. "It's already one-thirty! The shops will be packed!" she told her.

Richard decided he did not want to accompany Toshika and Page on their shopping trip, and did his best to see what he could of the city, using a standard chauffeur driven sedan from the hotel to get him where he was going. He managed to see Central Park and several museums, including the Metropolitan Museum of Art and the Guggenheim, each one rather rapidly. He drove through Harlem, through Soho, saw

Wall Street, took the elevator up the Empire State Building, wandered for a few minutes in Times Square, even got a look at the Statue of Liberty from near the Brooklyn-Battery Tunnel. But eventually traffic got the better of him.

"We've hit a logjam, sir," the chauffeur told him. "We aren't going to make no progress now."

Richard looked out the window. "Where are we?"

"That over there is Lincoln Centa," the driver said, bringing a grin to Richard's lips.

"Lincoln Center. I've heard of that. What is it?"

"It's classical music heaven, that's what that is."

"Okay." Richard got out of the car and gave the driver a tip after telling him he wouldn't be needing him anymore. He figured he would find his way back to the hotel himself after this final stop. Once outside he realized that he was happy to see the pace of the day slow down. He set off for the area the driver had pointed to, checking his watch to make sure he would not be late for their flight.

Having spent the better part of half an hour wandering aimlessly around Lincoln Center, happily absorbing the scent of higher culture that hung in the air, he needed a break. It was nearly six o'clock. The August heat had subsided to some degree, but the fountain in front of Avery Fisher Hall held considerable pull as he walked by. He went to the base of the fountain, hoping to feel some relieving mist. Looming like cathedrals, with soaring stone pillars and vast sheets of glass, the Center's halls had been both inspiring and comforting, bringing Richard back to his days in the university. The air by the fountain was noticeably cooler, but thirst soon drove him to a place he had seen before, around the corner from the Julliard School. He opened the door to 'Pat's Bar' and immediately felt relief at the rush of cool air inside.

Letting the door close behind him, he stood and took the place in. The bar was very simple: dim lights, dark wood, soft classical music. He chose a seat near the end of the bar, next to a man who sat fully absorbed by a book that lay open, flat on the bar in front of him. Ordering a beer, Richard turned his back to the bar to gaze out the window at the people coming and going in the late afternoon summer's glow. He sat, studying faces, occasionally trying to imagine scenarios behind the expressions he found. A humming sound from the man at his side made him glance over at the book he read. He noticed it was in fact a book of music. Suddenly the man's humming – his 'da dee, da dum' – nearly unnoticeable before, made sense. Richard wondered what it would be like to be able to simply open up a book and hear music, and continued to observe the man for a few moments. His attention did not go unnoticed, however, and soon the man returned his gaze. The man smiled, took a sip from his beer, and then turned on his stool toward Richard. "Scriabin," he announced, nodding openly at Richard in a way that people seemed to do in this city.

"Sorry?" Richard asked, unsure of whether the man was introducing himself or his book.

"Russian composer," the man continued, hooking his thumb in the direction of his book on the bar. "Nineteenth century. *Brilliant*," he said, leaning forward for emphasis. He settled back into his chair and smiled. "Not a musician, are you." Richard hesitated, wondering if his guitar playing would count for someone who carried music in books. "Let me guess," the man said, thrusting his fingertips towards him with an excitement Richard found amusing. "You play guitar! Rock music!"

Richard smiled and wondered at the luck of his guess. "Yes. But not professionally. How did you know?"

"Ah, it's always a good guess. Every other young guy has a guitar, you know? Heck, even I used to have one. Long time ago. But I play the cello. I could walk around the city all day, stopping everyone I passed before I found another cellist. It's a little different."

Richard considered the man's comment. "Well, I don't read music, but I really love music." He glanced out of the window at the halls across the street and nodded his head at them. "Do you play there?" he asked, feeling fairly certain of the answer.

"Twenty years!" came the enthusiastic response. Richard cocked his head. The man did not seem that old. And twenty years of doing anything at all was longer than he could imagine. "Yeah, I started playing Lincoln Center when I was twenty-two. You may not know this, but this is a great country for classical music. So many legendary composers wrote for European orchestras that we sometimes forget composers like Bartok wrote the 'Concerto for Orchestra' specifically for the New York Phil," he said, pausing to catch Richard's reaction. "You probably don't know who Bartok is. Well, Richard Strauss premiered several of his famous tone poems in Chicago. Who doesn't know 'Zarathustra' from '2001: A Space Odyssey'? Kubrick knew his music, that's for sure. Don't ask me exactly when it was written, but it was written late in Strauss' life and is great fun to play if you have the chance. And the silent movie, 'The Thief of Baghdad.' Watch it sometime if you can. Rimsky-Korsakov's 'Sheherezade,' if you want to hear the real stuff and kindle a love of classical music. They cut it up badly, but greatness is greatness, and it'll get you dreaming about harmonic minor whether you know it or not. Another one to watch – oddly enough – and not just for Basil Rathbone, is the Errol Flynn 'Robin Hood' music composed by the Viennese composer Korngold in the thirties. Those were the good ol' days. Before modern music took over." The man smiled at the faces that rushed by, lost in the past. "Yes, twenty years and I still love it."

"Really?"

"Sure, when I get a piece I really like to play. Which isn't often enough, to be honest with you." He held out his hand. "I'm Thomas, by the way."

"Hi Thomas. I'm Richard. Why don't you just play the music you *like*?"

"Well, it's not up to me to decide what we play, first of all. I'm just one of the gophers," Thomas said with a laugh. He looked at Richard, and caught himself before he spoke again. He turned on his stool and joined Richard in gazing out the windows at the people passing by. "It's hard to explain," he said, examining the rim of his glass carefully. "You see those people out there? They have no idea what I do. Well, right here, at Lincoln Center, there are plenty of musicians, actually, so it's not a fair comparison. Some of those people know what I'm talking about because they're *from* here. They're part of this place. But anywhere else in the city, forget it." He nodded towards the window. "See them? That crowd there across the street is seeing 'Tosca' at the Met, and the Avery Fisher crowd is seeing an out of town orchestra.

It's not Chicago. They've got more sense than to play with those terrible acoustics, but it could be Philadelphia. I think it is Philadelphia. They like Avery Fisher for some reason, and probably can't afford Carnegie. See that man in the tux right next to the teenager with a backpack and baseball hat?" he asked leaning toward Richard and pointing with his beer. "You can get a sense for how seriously people take their music by how they dress for concerts, don't you think? And you see a lot of dressing down. At least at Lincoln Center. I don't know. I don't want to say that our audience doesn't take us seriously, but... There's only so much they can handle." He saw Richard's expression and sighed. "It's difficult to have a conversation about classical music with the man on the street, or on the bar stool, as it were. No offense, but how do you talk about whole tone scales without understanding what they sound like? You can begin, I suppose, by relating classical music to the movies, at least to illustrate that everyone loves classical music. But technically there is little common ground, as you have, say, in the visual arts. Everyone knows what blue is, or Picasso's blue period, or impressionism, but who knows what a diminished scale is? Or the fact that there are three of them mechanically and more than a dozen of them theoretically?"

Richard's blank expression proved the point. "I guess I don't know very much about classical music, but I'm surprised to hear you say that you have to play pieces that you don't like. I mean, don't you like all of it?"

"Do you like all rock music?" Thomas asked. Richard nodded, getting the point. "I guess you haven't yet been subjected to any modern composers," Thomas said with a wry smile. "If you don't mind my asking, what do you do?"

Richard sat dumbly for a moment, his eyes wide, his gaze unfocused. "I studied philosophy. I graduated recently."

Thomas clapped his hands together. "Oh, philosophy! Perfect. Well, let me explain. Do you know Schoenberg? He was an Austrian composer who died about forty years ago. Actually, he was Austrian-American. Maybe we haven't done the world of classical music any favors after all. Anyway, he stands as a 'great' composer for creating 'twelve tone' or 'serial' composition. Instead of employing traditional harmonic progress and extending the traditional system to new levels, like Stravinsky did, Schoenberg chose to discard ninety percent of all that had previously come to make up our traditional system of harmony, amassed over the last five or so hundred years, and put his new invention in its place. As though one man would ever presume to speak for so many artists, and decide that painters of music will no longer use blue and red," Thomas said, an air of contempt in his voice. "Oh, it's not his fault that it caught on, and that it completely took over the classical scene, but he did invent it, after all. Schoenberg and his disciples – Webern and Berg for example – have to bear some weight and responsibility for leading classical music, and more importantly academic music, in a direction that audiences have simply not been able to follow. You see, 'harmonic' minor is basically common to the ears of most listeners. It's no more than a simple natural minor scale, where the minor seventh is altered by raising it a half step. This is true for movement both up and down the scale. The 'melodic minor' on the other hand, depends on the direction, up or down, for its aural impression. From the fifth moving up, the mode is Ionian; down, the mode is Aolian. Simple stuff as you know from your guitar playing," he said, nudging Richard's shoulder. "Anyway, Schoenberg's system is totally different. Not 'natural' to the ear, if you like. And to the great loss of audiences everywhere, everyone who was anyone went along with it, including virtually every university. And they went lock, stock, and barrel too, seeing an opportunity to make music a science project rather than a reflection of what we call pop culture. For more than half a century you basically couldn't compose 'classical' music using traditional tertian harmony without being bombarded with ridicule from every quarter of the academic world. And the musical elite bought into it as well, making traditional composition for orchestra virtually taboo. It has regrettably been the academicians who have assumed responsibility for the training of classical composers. I know from personal experience," Thomas said quietly. "You see, I'm a composer as well as a player. But, that was a long time ago. My compositions were, how should I say it? Not encouraged.

"Well, anyway, audiences have never come to appreciate in any significant way music that has no tonal center. I mean, Richard, most of the stuff sounds like crap unless you're a pro. It's relatively easy for schooled musicians to appreciate twelve tone, or pan tonal music for its technical complexity, but for modern audiences, it's like asking that Avery Fisher audience out there to hear white noise for a couple of hours and then feel as though they had a magical experience! The average audience member just doesn't get it. I don't even understand how your Milton Babbits of the world even find an *audience*. He's famous, if you didn't know. As far as I can tell, it's mostly for his audience callback chimes at Avery Fisher, but famous in any case. Anyway, Milton is known to have said that the audience is not all that important a component in classical music anymore. He basically didn't care if they liked his stuff or not. Imagine that! His assumption was that they wouldn't understand it, so it basically didn't matter what he wrote, except as far as it was appreciated by his fellow academicians. I just wish he had taken it a step further and not written anything at all. It's not that I don't like the music, Richard. For a professional like me, it's often interesting. And it's often a technical challenge. It isn't easy stuff to play, so if you can pull it off, well, it can be something to be proud of. But we have turned our backs on the audience, and that's not right. I'll tell you, there is nothing I dislike more than having to play to an audience that doesn't at all understand or appreciate what I'm playing." With that, he raised his glass and winked at Richard. "Cheers," he said.

"Cheers." Richard sipped his beer and pondered whether or not to raise the question that had occurred to him about what Thomas had said. He was not a musician like this man was, and did not want to wade into an argument that would leave him out of his depth. But the thought would not go away. "What about artistic progress?" he asked. "I would imagine that composers wouldn't really be interested in writing music in a style that had been pioneered ages ago and had already been praised, ridiculed, and lived. Don't these artists naturally search for something new?"

"Oh certainly! Absolutely! Listen, the requirement that composers stop using tertian harmony is like asking a painter – didn't I already mention this? – to stop using certain colors. It's not a matter of recreating Bach. Nobody wants to do that. But why should we be told that we cannot use some of the same tools he used? Some of the same colors? That's what the issue is."

"I think I understand now," Richard said, glad that he had spoken up. "But then again, something else. I don't know, of course, but it seems that when you say that something is 'common' to the ears of your average listener, I'm not convinced. Isn't it a learned or acquired taste? Are we really just born with a certain ear that allows us to appreciate some sounds and not others? Maybe progress means chucking certain things out the window that we thought all along were essential." The man raised his eyebrows. "I'm just suspicious," Richard continued, "that's all. Suspicious of that kind of talk. It's like 'common sense.' Sometimes I don't think there is such a thing."

Thomas nodded. "That could be, Richard. Could be."

The two of them sat quietly for a time, watching the people go by outside until Richard placed his empty glass on the bar, paid, and said good-bye.

Detective Ryan somehow sensed that his phone would ring as he turned to stare at the receiver. Nonetheless, when it did ring, he jumped before picking it up

"Ryan,"

"Hey, Ken? Gary here. Listen, we got word on your David Norton."

"Yeah? Shoot."

"Okay, well he's in the big apple."

"What?"

"Yep, caught a flight out there on United flight 711 yesterday."

"Shit," Detective Ryan said, chewing on his thumbnail. "Okay, well, can you get on the phone with someone out there and let them know we need him back?"

"No problem. I'll get on it right now."

"Thanks Gary." Detective Ryan placed his finger on the receiver, killing the line. Then he let it go and hit three numbers. "Hi, Marsha. It's Ken Ryan here. Look, we have probable cause on David Norton in my Swiss chocolate case. He's left the state. We need a warrant today to get into his

house and go through it, can you handle that for me please?
Great, thanks a million."

22

The large Mercedes taxi emerged from the tunnel and followed the road along the *Limmat* River into the city. Richard watched as the pointed spires of a castle-like building just opposite the river appeared, sitting atop towers built from stone blocks. It was something out of a fairy tale.

"Wow," he exclaimed quietly.

"That's the *Landesmuseum*," Toshika said, her delight in seeing the city once again apparent. "It's a museum covering the history of Switzerland. I'll take you there, if you want."

"Sure," Richard answered, already occupied with the next point of interest. Coming directly from a city like New York, Zurich seemed small. Even tiny. As they passed by the main train station, the *Hauptbahnhof*, he was surprised at how small it looked.

"There are only about three hundred and fifty-thousand people living in the city," Toshika explained. "It's only half the population of San Francisco. But if you include the surrounding area, it's about a million people. That's not small, but Zurich never seems big."

Everything about it was different. It was on a much smaller scale, the streets were narrower, the buildings had a smaller footprint and were not so high, the cars were smaller, the people were more smartly dressed. Toshika had been right. The buildings everywhere were made of stone, giving the city at once a solid, fortified feel. And although many of them were old, none of them looked worn down; they looked as though they could have been erected only recently simply judging from the condition of the stone itself. It was a perplexing sight.

"Here's *Bahnhofstrasse*," Toshika announced as they crossed an intersection. "All the major banks are here, plus lots of jewelry stores, department stores. Lots of shopping, right Page?" Page nodded her head vigorously. Richard noticed the street had streetcars on it, similar to those in San Francisco, only smaller. Everywhere he looked, he was impressed by the look of quality, from the shops, to the buildings, to the cars, to the clothing people wore, to the clean streets. Everything looked so well organized.

"Everything seems so... so perfect," he commented. Toshika laughed.

"It's beautiful," Page said, visiting the country for the first time as well. In Europe she had only ever been to London, a European city whether or not the Londoners thought so, and to Paris. Richard winked at her, happy to have a traveling companion who was as fresh as he was to their new surroundings. Richard finally had time to speak with Page on the plane while Toshika slept and found himself liking her more and more. Page was just a nice girl, he thought. Nice, simple, and easy to be with. It occurred to him that if he had met her before meeting Toshika, things might have been different. It was an unsettling thought to have at the outset of a long voyage with the two of them.

Minutes later they pulled into the courtyard of their hotel, the Baur au Lac. The taxi stopped as elegantly uniformed men approached and opened the car doors. "*Gruezi mittenand*," they said. Richard simply nodded as he exited the car, unsure what language it was that the men were speaking. "*Gruezi*," Toshika answered. Richard saw that she spoke with what seemed to be a perfect accent, and gave her a questioning look that she failed to notice. He stood a moment by the car surveying the grounds. The property of the hotel sat close to the lake of Zurich, just on the other side of the street that ran along the water's edge. A sprawling garden lay between the road and the hotel itself. A garden of that size in a city where things had seemed so compact must have meant that this was a special hotel. Page stood at Richard's side, also looking at the garden.

"Come on, guys," Toshika called.

They checked in and went to their rooms. Richard and Toshika's room – a deluxe suite – was suitably large and very elegant. Not exactly Richard's taste, but he was in any case still thrilled to be staying in such luxurious accommodations. He was beginning to realize that very little that he had experienced since the game was to his taste and wondered if he would get used to it, or if he would return to his old ways and preferences. No, he thought, I was the way I was because that was all that I could afford. Things are different now.

He watched Toshika with amusement as she immediately began unpacking her bags, putting everything away nicely as if she were moving in. She noticed his expression as he stood in front of his own bag that lay unopened on the floor near the bed.

"We'll be here a good two weeks or so, so you might as well get comfortable," she told him. "Go on and unpack your things. Otherwise they'll look like hell."

"Oh, and I wouldn't want *that*. Not here, in the land of neat and pretty."

"Oh, shut up," Toshika said, "you American."

Richard began unpacking after he had discovered the chest that was meant to be his. Very fine. Antique, he guessed. Having fewer pieces of clothing than Toshika, and being much more cavalier in his attitude towards them, he finished quickly and took a seat. Toshika was taking her time, inspecting her clothing, going over each garment as if she were thinking of all the different combinations of outfits she could put together with them.

"So," Richard announced, slapping his knees. "Tell me about this place! I want to know something about where we are." Toshika turned to him, surprised that he had unpacked so quickly. "All unpacked," Richard assured her. "Go on, tell me. By the way, what language is that that they speak here?"

"It's Swiss German."

"But you answered those men out there so well."

"Well, I *speak* Swiss German," Toshika said, as if it were understood.

"Wait a minute, now. How many languages do you speak?"

Toshika paused and took a breath. "French, Italian, Japanese, and Swiss German. I speak some German, too, but not very well."

"So what is this 'Swiss German'? It's got to be a Swiss style of German or something. Is that right?"

"More or less. It evolved from old German, but a German standing on *Bahnhofstrasse* in Zurich would hardly understand a word."

"Really? It's that different?" Richard asked, surprised. Toshika nodded.

"Absolutely. Many of the words are similar, but the pronunciation is often totally different, and that makes the big difference. It's also simpler, with fewer words and a simpler grammatical structure. No past tenses, for example. And it's not a *written* language. The newspapers and books are all in German. At least," she added, "in this part of the country they are."

"But how did you learn to speak these languages?" he asked her, assuming that Swiss German was probably not taught back home.

"Well, I speak Japanese because of my mother, I studied French and Italian in college, and I speak Swiss German because I used to spend time here as a little girl. We used to visit Swiss friends of my mother's. I used to play with their children. We came almost every winter for skiing, and in summers too."

"So you just picked up Swiss German by playing with these kids?"

"Well, I was about four when we started coming here. Kids learn languages much faster than adults, you know. But you're right. My mother always said that everyone was impressed with how fast I learned to speak it. It was as if I had been exposed to it since birth, they said. I guess I'm just extraordinarily talented."

Richard's mind wandered from Toshika's mild attempt at humour and he thought about the main reason for his being there. He felt a twinge of apprehension. What if Jeffries made up some story about the rest of the money? What if something went wrong with the transfer?

"So, when do we open this account?"

"Tomorrow. First thing. We'll be at the bank by ten or so, and set you up. It wasn't easy to convince them to do this you know, now with the IRS breathing down their necks. You're lucky I've got so many good connections," Toshika said. She saw the concern in Richard's expression. "Why do you ask? Are you nervous about it?"

"Oh, I just worry that it might not go smoothly."

Toshika closed the cabinet, finished with her laborious unpacking. "Don't worry, my dear. Everything will be fine, you'll see." She closed the blinds, removing nearly all of the light from the room, and quickly undressed before climbing into the bed. "Come get me," she whispered.

The yellow Toyota taxi slowed behind the dark red Mercedes taxi as it turned right off of *Talstrasse* into the Baur au Lac Hotel. The passenger adjusted his sunglasses and put the window up.

"What hotel is that that my friends are going to? I forgot the name." he asked the driver, pointing at the Mercedes.

"That is the Baur au Lac Hotel," the driver answered.

"Right. Well that looks way too expensive for me, can you just bring me around to another hotel nearby here? I need to find a room."

"Well," the cab driver began, hesitantly, "Near the lake here, there will be mainly not cheap hotels." They turned a corner and headed along the lake before turning right and then right again. "Here, for example. This is Park Hyatt Hotel."

"The Park Hyatt? Perfect, take me there."

"But, it is not cheap!" the driver cautioned. "Actually, it is expensive one too."

"Okay, well then I guess I'll just have to get used to it."

The taxi drove into the driveway and stopped. He turned toward the man in the back seat to wait for his money. Having received his fare and a decent tip, he nodded.

"Do me a favor and wait just a second before you leave. In case they don't have a room for me. After a minute or so, if I don't come out, just leave, okay?" The driver nodded, and the man slipped out of the car and shut the door behind him. Inside the hotel, he hardly bothered to take the place in, proceeding instead directly to the desk. He was in luck. They had a number of rooms available. "Seven fifty a night? Jesus," he told the young, attractive desk clerk. "Better have a gold-plated tub in there. Does it *have* a gold-plated tub?" he asked. He eyed her blond hair, her hands. The young woman smiled and admitted that it did not. "Well, that's okay. I'll bet there's some good Swiss chocolate in the mini bar, isn't there?"

The woman blushed and nodded. "Yes, there is."

"Okay then, I'll take it. But only if *you* show me to the room. I don't need anyone else. Can you do that?"

"Oh, well..." the woman whispered something to her colleague and then handed him the registration form. "Yes, that's no problem. Please just sign here."

He signed the check-in sheet and then waited for the woman to come out from behind the desk to escort him to his room. He followed her to the elevator. Once inside, he was less jovial. He searched for words but truly hadn't any idea what to say. He imagined she knew what he wanted. It was so simple, and yet seemed very far off, beyond the range of what could be real in his life. Real for him. Finally the silence got to him and he forced his lips to move.

"What's a nice girl like you doing in a place like this?" he asked. Unable to make eye contact with her. He regretted what he had said instantly. The woman laughed, but didn't answer. She was no longer smiling. They finished the trip in silence.

After being shown to his room, David Norton went out onto his small balcony, rested his elbows on the railing, and looked out over the city, trying to find answers to questions that lay elsewhere. After many minutes he took a deep breath and let it out slowly. "What am I doing?" he muttered to himself. He had been tailing Toshika without thinking, like an animal simply following its instinct. Perhaps it wasn't really very much more complicated than that after all. What had he planned to achieve? What was the point? Would he confront her? No answers came to him. Outside, the world was calm. He looked toward Toshika's hotel but it was hidden on the other side of the buildings directly in front of his own hotel. Looking over their rooftops at the evergreens on the *Züriberg* to the north, it seemed a peaceful place. What he wouldn't give for a little bit of that.

A few minutes later he went inside and retrieved a bottle of beer and a shot of whiskey from the mini bar. He opened the whiskey and downed it, then drank half of the beer. He set the beer down on the cement floor of the balcony, went back in the room and dragged a chair outside, along with a bottle of champagne from his mini bar, and a glass. Sitting down, he proceeded to get himself very drunk. Later, when he awoke, he went back inside, closed the balcony door and began pulling off his clothes. He flopped into bed and was awoken the next morning when the maid opened his door at ten o'clock.

Both of them had been dozing for some time as the effects of jet lag asserted themselves. Toshika glanced at the clock on the night table and rose from the bed.

"Richard, get up," she called over her shoulder as she entered the bathroom. "Have to get ready for dinner." Richard stretched, not sure at first if it were morning or evening. As he swung his feet over the bedside the events of the day flashed before him, bringing him up to date.

"Zurich," he said. "That's right." Waking up in one new place after another felt exciting. He went to the window as Toshika called to him from the bathroom.

"Shall we have a *Cüpli* before dinner?"

"A what?"

"A *Cüpli*. A glass of champagne."

"I think I'm off champagne for a while." New York was only a day old, yet it seemed to occupy a place in Richard's past ordinarily reserved for much older memories. Only his reaction to the mention of champagne served as evidence to the contrary. "Toshika," he called, unsure if he really wanted to ask the question.

"What?"

"Remember Rovna?"

"Yes, what about her?"

"She said you were with a policeman the last time she saw you." Now he had done it. He had begun the questioning of her past. Toshika emerged from the bathroom and began removing clothes from the chest.

"Right," she said, "At Todd's exhibition. That was David."

The name hit Richard like an unpleasant odor. "David Norton?" he asked, his face screwed up. "Why would you have gone to New York with *him*?"

"He wanted to go to the exhibition," Toshika said, as if it were perfectly natural.

"And you *took* him?"

Toshika pulled her blouse over her head and pulled her long hair out, tossing it onto her back and looking in the mirror on the inside of the chest's door. "What could I do, Richard? *Refuse?*" The strength of the word brought to him a picture of an awkward scene between Toshika and Mr. Norton.

"Well, you could have made something up." He left the window and walked slowly across the room towards the bathroom. "I mean, it's not like he's your *buddy* or anything, is it?"

Toshika made a noise, mocking the question, before answering. "Yeah, sure, they're *all* my buddies."

"There wasn't anything between you, was there?" He stopped at the door, placing a hand on the frame. Toshika looked at him in a way that told him what a silly question it had been. Better quit while you're ahead, he thought. His hand fell from the door frame. "Sorry," he said, and stepped into the bathroom. He turned the shower on and then called out to Toshika. "Hey, let's have that champagne after all."

They were seated at a table in the middle of the large room amidst the buzz of laughter and the clatter of silverware against porcelain that was the same in any restaurant. Richard felt again like a new man in his splendid clothing, and sensed that he fit right in. The restaurant interior was a mixture of white walls and dark, heavy wooden beams; the ceiling a mass of ancient wood. The structure itself, according to the date carved in the stone above the doorway, was from the seventeenth century.

Richard looked across the table at Toshika and Page after they had been given their menus and were left alone. "I love it!" he said to them. He looked around once more. "It's great! So old, and rustic."

He looked at the people sitting in the tables all around them, observing the differences to the way people looked back home: the style of clothing, the care people obviously took in preparing to leave the house, the hair styles, the jewelry that the women wore that, although not flashy or grotesque, nevertheless were noticeably more expensive than what any woman would wear at home.

"So far, I have to say that I really like it here," Page said, looking at Richard for his own opinion.

"Well, so far, I agree."

"Switzerland is a great country," Toshika said, "After traveling around other European countries you come to appreciate their stability and orderliness."

"The Swiss are known for being very efficient, aren't they?" Page asked her.

"Yes," Toshika admitted, her tone indicating that she held a different opinion. "The trains and streetcars and busses run on schedule, unlike what you'll find in some other places, but trying to buy a ticket in the *Hauptbahnhof* is another thing."

Richard laughed. "How many times have the busses run on time in San Francisco?"

Just then their waitress approached the table. After they had ordered and were waiting for their food to arrive, contentedly snacking on fresh bread and drinking wine, the conversation turned to what lay ahead of them.

"First," Toshika began, "How about Italy? Just over the Swiss border is the *Lago di Como* – the lake of Como. Beautiful. We *have* to go there. We can take a train and be there in a few hours. From there we can go into Toscana: Florence, Pisa, and Lucca. Lucca is small, but so charming. You'd love it. Does that sound good?"

Richard exchanged glances with Page and shrugged his shoulders. "Fine with me." Page nodded in agreement. "As far as I'm concerned, you know the place, so I'm perfectly happy to let you decide where we should go," he told Toshika.

"But don't you want to go to Greece? Go do some walking in Socrates' footsteps? See if the ghost of his brilliance rubs off on you a little?" Toshika teased. For a brief instant, the idea struck a chord in Richard's heart.

"No, I don't need to go there. But if you say it's a must see, then I'm all for it. Like I said, you call the shots."

After dinner they went to a local bar where they drank and talked. When they finally left, it was well past midnight. They walked quietly through the streets that meandered as if carved out over time from use rather than having been created according to any kind of plan. As the three of them went, they commented on the building dates that had been either painted or engraved on the homes and other structures that lined the streets, marveling at the sense of history invoked by them: 1749, 1632, 1271. Upon recognizing the Bar au Lac, Richard drew the back of his hand across his forehead.

"Home at last! All that walking has made me sweaty." They all agreed that it was still amazingly warm out. As the doormen greeted them, Richard turned to see Toshika walking away, out into the gardens of the hotel. He and Page followed. When they were deep into the green Toshika turned to Richard and Page and pointed at something.

"Come on! The canal!"

Richard and Page soon joined her, standing at the edge of the garden overlooking the *Schanzengraben* canal that bordered the hotel grounds. A rowboat was docked on a small landing just beneath them. Given the night's warmth, the water was enticing.

"Let's go for a swim!" Toshika said, as she stepped around the railing bordering the canal and descended the stone steps to the landing. Before Richard or Page could respond, she began to strip, tossing her clothing in a pile.

"Let's go!" Richard said to Page, taking her hand and heading for the steps. They joined Toshika on the dock below the garden. Richard looked around them to see if they could be seen. He saw no one, but heard voices up on the bridge just beside them.

"Come on!" Toshika hissed at them. "There's nobody around!" Moments later, the three of them stood naked on the landing. As Richard was about to ask who would go first, Toshika grabbed his hand and leapt into the water.

Page clasped her hands together and stood on the landing, anxiously. "Is it cold?"

264

Richard quickly swam back to the landing. "Freezing!" he cried, as he vaulted up the steps and grabbed her, pulling her with him into the water.

"Oh!" she cried, wiping her eyes and treading water. "You liar! It's nice!"

They laughed and splashed each other in the moonlight before climbing back onto the landing. Page was in the rowboat in an instant, grabbing the oars and doing her best to get the boat moving. Richard and Toshika joined her after Toshika had set the boat free. They rowed clumsily against the current, bumping into the concrete walls along the way that formed the foundations of buildings on both sides of the river. When they had traveled a good fifty yards they heard voices and looked up to see faces looking down at them from a room on the ground floor of the hotel. It must have been some kind of party room. As Toshika and Page laughed and waived, more and more faces from adjacent windows appeared and began calling encouragement down to them.

"Shit!" Richard cried, "Let's get out of here!" He took the oars from Page and began putting his back into it, managing to get the boat headed home against the cries from the windows for them to stay. *"Nai! Da bliebe! Da bliebe!"*

When they had safely reached the landing, they drew themselves up against the stone wall and looked into the moonlit night, waiting for the wetness to leave them.

"Do you think anyone will come out here?" Page asked, getting up and going up a few of the steps to get a look out over the garden.

"No," Toshika said, "we're not back home. We're not going to have fourteen people come running out here to see some boobs." The three of them laughed as Page returned and took her place against the wall. They laughed like children over Toshika's choice of words, their laughter building upon itself, rising and falling and rising again, as the joke shifted to one of laughing at the sound of their own laughter. When they were finished, sitting above the water catching their breath, massaging their aching stomachs, their attention was once more drawn skyward.

"Who believes in UFOs?" Richard asked. Neither Page nor Toshika said anything.

"I don't believe in anything I haven't seen," Toshika reported. The others looked at her briefly. Richard looked back into the night as he spoke.

"Do you believe in love?" Page turned to look at Toshika, apparently waiting for her answer.

"Of course I do."

"Really?" Page asked her. Toshika gave her a funny look. "No, I'm serious. Sometimes, I wonder." Richard regarded Page with surprise. What did she know about Toshika that he didn't? The thought made him realize how little he probably did know in comparison to Page.

"Don't be silly. Of course I believe in *love*. I wasn't talking about love, or about things... intangible."

"But love is tangible," Page said. "I certainly feel it."

None of them spoke as each tried to imagine what the other was thinking. Finally Richard couldn't bear it any longer. "Love, shmuv," he said, "What about UFOs?"

"A friend of mine said she saw one once." Toshika said. "She was in the mountains. She said at first she was surprised and excited, but then it was frightening."

"Why?" Richard asked her.

"Because she thought: who are they? What are they going to do?"

"And what happened?" Page asked.

"Nothing. It came flying along, stopped, stayed there a minute, then left. That was it."

"I thought I saw one once," Richard said. "Also in the mountains. I was with my dad. We went camping, the whole family. I was probably nine or ten. He and I had gone for a walk one night and I saw this thing and I tried to show it to him – there were lots of stars that night – and he didn't see it. It wasn't there very long, and he just didn't see it."

"Is that all?" Toshika asked him.

"Yes, that's all that happened, but I remember thinking that he was going to be mad at me when he didn't see it, and I kept saying 'But I saw it! I saw it!' I thought I'd be in trouble. But he wasn't mad at me at all, and I remember thinking, why can't I figure him out? Why, when I think everything is cool, does he go berserk and get mad out of *nowhere*, and other times when I think he's going to kill me for something, he isn't bothered. He just says 'Ah, it's okay.' I could never figure him out."

Toshika stood up and picked her clothing out from the pile of things that lay on the stone. "We should get going."

The next day Richard and Toshika left Page behind and headed out early. The sun was shining and the city was busy. They went to a small private bank where Toshika had an account of her own and, quite quickly, it seemed to Richard, opened an account for him. They had arranged that he would telephone Jeffries later that evening to give him the necessary information. With that taken care of, Richard left Toshika alone with the account manager so that they could discuss her account together. Toshika told Richard he should go wander outside, but he preferred to wait for her in the bank. He was shown to the lobby, where he chatted with the receptionist who spoke perfect English and wore jewelry of a quality that he was certain he would never have seen on any receptionist back home. He wondered how she could have afforded it. Was she really paid that much? Did she have a rich husband? He stole a glance at her hands and could see that she wore no wedding ring.

"So, how are things in California?" she asked him.

"Oh, fine, I suppose," he answered, unsure just how to handle such a question.

"Is there a noticeable change there, now that the housing bubble has broken?"

"Popped."

"Sorry?"

"You said the bubble has 'broken,' but we would say that it has 'popped,'" Richard explained. "A bubble doesn't break, it pops."

"Oh, pop," the woman said, actually pleased to have learned something instead of finding his comment rude or picky. "Thanks."

"Sorry, I shouldn't have mentioned it. Your English is excellent. Amazing, really." The woman was pleased at his compliment and thanked him. They talked about the dire situation back home, the woman responding in a way that made Richard realize that the suffering back home hadn't really touched them there very much in Zurich. He thought of asking her about it, but was silent instead.

"Have you been to California?"

"Oh yes, a few times. I love San Francisco, and Los Angeles."

Richard resisted the impulse to ask how anyone could love Los Angeles and settled for a knowing nod instead, something that gave him an instant feeling of betrayal that he found curious. Just then a middle-aged couple entered the room. The receptionist excused herself and tended to them. Richard occupied himself with the various magazines on the table before him until he heard Toshika's voice as she approached with her banker, Hans Peter.

They spent the rest of the day wandering the old quarter with Toshika enjoying herself explaining historical odds and ends. That evening, as they readied themselves for dinner, Richard made his telephone call and was relieved to find no argument on the other side about the transfer.

"How long should that take?" he asked Jeffries.

"By the end of the day tomorrow your bank should be able to confirm the transfer," he told him. "If there's a problem, just call me."

Richard thanked Jeffries once again and passed on Toshika's regards to him. Hanging up the phone, he turned to Toshika and smiled. "It's done."

"Great. I knew it would be easy," Toshika said.

"Yes, well all I have to do now is check with the bank here tomorrow to make sure."

"Good. You ready?" she asked him.

"Yes."

She paused at the door and turned to look at him. Her somber expression slowly melted into one of relief as she smiled, happy to be there with him. "I'll be out in a minute. Then we can go," she said.

Richard went slowly to the couch and sat down, lifting a magazine and flipping through the pages that advertised the paradise of being a tourist in Switzerland. Toshika's voice echoed from the bathroom.

"Why don't you make yourself useful and go see if Page is ready? I'll meet you both in the lobby, okay?"

Richard jumped up, happy to have something to do. "Sure," he told her. "Don't be too long." At the door he turned and saw the key on the table. He thought to remind her to take it with her, then simply turned and left the room, closing the door behind him.

23

They moved silently through the traffic over the bridge towards Bellevue. As he looked out the window of the cab over the lake, with the air so clear that the Alps seemed to emerge right out of the water, he squinted at the diamond-like reflections off the surface of the water lit by the golden sunlight of the evening. Suddenly he was reminded of home. It seemed funny to him then that the sunlight alone could link this place, distant and different in almost every imaginable way, with his home. He saw the blue triangle in his mind and the gaily-colored houses that surrounded his own bathed in this light, the light that stopped time. It occurred to him that he was not feeling the least bit homesick. Having verified the success of the bank transfer some days ago, he had quickly built up a certain momentum and had no plans to go back any time soon. Every day that came and went left him eager for yet another, far from home, fully immersed in the world.

Time was passing quickly. He was not sure what day it was and had to remember that Toshika had said earlier in the week that the party would be on Friday night. Already one week. He gripped her hand tightly but kept his gaze fixed on the passing scene. Here, people walked in the evening, feeling the earth beneath their feet. Not necessarily to get to somewhere. There were always a lot of them by the lake. The water had an effect on people. Like the sea, it was a place to sit and be reminded of one's hopes. Like the light, it too stopped time. A healing force.

They went around Bellevue and up *Rämistrasse*, past the *Kunsthaus* and up into *Züriberg*, passing private homes that in their stone construction looked as solid as medieval castles. "*Nächshti links, un den ishes tsershti huus raachts mit em grosse Tor.* Next left and then it's the first house on the right with the big gate," Toshika said to the driver. In a moment the cab passed through an open gate and entered a horseshoe driveway in front of an impressive house made of stone, as so many of the others were. Richard paid the driver, and then the three of them made their way to the door where they rang and waited.

Toshika had warned Richard against making the kind of gesture with the champagne that he had made for her friend Todd in New York. "Why not?" he had asked her. "Because nobody would do that." He did not really care, because he in fact had not planned to do anything of the kind, but was curious nonetheless. "Don't the Swiss do something extravagant from time to time?" he asked. "Of course, but to do what you did, to call attention to yourself by making a big splash at a party where you don't know anyone, that would look ridiculous here." Richard was not aware that his goal had been to draw attention to himself. He had merely told himself that it would be a nice thing to do and an amusing way to spend some money. Hearing Toshika's interpretation, however, he knew that she had been right about his motives, and the fact that she had seen through to them when he had not was annoying. He wondered what Toshika's own reaction to his gesture had been, knowing now that she had seen it for what it was, but he was not up to asking her, not wanting to hear her tell him that she had found it 'ridiculous.'

The party was being given by an English banker Toshika had met some years back, Rupert Sims. She had warned both of them that this was not going to be another wild party. "We'll probably be the youngest guests there. I hope it isn't going to be boring for you," she told Richard in particular, "but I don't think it will be."

When the door opened, he was surprised to see a man who appeared to be not quite forty, healthy, tall, and, something he never liked of Toshika's male friends: handsome. For some reason he had expected someone much older. Hadn't Toshika said that he was the director of a bank? Isn't a director someone old and gray?

Toshika and Rupert exchanged the customary three kisses on the cheek before Rupert gave Toshika a hug and held her back at arm's length to comment on how lovely she looked. Toshika introduced him to Page and Richard.

After greeting Page very warmly the banker turned to Richard. "Richard, I'm Rupert. How nice to meet you, do come in," he said, shaking Richard's hand firmly and with the kind of confidence Richard imagined the director of anything would exude. The four of them stood briefly in the foyer, Rupert smiling at Toshika and Page as if waiting for them to speak. Behind Rupert was a second, rather large foyer that led into several different directions. Directly at the rear of this second foyer were large glass doors leading into a garden behind the house, where they could see the other guests enjoying the warm weather. The house reminded Richard of the Victorians back home with its high ceiling adorned with fancy trim. Suddenly, a woman appeared from behind their host calling his name. She was very attractive and wore what Richard would have called a racy red dress. He hoped that this was Rupert's wife, as if being married to a beautiful woman would restrain a womanizer.

"Peggy, dear, look who's arrived," Rupert said to her, taking her hand and presenting her to the three of them.

"Toshika! Fantastic to see you!" the woman said as she and Toshika embraced lightly. When they had all met each other, they went to the back of the house and through the open doors out into the garden. A little over a dozen people were gathered on a large pebbled area just outside the house with beautiful wooden garden furniture including a splendidly adorned dining table. To the side was a large table with chilled bottles of water, soft drinks, beer, wine and champagne. Red wine and numerous liquors were present as well. The other guests were impeccably dressed, and rather older than Richard and the women. As it happened in New York, those who knew Toshika well came immediately to greet her, exchanging again the trademark kisses. Observing this, Richard realized that it seemed most of these people were in fact Swiss, as Toshika spoke to them in their mother tongue. Richard was about to slip around the throng of people hovering around Toshika and casually stroll about when Rupert spoke to the group.

"Everyone, let me introduce Toshika Tamura, whom a few of you obviously already know, and her friends Page Jenkins and Richard Peel. They've come from San Francisco."

Richard would have been happy to have left it at that, but immediately the other guests approached and introduced themselves to Page and to him. He hadn't understood many of their names, forcing the first two to repeat themselves before giving up on the rest. Finally, he stood alone with Page. The two looked back to those they had just met and tried to recall some of the names, but with little luck. Richard could only remember three names. One name he did remember was that of a Frenchman, Philip Boureli. Philip was very tall and had an iron grip. He was instantly likeable and made a joke about being 'another foreigner,' putting Richard at ease. He was just about to ask Page if she wanted something to drink when a hand gripped his shoulder.

"Well, you've suffered through the Swiss inspection line, how about something to drink?" It was Rupert. "Page my dear, what can I get you?"

"A glass of white wine would be nice," she suggested.

"Would you like that white wine to have bubbles in it?" Rupert asked, pouring on the charm.

"Oh, no thank you."

"Richard, what'll you have? A beer?"

"Yes, that would be fine, thanks."

"Very good then, be right back. Make yourself at home." With that he was gone.

"He's extremely pleasant," Richard commented to Page in a low voice. She laughed and put her arm around his shoulders, hiding her face briefly in his neck. Something in him stirred as he felt the warmth of her breath on his skin.

"This is fun, isn't it?" she sang into his ear.

"Page, come on now, I'm spoken for. Besides, you don't want these people to get the wrong idea, do you?"

Page laughed again and took a half step back, looking Richard in the eye this time. "And what 'wrong' idea is that?" she asked him.

"You know perfectly well what wrong idea I mean," he teased. "I mean the *right* wrong idea."

Page looked over Richard's head and spoke to him quickly. "Tall French hunk coming," she said, putting on a smile.

"So," he said to both of them, "Richard, you're a lucky man to be here in such beautiful company." When he finished he nodded appropriately to Page, who blushed, and, for the first time since Richard had known her, looked as though she were unable to find words.

"Yes, well, some guys have all the luck," Richard replied. "Philip, how long have you known Toshika?"

"Oh, not long. A few years, I guess. We met through Rupert, you know. On my boat." Richard nodded, and was about to ask where they had been sailing when Philip spoke again. "So tell me Richard, what is your job? What are you doing?"

This was no longer the awkward question it once was, having been called upon already several times during the week to explain it. "I'm working for myself. Asset management, primarily, but I plan to perhaps open a business soon as well. Restaurant, for example. I'm not sure."

"Ah, another banker," Philip said with a very bored expression that was obviously just teasing.

"Well, not exactly. I'm only managing my own assets."

"Ah, I see. A rich boy," he said.

"What do you do?" Page asked Philip.

"Well, I'm an *older* rich boy. But really, I'm a sailor. I sail a couple of boats, take the people out, sometimes for a weekend, sometimes for much longer. It depends."

Rupert brought them their drinks and remained briefly, joining in the conversation's laughs but saying nothing, eventually departing to other guests and greeting a few others who arrived late.

The evening went very much like that, as could be expected. Since many of the guests were involved in finance one way or the other, in many cases the discussion turned to speculation as to what the markets were likely to do next, and what one should do in the case that they behaved this way or that. When he was asked his own opinion of the markets or of currencies, Richard did his best to appear knowledgeable by simply commenting that it was a difficult time and that he was simply waiting now for a clearer picture to emerge. This tactic worked well, and he laughed to himself more than once for being praised as having the 'right instincts.' Although he had no knowledge of the subject, he of course was quite interested, and was happy to hear what the others had to say.

Soon they were called to be seated for dinner where the conversation continued along the same lines. Eventually the discussions moved into more personal directions: what one did in one's free time, what travel plans one had made. It was all very pleasant. Richard sat near the head of the table across from Toshika, with Page on his right and Philip on his left. He found it exotic to be seated at the dinner table of a private party where one pair spoke German, another French, another Italian. He was very pleased, wishing people at home could have seen it. He marveled at Toshika as she switched from Swiss German to French to Italian and to English with ease. He felt particularly drawn to her when she spoke in a foreign tongue, as the mystery of those enticing sounds combined with her beauty to create the most tempting kind of lure.

When the first course was brought out to them, Rupert rose and held his glass aloft. "Thank you all for coming, lovely to see you all again, especially those of you who have traveled from far and wide to be here. I wish you all good health and, especially in these times, a speedy return to wealth. No, no, just kidding. No, we've all had a good run, and while we're certainly a bit shocked at the recent events in the markets, I for one am sure that we are just experiencing a much needed correction before once again shooting off to the stars!" There was laughter all around the table. "Those of you who are my clients, I meant every word of that. The others of you, well you know I'm just full of hot air." Once again, laughter. Philip warned Rupert against shutting his mouth lest he rise up and float away "like a balloon of hot air."

"Anyway," Rupert continued, "Enjoy the food and drink and the lovely weather while it lasts."

With the toast completed, there followed only the very briefest of hesitations before people found their feet and the murmur of conversation returned. Richard had the feeling that Philip was in a sour mood, even though he had spoken to Rupert lightly. His feeling was confirmed when, halfway through the first course, Philip was asked how the sailing was going. "Oh, it's very well. Very well. I was in Morocco a few weeks ago. I stopped into a small port to let one of my clients off who was suffering a bit from seasickness. I saw the poor little children there, in this tiny village, with nothing. It is really terrible, that they are so poor," he said. "We are all so very lucky," he continued. "We should not forget about it, instead of feeling sorry for ourselves now." The others said nothing, feeling their way carefully around the awkward silence that Philip had brought upon them.

"I'm not feeling sorry for myself," Rupert told Philip. "Not at all. But I know that everyone will gain when things turn around once again. We'll all benefit, rich and poor."

"That's right," another agreed.

"Yes," Philip said, nodding. "Especially the rich. Especially us."

The group strangled the sentiment and the subject with their silence. When it was long dead, someone commented about the latest film to hit town, and things returned to normal. The meal proceeded from then on without a hitch, and everyone, including Philip, seemed to enjoy themselves. Some two hours later, after the dessert had been served and eaten, one by one the diners began to stand and stretch their legs. Richard followed Toshika over to a tall tree that stood near a small pond in the wondrously landscaped garden. She went to the tree and placed her hand on its smooth bark. She turned when she heard him approach. He took her hands and leaned forward against her lightly. She rested the back of her head against the tree and looked up into the darkening sky.

"No stars yet," she told him.

"Oh, but there *is* one. I have to tell you something," he said, bringing his forehead just inches from hers, unable to contain himself any longer. He looked into her eyes, searching them for any sign that would give him a reason to keep his mouth shut. "I love you," he whispered.

Because he still had her eyes in his own gaze, he saw it before it could be taken away from him: the light inside, the spark that told him that if she did not love him as well, she was at least happy to have received his love. The light was there. He had seen it. But it was fleeting. In an instant her gaze fell, and the space between them grew as she straightened up and then turned her head to one side, searching.

"Richard," she pleaded. The tone of her voice indicated not a total rejection, but merely an alternative. "I'm having a great time with you, and you know... I didn't expect this to happen. But don't complicate things, okay? Let's just keep enjoying it. Keep enjoying ourselves. Let's just not forget what this really is, all right?"

Richard raised his head, his eyes wide. "What do you mean what this 'really' is?" he asked, trying to keep his voice down. Toshika merely smiled. "What?" he repeated.

"It's just a game Richard, come on. And anyway, you know I told you I'm not ready for this kind of thing yet."

"What are you *talking* about?" Richard cried, unable to stop himself from laughing. "Of *course* it's just a game! Everything's a game! We don't know what's going to happen tomorrow, we don't have any guarantees. *Life* doesn't have any guarantees, but so what?"

Toshika held him in her eyes, a doubtful expression on her face as though she intended to disagree with him. Then she tilted her head and her doubt melted into something else. "Well, so we don't try to solidify things! 'I love you' turns into 'I need you' and then 'You're mine!' and then... Then we just lose in the end."

Richard did not know what to make of things. Part of him was joyous at the thought that Toshika was with him, wanted to be with him, wanted to protect things as they were. But part of him so badly wanted to hear the words come back to him. To be electrified by them. He could not conceal his disappointment, but began to persuade himself that all was not lost, and that he should perhaps see things as 'so far, so good.' As having a future. He held her and turned her around, taking her from the safety of the tree. Behind her he could see Philip coming. He had been jealous of Philip's ruggedness, of his accent, of his certain power over women. He cursed his inability to simply act himself out of his emotions as Philip affectionately wrapped a brawny arm around Toshika's neck.

"Who's that?" Toshika smiled. "Philip? *Ah, tu nous as trouvés.* You've found us."

"*Oui, un bon marin trouve n'importe quoi.* Yes, a good sailor can find anything. Hello you two," he said, patting Richard on the shoulder with his free hand. He saw at once things had been tense between the two of them. "Richard, how are you treating our lovely Toshika?" he asked good-naturedly. Richard could not answer, his mind blank. Philip turned Toshika so he could look her in the eye. "Toshika, how are you treating our Richard?" he asked, again with a disarming mock suspicion. As much as he wanted to dislike Philip, Richard could not maintain anything so unnatural against him. Toshika turned to look at him. He repeated his last thoughts of Toshika to himself, feeling a weight leave his shoulders. He returned her look and smiled.

"Oh, Philip," he said, "she's treating me very fairly. I just hope I can make it last."

The Frenchman threw his head back, laughing heartily. "That is what we all want, isn't it? Keeping the love going, eh?" he said, gripping Richard's shoulder firmly and shaking him. Richard found himself grateful for Philip's use of the word. "Ah, but it's not easy!" he continued. "It's definitely not easy, yes? Like a sailboat, you have to keep praying for just a *leetle* wind. Just a *leetle* wind." Philip released Toshika and pointed her towards Richard, like a father giving away the bride. Toshika put her arms around Richard and kissed him. With that kiss, and Philip's encouraging grin, Richard didn't give his feelings of love another thought. All he had, and all he would ever have, was now. And now he had Toshika, and she wanted it that way.

Philip stood with them for a moment before turning to see that the others were heading inside. Rupert stood at the door and turned, waving when he spotted them. "Philip!" he called. "Come now old boy and show us that film from your latest voyage you've been telling us all about, will you? Richard, Toshika, come on!"

Philip raised his hand and nodded, then backed away from Richard and Toshika, telling them with his eyes that they would now be left alone to enjoy the garden's peace. Not wanting Philip to feel that they had no interest in his film, Toshika looked at Richard and nodded towards the house. "Come on," she said, "Let's see what this is all about." She took his hand and gave it a gentle tug as she stepped away from him. As they followed Philip, Richard noticed for the first time the sharp crunching of pebbles beneath their feet. As they retreated along the path, Richard was struck by the intensity of the moonlight, casting shadows of them all against the landscape. He glanced up and behind himself, into the moon that glowed so brightly. It was nearly full.

24

The day after their dinner party the summer weather in Zurich abruptly turned around, as it often does. A beautiful summer day turned into a raging thunderstorm. The sky grew dark, the wind began to blow. Then came the lightning and the rain. Fierce winds blew until the early morning. The next day, the skies couldn't have been clearer. From the balcony at the hotel the mountains to the east behind the lake appeared to spring from the shore, causing tourists to mass on the shores of the lake, furiously snapping postcard pictures.

Toshika and Page began to run as they saw their tram pass them by, heading toward its next stop about fifty meters further down on *Bahnhofstrasse*. David Norton swore and tossed his cigarette into the street as he reluctantly began trotting after them. This wasn't ideal. It was harder to remain invisible when you were running. There were too many people on the sidewalk to run through them, so he swerved left into the street as Toshika and Page had. Luckily, they made the tram easily, allowing him enough time to linger behind just enough so that he could be the last one to enter the tram before it set off again. This wasn't ideal either. Being with them on a tram increased the chances that they would spot him, sunglasses and big hat or not. Luckily they sat in the back of the tram in the last pair of seats. David stood directly behind them with his back to them.

"So. You getting any ideas yet?"

"Toshika, I think I need to get off *Bahnhofstrasse*. There are only big names here. I can see that anywhere."

"Okay. Well, I know of a few shops that might be carrying smaller, or maybe even local designers. But first let's go to the train station to get our tickets."

"Okay."

"Are you having a good time?"

"Sure." Page took Toshika's hand. "I'm glad we're getting to spend some time alone."

"Yeah, I know. But Richard's been fun too."

"Toshika, I *really* want to go to Paris."

"We'll go, don't worry."

The tram stopped and they got off. David Norton followed them, but at a very safe distance. If they were going to the train station to buy tickets, he wouldn't need to be very close. They were at once at *Bahnhofplatz* directly in front of the station, waiting to cross. David stopped where he was and allowed the women to cross. In the middle of the street was an island with a tram stop. Pedestrians crossing to the train station had to wait there for a second light, while traffic heading in the opposite direction passed. When Toshika and Page were safely on the sidewalk David followed. Entering the cavernous station, he spied them immediately heading towards the ticket counter on the other side.

In recent years the ticket office had been completely renovated, with the original 1871 structure being joined by a modern extension and housing a travel bureau and a few restaurants. Despite having spent many millions and a few years to complete, the ticket office was still a throwback, with one queue per ticket window causing needless delays. David entered the line for the window next to the line that Toshika and Page had entered because it was longer by at least two people. He could observe them from behind more discretely. As he waited, he took out his Blackberry and checked his email. There were three new mails waiting for him. The sender of one of them leapt out at him: San Francisco Police Department. He glanced up. Toshika and Page had moved forward a step or two. There were four people in front of them. He opened the mail just as his own line advanced several steps. He hesitated. He would now be directly alongside them. He turned around. Three people behind him. He went to the back of the line. He looked down and scanned the email, quickly zeroing in on the punch line. '...requested to appear in person at the office of the headquarters...Detective Kevin Ryan... If you fail to contact the officer in the unit named below within 24 hours of this date, a warrant for your arrest will be issued.'

David Norton felt his neck and head grow uncomfortably warm. "Shit," he whispered, putting the phone away and checking the position of Toshika and Page.

Two people in front of them.

He thrust his hands in his pockets. What to do? He looked at the clock on the wall above the ticket windows. It was a little after 10:00 am. Too early to call back home. Advancing a few steps to within three people of Toshika and Page, he took his phone out again and began writing an email as quickly as he could.

Hey Bob, hope you are doing well and that McCormack is staying off your ass. I need a favor. I am being requested to appear downtown ASAP. I'm in a bit of a bind right now, could you let me know what this is about? Take care, Dave

As he hit the send button he put the phone back on standby and put it in his pocket. He looked up and then back down at his shoes as soon as he saw them. Toshika and Page had just turned around, facing him briefly as they left the window, tickets in hand. How the hell did they do that so fast? Did I take that long to punch out that email?

He waited a few seconds and then left his place in line and headed straight for the same window. He removed what looked like a wallet from his pocket, and pulled the silly hat from his head as he did. He placed a hand on the shoulder of the woman who had followed Toshika and Page and was speaking to the ticket officer.

"Excuse me, this is police business," he said to both the woman and the man behind the glass. He showed them his police badge, held in a leather cover. "I'm with United States police, department of the city of San Francisco, California. Sir, I need to know where these two women are headed with the tickets they just bought from you."

He turned and pointed to Toshika and Page, who were just 30 feet away, exiting the ticket office. He quickly removed his sunglasses, having forgotten that he had even been wearing them. He looked into the eyes of the man behind the glass and kept his police badge against the glass. The man's mouth had fallen open. David began to wonder if the man hadn't understood English when he closed his mouth and leaned slightly towards his microphone.

"Those two ladies are going to Aix en Provence, sir. Wednesday morning at nine-twenty."

David frowned. "Exxon what?"

"To France, sir. To Aix en Provence, in the south of France." He pulled a ticket envelope from a stacking file on his right. "Here, let me write it down for you."

In mild embarrassment David Norton turned to look at the woman whose ticket purchase he had interrupted. She was blond and fit. She looked slightly alarmed, but smiled faintly as if the episode had somehow struck her as being rather exciting.

"What lovely eyes you have," David told her, smiling confidently. He turned to receive the envelope that had been slid under the glass. His voice was now more forceful. "Thank you very much sir," he said with a nod of his head. "Excuse me ma'am," he said to the woman, his sunglasses now back in place. He left the ticket office quickly, and continued to walk briskly until he was outside. A line of cabs sat waiting at the curb. He entered one and threw his hat onto the seat next to him.

"You speak English?" he asked the driver, whose bull neck and crew cut did not fit David's image of what a Swiss cab driver should look like. The driver turned in David's direction. The broken nose profile completed the picture.

"Yes."

"Good. You got any casinos around here? Someplace where I can gamble?"

The driver hesitated. "Yes, but... closed now." His Eastern European accent was lost on David Norton. "They open tonight."

"Yeah? Okay, then in that case, the Park Hyatt please. They got a bar that's open all the time."

The driver faced forward and hit his turn signal. "Okay."

Richard found himself at the hotel unsure whether to be annoyed or worried. Toshika and Page had gone off on their own for the day, leaving him to find his own amusement. He had spent the day looking for, among other things, a book on investing, to begin educating himself on how to properly care for his money. Not used to shopping for such subjects, he had been surprised at the mild embarrassment he felt handing the book to the cashier at the large English language bookstore on *Bahnhofstrasse*.

He had been waiting in the hotel room for over an hour. There shouldn't be any reason to worry about them, he thought. This was Switzerland, after all. Toshika knows her way around. After calling the front desk for the second time and asking if they still had no message for him from either Page or Toshika, he decided that he had had enough. He would go out and find a restaurant alone. He took his book with him and left the room. Perhaps it would be nice to make an evening alone of it, he thought. In any case, he left a message for Toshika and Page at the front desk that he had gone out and that he would try calling later at the hotel for them.

It was still early for most people to go out for dinner. At the restaurant that he finally settled on, specializing in Swiss food, the lack of other diners meant that he could eat and read in peace. He opened the thick, hardbound volume and laid it on the table. The world, the book began, was an apple waiting to be plucked, if one knew what to look for. The problem with most investors, according to the author, was that they did not take the time to learn about the markets. Instead, they just dove in, and often lost money. Careful planning and some studying were essential to come out ahead. By paying attention to events that had ripple effects in the markets, and by anticipating those effects, one could effectively 'time' the markets, buying low and selling high. That was the secret. Although he had given Hans Peter the authority to make investments without his consultation with a portion of his account, Richard found himself looking forward to giving his own directions to buy and sell. To try his hand at this game.

By the time he had finished eating, the restaurant was filling up. With people came noise, and he found it difficult to concentrate. Besides, having finished his dinner, he now felt useless to the proprietors, taking for himself a whole table. He paid the bill and left. He had not gone far when he saw a bar and decided to stop in. It was a small place with a bar big enough for only eight or ten patrons. Opposite the bar were several booths where one could eat. Seafood was the specialty. Only one booth was occupied, and there were only two people at the bar. He took a seat in the middle of the bar and took out his cell phone to call the hotel. The phone in his room rang and rang. "Come on." He asked for Page's room. Also no answer. There was still no message from either of them. He put the phone away and watched the bartender. Seated against the wall, two seats over from him, was a man talking quietly with the bartender. It seemed they knew each other. He ordered a beer and opened his book, his eyes automatically finding the exact spot where he had left off. How did that work? He hadn't recalled where he had been, but his eyes knew. With that thought, he began to read, his mind setting itself once more to the task of absorbing a subject matter that was alien to him.

"What's he saying these days?"

He looked up from his book and looked straight ahead. As he was serving someone at the other end of the bar, the comment had not been directed at the bartender. There was only one other possibility. Why can't I just read my book in peace? Do I look like someone who wants to be bothered? Finally the silence made him turn to the man, who sat grinning, waiting for a reply. He looked Indian, seemed to be in his forties, was casually, if not sloppily dressed, and was otherwise unremarkable. Except for his eyes. Dark and piercing.

"Excuse me?"

"Mr. *Boros*," the man said, jabbing his finger at the book. "What's he saying?" He spoke with a British accent. It was faint, but there. Richard looked at the open book before him, wondering how to answer the question.

"Well, I've only just started reading it. I'm new to this sort of thing, actually."

"Really?" the man asked him, as if this presented him a significant opportunity. He again pointed at the book. "You're wasting your time with *him*." As if it could defend itself, Richard looked again at the book, and then back at the man. A smile spread across the man's face. He held his breath. "I know what you're thinking," the man continued, "Who am I to disagree with him!"

This was exactly what he had been thinking. He waited for the man to continue, but he simply smiled, his piercing gaze boring into Richard. Is that all? He nodded to the man in an effort to elicit his thoughts, but the man did not speak. The exchange was proving to be a waste of time. Richard reached for his beer and drank. When I set this glass down I am going to excuse myself and return to my book instead of having a staring match with this very strange man. He placed the glass on the bar and opened his mouth to speak when he was cut short.

"My name is Ravi Singh," the man said, offering his hand. "Call me Ravi."

"Hi. I'm Richard. Are you going to tell me why I should not pay this author any attention, or do you want me to guess?" he asked, annoyed at having been drawn further into the conversation.

"How about if *I* guess? You work in a bank, probably in trading or in sales, and you want to learn the secret to 'making it big,' am I right?"

"No," Richard replied flatly with a curt shake of his head. Ravi did not seem surprised, but did look a little disappointed.

"What do you do?"

"I'm into asset management."

"So I was *warm*," Ravi said, smiling. Then his eyes focused sharply on Richard. "But you said you were new to this!"

"I manage my own money. Or, I should say, I've recently come into some money, so I'm reading this book in order to find out what to do with it," he said, realizing he had nothing to lose.

"Well, where *is* this money?"

"In a bank."

"Doesn't the bank have someone who can manage the money for you?"

"Yes, but I do want to have some idea myself of what's going on. And I'd like to do some of my own investing."

"Ah, I see." Ravi sat quietly, evaluating Richard's situation. Richard was again impatient.

"What have you got against him?" He pressed, closing the book and pushing it towards Ravi, as if its presence would pry the words out of him. Ravi pushed his drink forward along the bar and stepped off his stool, taking the one next to Richard.

"Let me tell you something, my friend. Listen to me now, and listen carefully," he said, leaning forward, his eyes taking hold of Richard, a look of deadly seriousness on his face. His manner struck Richard as arrogant, even comical, and he immediately felt he would never trust a word Ravi said. "I have been in this business for a long time. Maybe longer than you've been alive. I know more about making money than anyone in this town!" Richard could not suppress a smile. "I'm serious!" Ravi protested, keeping his voice low and glancing around the room quickly. From where he sat he could see everything. "I'm serious," he repeated. "You can ask anyone." Just then he looked over Richard's shoulder and waved his hand. Richard turned to see the bartender approaching.

"*Ja Ravi, vas votch?*" the bartender asked him. The Indian man answered to him in English, pointing at Richard. "Tell this gentleman that I know what I'm talking about when it comes to money."

The bartender looked at Richard suspiciously, as if he had caused his friend trouble. "Mr. Singh is the *best*. If you want to know about investing, you listen to him."

Richard smiled at the bartender and nodded. "Okay, thanks for your advice." The bartender looked at Ravi and nodded, having put the young troublemaker in his place. He gave Richard a last look and stepped away from the two of them.

"You see?" Ravi asked Richard. "Listen to me, man."

Richard spoke quietly. "I should listen to you because the *bartender* said so? Is that it?"

"He said that because I manage his money. He has firsthand experience of my ability. That's what I do. I manage private clients. Never all of their portfolio – I don't want that much responsibility. I never take more than half. Of course, the client can always lie and tell me he has only given me half, but the principle remains. And, I never work for the wealthy. They don't need any help. Everyone is falling all over themselves to help them anyway, setting up 'family offices' to help the super rich. Whoever helps the common wage earner? Nobody, that's who. So *I* do it. I go only by word of mouth, and I never take a percentage fee like all the crooks out there. Flat fees are the only way I work. Same work, same fee," he said, now holding a defensive posture. "You think that because the man is just a bartender that he doesn't know anything? Huh? And what makes *you* so clever? You inherited some money and now you're something special? You're American, right? You graduated from university and that makes you better than a bartender?"

Although Richard felt that Ravi's attitude was more theater than true feeling, he did not like the way the conversation was going. "No, that's not what I think. I said that because I don't know him. But I don't think I want to discuss it with you anyway." he said, politely but firmly. "I think I'll just finish my beer and go."

"Wait," Ravi said, the smile returning to his face. "Listen to me now, listen. As I said, I've been doing this for years. I've worked in a lot of banks doing a lot of different jobs. Where are you from?"

"California."

"Hey! Far away from home, aren't you? Mr. Surfer, huh? Do you surf?" he asked Richard, his expression now one of near glee. Richard could not believe what he was seeing.

"No, I don't surf."

"Oh, so it's not true that all Californians are surfers?"

Richard laughed. "No, of course not!"

"Well, I was born in India, but was raised in London. That's where I started my career as a banker. But let me tell you, having dark skin meant that I had to start out as a lowly clerk on the trading floor, running around with order slips for the traders. There was a real hierarchy there back then, you know. It's probably changed now. Now that the Americans have spread their 'political correctness' halfway around the world, removing the human touch and turning everyone into a typical phony American that you meet at a party who says 'Hey, call me some time!' and when you call them they're all excuses. Politically correct. It's half good, half bad. Anyway, I don't want to complain about that," he said, showing Richard the palms of his hands. "The British can be very racist, let me tell you. I wasn't good enough for the likes of them. It worked this way: the more bent your accent was, the lower down you were. Of course, my accent wasn't like the others. They could tell that I was properly educated. Oy dint tawk loik, ya now, eh guv, roit? No. It was my skin color that forced me to work alongside those blokes, the traders. And then they had the 'gentlemen,' the Oxford types, working as stockbrokers. In the equi-tehs, old chap," he said, his fingers to his head in a crisp military salute. "The blue blooded club, that was." He shook his head slowly at the thought of it. Richard was starting to like him. "Eventually I became a trader myself. A couple of years later I met a Swiss woman, and left for Switzerland. That was, let's see," he said, surprised at his conclusion. "Nearly seventeen years ago! Boy, how time flies. Well, *here*, things were different. I was still a trader when I came over, and did that for several years, but eventually I moved into equities myself. And from there," he said, his hands spreading out from his sides, "everything."

"And you just learned all of this on the job?"

"Yes. Well I had to! I was thrown into it. I had studied mathematics in the university. One of my many interests. But it didn't help me much on the job."

"You still haven't told me why I shouldn't read this book," Richard reminded him. Ravi gave the book a long, cold stare, and then waved it away with his hand. He laced his fingers together and looked Richard in the eye. When he spoke again he spoke slowly and carefully, pausing between sentences to allow Richard to keep up with him.

"Let me tell you something my friend. Listen to me now. The market is like a living, breathing animal. It's not a robot. You want robots? Look into any big bank. Look at the best of them: UBS, Merrills, Goldmans – you name it. There's where you'll find your robots. You see, this is a Western game. They approach problems from a Western point of view." He leaned forward. "They say 'We have sixty-thousand CFA's working for us. Give us your money!' Do you know what the point of all of this is? Do you know what these so-called investment managers are trying to do?"

"They're trying to make money."

"Yes, but specifically they are trying to beat the markets. This is the game. They want to outperform the benchmark: the S&P Five Hundred, or the Topix, or the MSCI World – whatever their benchmark happens to be. They think that by throwing manpower at this animal, which they believe is really a robot, they can predict where it's going and can beat it. Do you know how many asset managers have consistently beat the markets over periods of many years?" Richard shook his head. "Basically, none of them have. A few, which amounts to none." He left Richard with that thought and called to the bartender. "Another Coke, please."

"So why do people give their money to these banks if they can't beat the benchmark?"

"Simple: greed. Just greed. You have a million dollars. You have twenty million – whatever. Are you just going to buy the market?" He could see that Richard did not understand. "Are you just going to buy a little bit of everything so that your performance is more or less in line with the market? Of course not. You're greedy. You want to earn more than that. You want to beat the S&P. You want to beat the Nasdaq. You want to be able to brag about it to your friends."

"I don't know what the S&P is," Richard admitted. Ravi smiled and sat up straight.

"I thought all Americans were invested in the stock market! Okay, look. First of all, we have only mentioned the stock markets. There are a lot of ways to invest money. You can buy gold, real estate, bonds, stocks, derivatives, and of course, funds. You can buy gold funds, stock funds, bond funds, hedge funds. You know what a fund is?"

"No, sorry."

"A stock fund is just a bag of stocks. A bond fund is just a bag of bonds. Let's say you buy a stock fund. Let's say it's a fund investing only in American tech stocks. You put your money in a big pool with everyone else that is buying that fund and the fund manager takes it all and buys a heap of American tech stocks. He buys a wide variety of them to spread his risk and so that he ends up with performance that is very similar to the benchmark, which is probably the Nasdaq. It's complicated, but let's just say the Nasdaq is a load of American tech stocks. More than a thousand of them. Put their price movements all together into one – with some having more weight than others, but never mind – and you have your benchmark. Anyway, your fund manager divides the pool of money, say a hundred million dollars, into one million units, each of which is worth a hundred dollars. You buy ten units: one thousand dollars. He goes out and buys all the stocks for the fund and then watches how they perform. The prices go up, down, sideways... He is free to sell off some of the stocks and buy others when he wants to, as long as they are stocks that meet the rules of the fund. So if his original hundred million dollars' worth of stocks gains ten percent in six months, each of your units are now worth ten percent more; one hundred and ten dollars each instead of the original hundred." Ravi stopped when he saw a light go on in Richard's eyes.

"Oh, so that's how it works," Richard said, "I've always wondered about 'funds.' "

"Boy, you really don't know much, do you?" Ravi teased. "Where were we? Ah, that book. The book. These banks, then, throw a lot of money at hiring thousands of young people like you, fresh out of university with degrees in finance, because they think this will help them to beat the markets and attract money from clients – from people like you. But you know what? It's all a game! Even before they've started, they know they can't beat the markets. Not for long. They might have someone working for them who can outperform the benchmark for a while – six months, a year, two years. This is common. And it can be enough to get lots of attention. They win some award for best performance for a one-year period, and spread the word around and people like you line up to give them money, hoping for the good performance to last. But they know they can't go on beating the markets. So why do they waste all the money on all these bright young faces? Because they know you're greedy. They know you want them to *try*. They know you will say 'Please try to beat the markets for me!' What are they going to tell you? Are they going to admit that in the long run it can't be done and that they could get the same long-term performance by just taking your money and making random bets? Would you give them your money if they told you that this was their strategy? Of course not! It would do just as well as all the carefully drawn calculations, but of course they won't do that. They have to look respectable. So they say 'Richard, we've got sixty thousand CFAs working for us. Your money is safe with us.' And you say 'Okay, here's my ten million.' That's how it works." Ravi sat with another hard expression, a penetrating light in his eyes. As he nodded to himself, a smile slowly appeared on his face. "That's how it works," he repeated. "But I do it differently."

It was clear that he would not tell Richard how he did things differently until Richard asked him.

"And how do you do it?"

"I tell you, it's a nightmare!" Ravi said, covering his face with one hand and laughing. It was a sneaking, almost silent laughter, given away only by Ravi's eyes, the smile on his face, the shaking of his body. "A nightmare!" he repeated. Ravi Singh wanted Richard to laugh along with him, but it was a joke that Richard had not heard. It was as if the subject had been changed while he blinked. "You sit in these trading floors, you know," Ravi began, struggling to contain his laughter, "And you listen to the same rubbish day in and day out. You listen to the 'experts' give you their analysis. God!" he said, laughing, "It's painful!"

What a character, Richard thought, sitting there, laughing at his own jokes. It was not exactly infectious, but odd enough still so that Richard found himself laughing haltingly as well. This only served to encourage Ravi. Richard wondered if Ravi realized that he was laughing at him, at the situation.

"Every morning you have the conference call. This is where you are imparted with your wisdom for the day. The jackass economist or strategist followed by the jackass head of sales telling you some nonsense or other." He stopped and stared out over the bar, a chuckle rising in his throat. "Do you know what they call a good salesman? It's the one who takes notes from the morning call and vomits this back at his clients all day long like some kind of bird, you know, feeding the little ones. Oh, the poor clients! Can you imagine? How would you feel if some weatherman called you every morning to tell you what the weather was like yesterday?" he said, his mouth laughing, soundless, his hand slapping his leg.

"So how do *you* do it?" Richard asked him. Ravi took his time to sober up at the question, sitting for a time shaking his head, smiling, his dark eyes on Richard. It was unnerving. Richard finished his beer and called the bartender over for another.

"Did I mention to you that I studied mathematics?"

"Yes, you did," Richard said. Ravi nodded.

"The markets, as I said, are not robots. They are thinking, breathing, undulating flesh; arms and legs acting independently but belonging to the same body, and of one mind. The mind comprising millions of brain cells: all of the market participants." Richard held that thought in his mind and examined the image that formed. He nodded. It made sense enough. "You are trying to beat the market – one of the arms, one of the legs. Where do you start? Do you focus on one company? One currency? Each one may move the market, or it may be moved by the market. But how can you know which will overpower or lead the other? And how far will it go? Do you know anything about chaos theory?"

That did it. The mention of an esoteric scientific theory immediately captured Richard's imagination. This was the kind of foundational approach to problem solving that Richard could appreciate. The kind that was so rarely used by the average person. It had to mean that Ravi Singh was not average.

"Barely," he told him, "I read a book about it once." Ravi's eyes widened and he nodded, impressed that he would have been acquainted with the subject.

"Linear thinking," Ravi continued. "That's where they all go wrong. All the armies of analysts. The beast doesn't behave. The structure cannot be mapped out like some geometrical puzzle, because the interactions are non-linear. Do you know what that means? It means that the effects will not be proportional to the causes. Not consistently, anyway. Not as a rule. It may happen that one action creates a proportional reaction, but most likely not. It would be exceptional, in fact, if the reaction were proportional. If it were linear. Exceptional. So we have to abandon traditional methods toward pursuing a picture, a forecast."

Richard nodded, seeing how this criticism fit. "Does that mean that it's not possible to predict the market?" he asked, feeling that he already knew what the answer would be.

"Yes, and no," Ravi said. "Yes and no, light and dark, left and right. Do you know anything about Eastern philosophy?"

"Actually, I majored in philosophy. But I know very little about Eastern thought."

"You studied philosophy?" Ravi asked him, a new appreciation for the young man appearing to flow from him. "Good for you. Well, then, you should appreciate this. When the stock markets cracked last year, I celebrated," he told him, nodding confidently. "I celebrated, I tell you! I called all my clients and I told them 'Hallelujah! Get ready! Get ready!' Of course, I had advised them all months before to go cash. Many of them did, reluctantly. Some thought I was mad – most of them, in fact. The few, the very few that I really, really trust and with whom I share some of what I am sharing with you now," he said, pausing to allow this gift to be appreciated by Richard, "did not think I had gone mad, and their laughter when I broke the news to them was one of anticipation. Of understanding. Not of ridicule or fear. These few understood." The unbounded laughter returned. "Yes, the stock markets were crumbling. And I was elated! Do you know why?" Ravi's hands once more came to his face as if to stop up a leaking dam. Richard shook his head. Of course he did not know why. How could he possibly know why? When Ravi had stopped shaking, he took a deep breath and composed himself before continuing. "I'm sorry," he said, placing a hand upon Richard's forearm in apology, "I'm sorry, but it's just crazy. Let me tell you. In Indian philosophy, which is far more closely aligned to religion or spirituality than it is in the West, we have a god of creation, Brahma, and a god of destruction, Shiva. This might surprise you, but there are far more temples to Shiva in India than to Brahma. Do you know why, my friend? To know why is to know why I am so happy that the markets crashed."

Richard shook his head. "No, I cannot imagine why."

Ravi held up his finger and tightened his gaze. "It is because destruction is a *creative* force." Richard raised his eyebrows at the paradoxical explanation but felt he understood immediately. Ravi continued when he saw the understanding in his eyes. "The ancient Greek philosopher Anaximander said it well when he drew his picture of the cosmos, in which, contrary to our modern view, chaos and destruction arise from order. The birth of this world is a destructive event, disturbing the original order of nature and must inevitably – justly, he felt – return to order. His view was similar to the Indian view, but significantly different, for Anaximander saw this destructive creation as being offensive, and unjust, to the order of nature."

Richard's expression was calm, unperturbed. But inside he was shocked at what he heard. This man? This banker knew something of ancient Greek philosophy? Was this brought to him through his studies of his own Indian philosophy, or did he purposefully study Western philosophy? He was about to pose a question along these lines when Ravi spoke again.

"People in Western business know of it in a very simple sense as 'creative destruction.' The Indian view is that with destruction comes the ability to create anew. The aftermath of destruction is a breath of fresh air!" Ravi said, puffing out his chest, his hands against his ribs. "Look at the stock market: as we climb higher and higher, month after month, we continually run out of possibilities. We have fewer and fewer reasons to push forward. Not simply for the obvious reason that when we have reached a high level the chances of a fall seem to increase. A correction, an adjustment, profit-taking, or whatever you want to call it. No. It is because the momentum of the world, the creative momentum of new business, the entrepreneurial spirit, begins to die. We become stuck in a groove. Market crashes force people to rethink everything. Maybe not everything, but we go back to basics. We look again at fundamental issues and ask ourselves what went wrong. We say, 'How can we do it differently this time?' And this is exciting!"

"I see," Richard said. "So you're expecting great things to come out of what most people are seeing as simply a lot of grief."

Ravi continued as if he had not heard a word Richard had said. "You know, one thing that is very interesting is that the so-called new thinking of the nineties – the casual attitude that originally spread from creative genius types in high-tech companies right into mainstream corporate America – wasn't the result of any kind of destruction. Like so much of why we find ourselves where we are now, it was the result of arrogance and over confidence. People began to think that they could simply do anything they wanted because they felt they were participating in a new age. And they all thought they could claim partial responsibility for this if they behaved like a bunch of nutty professors."

"But don't you think that they learned from their mistakes?" Richard asked.

"The nincompoops! The idiots! Do you know they're saying it's going to *change* now? You can read it in the papers every day. 'We've learned our lesson now and will create a new system to replace the old one,' they say. Well, I wish they would, but of course, they won't. Mark my words," he said, a finger held aloft. "The Americans are now throwing billions at the criminal banks to prop them up. Well, they're going to cut their losses and get back on track and have another record-breaking year. Where's the incentive to change?"

"How do you know so much about America?"

"Oh, because I spend a lot of time there, of course, to see clients. Yes, I travel a lot. I spend about two months a year traveling. I don't know. Maybe if your people traveled more, if they could see life in foreign countries, maybe they would have something to compare themselves to. It's a powerful deterrent, you know. A country that looks inward. A country where people don't know and don't seem to care what happens outside. You've got two weeks' vacation in most jobs, haven't you?"

"I guess so."

"Right. Not enough time to get away. Barely enough time to relax. It's an interesting thought. Yes, the American Experiment." He stared into his Coke, watching the bubble rise. "Where were we?" Ravi Singh asked, sensing Richard's dismay. "My investment method! Right." Richard waited while Ravi reached into his pocket and handed him his business card. "Give me a shout when you're done with your travels and I'll tell you all about it.

Richard shrugged his shoulders. "Okay."

"For me, it's not about greed. I don't need the money anymore. I have more than I'll ever spend." Ravi at last seemed humble. Vulnerable. "I amassed a fortune that I eventually had to give away, it made me so sick. So sick!" He placed his hand on his stomach and his dark eyes searched Richard's face for a sign of understanding. "I tell you, man is a cruel beast. Man's destiny is cruelty."

His gaze lingered, making sure that the message was received. But talk of destiny never sat well with him. He immediately found himself annoyed that their conscientious discussion had suddenly been marred by such a thoughtless interjection.

"You know there are so many things wrong with this world," Ravi began again. "I said I used to be wealthy. Well, I still am, but not nearly so much as before. When I reached fifty million dollars of personal wealth, which is simply peanuts compared to hundreds of others, I came to the realization that I could not live with myself. I simply could not," he said, his eyes smoldering like lumps of coal. "So you know what I did? I decided to place a cap on my wealth. First I made sure that my family were all comfortable, and then I capped my liquid wealth at ten million. My illiquid wealth is a couple times more than that. It's a lot. It's more than I need. But I had to start somewhere. I created a charitable organization with the rest of my money and assets. This organization does many things: builds schools, provides food, shelter. We target people in many countries, but mainly in non-industrialized countries. Everything I manage to earn in excess of my cap is given to the organization. We also solicit donations, other things. And it's amazing."

"I can see why you would do this, but what about the idea that because of your hard work you are deserving of the rewards you receive?"

"Hard work? Yes," Ravi sighed, "sometimes it has been hard work, but mostly not. Not so hard. I never was one to work late at night and at the weekend. When I did that, it was an exception. But even if I had worked seventy, eighty hours a week, the rewards I received are far more than I or anyone else would deserve. I mean really, people are starving to death in this world by the thousands. How can we still look up to multi-millionaires and billionaires with a sense of awe and respect? It is obscene! That anyone should be allowed to be a billionaire, for example. It's just a tragedy. Greed is good only until it gets you to safety. After that, after it becomes nothing more than stockpiling our world's finite resources, it is obscene. You know, I have a little fantasy. I know it's wishful thinking, but it could be done. We could make it a sort of contest. A game for the elite. Each year, or even every few years, it wouldn't matter, you rank all of the income of the period and you come up with a list of winners. The software giant earned more than anyone, good for him. The oil tycoon came in second. Bravo. And on down the line. You print up some fancy magazine with everyone's picture. You have a big television song and dance where trophies are presented. And then all the income over that ten million or twenty million cap – whatever it is – is pooled and put to work immediately to better the world. To help people to better themselves. To give opportunity where none exists. Maybe it wouldn't work, I don't know. But why not try it? Why not do something?" Ravi watched how his words affected Richard. Happy with the result, and fearful that he may be placing too much gloom on Richard's shoulders, he considered him freshly. "So tell me, why did you study philosophy?"

Richard wondered if he had not known, just a split second before the words had escaped Ravi's lips, that he would ask this question. What would he have done if he had known? Ran? Leapt off his stool and ran? The image made him laugh. He fought to control his quiet laughter, but it simply escalated as he replayed that image over and over, creating a snowball of hilarity that spun out of control. He laughed, but it was embarrassing. He stole a glance at Ravi and was pleased to see the tables turned, and Ravi's expression one of confusion. He was off balance, despite his own accommodating grin.

"What?" Ravi finally asked in desperation.

"Nothing. Nothing. Forget it. Sorry about that. I was thinking of something else." Ravi allowed Richard time to regain his composure, waiting for his question to be answered. "Can I buy you a drink?" Richard asked him, his own drink finished.

"Sure. Another Coke." When they both had their drinks Ravi thanked him. "Cheers," he said, raising his glass before taking a sip. "You were saying?"

"Yes. Sorry, your question. Why did I study philosophy?" He gazed into his beer looking for some new angle to amuse himself with. In the end he simply stuck to his standard answer. Ravi accepted it without any argument. In fact, he approved of the answer quite readily.

"Me too," he told Richard. "I meditate regularly. I know that's not a part of the Western approach, but, nonetheless. I am dedicated to it as well."

"Well, I wouldn't say I'm 'dedicated' to it," Richard admitted. He felt a creeping shame at hearing his own comment.

"Oh? Why not?" Ravi asked. Richard found his manner touching, as if he were reacting to a friend who had declared that he had lost the will to live. Richard saw the possibility to explore his frustration with his search with Ravi's help. He stood at the door, looking into this opportunity, but then turned away, saying nothing.

Ravi watched Richard, a smile slowly warming his expression. "You want to know my own philosophy of how to deal with this life?" he asked. "I move, I must say, like a man lost in the world. I know it sounds void of hope, but listen: you continually realign yourself, like a bird flying through a broad mountain range. You aim for the top of one and as you make it, you find the next one and head off for it, making sure that by reaching all of those minor goals, you eventually find your way to the place it is that you are trying to get. Understanding the secrets and the mysteries of this world may well be beyond us all," Ravi said, with a kindness in his voice that surprised Richard. "Insofar as we can know – and I mean this in the crude, modern sense of knowledge involving proof and facts and all of that – a pragmatic attitude is useful. But for the spiritual life, ask yourself: What am I really looking for?" he said, his intense gaze finally softening as he searched Richard's own ready expression. "Many people simply want to know if there is life after death; if death as we know it means that there is no kind of life for us after this one. Is that what you want to know? If it is, imagine receiving the answer: yes! There is life after death!

300

But then ask yourself: what now? Many might think that there is no need to ask that question and would feel relieved and overjoyed that they have 'something to look forward to.' But really, I ask you: what now? Assuming there is life after this one, what will it be like? What struggles will it hold for us? What responsibilities?"

Richard once again felt let down. Once again, he felt was being advised not to seek what he could not help looking for.

"And so you see, it's not that simple. Our quest is not about finding 'answers,' as if these answers were finite and complete all by themselves."

"You mentioned wisdom," Richard said. "I have been thinking in the past couple of weeks about this talk I had with my friend back home. It occurred to me that perhaps we once had wisdom, but we now have only knowledge."

Ravi smiled, encouraged by Richard's vision. "Or that we now only value knowledge?" he suggested. Richard agreed. "It is an interesting idea, my friend. You probably have not studied Eastern philosophy," Ravi said, changing the subject.

"Not really."

"They don't often use argument. To a Westerner it can be truly frustrating. One senses from time to time that something important is being said, and yet one has no argument with which to test it. Nothing with which to satisfy this skeptical drive we now have. The Easterners profess wisdom, not knowledge. Wisdom, and wise sayings, have an intuitive appeal that makes them powerful. Yes, powerful but dangerous. The danger lies in the very fact that people may accept things because of their intuitive appeal without subjecting them to the filter of what we might call 'better judgment.' Do we give praise to wisdom out of some unconscious assumption that one who speaks of truth without resorting to argument surely must know what they are talking about? Yes, frustrating it can be. But I recommend it nonetheless."

"But there must be more to it than that," Richard said.

"What do you mean?" Ravi cautiously ventured, his eyes narrowing.

"There must be some real wisdom there, despite what we might feel are weaknesses in logic. Or an absence of logic, I guess."

Ravi raised his hands. "Okay, you got me," he said, "Let's take a closer look. You may be ready for it." He removed his attention from Richard for a moment and gazed absently into the room. "Why do Eastern thinkers communicate in riddles? Why don't they provide a step-by-step, logical approach? Build up to a solid conclusion? Well, think about Socrates, and his questioning. His claim to know nothing. Clearly, he felt that the nature of the quest required that one do it themselves. Perhaps this was what he meant when he said that the unexamined life was not worth living. Perhaps the emphasis is incorrectly placed on the act of simply examining one's life, and is properly placed on the idea that one is going through the process on one's own – not just going to the local wise man and asking for easy answers. One cannot simply ask questions about life's mysteries and have them answered, like using a dictionary or a telephone book. Many of the early Greek thinkers handled things this way, not just Socrates. Heracleitus, Empedocles, Parmenides and Protagoras. It is the same with Eastern thought."

"But why?"

"Because it doesn't work to simply lay it all out, like a roadmap. It doesn't. Look, we have to, each of us, be ready for this knowledge, this experience. If I were to explain everything I know on the subject as clearly as I knew how – and it isn't easy, by the way, it is very difficult to put into words – those who weren't ready for it would not accept it anyway. They would resist it. They would not see the logic in it, the value, and would be no better off. So it doesn't make sense to do this; they will simply have to wait. There'll be another time for them."

"What, you mean life after life?"

"Well, or perhaps later in this life. But since you brought it up, I do believe that we live many lives. You know the first law of thermodynamics? Conservation of energy? Think about it. No thing becomes *nothing*. It isn't like one comes back as the same person one was, with the knowledge that, oh, here I go again. Not at all. It's a kind of starting over more than a continuation." Ravi's face became pinched as Richard saw that he was not comfortable with this discussion. "I don't want to get sidetracked. It is enough to say that if you aren't ready now, you'll have another chance. But there are always those who are in a gray area. On the fence, so to speak. And for these people, sometimes a little push is very useful. A little wind, helping one to complete the step one is already poised to make."

Richard waited for Ravi to continue. A lull in the conversation in the bar gave him the courage to go in the direction that only part of him resisted, and so he spoke. "And what do you say to someone in this case?"

"Everything and nothing. Listen, when you are on a journey, what is the most important thing for you to know?"

"You have to know where you're going," Richard answered, easily.

"No. You must know where you *are*. You must know where you're starting from. Energy is wasted when one sets out to arrive at the place one is."

"I don't follow you."

"It's all a matter of becoming properly oriented. When one is ready, all one needs is this orientation. Have you ever heard of the famous Zen koans?"

"Yes. I read about them once. They're a kind of riddle."

"Exactly. Have you heard of any of them? Do you know any?"

"I can remember just one. 'What is the sound of one hand clapping?' "

"Was an answer given?"

Richard laughed. "Yes, but it didn't make any sense."

"What was it?"

"The teacher asks, what is the sound of the one hand clapping? After going away and returning and giving one wrong answer after another, the student returns, is asked the question, and thrusts one hand forward, palm up, and says 'Mu!' "

Ravi looked as if he'd been reminded of an old, familiar song. His eyes danced as his laughter returned once more. "And you read this and thought, what the hell is going on, right?" he asked. "Oh, Richard. It's funny," he said, regaining his composure. "Let me just tell you why this answer is correct. Do you run?"

"Sorry?"

"Do you run? Jog?"

"Oh, sometimes. I'm not a big runner, though."

"Think of it this way: when you're running a familiar path, say a set course that you know well, you might start out mindful of the goal. Out to the big meadow and back, or whatever it might be. On your way out, if you aren't having a good run and you're feeling tired too early, you find that the goal becomes an obstacle. The thought of it weakens you. Wears you down. In that case, you must stop thinking 'I am going to the meadow,' and instead you allow your attention to center on yourself. It is you, running right where you are, and no thought is given to a goal or stopping point. The answer to the koan is not what the student said. It was never what the student said that made all the other wrong answers wrong, it was how the student said them. The teacher, at some point, sees that the student has learned that the answer to the question is of no importance whatsoever. The goal was meaningless. The student answers, says some words, but this intent or awareness is expressed and is intuited by the teacher. The teacher sees that the student has finally answered the question with no answer. He has reached the destination without having gone anywhere. This is the way I see it, anyway. One says 'I've just made a fabulous journey.' The other asks, 'Where did you go?' And the guy answers 'I stayed home.' This is it, Richard."

Richard said nothing, but Ravi could see that he was in the right place. "You said you meditated," he told him.

"Yes."

"What happens when you meditate?"

"Let me try to explain. You have probably heard the Eastern advice to 'stop grasping.' This is the key. When I meditate, I try to let everything go. I want to be left completely alone. No thoughts, either. I want to be alone from the world and alone from myself. It sounds odd. It *is* odd! But that is the exercise. It is a paradoxical exercise. I can say that this is what I strive for, but one who strives will never know. It is the goal, but if one sets out to pursue that goal, it isn't met. One must wish for everything to fall away, and yet if one pushes things away, one finds oneself in the end at the center, pushing, and that is all. When we meditate we don't ask 'Who am I really?' We have to lose this 'me and the outside world' point of view. We have to shift from 'me' to nothing, and then we see that 'me' becomes everything."

"And this meditation works for you? I mean…how can I say it? Were you successful?" Richard asked, unable to escape from formulating his question in a way that seemed to go against what Ravi had tried to show him.

"It's okay. I told you it was difficult to put into words, didn't I? Let me tell you. It only happened once for me. If you are lucky you will be there, and you will experience something that at once is and is not your inner nature. It is the oneness of the world and of yourself. It is clarity. It is knowledge. It is beautiful, and powerful. Perhaps it scared me away," Ravi said to himself in a voice that was barely more than a whisper. "Yes, maybe that is why I haven't found my way back," he said, his voice sounding weary. "And now, my friend, I must say good-night. You have my card if you ever want to reach me."

Richard got off his bar stool and stood next to Ravi, indicating that he would also be leaving. He followed Ravi to the door where they stepped outside and then shook hands. A question formed in his mind that he was scarcely aware of until he had heard himself ask it.

"So what should I do with my money?"

Ravi smiled at him. "Leave it in the bank, in cash, for now. Then, like I said, call me when you're ready."

Richard saw the seriousness in Ravi's eyes. "Listen," he told him. "I'm talking about several million dollars here. Are you sure?"

Ravi changed the subject. "Richard, why not join me? Why not become a partner with me in my charitable work? You could be my American counterpart!"

"Me? But I don't know anything about this kind of thing."

"That doesn't matter. You're the right kind of person, and *that* is what matters."

Richard fingered Ravi's card, but said nothing.

"Think about it. You know how to reach me. Good-bye my friend." The man stepped down to the sidewalk and stopped short. "And Richard," he said, his expression indicating that he was no longer talking about money, "there is no hurry." He waved, turned, and continued down the sidewalk.

Richard watched him go for a moment before setting out to walk in the warm night air back to the hotel. It was nearly eleven o'clock. As he made his way down the road he tried to talk himself out of his slump. " 'Oh where is the girl I love?' " he sang. "Boy, talk about a 'walking torture chamber.' Sheriff, I'm yer man." He crossed the center of the city quickly, and was soon near the hotel. Ravi had said it, he thought. Stop grasping. He passed by the hotel and went straight across General Guisan Quai to the docks where the ferries sat, ready for another day. He walked down to the end of one of the docks and sat down, folding his legs underneath him. He looked out over the water and listened as the tiny waves fell against each other. The sound soothed him, helping him to find some peace. But soon, he rose and took one last look on the undulating moonlit brilliance before him. Out there, he thought, is only water.

25

Page waved and smiled when she saw Richard standing in the entrance to the restaurant scanning the tables for her. He smiled back, surprised at how glad he was to see her, and crossed the room to join her for breakfast. He sat next to her at the small round table set for four.

"She still sleeping?" she asked him, her voice hinting an apology.

"Still sleeping."

"Coffee?" she asked, the pot in her hand. He nodded and she poured. He watched her, noticing her still barely wet hair tucked neatly behind her ears.

"Thanks," he said. "Page, if she never wakes up, will you marry me?" Richard watched as he saw her blush for the second time. She looked at him again and searched his eyes. He leaned over and put his arm around her. "You're just so great, you know? And I'm sorry to say that at first I was upset when I found out that you were coming with us. But now, I'm so glad you're here."

Page rested her head on Richard's shoulder for a moment. "I'm glad too," she said. She looked him in the eye, squeezing his hand. "And if she never wakes up, then yes, I'll marry you."

"Okay. I feel better now."

The two of them had a quick breakfast and then went for a walk through town. Page and Toshika had had a long night, going to dinner with friends and then out to several clubs, returning only at four in the morning. The note that Toshika had written and placed on the bathroom mirror informing him of their plans had fallen and gone unnoticed by Richard.

The two spent the day talking as they wandered the city. There was little they had not already seen, making it difficult at first to decide where to go. In the end, having no plan suited them both fine. As they worked their way down *Bahnhofstrasse* they entered few shops, and while in those few, they kept their hands in their pockets, content to poke around with their eyes only. They also struck out on some of the alleys near the river, strolling the cobblestone streets, and finally taking in a view over the old town, with the river running through the middle of it, from the *Lindenhof* hill where, according to an excited old woman who correctly took them for tourists, nearly a thousand years before when the soldiers of the city were away in battle and opposition forces began their march on the city, local women took whatever military paraphernalia they could find and massed upon the hill where they could be easily seen, successfully delaying the attack upon the city until the soldiers returned.

In the afternoon, while in the neighborhood known as the *Niederdorf*, they stopped in for a late lunch at a small café where they ordered sandwiches and mineral water. They ate quickly, having worked up a healthy appetite from all the walking they had done.

"This has really been fun," Page told Richard, licking her finger and pressing it to the crumbs of bread on her empty plate.

"Yes. I only wish I had come here years ago. Seeing a foreign country where everywhere you look you see something new and interesting is just fantastic."

"I meant today. Being with you." Page watched Richard's blank expression and then flashed her eyes wide open at him, forcing his reply.

"Oh! Yes," he said. "Me too. It's nice to…" He searched for the words for his thoughts but came up short. "It's nice to be with you." Naturally, his thoughts turned then to Toshika. He wondered if she was still sleeping, and pictured her spread out on the bed, her black hair soft against the white sheets. He remembered their moment under the tree at the party, and Philip's generous comment. "Just a *leetle* wind," he said quietly.

"What?" Page asked him. Richard looked up from the table at her.

308

"Oh, nothing. I was just remembering something Philip said at the party. You remember Philip, the sailor?"

"Yes, of course."

Suddenly he felt the urge to tell Page of that moment under the tree and of his feelings for Toshika, even though the thought of doing so drew from him warnings not to spoil things. But why can't I tell her? Can't people talk to their friends? I want to tell someone. Finally, it was the vague notion that by revealing his feelings to Page he would lay a firmer ground for all of them to walk on that made him speak.

"I suppose that, you being a woman, and possessing a woman's instinct for these things – I know it's a stereotype, but I also know you have it – this won't surprise you," he said, speaking in a quiet voice, mindful of the strangers all around them. "Well, anyway, I'm in love with Toshika. I've been fighting with this for a long time, because I've felt this way with other people so many times that I had become convinced that it had never really been true, and that something so special couldn't happen like that. Like finding pearls in every oyster you open. But what can I say? What else can it be?" He looked at her, his eyes asking for an answer. "But in any case, it doesn't matter, because it's just a word, right? I feel what I feel, regardless." As he watched Page's expression, the fear that had presented itself to him a moment earlier about speaking from his heart returned. Page brought her hands to her head, resting her elbows on the table between them.

"Don't tell Toshika," she told him, her eyes now moist. "But I feel the same way."

Richard stared at her blankly for a moment. "Oh, Page, I-"

"Not about you, Richard, get it?"

Richard held his breath. His mind returned to his first visit to Toshika's house, of the three of them, and everything since. Page's admission made everything different, but clarified nothing. Nothing except the feeling that he ought not have spoken.

"Page, I had no idea."

"Yeah, well, men never do, do they? Sorry, I don't want to attack you or anything." She put her elbows on the table and held her hands over her face for a full minute. Richard hadn't a clue what to do, so did nothing but sit there, waiting for her to burst out in tears or start screaming obscenities at him any moment. Finally she took a deep breath and sat up straight. "I have to go home," she said. "I've got to get back home."

"Are you sure?" Richard asked her, realizing that explanations and apologies were not called for.

"I can't keep going around with you both. Not now. Besides, I don't know how long you want to travel, and I have a few projects that I should really finish," she said, wiping her eyes and sniffing once loudly. She sat up straight and looked over her shoulder. She raised her hand to the waiter and turned again to Richard. "No, I have to go. I have to stop quickly in Paris for work, but then I'll head home. But listen," she said, reaching for Richard's hand, her fabulous smile returning, amplifying Richard's feelings of guilt. "Don't worry about the game, and that whole thing, okay? I don't know if Toshika loves you, but I think she likes you enough to stay with you, game or no game. So don't worry about that."

"Oh, I'm not worried about that," he assured her, surprised that she would even mention the game at that particular moment. What did she mean, anyway? "I never even think about it."

"Good," she said. The waiter came and stopped at their table. "I'll get this," she told him.

"No, you don't have to."

"No, really. It's nothing."

Having settled the bill, Page stood up and swung her backpack over one shoulder, quickly finding the other strap and settling it properly in place. They went outside and stood in the warm air a moment without moving, as if waiting to be swept up and carried on to their next destination.

"Come on," Page said, "let's go."

Page stood in the doorway, feeling pulled in two directions at once. "I'll wait for you outside in the garden," she told them as they finished packing.

"Okay, we won't be long," Richard called after her as the door to their room shut. "We won't be long, will we?" he asked Toshika.

"Oh, come on!" Toshika protested, still wearing a bathrobe as she packed. "I've never missed a train in my life." Unable to confirm or deny her claim, he shrugged and waited on the balcony for her while she threw some clothes on. Their train was an early one, disrupting the leisurely pace they had all enjoyed during the past two weeks. Although it had been difficult initially to raise himself from bed at such an hour, he now felt happy once again to have most of the morning ahead of him and was eager to get started on their journey. Soon Toshika was ready, and called the front desk to have someone fetch their bags. In the elevator Richard thought she seemed a little nervous.

"You look beautiful," he told her. She smiled and wrinkled her nose at him.

"You don't look so bad yourself."

They went to the front desk and left the key, having already settled the bill. "Have a nice trip," the clerk said to Richard as he turned to find Toshika already out the front door and joining Page in the car that was to take them to the train station.

When they arrived at the station there were so many taxis massed around the entrance that their driver could only let them out beyond the entrance in a loading zone, forcing them to walk a minute back into the station. Once inside, Richard found their train quickly.

"Be careful, okay?" Page told Toshika as she gave her a hug and smiled at Richard over Toshika's shoulder.

"I wish you were coming with us," Toshika said. "Are you sure you'll be okay here alone before you go on to Paris?"

"Of course! What can happen in two days? Anyway, Philip will take good care of me."

"Well, you watch out for him. He seems harmless, but he is a man, after all."

Page stepped away from Toshika and hugged Richard warmly, making him promise her he would have fun before sending them both up the steps onto the train bound for France. Richard told himself that she seemed okay, and tried to forget about things and to forgive himself a little for his bad timing.

He and Toshika then stepped up into the train and turned, waving to Page before entering the car. They quickly found their seats and sat down before looking out the windows, the excitement of setting off once again building. As the train pulled away, Toshika took Richard's hand.

"Now it's just you and me!" she said, a surprised expression spreading across her face as if she could not quite believe it. She laughed once and clapped her hands before sliding off her shoes and putting them in the empty seat facing her. "You and me," she said quietly, her voice nearly lost in the rolling hum of the train.

26

It was their third and final day in Aix en Provence. Toshika had put off seeing her until today, their last day. She had been avoiding it, hoping instead to somehow simply bump into her to remove the necessity of going to see her. But it hadn't happened. She held her arms crossed over her chest with her head down as she headed to the house. Rounding a corner, she entered the town square, smiling a greeting as she passed a man wearing rubber boots who stood hosing off the old stone street in front of his restaurant. She could still taste the coffee in her mouth, but its warmth was long gone. Oh well, she thought, at least the sun is shining. As she left the square and began to climb the alley that rose sharply and disappeared in a gentle curve, pulling the petit and charmingly tilted stone houses with it, she wondered what Richard would do until they met for lunch. He had not at all minded her suggestion that they meet only later at the Café Moon, which suited her just fine. But she felt his reaction was a little odd nonetheless. He had not seemed even remotely curious as to what she planned to do with herself in these few private hours. Of course, it was better that way. Had he asked her, she would not have told him the truth anyway. He would want to meet her, and that was something she was not prepared for. Not yet.

The angle of the alley eased. She was close. She looked up and spotted the blue window frames of the house and had to smile. It was no ordinary blue – if there was such a thing. It was a blue that caused one to stop and wonder if it weren't some other color after all. A green, perhaps. Or was it violet? It was clearly the work of someone who knew color. Someone who knew how to manipulate and play with what color could do.

The door was oiled, but not painted. A heavy French oak, it was carved and fitted in a style long since gone, but was not itself antique, having been specially made for her. Toshika gripped the heavy iron knocker and winced as she brought it against the door twice, the harsh flatness of the sound combating the lazy stroll of a piano from a nearby radio. Toshika breathed deeply and smoothed her sweater. She heard footsteps, and then the shunt of the lock in the door.

The woman's eyes gave away her surprise. "Toshika."

"Hi mom."

The woman allowed her eyes to roam down and then back up, taking her all in before stepping away from the door. "*Entre*," she said without thinking, and turned and walked back into the house. She had not taken five steps when she stopped and turned, placing her hand on the table that stood beside the doorway into the living room. She crossed her arms over her chest and brought her chin down, her eyes locked onto her daughter. It was as close to a smile as Toshika would get from her mother.

"You look well," the woman told her. "Rather dark, but..."

"It's summertime, mom."

"Yes, of course. And I'm sure you're still..." she hesitated, looking for the right word, "shameless, about putting yourself out in the sun." She averted her eyes, knowing she had tempted a hostile reaction. "Would you like something? Some coffee?" she asked over her shoulder as she slipped silently into her home and disappeared through another doorway.

"No, thanks," Toshika called after her, looking around the house as she entered. Through the windows painted so carefully, she looked once out onto the rooftops of the village before stopping at a chair. It was not a large room, but big enough, she imagined, seeing as how her mother lived alone there. The room was simple. A few pieces of furniture, most of them rustic older wooden pieces, probably from the local countryside. There was a small round table with four chairs, a wide, low bookcase, a coffee table, and then a pastel blue leather sofa. No clutter existed anywhere. In fact, the only part of the room that looked lived in was the corner where the easel stood on the other side of the room surrounded by paints, brushes and what looked like a bed sheet speckled with a rainbow of color, spread out on the floor. Through the open windows, the piano danced softly through the room, freezing everything in time.

In the next room, the kitchen, she could hear her mother's careful preparation of something to drink. Tea, she guessed.

"What brings you to Aix?" her mother called.

She hesitated. "I told you I was coming."

"Yes, you did. Did you just arrive?"

"No, but we won't be here long. Just came to see you, really."

"We?"

She ignored her mother's question. "Hans Peter sends his regards, by the way."

"Oh. I'm not using him anymore," her mother said, as if it were understood.

"Really. I guess that explains it."

"Explains what?"

"Oh, nothing. When he mentioned you he waited, as if I would volunteer some kind of information about you. I even thought at the time that you might have gone somewhere else, but I didn't go into it with him."

The stirring of water reaching a boil was followed by a whistling that Toshika's mother silenced immediately. In a moment, she returned to the living room and took a seat behind her easel.

"Yes, well, it's better that way, isn't it. None of his business." She placed her tea on a small table that stood nearby and leaned back into her chair, staring into the canvas before her. After a moment she breathed in deeply. "Well, that's not working," she said. Then she leaned right and peeked at Toshika from behind the canvas. "You don't mind if I work a bit, do you?"

Toshika smiled at her mother's face before it retreated back behind the rectangular mass. "Of course not."

"And? Anything new? How's that friend of yours? The painter."

"Todd. He's fine. He's still painting."

"Still trying anyway, I suppose. Well, good for him."

"I'm fine too."

Her mother lowered her brush and leaned over enough to consider her daughter with one eye before returning her attention to her painting. "Of course you are."

"I'm seeing someone now," Toshika ventured. She held her breath. Her mother took her time before responding.

"Another one of those poker players?"

"No. Not really."

" 'Not really,' " her mother echoed.

"He played once," Toshika said in her defense. She knew it would not suffice. "Hans invited him," she added on impulse. "He *liked* him."

"Really? And that means a lot to you?"

"Yes, as a matter of fact." Toshika could see her mother's elbow moving fluidly from left to right, as if buoyed by waves, as the sound of the bristles of her brush against the canvas interrupted the rhythm of the piano. The movement stopped. Then it began again, this time more slowly.

"I'd rather not discuss Hans."

"Yes, well. I'm sorry about him," Toshika offered. The flit-flit-flit of the brush was not interrupted. Undisturbed. She looked again out the windows onto the rooftops and wondered how she had managed to get by for so many years in the presence of such loving neglect.

"No need to be."

"His name is Richard."

"What?"

"The man I'm seeing."

"Is he here? In Aix?"

"Yes. Would you like to meet him?"

"Don't tell me: he won the game?"

"It's different this time!"

"Is it really?"

"I have feelings for him," Toshika said, unwilling to expose herself any further.

Her mother breathed deeply and then made a stuttering hiccup sound that was only barely audible, and which only Toshika knew to consider a laugh. "Oh, love. Yes, it's so wonderful when it bites, isn't it? Until the blood flows." Her elbow was leaping back and forth now, a gazelle pursued by an attacker. "There," she whispered to herself. "That's better."

Toshika stared into the weave of the canvas, her eyes failing to penetrate the heavy fabric to see the woman who sat behind it, lost in her own world, and then suddenly the canvas wavered and wrinkled before her eyes as her fists clamped down on the air and pressed themselves into her lap before the tears fell helplessly against them. "Mother, why won't you tell me who my father was?" she cried, wiping her eyes quickly once before jumping to her feet. She took two steps forward and wrested the brush from her mother's hand with her eyes. "How can you do this? Year after year?"

Her mother stood and went to her, taking her gently around the waist and leading her to the couch where they both sat. She stroked Toshika's hair once before placing her own hands neatly on her knees. "Your father," she began slowly, "caused me great pain when I came to know who he really was. What he was. Our marriage turned to tragedy overnight because of his deception. Toshika, I don't want this pain to be yours, too."

"You can't protect me by hiding me from myself! Whatever he did, I still want to know who he is! Mother, can't you understand? My own father?"

"Of course I do," she said, rising and going to the middle of the room. "I also understand that when you know, I can never see you again."

"Oh, and how often do you see me anyway? When was the last time you called me?" Toshika got up from the couch and crossed the room, taking her bag from the floor near the doorway and slipping it over her shoulder before turning to look at her mother. "It's always me, isn't it, mom? I don't even know why I bother to make the effort. Unless you tell me who he is, this may be the last time you see me."

Her mother did not paint. She found a concentration point on the floor and attached her gaze to it as she spoke. "Toshika, a mother prepares herself for the day when her children will leave her. This is normal. This is life. It will not be with sadness that you leave me, or that I release you to live your life. You already know that life is not an easy place to be. It is my duty not to allow things to enter your life that make it even more difficult, unless those things build character. Like–"

"Like all the hard years in school – mom, I know this speech."

Toshika's mother paused, then carried on. "Like your schooling." She took a deep breath. "Your father brought nothing but shame," she said. She turned back to her painting and fixed her hand just inches from the canvas. "Only shame."

"Jesus! You and your Japanese *shame*! Does he even know that he has a daughter?" Toshika cried out, feeling the impulse to fling her purse at her mother with all of her strength.

Her mother did not answer immediately. Toshika, looking at her mother's hands clenched onto fists in her lap, imagined that she had simply been drawn back into her work. Her mother looked up at her. "No," she whispered. "Never."

Toshika could not remember the last time she saw such emotion in her mother's eyes, and for a moment she thought she might change her mind and stay. Try to talk things out. But if there was anything she had inherited from her mother, it was her stubbornness. "You know how to reach me," she said. She opened the heavy door with a yank and stepped into the street. As her heels echoed through the stony alley and she noticed that the piano no longer hung in the air, she felt eyes burning into the back of her head. She turned, having promised in an instant that if her mother were there at the door, watching her, she would go back. Looking at the door, and then the windows, she found nothing. She turned again and hoped that Richard would be at the café early.

By the time they reached Portugal, nearly three weeks and several countries later, the two of them had fallen into a rhythm that Richard had trouble imagining doing without. Every morning they would sit over coffee and croissants or pastry reading a newspaper and chatting about the plan for the day, which would either involve going together to see a particular site, or splitting up, each doing their own thing before meeting up for lunch or for a drink later at the hotel before dinner. They were perfectly happy this way, each having their own time and space, and enjoying the time together or alone, before finishing each day by discussing what had been memorable.

On a secluded beach near Lagos that was accessible only by boat and encircled by tall, rocky cliffs, the two of them dozed in the lazy afternoon heat. It was their third such day in the Algarve in Southern Portugal.

"Richard," Toshika ventured quietly, unsure if he was asleep. He did not answer. She waited a moment before sitting up and hugging her knees, looking up and down the beach they shared with perhaps just twenty others, all of them with their boats anchored in waist deep water off to one side so as not to block the view of the sea. Looking beyond the breaking waves, she spotted a grand sailboat with its tall white sails, pressing along parallel to the coastline, having managed to find a wind unknown on their little spot of sand. She thought of Philip. He would be somewhere in the Caribbean by now, with his load of wealthy guests island hopping and playing at being sailors.

"Richard," she said, loud enough this time to bring him back from wherever he was. Richard raised his head with a start and then let it fall back onto his towel gently.

"Yes?"

"Look at this sailboat." Richard groaned and raised himself onto his elbows, bringing a hand to his forehead and squinting in the sun. "See it?"

"Oh, yes. Big one."

"Philip's larger boat is about that size, I would say. Gorgeous boat," she said, remembering countless days spent on it back when she too was fond of playing sailor. "Richard,"

"What?"

Toshika turned to him and grabbed his hand. "Let's go somewhere different, shall we?" she said, her eyes sparkling, seized with the spirit of adventure.

"Different? Like where?"

"Well, I was thinking about Morocco. Remember when Philip told us about going there?"

"He told us about the poverty he saw that made him sick to his stomach," Richard said dryly, sitting up now at Toshika's side.

"Yes, but later he and I talked about his stay there. After he left that little port he mentioned, he went on to Tangier and docked the boat for about ten days. He hired a car and did some traveling. He said it was fantastic!" Richard did not have much of an impression of the country, other than that of a hot, dry place. He was not inclined to go on from Portugal just yet, and the look on his face told Toshika as much. "Come on," she pleaded, "We'll ride a camel! Run around in the sand dunes!"

He saw the gleam in her eye and it caught him. "Well," he said, smiling wryly, running a hand over her bare breast and then seizing her around the waist, pulling her to him. "I suppose a little adventure wouldn't hurt."

"Yay!" she shouted, jumping up and bringing her hands to her mouth with excitement. She hollered once more and then raced into the water, diving into an oncoming wave. As fast as she was in, she was back out, glistening in the sun, wringing her hair out over the sand.

"Richard?"

"Yes?"

"Do you feel like an American now?" she asked him, sinking to her knees at his feet.

"I get it," he said, the look on his face thanking her. He looked out over the waves and closed his eyes for a moment against the breeze. "It doesn't mean very much anymore, does it?"

Toshika smiled. "Nope."

"Yeah. What's the point? American, French, Portuguese. Here, there... anywhere."

"Everywhere."

"Exactly."

Toshika glanced at her watch and looked briefly after the sun. "It's five already. Shall we go?"

Richard watched the sailboat as it disappeared beyond the rocky shore. "Sure," he said, trying in vain to suppress a yawn before rubbing gently at his eyes.

"Great! I'll go tell Miguel to get ready!" Toshika cried, and broke off in a trot toward the cluster of boats with their drivers sitting around smoking and talking with each other. Before Richard could utter the words that had formed in his throat, Toshika turned on a dime and with a look of fright on

320

her face, scooted back to him. "Forgot my suit!" she said, taking it from Richard's outstretched hand. She slid her panties on and then began working on her top as she walked slowly towards the boat.

Richard stared after her in surprise. "Well, well," he called out. "Good for you."

"Your turn," Toshika said, stepping from the shower and throwing on a robe. Richard entered the bathroom and stood under the shower head. The cool water was a relief, removing a layer of lotion, sun, and sand from his skin. Wrapping her hair quickly in a towel, Toshika took a seat at the desk in the corner of the room and picked up the phone. She called the concierge and enquired about flights from Lisbon to Morocco. By the time Richard had emerged from the bathroom she had lined up a flight to Casablanca and taken care of the first few nights' lodging.

"Good job," Richard told her. "When do we fly?"

"Tomorrow night. We don't have to get up early. If we're up by nine or so, have a quick breakfast, we'll be in Lisbon with time to spare. We return the rental car directly at the airport, so it's all pretty easy."

"Great."

As Toshika removed the towel from her head and returned to the bathroom, Richard pulled a pair of underwear from his closet and a minute later stood dressed and ready. "Shall we have a little stroll through the village before we go to the restaurant?"

"Yep," Toshika called from the bathroom. "I'll be ready in a minute."

27

The plane landed heavily, tearing Toshika from her slumber, bringing her back into the world wide-eyed. She looked across the aisle and then back at Richard before settling her head once more against the seat, her fingers relaxing their defensive grip on the armrests. Noticing her reaction, Richard placed a hand on her arm.

"Scared you, huh?" Toshika nodded and then smiled, feeling silly.

"Hey, we made it," she said, leaning forward and looking across Richard through the small window, hoping to see something exotic but seeing only an airport at night. Stretching, she gripped the armrests tightly once again, her whole body stiffening, then relaxing. "Wow. I think I must have slept more or less the whole way. Did I miss anything?"

"Oh!" Richard gasped, "Everything! I'd better not tell you all the wonders you missed. You'll never forgive me."

"Ha ha. Hey, we're in *Casablanca*! Are you excited?"

Richard thought for a moment. "Yeah, I am. I'm a little apprehensive, actually."

"Apprehensive, why?"

"Because I don't have any idea what to expect, except that life here should be really different than anything I'm used to. I don't know, it's a little scary."

Toshika laughed. "Come on, it'll be fun! You wait and see."

Moments later the plane halted. Everyone jumped up and began pulling things from the overhead compartments, each one imagining they could leave the plane before the others. After a long wait they stepped through the door of the plane and onto the rolling staircase that had been wheeled over to assist them. "Boy, and I thought Portugal was hot," Richard said, frowning.

"We'll get used to it."

Once inside the airport they filed off to claim their luggage, find a cash machine in the airport to get some local currency, and get to their hotel.

They found a cab immediately. The driver knew the hotel, and in minutes they stood at the front desk, checking in. The hotel was without charm, but was one of the biggest and most luxurious in the city. Casablanca was not anything like what either of them had imagined: modern, clean, tall new buildings and wide boulevards. Once in their room, Richard and Toshika shared a cool bath before lying in bed watching satellite television until they fell asleep. It was the first time they had been in bed before midnight in weeks.

Richard was up early and went down to the lobby to the hotel's kiosk where he found a guidebook to Morocco. Later, after Toshika had roused herself from bed and gotten dressed, he read from his new book over breakfast. At one point, he peered out from behind his book and looked at Toshika, then leaned out sideways to get a look at her legs under the table. "Listen to this," he said, reading from the book to her. "Notes for the traveler. Local customs: As Morocco is largely a Muslim country, travelers are advised to observe local customs discouraging public sexual behavior."

"Hmm, we'll have to teach them a few things, won't we?"

"Yeah, right. It also says that women should not dress 'provocatively.' I guess you'll need to buy some new clothes. All you've got are these skimpy summer dresses." Toshika looked beyond Richard at the people milling about in the restaurant. "Did you hear me?"

Toshika looked at him and then continued to eat her fruit salad. "Yes. Buy some new clothes. Sounds good to me. We can go as soon as we're done. But you need to buy some too. Neither of us have appropriate clothing for this trip."

"I know."

When they finished eating they set off in search of a good clothing shop for tourists. They found just what they were looking for in a busy shopping area near the center of town. With much amusement they each bought two complete desert outfits that looked like something out of Hollywood, equipped with loads of pockets, flaps, and zippered compartments. As they wandered the busy shops, Toshika grew impatient with the city whose name spoke of a romance it failed to deliver.

"This certainly isn't very exotic," she complained. "Let's go to the old town, shall we?" Richard nodded, opening his book and locating the city map, tracing the streets with his finger.

"Okay," he said, "Here we are, this way." They found the old district quickly but found little that was very old. As they entered, Richard considered once more Toshika's attire: a light dress that stopped above the knee, and sandals. He was slightly apprehensive about her appearance, aware that they were stepping into a different way of life and living. A way that might not take kindly to failures to observe its traditions. They visited the area without incident, however, roaming the streets and alleys, getting a glimpse of life away from tourism. The old town was nice, if small, but did not strike either of them as anything special. They stopped for a late lunch in a small café. There Richard made some progress with his book in finding suitable destinations. Toshika tried to make the best of things.

"Well, this is the largest city in the country. What did we expect?"

"Right. Okay, here it is. You want the desert, right?" Richard asked, drawing his finger across a map in the book. Toshika nodded. "Okay, so we head down the coast road to Essaoria, which is supposed to be nice. Then we cut east to Marrakech."

"Marrakech! Sounds great."

"It's supposed to be pretty amazing. From there we head over the Atlas Mountains to Zegara, or Zegora, which is known as the gateway to the Sahara. We can set up a desert tour from there. Sound good?"

Toshika was pleased that Richard had gone to the trouble to find a route that would suit her. "Yes, but is it okay with you? What would you like to see while we're here?"

"Oh, don't worry about me. I'm all set."

"Okay, then can we set off tomorrow? I think we've had enough of this place," she said, seizing the shopping bag from under the table and pulling out her new desert trousers.

She stood next to the table and held them to her waist. "What do you think?" she asked Richard. "Do I look rugged?"

"Oh, very," he assured her.

Following the advice in their guidebook as well as that offered them at their hotel, they arranged their accommodations ahead of time for the next several nights, including a flight from Marrakech to Ouarzazate. "It's an awful drive through the mountains," their concierge had told them, "and it takes ages." That was convincing enough for Richard. The hotel arranged a car and driver for them as well; a young, likeable man from Tangier named Massoud who would take them to Marrakech. It was all very convenient and, Richard would tell Toshika later, civilized. They planned to take a scenic route to Marrakech before moving directly on to the desert region beyond the Drâa Valley.

They began the next morning by heading along the coast road south, stopping at the seaside town of El Jadida. The driver, Massoud, informed them that El Jadida was a haven for Moroccans in the summer months who fled to the city from the hotter regions inland to relax and swim in the ocean. Stopping near the center of town, he was especially protective of the new-looking Japanese car of theirs. "I must stay with the car," he told them, "It is everything for me." Toshika and Richard bade him farewell and set off for a walk.

"This is more like it," Toshika exclaimed, gripping Richard's hand tightly with excitement. Just then she stopped and took out her cell phone and snapped a picture. "For Jeffries," she told Richard as she began punching out an email to him and attaching the picture to it.

The city, with its white walls and genuine appearance, was a far cry from the gleaming modernity of Casablanca. But after about an hour, having toured the old Portuguese remnants of the city, the two of them had seen enough and returned to the car. They headed on, still hugging the coastline, to the city of Essaoria, where they would stay for the night.

Nearly three hours of unimpressive views of the flat countryside and the hypnotic droning of Moroccan music on the car's radio found Richard and Toshika in and out of sleep that brought no rejuvenation. At one point Richard leaned forward and asked Massoud if he would mind turning the music off.

"No," Massoud replied, smiling eagerly, clearly having misunderstood. "I don't mind."

Richard thanked him anyway and turned his attention to the blurring scenery out the window. He found himself laughing weakly as the world rushed by outside.

Upon arrival they had some trouble finding their hotel, necessitating an irritating sequence of aimless driving punctuated by Massoud hopping out of the car every five minutes to spend an amazing amount of time receiving directions from innocent bystanders they happened upon, with lots of arm waving, head shaking, and vigorous talk. These episodes did, however, allow Richard and Toshika ample time to view this even more exotic and fascinating city.

Finally they arrived at their hotel. Although not impressive, but was one of the nicer buildings they had seen. They checked in, visited the room quickly, and then went out to explore on foot. 'Essaoria is a trading post with a three thousand year history,' Richard read from his book. Although nothing they saw looked anywhere near that old, the city had an ancient feel to it that they had not yet experienced in the country. The white homes with their blue windows reminded Toshika of the Mediterranean. A red stone wall surrounded the city, a feature common to cities in Morocco. On their walk they found a restaurant that they decided would be theirs for the evening.

They did not know if it had been a poor choice of restaurant, or if it was simply evidence of the quality of food away from Casablanca, or if it was just their weak tourist stomachs, but they had an unpleasant night that involved making constant trips to the bathroom where they wretched until their muscles ached.

In the morning they skipped breakfast and stayed in bed as long as they could to make up for lost sleep. Feeling weak, they checked out in the afternoon and set off for Marrakech, a drive inland of about two hours through which they slept off and on. They awoke to shouts from Massoud.

"Look! Here it is! Here it is!"

They sat up and looked ahead at the great walled city that lay before them. They had arrived in Marrakech. "Wow," Richard began, rubbing his eyes, "they must be thirty feet high!"

"And the mountains," Toshika exclaimed, pointing at the range of snowcapped peaks clearly visible some distance behind the city. "What a contrast!"

"That," Massoud said, his finger pointing into the mountains beyond, "is Atlas." They were immediately thankful that they had decided to fly through the mountains that lay ahead instead of making the journey by car. The arrival proved much easier than that at Essaoria and they found their hotel quickly. It was again one of the most luxurious in the city. Not the modern skyscraper variety one finds in Casablanca, the hotel was not impressive. Instead, it was beautiful.

Marrakech proved to be a city of extremes. Mystically beautiful, romantic, exotic, and even charming at times. It was also a very large city and therefore noisy, foul smelling, and not without vivid scenes of poverty. It was filled with prostitutes, and pushy salesmen who were often willing to follow tourists through the streets if one made the mistake of paying them the slightest attention.

On the first day, the sizeable square of *El Fna*, with its food stalls, assorted merchants and entertainers, including dancers, musicians, snake charmers, jugglers and fakirs absorbed almost the entire afternoon, as Richard and Toshika nourished their drained bodies with fresh fruit juices, dates, and baked sweets that Massoud, now acting as their guide, promised were safe to eat.

That evening they dined in their hotel, where the food proved to be almost as captivating as the décor. "Finally, a bit of romance," Toshika said to Richard as they sat barefoot on pillows with the other diners in a semicircle and watched as the night's entertainment was announced. At the front of the restaurant, a group of people in brightly colored clothing stood waiting near the hostess's podium. A man from the hotel came to the center of the large room.

"We are very lucky and pleased tonight to have four groups of dancers who will perform traditional Moroccan dances for you. The dances, costumes, and music are all traditional, so please enjoy them."

Uncertain applause followed the man's exit. At once, the people who had been waiting filed into the restaurant. Six musicians took up their positions impassively, while eight dancers, an even mix of men and women, smiled radiantly at the guests. One of the dancers, a man, stepped forward and announced the name of the dance, a word that neither Richard nor Toshika were able to catch. He returned to his place and waited for the music to begin. The music was performed by a combination of drums, flutes, and stringed instruments.

The performance was brief, not lasting more than six or seven minutes, and was quickly followed by another from a new group of dancers. "No wonder the dinner package was so expensive tonight," Richard whispered as they waited for the next group, a slightly larger one than before, to begin their dance. This one was more elaborate and impressive than the first, and involved some surprising acrobatic maneuvers from the dancers.

At the next performance, the announcement of the dance was clearly heard. "This is *Houara*," said a woman who stood in the center of the floor with a row of six men standing shoulder to shoulder behind her.

"This should be interesting," Toshika said. Richard raised his eyebrows at her and nodded. The music began and immediately impressed the audience with its deliberate power. As with some of the other dances, the rhythm built upon itself, pushing the dancers faster and faster. The men danced articulately and with quick, but fluid movements around the woman. The woman, flauntingly beautiful and with long, dark hair, stood quietly, paying little attention to the male dancers that hovered around her. After a lengthy show from the men, including a solo performance from one of them, a man dressed all in white, the woman moved to one side of the floor, as the men continued their dance, and began to move slowly in an arc in front of the tables, a serene expression on her face as she looked into the eyes of the guests sitting in front. When she reached the middle of the floor, directly in front of Richard and Toshika's table, she stopped. She looked into Toshika's eyes, with just the hint of a smile on her lips. The music had built up to a frantic pace. Suddenly, the woman leaped into the center of the floor while the men formed a semicircle around her. She spun with terrific energy, throwing out her arms forcefully in a defensive posture. Her energy was startling, having arisen from such splendid calm only moments before. Finally, the woman issued a sharp cry, collapsing onto herself, drawing her arms and legs inward as the music ended with a final mighty report from the drum. The audience sat in silence, awestruck, before bursting into hearty applause and whistles. Richard looked at Toshika, eager to see her reaction. She merely looked on at the woman and clapped mechanically.

"That was something, wasn't it?" Richard asked.

"Yes," she said, "but *what*, exactly?"

Richard smiled and shook his head. "I don't know. I'm not sure I want to know."

As the performers left the floor, the last group entered and took their positions. "*Tissint!*" a young woman cried before returning to the group. Several men and women, including a young boy and girl, all of them dressed in costumes of a brilliant blue, began the dance. The dance became faster and faster, with the young pair leaving the group to perform a duet. The boy pulled a dagger from his belt and held it outstretched towards the girl while dancing around her, encircling her. Finally the boy held the dagger at the girl's throat while the girl danced obediently. As the music reached a feverish pitch, the boy collapsed in front of her, bringing the music to a ringing halt.

"Wow," Toshika said, clapping loudly. Richard and the other guests joined in, providing the largest reward of the evening.

28

Jeffries awoke to the utterly charming sound of his alarm clock with a start. He swore, reached over to it, and shut it off. He lay there for a moment until he began drifting off, then forced himself up, swung his legs out of bed and put a pair of sweat pants on. He picked up his slippers with his feet and closed the door quietly behind him, careful not to disturb his wife who lay buried under the covers, oblivious. He crept past his daughter's doorway, looking in at her. She lay sleeping in an odd position, covers kicked off long ago, looking as if she had just been dropped onto the bed by some giant hand. Minutes later he sat sipping his coffee and reading the newspaper. He checked the kitchen clock. It was time.

He went upstairs and gently scooped up his little princess in his arms. "Yes, yes, yes," he said to her in answer to her sleepy protests. "Yes, yes, my Peeps." He held her in his arms for a minute or so as he sipped some coffee and looked out the window at the ocean with her.

"Okay now, some breakfast, shall we?"

Penelope nodded. "Mmm hmm."

He sat her down at the table on her chair. "Okay, so what'll it be my love? Some cereal? Some toastie toast with butter and jam? Some yogurt?" He stood in the doorway of the kitchen and waited.

"I'm not hungry."

He turned and went to the refrigerator. "Okay, then it's eggs."

"No!" the little girl shrieked. "Okay, toastie toast. With strawberry, no, with apricot jam. And butter."

"Okey dokey."

The two of them sat together eating their toast and jam as Rachel began mourning the loss of the darkness and of sleep upstairs. A little later Jeffries gave Penelope a hug and wished her a great day as she set off with her mother to school. He went back to the paper, then took it outside onto their deck in the backyard. He read for a few minutes before he thought of Hans. Then his mind began to wander. The police hadn't phoned him in ages. They must not be getting anywhere, he thought. He thought of David Norton, wondering if he had had anything to do with Hans' death. He remembered the champagne he had given to everyone at the game. At the last weekend Rachel had served that champagne to some guests they had been entertaining. Several people had commented on it. It was quite good. Jeffries started thinking, and the next thing he knew he was in the kitchen with the phone.

He would call David to ask about the champagne, but that wouldn't really be the reason for his call. The phone rang, but there was no answer. After nearly twenty rings he hung up. He retrieved his cell phone and rang David on his cell phone. Also no answer. Later that day he swung by David's house in North Beach. No one home. He started off and then stopped the car, reversed into a parking spot, and got out. He approached the house and squat down in front of the mail slot in the door and lifted the flap. A pile of mail lay inside the door.

Jeffries headed towards his car while he rang the police.

"Hello, Detective Ryan please." Jeffries waited, feeling more sure of himself as he did. Finally there was someone on the other line.

"This is Kevin Ryan."

"Hello detective, this is Arnold Jeffries."

"Oh, hello Arnold. What can I do for you?"

"Detective, have you any leads yet? Or I mean, forget leads. Do you *know* anything yet? Are you making any progress at all?"

Detective Ryan paused. He didn't know how to take this question. "Arnold, is that a simple question, or are you trying to suggest something?"

Jeffries checked his temper. "It's a question."

"Well, we're working on several leads, in fact. Sorry that 'leads' is all we have at this point, but I can assure you, every arrest starts with a lead."

"Detective, has your investigation involved any kind of focus on David Norton?" Jeffries asked. To hell with it. If they weren't going to think of it, he would think of it for them.

"We have considered everyone, including David Norton. In fact, I'm glad you mentioned him. We'd like to check some details with Mr. Norton but we haven't been able to locate him. Would you have any idea where he is?"

"In fact I do. I mean. I don't know where he is, but I think he may be abroad."

"Really?" Detective Ryan asked, his pen poised to take notes. "Any idea where?"

Jeffries stopped as he arrived at his car. He reached into his pocket and took out his car keys. "Yes. I think he may be in Morocco."

The next day Richard and Toshika visited one of the souks, the marketplaces comprising shop after shop nestled within a curious maze of earthen streets and structures. They left Massoud, eager to experience the souk on their own. It was a fascinating place, with all manner of goods for sale, each shop specializing in something. They wandered the streets aimlessly, taking in the smells, colors, sounds, and odd sights. At one point they stopped in a little shop selling lamps, furniture, and exotic decorative crafts. Richard asked to see an ornate metal pipe that lay with similar items in a glass-covered case. The proprietor happily offered it for his inspection.

"*Sipsi*," he told Richard as he handed it over to him.

"Look at the small bowl," Richard said to Toshika. "It must be for hash."

The man heard him and leaned forward, speaking softly. "Hashish for you? I have."

Richard looked at Toshika and smiled. "Why not?" Toshika said.

"Yes, sure. Can we smoke in the street? Is it okay?"

"No," the man said, gesturing behind him to a doorway at the back of the tiny shop. "Smoke here. Then go."

A price was negotiated quickly, as Richard had no patience for laborious haggling, and they soon found themselves seated on a couple of small stools in a room behind the shop. They had purchased only enough hashish for them to consume on the spot. They filled their lungs with the delicately fragrant smoke three or four times each. They did not quite finish the bowl.

"Enough?" Richard asked Toshika. She nodded her head and let out a fine stream of ash blue smoke from her mouth. They packed up the *sipsi* and left, thanking the man kindly on their way out. As soon as they were outside they knew they had been wise to stop smoking when they did. They could feel it already.

"Oh, my," Toshika said as they picked a direction and set off. Several streets and sharp corners later they began to laugh quietly to each other at things that they knew were not especially funny. The sight of a man coming the other way wrapped in blue, just a slit in his turban for his eyes that burned into Richard and Toshika as they passed one another, silenced them until, each of them having turned to watch him go and to make sure that he was in fact gone, they breathed a sigh of relief and then erupted in quiet, choking laughter that made them stop in their tracks. When they set off again, they immediately came upon a tea shop and went inside, each ordering a tall glass of sweet mint tea. Toshika winced upon taking her first sip. "Oh, it's quite sweet," she said, making an expression Richard had never seen her make before and that made him laugh as he tried to show her what she had looked like. They giggled at each other until it hurt and everyone around them, they were sure, knew why it was that they laughed so much. They had better not laugh so much – who knows? Maybe there is a severe penalty if you're caught with hashish in Morocco? They pondered the idea, then laughed some more and paid the bill so that they could escape into the labyrinth. Hurry, let's go, stand up straight, take a deep breath. "You know those hats they wear look like ski hats. Can you imagine! But it's so hot!" They laughed with their fingers pressed against their lips. Everything is okay. They passed by a man selling meats. "In India, cows are sacred. Can you imagine? Praying in some temple, muttering, 'Holy cow, holy cow.' Can you see it?"

Toshika let go a giant hiss of air between her lips. Richard joined her as they rounded the corner into the sun, with red earthen walls all around them. "Wow, it's really *hot!*" They laughed and laughed at the heat that held them tightly, as firmly as a wool carpet wrapped around them. Everything is okay. Everything is okay.

They sat on the ground against a stone wall under the shade of a tall palm tree gazing into the pool of water before them in the Menara Gardens, feeling pensive, happily lost in their own world, not speaking. They had spent half-an-hour exploring the extensive gardens before coming back to the water to rest. It was beautiful there. Soft, green, quiet, fragrant. The water of the menza, the mammoth pool forming the centerpiece of the park, was flush with and almost overflowing onto the cement path that framed it. Brilliant orange flowers floated on the surface of the water, the same ones that hung down over the wall above their heads.

"It's so full. I wonder what happens when it rains. If it flows out, flooding the paths, bringing everything together," Toshika murmured, closing her eyes and resting her head once more against the wall. "I'd just love to fall into it."

Richard smiled at the thought. "I'm sure it's not allowed."

As Toshika realized she was close to dozing, she looked at Richard, at his Buddha smile. She delicately removed an orange blossom that lay on his shoulder and, placing it behind her ear, nudged him gently. They rose and left the park, holding hands, exchanging glances, happy to have no words to say to each other.

29

From the air, they could see the whole world. The engines buzzed on the other side of the glass as Toshika rested her head against the window frame. Richard sat opposite her, minding his own window. He was in a special place of his own, a place of detachment, of freedom from feeling bound to any particular place, any particular scene. A citizen of the world, and nothing more. Fluid, guided by his intuitions. Looking at her, he wondered if Toshika had reached that place as well.

They had already begun their descent on this twenty-minute plane ride that felt like nothing more than a hop over to the next place. The Drâa Valley, on the other side of the Atlas Mountains, was visible as they approached Ouarzazate, a town nestled in the mountainous region, and famous as a Hollywood film site. With only about 40,000 inhabitants, it was dwarfed by Marrakech. The kasbahs of Ouarzazate were beautiful and exotic and presented Richard and Toshika with an easy choice for an afternoon stroll before settling down for dinner at Dimitri's, Ouarzazate's oldest restaurant. In the morning, eager to move on further south into desert country, they hired a car and headed off for Zagora.

The drive to Zagora was long and uncomfortable, but they found the city itself to be fine, perhaps even better equipped than either of them had anticipated. Their hotel was more than adequate, and the service surprisingly good. When they arrived and checked in, they immediately kicked off their shoes and managed a short nap, not bothering to unpack. Later they had something to eat at the hotel restaurant before setting off to explore the village. They wanted to see what kind of guide services they could find for the region, beginning with the one that was recommended in their guidebook.

After meeting the founder and main guide of Adventure Treks, it was a clear choice. Mike Trimble invited them to have a seat on a couch in front of a coffee table. Mike was an American who had been living in Morocco off and on for nearly ten years. He had started his company more than five years before. That fact was important to Richard, who did not want to end up in the hands of someone who did not know their way around, or who might even take them to places that they would regret having visited. After all, it was clear that the region held its own dangers, like any other place.

Mike sat opposite them and began explaining what they could see with the help of a photo album of pictures he had taken of the various destinations so that they could get a precise feel for what they wanted. The choices were numerous, including day trips to both the mountains and the desert, as well as longer trips in both places. They could go by four-wheel-drive truck or by mule into the desert, an option that appealed neither to Richard nor Toshika.

"What could we see of the desert in a full day, if we rose early and took a Jeep?" Richard asked.

"Well, the Tinfou dunes I mentioned are not far, but you don't need a whole day for them. This area here is near the desert but our tours are more geared to the mountains you came in through. The most spectacular dunes in Morocco are farther east at Merzouga and Erg Chebbi. But if you want desert, and you don't mind a bit of a drive, there is an oasis across the border into Algeria that is spectacular. I've only just started going there this year, and I don't have pictures of it yet, unfortunately. There's a nice little village there with a place to get something to eat that won't kill you, and the scenery is fantastic. It's two hours by car but the drive takes you through some amazing territory."

Richard looked at Toshika. "Sounds good to me," he said. She nodded and began flipping through the photo album that lay in front of them.

"The only thing is, since it's a hard drive for the trucks, compared to my more local tours, it's a bit more expensive," Mike told them.

"Oh," Richard said with a gentle shrug. Toshika finished looking at the pictures and closed the book, smiling at Mike and putting her hands together.

"Yeah. Algerian desert oasis. Let's go."

They agreed to meet at the hotel the next morning at seven, thanked Mike, and took the scenic route back to the hotel. After a meal of an unidentifiable meat and some vegetables that neither of them could stand to finish, they went to their room for some reading, and then went straight to bed, sleeping soundly and without a care.

"Did you sleep well?" Mike asked them as he took Richard's small backpack from him and helped Toshika and then Richard into the Land Rover.

"Very well, thanks," Toshika said. "I don't think either one of us will be sleeping on the way there."

"Oh, I don't think so either," Mike said with a laugh. "It's not a roller coaster by any means, but the drive we're taking isn't really smooth enough for sleep, I'm sorry to say."

"No problem, we're up for some adventure," Richard said, taking a firm grip of Toshika's knee and then giving it a slap. "Right?" he asked her.

"Right."

Soon they were cruising over the sandy roads towards Algeria, with Mike explaining everything about his life there and how he had come to be there in the first place – to seek adventure – his love for the desert and its wildlife, and of his occasional homesickness. He went through a long list of things he missed from home, which consisted mainly of different types of food. The three of them laughed together at their common feelings about life in the country. At one point the Land Rover left the road and sped over the sand as they headed up a long, gentle sand dune.

"Where are we going?" Richard asked Mike, looking back at the road behind them.

"Shortcut," Mike said. "A great road. We go over a few easy dunes and through some remarkable country. We end up back on the new road a little while before we get to the oasis.

Saves us a good twenty minutes, too. Don't worry, I know this place."

The way was indeed beautiful. Beautiful, but haunting in its stark severity. The vastness of the spaces, the harshness of the soil and the vegetation impressed upon Richard and Toshika that they were indeed in another world.

The time saved by the detour was diminished by a number of stops they made so that Mike could snap some pictures for his tour book, but Richard and Toshika did not mind at all and actually appreciated the chance to get out from time to time to stretch their legs and get a more intimate feel for the area.

They had already had two such interruptions when Mike suddenly slowed the tortoise-colored vehicle to a stop and swung the thin door out, grabbing his camera as he called to Richard and Toshika over his shoulder. "Last one, I promise."

Toshika took Richard's hand and took a deep breath. "Heat wave number three," she said, then opened her own door and pulled Richard outside with her before letting go of his hand and taking a few halting steps forward. "*Man*, it's hot out here," she said, placing her hands on her cheeks.

Richard could only manage a faint groan at her remark, but kept walking ahead past and around her as if he were seeking to cool himself by creating a breeze with his stride. After a dozen steps he stopped. Spread out before them, all around, was really something. A mule ride might not be such a bad idea, Richard thought to himself as he stared out over the barren country.

No sooner had he had the thought than he was struck by the fear, although not the sensation, of something akin to falling from a great height, looking up from where he had come, unable to see where he was to land. He knew then that he had been wrong. The questions were not going to fade away. Love could make him feel drunk, and money could help him to run faster and faster. But he could not leave behind what was part of him.

Looking out through the heat waves that rose up from the scorched and broken surface that stretched out all around them, his hands rose in the air. "What is all of this?"

He felt a hand on his shoulder. "Hey man, you okay?"

He turned. Looking at his almost panicked expression reflected in Mike's sunglasses, embarrassment gripped him as he wondered what it was he had said.

"Don't worry, I'm not going to leave you here," Mike said, grinning as he slapped Richard on the back. The sound of the dirt and stones crunching beneath Mike's boots as he returned to the Land Rover reached Richard as if from miles away. "Come on," Mike said, "before your brains get cooked." But it was the sight of Toshika, her back to him as she made her way around the truck, that jolted Richard into action.

"Coming."

It was not yet ten o'clock. When they made their final stop an hour later on the fringes of the village, Mike waited a moment to look around them before shutting the engine off.

"Here we are," he said, turning around in his seat. "Now listen. We're far away from anything out here so be careful. We'll go up together to the place where we'll have lunch, to say hello and find out what our choices are today for food, but after that if you want to walk around a bit, stretch your legs, that's fine. Before we eat I'll show you a few things, show you some of the agricultural activity of the place. And then after lunch we can see some more. There's a beautiful pond just five minutes' walk from here on the other side of this strip of date palms," he said, indicating the direction with a wave of his hand. "It's set in the middle of a field of stunning red rock. In the last week there's been a lot of rain back home, and probably here, too. Freak storms. So the pond may be pretty big right now. Anyway, it's something to see. We'll also see some things by car."

When their boots hit the dusty ground, they had to stop a moment before leaving the Land Rover as the simmering air they had been sheltered from for the past two hours hit them with full force.

"Holy cow," Richard exclaimed. Toshika could only grunt in agreement, gathering her hair in a ponytail and quickly placing a band around it. The two of them began to follow Mike into the village as a small crowd of children approached, encircling Mike, laughing and grabbing onto his hands, arms, and waist. He laughed with them and spoke to them in their native tongue. No sooner than they had seemed permanently attached to him when they began at once to fall away, focusing instead on the strangers, approaching them eagerly, although more cautiously, with the same smiles, seeking physical contact with them, especially with the pretty girl whose hair was the same color as their own.

"Hi," Toshika said to the children, "How are you?" The sound of a foreign language brought instant laughter from the delighted children, who responded as best they could.

"Hi!" they answered, "Hi!"

Toshika squatted before a small boy and held his hands. "Hello," she said, fully aware that he would not understand her but unable to stop herself. "What's your name, sweetheart?" The boy nodded, smiling shyly, before looking to the other children with wide eyes.

Toshika stood and waved as the children ran away, racing ahead of the newcomers, anticipating their destination, leaving them in the quiet of the dust as they walked in a line like mules tracing a path across the desert. The grind of the engine of another vehicle arriving somewhere behind them was the only sound they heard. They saw no one else until rounding the corner of the road which began to run uphill when the village immediately came to life, with people walking in the streets, selling fruit and other food on the roadside, as well as assorted goods, bargaining over tools, rope, radios.

Soon they stood in front of a small earth and stone structure where Mike was instantly greeted by an old woman who sat in the shade of an awning in front just next to a doorway. The two of them spoke for a moment, the woman nodding and smiling at Mike's guests. They entered the structure, which turned out to be the woman's house, and went straight through it into a small garden behind the house with a large table and chairs and shaded with a canopy of sorts. They were invited to sit and have something cool to drink. Mike talked with Richard and Toshika about the choices for food and then conveyed their wishes to the old woman, who nodded and smiled to them as she turned and disappeared into the darkness of her home. Richard and Toshika thanked the woman as they passed back through her house with Mike to the road in front of it.

Once there, a teenage boy passing by with several friends his own age stopped and approached Richard and Toshika. "You! Where you from? You!" he asked them, smiling shyly.

Richard grinned at Toshika and then at the boy. "Disneyland," he told him.

The boy's face lit up. "Disneyland! Americans!" he cried, returning to his friends as they began pushing and shoving one another playfully before they trotted away in a din of laughter.

"Hey guys," Mike called to Richard and Toshika as they began to move down the road. "Don't be longer than an hour, okay? And don't go far." They waved to him once and were gone. As soon as they were out of earshot from Mike, Toshika took Richard by the hand, squeezing it urgently.

"I want to go find that pond Mike told us about," she said. "This heat is awful!" She took a good look at what appeared to be a woman clad head to toe in white as she walked briskly by them. "I wonder how they do it?" she said. "Maybe those *jalaba* they wear make all the difference."

"I'm not sure going to the pond is such a good idea," Richard told her, hesitant already to simply wander the village without an escort who knew the way around.

"But look, he said it was just on the other side of those palms. Why don't we just hop over?" she asked, pointing to a line of trees that began on the next hill and ran up to the top, stretching nearly as far as they could see in either direction.

Richard looked at the hill and put his hands on his hips, thinking. "Okay, look. Let's go up the hill to the top, and we'll see what we can from there. If all we see are more date palms, then I say we forget it and wait until we can go with Mike." Toshika agreed.

They continued down the dirt road as it twisted and turned among the earthen structures on both sides of it. Several times they were approached by men who offered services of some kind. Toshika thanked them each time in French and told them that they already had a guide.

"I don't know which is worse," Richard told Toshika, keeping his voice low, "These buggers or the damned flies."

"Well, we can't talk to the flies."

Richard looked at her and laughed. "Of course we can talk to the flies! Go away! Get out of here!" he cried, waving his hand in front of his face.

"Stop it!" Toshika said, laughing, trying to sound serious, "They'll think you're talking to them. The last thing we need is to get chased out of the village by an angry mob."

"Yeah, right."

In just minutes, they arrived at the top of the hill, having walked a straight line through a row of date palms that at least offered some shade from the heat. Standing on the top of the hill they could only see more trees for hundreds of yards, and beyond them only desert and scrubby, desolate-looking land punctuated by similar low hills. Then they looked east, and there it was, a shimmering mirror perfectly placed in the midst of rolling red rock about a quarter mile away. There were no roads, no houses, no people to be seen. All was perfectly quiet. Serene.

"There it is!" Toshika whispered, pointing to the glassy water above the trees that spilled down the hill all around them. "Let's go!"

Richard's concerns about their safety vanished when he lay his eyes upon the water that looked as cool and refreshing as any he had ever seen. They tramped down the hill and then turned, staying within the shade of the trees as far as they could. Finally they came up alongside the pool that lay not more than fifty feet from the shelter of the trees.

They left the shade and strode onto the uneven, rocky ground that formed curious knobs and lumps that seemed to give evidence to it having been under water at one time. It was like being on another planet; a scene from a science fiction movie. The pool itself was larger than they had expected, covering an area nearly a couple of hundred feet long and easily sixty or seventy feet across.

"Now, *this* was worth it," Toshika declared, sitting down at the water's edge and unlacing her boots. The water was still and clear. Richard joined her but remained standing, his hand to his forehead as he took in a three-hundred-and-sixty-degree view of their surroundings. Seeing no one, and nothing out of the ordinary, he looked down at the sound of water swirling below him.

"Ah! It's nice!" Toshika groaned, both of her feet in the water. "It's warm right here, but it's got to be cooler farther in where it's deeper."

"*If* it's deeper," Richard said. "It certainly *looks* deep."

In an instant Toshika was on her feet, walking quickly over to a spot where the rock formed a small table near the water. She pulled her T-shirt up over her head and dropped her bra after it onto the rock, a smile of pure delight forming on her face as she looked Richard in the eye, making very clear her intention. She unzipped her pants and slid them off before pausing just for a moment, her thumbs hooked under her panties. "Last one in is a rotten date!" she said, letting her panties drop and then quickly stepping into the water and heading immediately for cover in what she hoped was a much deeper pool farther out. "Oh! It's fabulous!" she said, already waist deep.

Richard took another quick look around them and then joined her as fast as he could get undressed. He stepped into the pool carefully, unsure of what kind of bottom it held. To his surprise, it was just more rock, making it very easy to negotiate. "Ahh," he moaned, quickly entering and following Toshika. In just seconds the water was at his neck. "I thought it was going to be all slippery and muddy on the bottom, but I guess it really isn't very often that it fills up like this." The water was much cooler away from the shore, and approached something next to chilly down at their feet. "Oh, *man* that feels great! I can't believe this. They should charge people admission."

The two of them swam quietly, thrilled to be outsmarting the heat. As they approached the middle of the pool, Richard could still stand, but Toshika was forced to tread water. "It sure is deep," he said, stopping where he was, watching Toshika doing a backstroke, slipping slowly away from him as she headed for the other side of the pond. Before she reached the opposite shore she stopped and began swimming along the edge of the pond toward what looked like the deeper of the two ends. She swam on until she could walk, then emerged from the water once again into the hot, dry air. She sat down a few feet from the shore and waved at Richard to join her before lying on her back, the sun quickly removing the moisture from her skin. Richard began a slow walk towards her, curious to see if he could in fact walk the whole distance to her or if the water would become too deep.

As she lay in the penetrating heat, Toshika noticed the effect of the swim already leaving her. The heat from the stone beneath her and the relentless sun above warmed her on both sides. She turned her head to one side, trying to spare her eyes from the sun's brightness. In her stillness she opened her eyes for a moment, looking at the low wall of rock nearby, a sharp line contrasting against the deep blue sky above. She was about to close her eyes when she noticed movement on the wall. She sat up abruptly and looked to see a young boy, not yet a teenager, sitting atop the stone just fifty feet from her. She sat there, motionless and exposed, goose bumps forming on her skin, heart pounding, eyes quickly scanning the entire length of rock as well as the surrounding area. When she was sure he was alone, she allowed herself to relax.

He's harmless. If he likes what he sees, then let him look.

She waved once to him and smiled before settling back down onto the rock. As she did, she looked to see Richard approaching. He would be at her side in a moment. Resting her head against the warm rock, she opened her eyes once more. The boy was gone. "Good-bye," she whispered.

Moments later, the swirl of water nearby told her that Richard had arrived. She heard his footsteps and the water dripping from his body as he approached and took a spot next to her. "That was excellent," he told her. He lay down next to her and breathed deeply, his body feeling the heaviness from their early start that morning. Toshika's hand found his, and then all was quiet once again.

The sand was hot against his bare feet as he struggled up the large dune, each step being robbed as the sand gave way underneath his weight, making his progress slow and frustrating. He looked up from time to time, checking the distance between himself and the little tea stand at the top of the dune. After some time, the little shack that had at first appeared so very far away seemed suddenly within his reach, and with a burst of energy he stepped faster and faster until he stood in the shade of the tiny structure, his heart pounding, his feet thankful for the coolness the shade brought.

"Come in," a voice called to him. "Have a seat and sample my famous tea."

Richard looked after the voice, his eyes still adjusting to the sudden change of light. He stepped forward and rested his hand against the doorway and saw a young boy beckoning him to enter, his hand holding the back of a chair that stood next to a solitary table.

"It's very hot," Richard ventured, "Is your tea cold?"

"It is not hot tea," the boy told him. "Come and rest, and I'll fetch you a cup."

"Thank you," Richard said. He entered the small shop and sat down, removing his hat and setting it on the table in front of him. The boy returned with a tall glass of tea which he placed in front of Richard before sitting in the other chair, facing him. Richard eagerly lifted the glass to his lips. "Thank you very much," he said, and then promptly drank the entire glass of tea. It was delicious, and felt cool and refreshing as it entered his body and filled his stomach. He set the glass down and looked out through the doorway at the view from the shop. He could see the sand stretching on for miles before disappearing into the green of an oasis far away. A brisk wind blew outside, sending light wisps of sand by the door.

"I can see that you are troubled by something," the boy told him, folding his arms across his chest.

"Well, I suppose I am," Richard said. "I also suppose that that isn't surprising, people being the way they are, living in this world as it is."

"I can help you," the boy told him. "If you would only listen to my advice."

Richard looked into the empty glass. "Tell me."

"You must follow your destiny," the boy said, raising a finger and sitting up straight, his voice a little deeper than before, as if this message were given to him from some higher authority. "No one can be happy unless they follow their destiny. That is all I have to tell you."

"Who told you that?" Richard asked. The boy gazed wistfully out over the dunes below and pointed to the sky that spread out over the desert.

"A bird told me," he said. "A bird that lives in the skies of the desert."

Richard thought about the boy's advice and lifted the glass, setting it down in front of the boy and smiling. "Well, thank you for your advice, although I am sure that it has been told before. But let me ask you something," he said, watching the boy for his response.

"By all means. Go ahead and ask."

Richard folded his hands together and rested his arms on the table. "Wouldn't you say that, assuming that life is a matter of destiny, as you say, by definition then, we would live out our destiny whether we chose to follow it or not?"

The boy raised his finger to speak, and then tapped his chin with it instead. He leaned back in his chair and folded his arms across his chest, looking at the empty glass before him, unable to speak.

"Well?"

Finally the boy stood up and took the glass away, placing it on a tray and wiping it carefully. "I do not know about such things," he said uneasily. "I am just a boy, with much life ahead of me."

Richard thanked the boy for the tea and went to the doorway, ready to resume his trek across the sands. At the doorway he paused, looking once more at the boy who sat alone now at his small table. Looking at the boy's face, Richard was struck by the feeling that he had changed. He looked the same, but he was no longer a boy. His eyes were infused with a confidence they had not revealed before.

"Tell me, kid, do you believe in God?" the boy asked. He waited a moment for Richard to answer, and then stepped back into his shack, walking slowly into its depths before slowing to turn, offering Richard one more chance.

Why is he calling me 'kid'?

"I don't know," Richard told him. "I don't know." He turned and stepped onto the sandy dune.

"Hey," the boy called out. Richard did not stop, but merely turned and raised his head to hear the boy. But in the shack, instead of the boy, Richard found an old woman staring back at him. Plodding as he was through the sand, his gaze fixed on the woman, he suddenly lost his footing and tumbled headlong down the dune. When he rose, he looked back to the shack, the question already forming on his lips. But the shack was not there. Atop the dune was only blue sky. He looked once down the dune and then back up, but there was still nothing. As he stared into the blue above the dune, the cry of a bird circling high overhead broke the silence.

Toshika opened her eyes and sat up, the heat hitting her as if she had been thrown into an oven. She stared out over the water, wondering if she had dozed. How long had it been? She looked at her watch. They left Mike forty minutes ago.

"Richard," she said, placing her hand on his arm and shaking it gently. "Hey," she said to him softly. "We should get going."

Richard sat up and rubbed his face. "Wow. I must have fallen asleep. Goddamn, it's hot!"

Toshika rose and stretched before stepping toward the water. "Race you!" she said, wading noisily into the water and glancing over her shoulder at him.

Richard was instantly on his feet and ran into the shimmering water before leaping forward and diving into its depths after her. Opening his eyes, he swam briskly beneath the surface of the water and grabbed her by the ankle, causing her to shriek with delight. They headed directly across to where their clothes lay in a heap on the other side, stopping for a moment when they reached the middle where the water was the coolest, trying in vain to collect as much protection as they could before going out into the desert once more. Having lingered there a minute they moved on, Toshika swimming ahead of Richard on her back, kicking playfully, splashing him once, and then again.

"I bet you'd like to stay here all day," Toshika said. Richard smiled at her. She watched as Richard's eyes moved away from her to something else, something above and behind her. The smile on his face was suddenly gone.

She wheeled around and stopped, her feet quickly finding the ground in the now shallow water. Without rising up she looked to see a man on a mule dressed in a white *jalaba*, a sober expression on his face, standing perfectly still a hundred feet away at the point where the rocky mound, the one upon which the boy had been sitting, began.

The three of them stayed as motionless as the desert air, as soundless as the water that had collected on the rock. As quietly as he came, the man prodded his mule and began moving closer to Richard and Toshika. As he did, another rider emerged from behind the rock wall, followed by another, and yet another.

"Shit," Richard said, finding Toshika's hand under the water and holding it tightly. "Don't move." Richard cursed their decision to stray from the village. He cursed Toshika for having encouraged him to go to the pond, and then cursed Mike for having told them about it. He was frightened, almost panicking, thinking of how far they were from Morocco.

The six riders stopped their mules thirty feet from the water All wore *jalabas*, some black, some blue. The boy whom Toshika had seen followed directly behind the leader. He spoke quietly to the man in white. As the tone of his voice grew more excited, the man frowned, barking a command and with a sudden wave of his hand silencing the boy.

"Is this your pond?" Toshika asked the man in French. There was no reply.

"If this is your pond, we're sorry. We will leave right now," Richard added.

The man in white simply sat and stared, his face expressionless. One of the other men spoke quietly to the leader, bringing a brief smile to his lips, and then a laugh, before his expression returned to one of disapproval.

Suddenly the leader spoke roughly to Toshika and Richard in a language they could not understand, his finger pointing at Toshika and then at the boy, who nodded in approval. He went on at some length, slapping his leg as he spoke and holding a finger aloft more than once, as if pointing to the sky. When he stopped, the other riders turned their mules around and took several steps back toward the field of palms just behind them, leaving the boy and the leader, turning again to face them before stopping.

Again the man shouted, startling Richard and Toshika. He waved his hand, his arm held out stiffly. Once, twice. It was enough for Toshika.

All at once she pulled her hand free from Richard's and stood up, her feet gripping the rock as she rushed forward against the water. "We're leaving!" she cried, "We're leaving!"

350

She pressed on, unaware that the man's gestures had not been a command to leave the water. Richard cried out for her to wait, but in her fear Toshika heard nothing except the noise of the water she so violently stirred. In her panic she did not hear the renewed shouting of the man, who was now furious that she had once more exposed herself to the boy and to all of them so shamelessly, directly against his call for her to stay right where she was until they had gone, and to never behave that way again. He came down off his mule at once as Toshika left the water, followed by the others. The boy jumped down as well but stayed rooted in place, afraid of what his elders might do.

The man was swiftly upon Toshika, as the others raced to meet Richard as he made his way out of the water, shouting for Toshika to run, to just run. Toshika stood over her clothes and struggled to pull on her pants over her wet feet when she felt a powerful tug on her head that knocked her off balance. With her feet in the legs of her pants, she fell to the hard stone, her hands outstretched breaking her fall. She screamed as the tug came again, bringing her to her feet, her hands searching for what it was that held her by the hair and pulled with such force. Richard shouted in fury with a voice he had never known as he was pushed roughly to the ground, a kick on his back sending him back down when he tried to get up. Then the weight of at least one man came down upon him and stayed there as his hands were pulled up behind his back. Something kept his face pressed down sharply against the stone. He watched as the man in white held Toshika by the hair, one arm around her waist and arms, holding her tightly. The man shouted something toward the mules where Richard could not see. Another man appeared in front of Toshika and squatted down, binding her feet together. Richard struggled violently against the weight upon him and managed to stand up, swinging his fist blindly at whomever was near him. He caught one man against the nose, but only with his wrist. It was enough to bring a sudden and violent response from the men who surrounded him, bringing him swiftly to the ground once again, his head thumping painfully against the stone, causing him to be still once more.

Toshika cried out to Richard, but there was no response except that from the three men sitting on him, staring at her wildly. She swung her arms with all her strength as her fingers clawed at the air, trying to find something to punish. The force that held her head pushed forward, taking her carefully, face down, onto the ground. She gasped and struggled as her arms were brought behind her back and tied together with something soft, like leather. Powerful hands gripped her arms and pulled her once more to her feet before releasing her, leaving her to stand on her own, unsteadily, feet bound together and crossed at the ankle, facing her captors.

A startling quiet returned, forcing her to think very carefully about her next move. The man in white emerged from behind her and looked at her – sadly, she thought – before walking over to where Richard lay. "Please don't hurt him," she heard herself saying. She repeated her plea in French, finally realizing that she had been speaking English to them. The man stopped and turned toward her, then waved his hand as he once again approached Richard and spoke quickly to the men who sat on him. At once they got up and turned to look at the young man they had contained, who now lay motionless on the ground. The man squatted and examined Richard's head, then stood, saying something to the others quietly. At his words, the men seemed to relax and began to laugh, quietly at first, and then more loudly as they held on to each other and patted each other on the back, one of them rubbing his nose and recounting the tale of how he had been hit. The others laughed at him.

"You fucking bastards!" Toshika hissed at them, suddenly afraid for Richard.

The man in white approached and stopped a few feet in front of her. "*Non, non*," he said in French, his finger held up for emphasis. He brought a hand to his chin and stroked his beard in thought as he considered what to do with her. Suddenly she lost her balance, sitting quickly to avoid falling hard and out of control. The man promptly helped her back up. He stepped away and asked something of the boy who stood next to his mule, his face still showing fear. Whatever the man said brought a smile to the boy's lips. He answered the man, and then another said something as well which made all six of them laugh. Finally the man said something to the others. They all spoke and nodded, and Toshika was surrounded and lifted into the air, face up and squinting in the sun.

She cried out as she struggled weakly, tears running down her cheeks. She felt the rough, weathered hands that gripped her naked body and cried for them to stop, cried for Richard to help her. She was carried a short distance and then turned face down as she was placed over a mule and laid down across its hairy back. She saw the shoe of its rider as he climbed on his mule. There was a slap on Toshika's bare behind and then a hand that gripped the back of her thigh, steadying her, as the mule beneath her began to move forward. The six men called out to one another as they began moving together. Her fear having sapped her of her strength, Toshika lay still, watching the ground beneath her pass by through watery eyes, the world as she knew it rushing away from her, as the hand on her leg slapped her on the behind, as if to announce the coming of a new world for her.

The laughter from the men never let up but in fact only seemed to grow as their mules moved along slowly in their tumbling gait. After a minute, Toshika began to feel that something was not quite right. The ground below seemed familiar. Arching her back slightly, she raised her head and looked about her. She was shocked to see that they were in fact still at the pond, that they had simply been traveling in a circle. She looked at the face of her driver as he turned to her and laughed mightily, his hand coming down again upon her behind.

Suddenly, there was a sharp cry from one of the men, and all motion stopped. Toshika raised her head and listened as the grinding sound of an engine, far away, grew louder. The men turned and watched until they could see the vehicle approaching. The man in white seemed unconcerned. He laughed gently and then barked orders to the others, who immediately broke into action. Toshika was swiftly brought down and set gently on her feet. The animal skins that had held her bound were swiftly untied. She looked toward the sound. A green Land Rover was approaching slowly, taking a path parallel to the field of date palms.

"Mike!" Toshika cried out. She backed away from the men toward the water and looked at the man in white, who held up his finger and spoke to her quickly in French.

"*Tu vois,*" he told her, "we were just going in circles, to teach you a lesson." He glanced at the approaching Land Rover, then pointed to Richard. "Your friend is okay. Splash some water on him and he will wake up. Now go and put your clothes on. Hurry! And never come here again!"

At once, as the man in white urged them to go, the others mounted their mules and began a steady trot into the field of palms, surmounting the hill and moving swiftly out of sight.

Toshika watched them go and then turned to face the Land Rover as it came to a halt in front of her, the dust in its wake filling the air briefly before settling. The driver swung the door open and hopped out, smiling at Toshika's shocked expression as he approached her slowly.

"David!" Toshika cried, looking once more into the Land Rover for signs of Mike. "What are you doing here?"

David Norton grinned at the scene before him. "I'm saving your bare ass, that's what."

"But how did you find us?"

"Ha!" David said, giving the gritty earth beneath his boots a kick. "How did I *find* you? Don't forget I was a cop. I've done my fair share of sleuthing." Toshika continued to stare at him in disbelief. "It wasn't so tough, believe me."

"But what do you want?"

"You know what I want!" David barked.

Toshika regarded him angrily for an instant before rushing over to Richard. "Help me!" she cried. She turned Richard over and called his name. Richard groaned and brought a hand to his head. Toshika went to the water and scooped up as much as she could carry, bringing it to Richard and pouring it over a bloody cut on his forehead at the hairline. "Richard," she called to him, returning to the pond for more water. Finally he opened his eyes wide and wheeled around, still fearful of the men who had come and gone.

"Howdy, Peel," David said to him as Richard stared, open-mouthed.

"You!" he cried.

"Can you stand?" Toshika asked him, helping him to his feet.

David retreated to the Land Rover, calling to them over his shoulder as he opened the rear door. "Come on, Adam and Eve, get your clothes on and let's get out of here."

"What are you doing here?" Richard demanded.

"Come on, hurry up and get dressed," Toshika told him. "We can talk in the car."

None of them spoke as David drove back into the village and parked near Mike's vehicle. "Stay here," he told them. "I'll go and get your guide and we'll get ourselves out of here."

When he was gone Richard looked at Toshika, squeezing her hand gently. "What happened to you back there?" he asked, fearful of what she might say. She paused and then began to cry, pressing both hands to her face. At once she breathed in sharply and held her breath for a moment, forcing the tears away, her hands falling into her lap. She smiled weakly at him to tell him she was okay and then quickly explained the merry-go-round she had been taken on, and how that was all that had happened. Richard breathed a sigh of relief and held her tightly in his arms, stroking her soft hair, and promising to himself not to be so stupid with her again. Then he thought of David Norton.

"Toshika, what about David? What the hell is he doing here? He must be *following* us!"

Toshika did not answer, but merely kept her eye on the terrain around them, fearful that the men would return. "Oh, God. I don't know. He's probably here to persuade us to go back so that you can play the game and he can win back some of his money."

"But the game isn't for another month! And why would he care anyway?"

"Richard, how much money did you win from him? A million? More? Don't you think that's worth anything to him?" she said, irritation showing in her voice. Richard looked away from her out the window. He, too, was worried about the return of the men. She was right – it was a lot of money. It was not as crazy as it sounded at first.

"Maybe you're right," he said. "Maybe I'm just trying too hard to forget everything that happened."

They sat in silence for a few minutes before David came back with Mike, looking very worried. "What happened?" Mike asked, looking at them to make sure they were all right and then looking at the cut on Richard's forehead. "That must hurt," he said.

"Yes, quite a bit actually," he said. He took a deep breath and, knowing how stupid it would sound, began to explain. "We went to that pond you told us about and took a swim. We didn't bring bathing suits, so..."

"Oh, brilliant," Mike said, shaking his head in disbelief.

"I know. Anyway, when we were on our way out of the water six men appeared from out of nowhere riding mules. They saw us and came right up to the water. They started yelling at us, but of course we didn't understand a word of it. Toshika panicked and got out of the water, and that was the last straw for them, I think." Richard looked at Toshika, who sat holding her arms, her head bowed. Recounting the incident probably was not doing her any good. "I don't want to talk about it anymore," he told Mike, quietly. Mike frowned and stole a glance at Toshika before looking at Richard once more. "Nothing happened," Richard said.

"Yeah, you were *lucky*," David said, throwing his head back once and giving a crisp laugh. "Believe me, back home it would have been a different kind of merry-go-round."

"Well, I guess we should head back," Mike said. "I don't know who those men were, but it's better if they don't see you again."

"Yes. We just want to get out of here and back to Zagora," Richard told him.

"Sure. But how about taking something for that head. Let me get a painkiller for you," Mike said, leaving Richard for his Land Rover before he could respond. He returned with a bottle of pills and a bottle of water. "Here you go, this should help." Mike gripped the door of the Land Rover and hesitated, shooting Richard a troubled glance. "You know, this event may make it harder for me to bring people out here. Now I'll be known as Mike, the American who brings foolish and arrogant tourists with him." He looked at Richard, trying to balance his anger at being placed in this predicament with the sympathy he felt for him and Toshika.

"I'm sorry, Mike. I'll make it up to you," Richard said vaguely, raising his hands in a kind of promise before letting them fall loosely at his sides.

"We'll follow you," David told Mike as he climbed into the Land Rover. Mike nodded and got into his own vehicle, starting the engine and turning around in the small space at the end of the road. David did the same, and then stopped suddenly, lowering his window and waving at Mike to stop. "Maybe it would be safer if you had someone in your car too. Another pair of eyes," he suggested.

"I don't think that's necessary," Mike said. "It's up to you."

"I'd prefer it," David said. "Toshika," he said, looking at her in his rear view mirror, "Why don't you go with Mike so you can help him keep an eye out for any unfriendlies." At the thought of driving back with David, Toshika quickly agreed. Richard held her in his arms, reluctant to let her go.

"Will you be all right?" he asked her. She nodded. "Are you sure? You can stay here with me if you want."

"No, it's okay. I'll be fine," she said, giving him a kiss before jumping out of the Land Rover to join Mike.

David Norton looked over his shoulder at Richard. His face betrayed no emotion. "Peel, why don't you sit up here next to me so you can watch things better."

Richard hesitated, then gave in when he could not think of any excuse to refuse. "Sure," he answered, and let himself out of the car to get into the front passenger seat. He closed the door and put his seatbelt on.

They set off at a slow pace until they were outside the palm fields where they quickly settled into a good cruising speed, raising long trails of dust behind them. As they drove on, David did not offer any explanation of just what he was doing there, and why he had arrived in this remote village at the same time as Richard and Toshika. Richard did not ask, weary as he was from the incident at the pond, his head still pounding from his fall. He brought the back of his seat down a bit and made himself comfortable, as he suddenly felt unusually tired.

He had started to nod off when the sound of David's voice brought him back. "Hey! You probably shouldn't sleep with that lump of yours there. You never know."

"Yeah, okay," Richard said, raising himself up a bit and trying to concentrate on the road ahead.

David gave Richard a hostile glance. What the hell is his problem, Richard thought. All at once he decided to ask him about his presence there. "So what are you doing out here, anyway? I mean, it looks pretty obvious that you're following Toshika and me."

" 'Following Toshika and me,' " David echoed. He looked at Richard and his face grew red. "What the hell are *you* doing here is more *like* it," he said angrily. "Skipping all over the world with my money, dragging our sweet thing Toshika with you."

" 'Dragging'?" Richard asked him.

"Internet start-up? You *lied* to us, Peel. You never had any money. Hans invited you to that game and fronted you the money that you used to clean us out. I don't know how you did it, but I'm willing to assume it was beginner's luck. The next game is coming up soon, cowboy. You won a lot of money off me, isn't that right?" Richard said nothing, merely watching the dust that came from Mike and Toshika up ahead of them. "Damn right. You want to know why I'm here? I'll tell you why I'm here. I want what's *mine*. I want what I've been *waiting* for." Richard was about to tell David that he was not obligated to play in any more games if he did not want to. He even thought of mentioning that these games were illegal, implying that he could blackmail the whole lot of them, until he realized that this would now include himself, too. In the end he remained silent, hoping that David would take this as a sign that he was at least considering participating in the games so that he would leave him alone.

"Tell you something else, too," David continued. "You weren't supposed to leave town, were you?" Richard looked at him, realizing that, having been a police officer, David could easily have learned much about the status of the investigation into Hans' murder. Richard had pushed all of that so far out of his mind that the mention of it now was something of a shock to him. David nodded, clearly enjoying himself. "That's right. You were told to stay put. Do you realize that you appear to be running from something now? Do you realize that you are the prime suspect at this point?" Richard looked at him, feeling a protest rise in his throat that he could not find words for. "Do you know that the detectives covering the case think that you might have killed Hans in order to profit from the game?"

Richard was shocked. "The game? How would they know about the game?" he asked David, suddenly feeling suspicious of his suggestions. "If they know about it then you're all in a bit of trouble, isn't that right?"

David merely laughed. "Trouble? There's no trouble! Those boys are friends of mine. Hell, I've got a game going with them too! Lower stakes, of course. They'll wheedle me out of the whole thing, but they need the game because it gives them a reason to look for any evidence pointing to you. It makes them concentrate their investigation on you, because at this point, you are the only one they see with the motive and the proximity to Hans at the time of his murder. The evidence they have points to you, even though it isn't overwhelming. But that's not a problem," he added, pausing to increase the pressure on Richard. "They've been successful many times with slimmer evidence than what they have on you."

Richard did not know what to believe. He could not even think straight anymore. He looked again at David, surprised to see him now as perhaps someone who could help him if what he were saying was in fact true. David could feel his gaze, and could not help but smile.

"Yes, Peel, those boys are *friends* of mine. And friends do help each other out, don't they?"

Richard felt caught out. Stuck. "Yes, that's what friends do," he admitted, turning his gaze out onto the desert. A hard place to seek comfort.

Some time later David sat up straight and watched as Mike took a sharp left, turning off of the main road. "What the hell's he doing?" he cried. Richard's head snapped up, as he strained to see what was happening. Mike was about a quarter mile ahead of them and disappearing fast behind the dunes to the west off of the road. "What's he doing?" David cried again. Then Richard remembered.

"Oh, right," he said, relaxing in his seat and laughing to himself. "Follow him, it's just a shortcut. An old road that nobody uses anymore. It's got a couple of dicey spots, but otherwise it's fine. We went the same way when we came out here. Don't worry, just follow him."

David turned the wheel and slowed the vehicle as he searched for the spot at which Mike had left the road, not wanting to enter a spot of soft sand and risk becoming stuck. He leaned forward, his eyes squinting to see the condition of the road ahead. At that moment Richard noticed something above David's belt underneath his shirt.

It was the barrel end of a holster.

Richard felt a stab of heat in his chest at the sight of the gun, looking away from it before David noticed. Having sorted himself on the old road that stretched out before them, covered here and there by sand drifts and other debris, David accelerated sharply until he brought Mike back into his sight. "Holy shit, that son of a bitch isn't making this too easy," he said roughly. "Doesn't he know that this ain't my town?"

"Yeah," Richard said, trying to sound as casual as possible, "He probably drives it so much that he doesn't even think about it. But he said it would take at least twenty minutes off the trip."

"Well, that's something, then. As long as we don't have a breakdown out in this shithole, that is."

Richard was happy to have found something with which to agree upon with David. He was suddenly filled with the determination not to provoke him in any way. He would simply get himself and Toshika away from David and from Morocco as fast as possible.

When they pulled up in front of the hotel, Mike and Toshika sat waiting for them in Mike's Land Rover.

"Here it is," Richard said to David, watching him turn the engine off and remove the key from the ignition. When he realized that David Norton might not be heading off somewhere else, he stiffened. "Are you staying here too?"

David nodded. "Best place in town," he said, sarcastically. Richard got out of the car and went straight over to Toshika. He opened her door and looked across her lap at Mike, who was writing something down in a small notebook he kept in the car door.

"Mike!" he hissed, keeping his voice low, "You've got to drive us on to Ouarzazate right now! I'll pay you a thousand dollars US." Mike and Toshika gave Richard puzzled looks but did not say anything. "Listen, this guy is after us and he's got a gun."

"A gun?" Toshika asked, her hand coming to her lips. "What?"

Richard looked through the car windows over at David Norton, who had begun inspecting the wheels of his Land Rover. "I saw it under his shirt," Richard said. He looked at Mike. "Will you do it?"

On the drive back into Morocco, Toshika had explained the poker game to Mike and had told him that David was rather unpredictable, but neither one of them were prepared for this. Mike looked over at David, who by now stood on the steps of the hotel with a backpack slung over his shoulder. Mike waved a hello to him.

"Sure, Richard," Mike said. "No problem, but how do we do it?"

"Okay, thanks. Listen, stay out here. Look under your hood or something, or use the toilet in the hotel. Anything. I'll call down from the room and tell them to prepare the bill and that you'll be paying it for me. In fifteen minutes, be ready to drive off."

Richard nodded as David stepped down from the stairs and approached the vehicle. Mike got out and greeted him. "Hey, I'm sorry I drove so fast back there on my little shortcut. I had practically forgotten about you."

David shook his head and laughed. "Well, you had me going there for a minute, but we figured you were probably just so used to that old road that you forgot how some city slicker like me might have trouble driving it, didn't we Richard?"

Richard shut the door of the Land Rover and hoisted his pack over his shoulder as Toshika walked up the steps of the hotel.

"That's right," he said, making a point to make eye contact with David. "But you did a pretty good job out there David, don't you think so Mike?"

"Oh certainly!" Mike grinned. "As a matter of fact, if you're looking for a job as a driver, I might be able to help you out," he said, laughing and slapping David on the shoulder.

"Well, I sure feel better now that we're back here and far away from those bastards," Richard said, nodding his head in the direction they had come from. "But I think Toshika is a bit shaken up. She needs to lay down and have some peace and quiet," he told them. He shook Mike's hand and said good-bye. "So, we'll call you in the morning about that tour of the Tinfou dunes, okay?"

"All right."

Richard turned to David and looked at his watch. "Shall we meet for a drink after we've had a chance to relax a bit, say at six?"

David looked at Richard, then at Toshika. "Yeah. Sounds good," he said, returning to his Land Rover and opening the door. He took out another bag and closed the door, locking it. Richard quickly went up the steps and met Toshika, who stood waiting at the door.

"Thanks Mike, see you tomorrow," she said. The two of them went inside, going upstairs to their room straight away. Once inside, they quickly packed up their things. "Are you sure he has a gun?" Toshika asked Richard.

"Yes. I saw it under his shirt. I saw a holster, anyway, and I doubt he's carrying pencils in it."

"God, he must be crazy."

"I wonder how he *got* it here?" Richard said.

When they were finished, Richard looked at his watch and then picked up the phone, calling the front desk. With everything arranged, the two of them sat down on the bed and waited until it was time to go downstairs.

"I just hope to hell that David isn't sitting there in the lobby when we go down," Richard said.

"Why don't you call the reception and ask just before we leave?"

"Good idea," he said, putting his arm around Toshika and giving her a squeeze. "I knew you were good for something," he teased.

They waited silently, holding each other, waiting for the time to pass. Richard felt awful for what had happened to Toshika, and though he knew that it had been her idea to go to the pond, he felt he should have known better, that he should have protected her from getting into that situation in the first place. And then his thoughts swiftly fell upon the murder of Hans Kienle, and of what David had said in the car. Part of him felt secure in the knowledge that he had nothing to do with Hans' murder, and that there should be nothing for him to worry about. But another part of him realized that if the available evidence, as slim as it was, pointed to him, the police might be forced to go after him. What if they won? Somehow the notion that he might actually be convicted and placed in prison for a crime he did not commit failed to strike home. It just was not real. It couldn't happen to me, he told himself, not to me.

Toshika was terrified of what David might do if he managed to catch them, unprotected. She told herself over and over that they would go downstairs, and that David would not be anywhere in sight, that they would get into Mike's waiting vehicle and speed off, putting time and distance between themselves and David. But where would they go?

"Richard," she asked him, suddenly realizing that the plan was not complete. "Where will we go from Ouarzazate?"

"I don't know. I don't imagine they fly outside Morocco. But we can at least get back to Casablanca and then fly out immediately. Where should we go?"

Toshika rubbed her forehead gently, realizing that it was not that important to know yet. "I guess we can figure it out when we get there," she said. "As long as we are away from David, we'll be okay."

"Right." Richard looked at his watch. "Okay, we go in one minute."

"I have to pee!" Toshika said, rising quickly and rushing into the bathroom.

"Oh, great! *Now* you realize this?" Richard cried. "Do it fast!" Moments later the sound of water running told him that they were ready. The time had come.

"Okay!" Toshika said, lifting her bag and taking a deep breath. Their hearts raced as Richard quietly opened the door and looked into the empty hallway.

"All right," he whispered, "come on!"

They fled without closing the door, both of them moving quickly, almost running down the hallway to the stairs. As he approached the stairs that began around the corner to his left, Richard thought he could hear something ahead. His suspicion was confirmed as he watched David take the last step up, emerging directly in front of him, turning as he did towards both of them.

Richard's heart froze at the sight of David, who stood rooted in place with a surprised look on his face. As he tried to slow himself down, the weight of his bag kept moving, giving Richard an idea that he was not even aware of until it was all over.

He broke his pace and shifted his momentum into the bag, swinging it back and up, like winding up to throw a baseball, bringing it forward over his shoulder with all of his strength, catching David square in the face with it, the blow sending him reeling back to land on the bare wood floor with a loud thump.

Toshika, who was running behind Richard, had not noticed that the person rounding the corner was David Norton. As Richard stopped short in his tracks, she crashed into him, sending him right down on top of David. Richard scrambled to his feet to defend himself, but David did not move.

He was out, cold.

His shirt had risen up when he hit the floor, exposing once again the gun against his ribs. Richard quickly reached under his shirt and pulled the gun from its holster.

"Go!" he shouted to Toshika, picking up his bag and following her down the stairs. They raced through the lobby, down the steps, and into the waiting Land Rover outside.

"Everything okay?" Mike asked them, seeing the panic in their faces.

"Yes, just go! Drive!" Richard cried, his eyes glued to the doorway of the hotel as they backed up and then began hurtling down the road sending clouds of dust into the air. Ten minutes later Richard showed Mike the gun and then held it out the window, tossing it into the dust and boulders near the base of the Atlas mountain range. With the gun gone, he looked at Toshika and they both laughed, shedding themselves of the fear and panic that had gripped them. As they laughed, Richard remembered that David could still follow them.

"Jesus, I hope to hell he stays out for a long time," he said. "Maybe we should have tied him up or something?" he said, looking questioningly at Toshika.

"Don't worry about him," Mike said, "With two flat tires, he won't be going anywhere soon."

"Hey, way to go Mike!" Richard cried. "For that, you get an extra thousand!"

As they wound their way up the mountains the sky grew dark, and then rain began to shower the land, putting a damper on their progress, but not their spirits. They had made it.

At the sight of Richard and Toshika running through the hotel lobby and out the door, their eyes wide with fear, Mohammed Slaoui came out from behind the front desk and went to the doorway, watching as the Land Rover was thrown into a forward gear, the tires spitting out small stones and sand as it carried on the hazardous retreat that the young couple had started. The American who ran the trekking company had paid their bill, so he was not concerned about that. But what on earth had made them hurry so? He had seen foreigners late for busses or planes, but none of them had looked quite like that. Curious, he slowly went up the stairs of the hotel that he was so proud to work in, stopping at the first floor to look up and down the hallway. Seeing and hearing nothing, he continued up the stairs to the next floor. As he neared the landing, he saw something that made him freeze. He brought his hand to his mouth. A man lay at the top of the stairs flat on his back. He hurried up to the top and looked at him. The man looked to be sleeping peacefully. Then Mohammed Slaoui recognized him: it was the other American. He had checked in the day before. He was about to bend over and rouse him when he noticed something under his shirt. Squatting next to him in the hallway he cautiously raised the shirt until he was sure that it was what he had thought it to be. He reached under the shirt to discover that the holster was in fact empty. Immediately he remembered having seen something in the hand of the young American man who had just run off. He could not be sure because his arms were moving quickly as he ran across the

365

lobby floor, but it could certainly have been the pistol that belonged in this holster, he told himself. Guns. Guns! Why must Americans always have guns? He quickly ran down the stairs and called the local police before returning to try to get the man to his feet. He was able to wake him easily, but the man was not very happy when he realized where he was and what had happened. Mohammed Slaoui explained that the young couple had indeed left and were not likely to return, suggesting that the American should go to his room and get some rest. But the man did not seem likely to do that. He thanked Mohammed Slaoui and asked him to prepare his bill and then went off quickly to his room. Mohammed Slaoui returned to the front desk and warned the police that the American was now awake and would be leaving soon. They asked him to take his time preparing the bill, should they fail to arrive fast enough.

But it did not take long. As he finished with the bill, a car pulled into the parking area in front of the hotel. Mohammed Slaoui felt greatly relieved that he would not have to become involved with any difficulties with this American all by himself. He felt sorry for the American, as he would soon have some explaining to do, but it was not a matter for his concern. The American should have known better than to have an illegal weapon with him. It was his own destiny that he would have to face.

For the first time, David Norton was worried that things might not be quite as easy as he had imagined. He sat in the front seat of a plane en route to San Francisco via New York from Barcelona. It was business class, but in this case he received no special treatment. His hands sat helplessly in his lap with heavy handcuffs securely fastened around each wrist. Next to him sat a hefty policeman dressed in plain clothes. David didn't look at the other man. Had no interest in speaking with him. He had entertained thoughts of explaining himself, of relieving the humiliation of being on the other side by telling him the truth, and by reasoning that it was all just a mistake, but he knew how pathetic those words sounded to a cop. How they reduced a person. The more earnestly those words were spoken, the more one shriveled. He was not going to be an object of that kind of scorn.

There was nothing to do but wait. When the time came he would explain himself to those who had no choice but to listen to him.

The Atlas Mountains were just wrinkles in a wide expanse of sun-baked earth as the plane climbed higher and higher. Richard looked at the crystalline formations on the surface of the window before sitting up straight and looking straight ahead in his seat. Soon they would be back in Casablanca, but he wondered if it might not be time now to go home. If what David had said were true, it would look better for him to return and to go directly to the police to explain why he had gone. But what would he say? He did not want to mention the game unless absolutely necessary. His eyes roamed the cabin in search of answers before coming to rest on Toshika. Of course. He would tell them that he had met this fabulous woman, that she had asked him to go to Europe with her, and that he just could not resist. Simple as that. "I planned to call but never found the time," he imagined himself explaining. Sure that this was the best plan, he smiled at Toshika as she sat next to him, her eyes closed. Then the memory of the scene at the oasis entered his mind. He placed his hand on hers and watched over her.

Later, with nothing better to do, he removed his guidebook for Africa from his bag at his feet and began flipping through it. He started at the back of the book, bending the pages backwards and flipping through, looking for pictures. He came upon a batch of color plates and stopped, finding the last one so that he could flip through them slowly. The last one was a photograph of a beach: stunningly blue water, immense round boulders in the surf, a couple sunning themselves with umbrella drinks in their hands. "Where is that?" he muttered. The caption at the base of the photograph read: 'The sunny splendor of Clifton Beach, South Africa.' He knew next to nothing about South Africa. He found the section on this southernmost country on the African continent and began to read. He was surprised. Cape Town looked like nothing he would have expected to see in

Africa. The elegant Victorian architecture of the city, the beaches with their restaurants overlooking the surf, the wine country nearby. He was soon convinced that this would be an excellent place to relax and think about the next step. But it would be completely up to Toshika, he told himself. He would ask her where she wanted to go, and if she put the question back to him, he would simply offer it as a suggestion.

When she awoke later, Toshika seemed to be in much better spirits. Richard waited until the time was right before mentioning their next destination. "Shall we talk a bit about our next move?"

"I want to go somewhere to relax," she said. "Just relax. I've had enough of roughing it. Maybe we should go home. We could go to the beach, go for drives up the coast. I know a great health spa up in Napa. One of the bigger wineries owns it."

Richard saw his own idea shrivel. "That sounds good," he said, "but we can have that here, if we want to."

Toshika frowned. "*Here?* Are you crazy?"

"Not *here*," he said, his voice soothing, "Look," he said, taking his book from the pouch on the back of the seat in front of him. He found the picture of Clifton Beach and held it for her to see. "How does this look?"

"Yes, that's what I want, but where is it?"

"Near Cape Town, South Africa. Look, it's all here," he said, the excitement of a new place once more taking over. "Cape Town looks great, there's a wine-growing region not far away, I mean, we could try it anyway, don't you think? One last stop before we go home? We don't have to stay long."

Toshika took the book from him and began to read it for herself. Richard watched until it was clear that she would not be giving an answer immediately. He looked out his window over the vast flatlands between Marrakech and Casablanca and felt glad to be leaving.

"Okay. If we can book a straight flight to Cape Town from Casablanca, let's go for it. If not, we go home. It looks wonderful, so, why not?"

"It's a deal," Richard said. He looked out the window at what he thought was the sea in the distance. When he was sure that it was, their decent to Casablanca Airport was announced.

"Direct to South Africa?" the man at the ticket counter echoed, "Of course we do. Where would you be headed, Johannesburg or Cape Town?"

"Cape Town, first class," Richard said, turning to give Toshika a victory smile.

"All right, yes sir. And how will you be paying for that?"

Before Richard could answer Toshika thrust her debit card toward the man. Richard turned to look at her, a puzzled expression on his face. "It's okay," he told her, putting his hand on hers. "I got it."

"No, this time it's on me," she told him, pushing her card nearly into the hand of the man at the counter. Richard shrugged and put his arm around her. She leaned into him and looked up into his eyes, then reached up to straighten the collar of his soon-to-be-retired desert shirt. "One more stop, and then home, right?" she asked him. All he could do was nod. In that moment he never felt more at home or at ease with her. As the man began the seemingly endless series of keystrokes on his computer terminal, Richard smiled. It was the first time that he did not mind at all how long it took to buy a simple plane ticket.

30

Detective Ryan closed the door behind him and stepped into the center of the small interrogation room at the police headquarters. He reached into his coat pocket and offered David a cigarette. He knew of David Norton from his time on the force, but he hadn't ever worked with him.

"Thanks. I don't smoke."

"Okay, well then."

He sat down opposite David on a hard metal-framed chair with only a modest amount of padding on the seat. David looked around the small room. He couldn't hold back a small grin. Now he knew.

Detective Ryan hesitated when he saw the look on David's face, but then it hit him, too. "Not so pleasant, is it?" he asked him.

"No. It isn't a place that calms you, that's for sure," David told him. "Don't worry," he said after a moment. "I ain't changed my view of things here. You're the good guy."

Detective Ryan nodded. "Okay then, let's start."

David Norton took a deep breath. It was going to come out in one go, because it was simple.

He was innocent.

"Okay. It's like this. I went to Hans Kienle's house with the intention of talking with him. Not hurting him. I hadn't been drinking. Not that much anyway. I was upset, but under control. I arrived at about one a.m. He wasn't home. I sat in my truck outside the house and listened to music until I fell asleep. I woke up a little after two when Richard Peel dropped him off. Must have woken me up. I watched Peel drive away and then I sat there for a few minutes rehashing what I wanted to say to Hans. I went to the front door and knocked, then rang the bell, but there was no answer. I knew the house, you know. I had been there a few times before. I went around the back and looked inside. Then the light comes on in the living room right in front of me, and then here comes old Hans down the stairs. I could see him across the living room on the staircase. I knocked on the window. I didn't want him to see me first, you know, scare him half to death. So I tried to get his attention. But he couldn't hear me 'cause he was listening to his damned iPod. I could see it then, you know, the little white headphones, the wire hanging down his chest. He was wearing a bathrobe and had a toothbrush in his mouth. I waved my hands a bit and he, he must have seen motion because he looked over in my direction. Anyway, with the room lit from the inside he must not have been able to see me so good through the glass, because the light would have been making the glass glare a bit, you know."

Detective Ryan nodded, his expression showing no emotion. "Right."

"So he's there on the stairs, he looks over, and I waved to him, and then he saw me." David stopped speaking. He swallowed, and began again more slowly. "He saw me, and took his hand up to pull out the earphones. Took his hand off the banister, I mean. And he yanked down on the earphone cable, and they came out of his ears, and he's looking at me there, and he took another step because he hadn't actually stopped coming down the stairs. He hadn't stopped moving." David paused again. He pursed his lips. Shook his head slowly. "He was almost at the bottom, for Christ sake. Jesus. He was on the third or fourth step up from the bottom at the most. Anyway, then he lost his balance, lost his footing, his hand flashed out and he stumbled down those last steps. He didn't fall, he stayed on his feet but he had lost his balance and pitched forward and when his feet hit the landing next to the front door he was all bent forward and moving fast, with his head down." David wiped his face with both his hands in one swift downward motion. "He went head first, straight into that goddamned bottle of champagne I gave him the night before. Son of a bitch. It was sitting there on this little table he had there by the door. Where he threw his keys and whatnot. Bam! Right into the bottle, head first. Then he fell down onto his knees and then backward into the living room. Landed on his back. The champagne bottle fell off the table and landed next to him. Pressure must have done it, cause it didn't fall from that high up, and the floor is a wooden floor, you know. Not as hard as marble or tile. Anyway, the bottle broke. I shit my pants and went running around to the front of the house. Fucking door was unlocked, believe it or not, so I went in and pulled Hans a little further into the living room, just got him under the arms from behind and dragged him back, you know. Get him out of the champagne that was all over the place. I don't really know why I moved him like that. Didn't really make no difference. He was alive, you know? He was still alive, but I could tell he was, I mean, he was grabbing at his chest and I figured it was probably his heart. But then he passed out. I went for my phone to call an ambulance but I had left it in the truck on the dashboard. I looked around the room and didn't see a phone, and didn't want to start looking for one, so I dashed out the door and ran to my truck and got my phone, and when I got back inside, I don't know. He looked different. I took his pulse, and he was dead." His story told, David sat back and stared into nothing, his eyes wide. "And that was that."

Detective Ryan didn't move for a long time. Then he sat up straight, placed his hands on the top of the table, and stood up. He turned his back on David and stepped toward the door of the small room. He turned again to face Norton. "Okay, so why the burglary crap? What was all that about?"

David smiled weakly. "Yeah, I know. I know how dumb it really does sound, but I panicked a bit. I figured that with the way things looked, I might have been fingered for killing the bastard. At the poker game – you must know about the game?" Detective Ryan nodded once. "Well, everyone knew I was pissed off at Hans. So yeah. I thought I would make it look like a burglar done it. Took some electronics. Just some stuff that was sitting on his desk upstairs, and dumped it later. Must have been seen doing that, I guess," he added, eyeing the detective for a sign of acknowledgement. There was none. "Okay," he continued, "well, in any case, that's probably what happened. Someone saw me and found the stuff and gave you all a ring."

Detective Ryan gave in. "Shit, David, that was pretty stupid."

"I know. Am I going to get charged with obstruction?"

Detective Ryan regarded him for a moment before answering. He shrugged. "I don't know," he said. "Okay, well look, if what you say is true the guys in forensics should be able to corroborate it." He stood with his hands on his hips looking at David. "I mean, we thought it was pretty straightforward," he explained. "It was all there, broken bottle, bump on the head, missing computer, wallet. The autopsy showed the heart attack, but that doesn't mean there wasn't a crime."

"You don't have to defend yourself," David told him. "I would have thought the same."

Detective Ryan nodded. "Okay, look Norton. You're going to have to stay here tonight. We'll get you a private cell, but there isn't any way out of it." David Norton nodded. "I have to get forensics back into that house to check your story out."

"Have the doc check the body again. See if that collision with the wall didn't leave something behind."

Detective Ryan nodded, and left the room. He stopped outside the door and looked at the officer waiting there. "Take him down to Jack and get him processed. He'll need a bed for the night at least." He turned for another look at David and then set off down the brightly lit hallway at a brisk pace.

Do the waves move in cycles, Richard thought to himself as he lay on the beach, listening to the advance and retreat, advance and retreat. Or do the cycles move in waves? His eyes were held shut against the brightness of the sun. Listening to the waves was like noticing the sound of the ticking clock on one's night table when one wanted to sleep: once it's there, you cannot make it go away. You can only hope that you become distracted by something else, and then the problem takes care of itself.

Cape Town was even more beautiful than the pictures they had seen in his guidebook, and the stunning sight of Table Mountain as they taxied into town was unforgettable. Looming high above both the sea and the city itself, the mountain looked as though its peak had been sheared off by some giant, invisible hand. Coming from the desert heat just the day before, they both found the temperature of Cape Town to be perfect.

They stayed in a small guesthouse with six rooms run by a charming older woman who hailed from a neighboring country and had relocated to South Africa some years before. As luck would have it, the nicest room had just been made available when they called from the tourist center, so they grabbed it before it got away. The room had a glorious view out over the ocean from a wide private terrace. The house was within walking distance from the famous Clifton beaches, a fact that Richard and Toshika took advantage of every morning after breakfast. They read, dozed, talked, and strolled the white sand without a care. Toshika was over the episode in Morocco enough to have begun calling everyone to tell them of their adventures. Jeffries had asked her to make a point to take lots of pictures in South Africa because he had been thinking about taking his family there and was curious to know everything about it. In the evenings they dined in the restaurants that dotted the coast, many of which offered direct views onto the sea, making it nearly impossible for travelers to forget where they were. Enjoying fires on the beach after hours, or informal gatherings at the guesthouse provided pleasant finishes to each wonderful day. It was just the paradise that Toshika had wanted. In no time, the incident in Algeria had nearly ceased to be even a memory.

On the fifth day they made their way again down to the beach after breakfast and spread their things out in the spot they had come to call home. Later, when the sun and the waves had worked up a hunger within them, they headed for some lunch. As they sat in a sandwich shop up above the beach Richard stared out over the beautiful paradise surrounding them and shook his head. "You know, Toshika, I love this. I mean, I *love* it."

"Isn't it great?" she asked him, thinking for the first time in days about where it was they had been before they arrived.

"Yes, it's fabulous. But it isn't Africa. I mean, where are the lions, the elephants, the wide-open plains, and the mystery? Where?"

She looked at him, an excited expression on her face. "I know what you mean, and you know what? I was thinking about this, but I was afraid to ask you. Why don't we go on a little safari?"

"That's exactly what *I* was thinking!" he cried. "I've been reading in the guidebook and there are some great opportunities here up near the Kruger National Park. We could stay in one of these exclusive luxury lodges for a few days and experience the real Africa!"

"Absolutely! Oh, I'm so glad you agree. But then again, we've got a pretty good rhythm going now, you and I, don't you think?"

Richard leaned forward and put his arms around her neck. "Yes, I certainly do." He closed his eyes and adored every fragrant hair on her head that touched his cheek.

"So, when should we go?" she asked him.

"I don't know, when would you like to go? I could leave any time. I mean, this is great, but it's been five days." Toshika's eyes told him when she wanted to go. "You want to go now? As soon as we can?" he asked her. She nodded. "Well, then it's settled. I'll make some calls and set it up."

Toshika looked out over the water and rolled the idea over and over in her mind. "Safari," she said softly, absorbing the images the word evoked. Richard watched her, pleased that he could bring her happiness, and that with her happiness he found his own. He told himself there was nothing more that he could want.

31

David Norton sat at the bar of the St. Francis Hotel, staring into his whiskey. Part of him told him that he should feel damned lucky. The other part of him said that it was clear, that it was bound to have turned out this way. He didn't kill Hans, after all. And having been a cop in that city, he would never have been railroaded into prison. Not an ex-cop.

The evidence was there, and, as he had figured, they were able to find it. A small but clear indentation in the soft wood paneling of the wall next to the table where the bottle of champagne had stood, showing clearly that the bottle had been pressed with considerable force against it. And the pathologist examining Hans Kienle had found what he called 'a subluxation of his fifth cervical vertebrae.' Whatever. They had their evidence.

The lucky part was that they had allowed him to go free on bail to await any potential further charges. David was clear about that. It was lucky because even with a private cell, jail was no place for a human being. David considered the living hell that must be. He ordered a beer as he noticed an Asian woman appearing on his right and pulling up a stool. She sat with her back to him, talking to someone. Her long black hair reminded him of Toshika, and he sat there staring at her hair, oblivious.

On his left, Margie Clarkson sat alone, one stool apart, waiting for her glass of white wine to arrive. She was on tour. Another bloody tour. Oh well, she thought, it wasn't so bad. This one, anyway. San Francisco had been lovely. Too bad she would be leaving already tomorrow. Here today, and heading home tomorrow. Her mood slipped at the thought.

Would he be happy to see her when she returned home? Would she be happy to see him? She knew the answer to that one. At least, she thought she did. Her wine came and she decided not to think of home anymore that evening. It was her last in the city. She would enjoy it.

She noticed the loneliness at the bar. No one on her left, and some bloke on the right who seemed to be another one of those types who have a thing for Asian women. That, and no sense of tact. He was just sitting there, staring, for Christ's sake. Had he no shame? With her eyes drilling holes in the back of his head, he suddenly swiveled round on his stool to face her.

Margie's eyes went wide in panic just before his gaze met hers, which had returned to something approaching normal. Or at least she hoped she looked normal in that split second. The suddenness of his movement seemed to demand a response from her.

"Hello," she said, smiling and realizing with a small shock that she had tilted her head in a stereotypically coy manner. But he was kind of cute.

David smiled. "Hello." Before the oddness of the ensuing silence could develop, the bartender placed David's beer before him and removed the empty whiskey glass.

"There you are, sir," the bartender said with a smile.

"Great, thanks," David said. He looked at Margie as if asking her to reflect on the nature of the pleasure of having one's drink deposited within reach. "Well, cheers," he said to her, holding up his beer.

"Yes, cheers," Margie replied. She took her glass over to his bottle of beer and waited for him to reply in kind. She noticed that the label on the bottle was completely foreign to her. It provided a way out, so she seized on it. "What kind of beer is that?"

David didn't take his eyes off of her. She spoke with some kind of accent. What was it?

"Where are you from?" he asked her before he realized that she had asked him a question.

"I'm from Liverpool. England." The man hadn't given any sign that he comprehended what she was saying. "Home of the Beatles," she added with a tinkle of laughter.

"Oh, okay," David replied, glad for some reason that his guess had been correct. "Right. I thought I heard something there in your voice."

"Yes," Margie added. Stupidly, she thought.

"You have a lovely voice, I mean, it's a very charming accent is what I mean." David was still holding his bottle of beer aloft. Her question. She asked you a question. He looked at the beer and then back at her. "My beer? It's an Anchor Steam. It's a San Francisco beer."

"Oh," Margie said, studying the bottle in his hand now carefully. "Not a beer that makes it across the Atlantic, I guess."

David looked at the beer and set it down on the bar. "Oh, yeah, that's probably true. But it's a damned good one."

Margie took a sip of wine to buy time. To think of her next comment. "So, what do you do?" That's it, keep it simple.

"Well," David began, unsure, as ever, how to handle the question. "I used to be a cop," he said, accepting whatever consequences that answer might bring. He had tried in that split second to sum her up. To see what she might think of his having been a police officer. Her overall look, with her hair, her clothes, even her face, had told him, for whatever reason, that she was not a flashy person and, at the same time, not an overly educated or intellectual type. Not the type who would look down at being a cop. He hadn't time to think further than this. "And you?" he added, reminding himself to be polite.

Something had changed in her. David could see that right away. He could also see that unless she was planning some kind of cruel attack, this change had been for the better. She smiled in an odd sort of way at him, put her glass on the bar, and laced her fingers together, resting her hands on the bar as well.

"I," she began slowly, "write crime novels."

David felt relief. "No kidding?"

"No kidding."

David gestured toward the empty stool that stood between them and picked up his bottle. "Do you mind?" He rose and sat down next to her as she shook her head.

"I'm David, by the way," he said. He offered her his hand.

David opened his eyes into the clean, white pillow case that lay pressed against his forehead. His breathing was slow, steady. He lay there, coming back, when he noticed the smell of the sheets. Not like home.

Then he remembered: Margie Clarkson. The memory of the evening, of having met her of all people there in the bar, and the realization of where he was brought a smile to his face.

He turned in the bed to find her, but she wasn't there. He sat up just as she came out of the bathroom, wearing a t-shirt and panties. She was rushing, but when she saw him sitting up and grinning at her, she stopped. Stood still with a violence that shocked the joy in him. He saw her expression and felt himself turn to stone. He had seen that expression many times before by people who were caught. Exposed. When something dreadfully wrong in their world was suddenly on display in the broad light of day.

She did not make him wait long in that state of bewilderment that he was in.

"I'm sorry," she told him, her voice breaking for an instant before she managed to pull it back together. And then she was back in action, hurriedly, almost madly, getting dressed and putting her things in order as she spoke. "I've never done this before," she explained. "It wasn't meant to happen. I wasn't here to pick up anybody. This was business," she said. "I was here for *business*. Nothing else. This isn't who I am." She stopped then and looked at him to check, to make sure that he was following her, because she was hardly following herself in the state she was in. The look he gave her caused her shoulders to slump, along with the corners of her mouth. "It was wonderful," she pleaded, suddenly. "But, my god. I'm *married*. I'm a married woman!"

David saw the lightness in the room become crowded out by all the darkness that had also been there when he awoke, lingering in the corners of the ceiling, behind and on either side of the drapes that hung half open now, under the chair and the desk that stood across the room in the corner as if in punishment. "What the hell did I do?" he heard her asking herself as she rushed here and there. How quickly the world turned around. He felt the life rush back into him. He brushed aside the heavenly down duvet and rose from the bed to stand on his feet.

"You're married?" He watched as her eyes widened for an instant before she went back to her task. She is afraid of me.

"I am," she said, squatting down and running the zipper round the corners of her bag.

"Do you have kids?" he demanded. He felt the anger rising in him. He was beginning to feel himself again.

"Three."

She was no longer anything to him now. He crossed the room to the desk and took his clothes that hung off the back of the chair and dressed himself. He pulled the chair out from the desk to sit on it. Socks. Shoes.

When he rose she stood in the middle of the room. She was having trouble getting her watch band fastened. She stood between him and the door. He aimed to leave, and as he did, she looked up from her busyness. Eyes wide again. She let out a peep of fright – there was no other word for it – as he went round her to the door. He stopped and turned, not yet having reached the door.

"What?" he asked her, wearily. "Do your cops kill their lovers?"

He closed the door as he left the room, and stopped. He felt his knees nearly buckle under the weight of having to endure another one of life's miseries. If an open window had been nearby he might have hurled himself right out of it. His hands traveled up to the top of his head and rested there as he began to force himself to get moving, to get the hell away from there. He went to the elevator and pressed the button. He finally let the air out of his lungs in a rush and let his hands fall at his sides. He reached into one of his pockets and fingered his keys. A plan was forming itself. He would need to get home and begin listening to the phone tapes if he was going to have any hope of finding her now.

By lunchtime it would have seemed as though David had gotten Margie Clarkson out of his system. He sat at his desk munching on a sandwich. He hadn't eaten since the previous night. He sat staring at his computer while the recording from his one terabyte external hard drive played all of the phone conversations from the phone in Jeffries' study for the past several days. Every time he heard her voice, he felt a bolt of adrenalin. And every time, it failed to be the message he needed. There was no word search facility with the crude software he was using, and he had no idea when the call might have been made, if ever, so he had to simply listen and wait. No longer being a cop with access to their technology had its drawbacks. He was reaching for his Coke when the call came.

"Hello?"

"Hey, Jeffries! How are you?"

"Toshika, hello! I'm fine dear, and you? Where are you now?" David glanced at the screen to check the date of the call. Yesterday.

"We're still in Cape Town. But listen, I wanted to tell you we're finally going to see some of the real Africa. We're going on a safari!"

"Oh, marvelous! Well, you should, you know. One can't really say they've been to Africa without having laid eyes on some lions and zebras, now can one?"

"That's right."

"So where are you going? To the Kruger Park?"

"No, we're going to a small private place nearby Kruger called Motswari. We're flying out here the day after tomorrow."

"Well, I hope you're still taking lots of pictures for me!"

The conversation continue on for another minute or so before David stopped the playback. He Googled up Motswari and began printing out details from the website. Then he got online and within minutes had his flights booked. He had to pack and go. The flight would leave in four hours.

32

The tiny plane touched down. Richard leaned over to Toshika and spoke loudly above the buzz of the engines. "We made it!" The airport at Hoedspruit was so small that they could not help but laugh as they walked in off the tarmac alongside a family of four with two teenaged children. "This is perfect," Richard said, "I half expect someone to ramble up in a little bamboo car and offer us a ride to the park."

Soon they met their driver, an African who called himself Robert and smiled so pleasantly that Richard instantly felt guilty. I'm going to give him a big tip, he told himself, as he wondered at the source of his discomfort. Robert helped them into the minivan and shut the door. It appeared that they would be the only passengers.

Almost immediately after setting off from the airport, just minutes after the pavement had turned to gravel, wildlife that they had only ever seen before in zoos or on the National Geographic television shows that had held both of them captive as children began appearing amongst the trees and shrubs. They saw zebras first, just a stone's throw off to the side of the road. Several antelopes stepped onto the road far ahead of them, bounding across as they noticed the approaching vehicle. Soon after that they saw the heads of giraffes peering out over the trees. Robert pointed animals out long before either of them had seen anything. There were no fences anywhere to be seen. It was the real thing.

"Now *this* is Africa!" Richard told Toshika, who nodded, nearly bouncing on her seat with excitement. The drive, Robert had told them, would take about forty minutes to the first camp. They would briefly stop there to sign in before departing for the smaller sister camp where they would be staying, a drive of about another twenty minutes. "Wow," Toshika had said, "We'll really be out there!" "Yes," Robert had told her, his speech very clear and careful, his voice as pleasant as his smile, "It is very remote, this place. You will enjoy it."

After signing in at the main camp, which, with a capacity of about twenty people, was twice the size of the camp where they were headed, they said good-bye to Robert and met another driver, Tholo, who showed them to his open Land Rover and helped them in. The engine sounded like it was filled with marbles as it fired up and then carried them away from the camp. In the open car they felt even more exposed and present in their new environment. Tholo did not speak to them as they drove over the dirt road. It was rough in some places, requiring him to come to a near stop to negotiate awkward bumps and other obstacles. They did stop once when they rounded a bend to find a small gray tree lying across the road in front of them. Tholo hopped out and swung one end of the rotten tree aside. "Elephant," he told them, an almost embarrassed smile on his face. He climbed back into the truck and off they went. They continued on, eventually driving steeply downhill to cross dry riverbeds several times. The terrain gave Richard and Toshika pause more than once as the ground ahead looked troublesome, but every time, Tholo would slow down and shift into first gear, gently tractoring his way over and through everything.

Finally the camp was in sight. It sat perched atop a small and lonely hill fifty yards from a river that neither Richard nor Toshika had noticed before, its green water lying heavily in the bed like some great snake. As they pulled up to the camp, they once again noticed that there were no protective fences anywhere. When they hopped down from the Land Rover, they heard a voice and turned to greet it.

"You must be Richard and Toshika," a tall young man said to them as he held out his hand. He was dressed in green clothing that looked like something a park ranger would wear. "I'm Tom. Welcome." The three of them shook hands and Tom escorted them to a large round space with an open fire pit in the center. There was a house on the right and a covered lounge with several tables and a bar straight ahead, a small swimming pool just behind it and to the left. In front was a fresh-looking lawn that had clearly been planted, surrounded by a very low stone wall. "I'll get the others," Tom said as he disappeared into the main house.

Tholo remained standing there and invited Richard and Toshika to have a seat at the large dining table that sat in the open area near the fire pit.

"Can I get you something to drink?"

Richard looked questioningly at Toshika. "I'd like a glass of white wine if you have it," she told Tholo.

"Certainly." The African turned to Richard and asked him once more with his eyes.

"If you have a cold beer I'd love one."

"No problem. I'll be right back." He headed over to the lounge and disappeared behind the bar.

"Well, the guests have arrived." Richard and Toshika turned as another young man approached with Tom and two young women behind them. Soon they were introduced to Adrian, Jane, and Monica. Tom explained that the four of them were qualified rangers, but that Jane and Monica generally did not accompany guests on the "runs."

"What sort of work do you do here?" Toshika asked the women. "Not cooking and cleaning, I hope."

The taller one, Jane, closed her eyes in a long blink as she answered. "We're more in charge of the management of the camp. The boys are sometimes gone nearly the whole day, so we're here making sure the facility is running smoothly while they're gone," she told them, sleepily, as if recounting a dream that she'd been telling over and over. The four rangers were like something out of a television show, all young, attractive, and healthy-looking. As Richard looked them over, imagining how their lives might be intertwined considering the poetry of the combination, Tholo arrived with their drinks.

"Thank you," Richard told him.

"Pleasure." he said softly.

"And of course you've met Tholo," Tom said, "He's our tracker. Tholo can find anything, right Tholo?" he asked.

Tholo smiled and nodded. "Almost anything."

Adrian took Richard and Toshika's bags and nodded towards the river. "I'll just bring your bags down to your tent. But please, relax here and enjoy your drinks."

This is service with a smile, Richard thought, as he nodded to Adrian and watched him head down a path between the lawn and the lounge and then disappear as he followed the sloping grounds down towards the river.

"So, was your flight okay?" Jane asked them.

"Yes, fine," Toshika said.

"Good. Where are you both from?"

"California," Richard answered, prepared for raised eyebrows and exclamations of envy.

"Oh," Jane said, nodding and smiling politely. "Is it nice out there?"

Richard glanced at Toshika. "Well," he stammered, "yes. *We* like it, anyway."

"Great," Tom told them. "Well, here's the schedule for today: we'll show you to your tent and you can freshen up there a bit – sit on your balcony, get your cameras ready – whatever you need to do. Then at three we'll have tea here in the lounge, and at four we'll go off for your first run. It's about three hours in the Land Rover, which should bring you back at around seven o'clock. Dinner is at eight. Tomorrow morning, if you like, we'll have breakfast here at eight and we'll set off around nine for the morning run. The drives in the bush are always about three hours, and we stop midway for a break for tea or soda. We have some small things to eat, too, and you can get out of the Land Rover and stretch your legs. Does that sound good?"

Richard and Toshika exchanged glances before agreeing that it sounded fine to them. "Sorry," Richard began, unable to help but notice the dearth of other people at the camp, "but where are the other guests?"

Monica, the blond ranger who had been carefully noting the manner of the foreigners who came from faraway places that she had promised herself one day to visit, cleared her throat. "Well, we had another party of six reserved, but they unfortunately have just cancelled. So right now, you're alone," she said.

Richard and Toshika accepted the news easily, but both of them instantly felt a bit odd now that "private and exclusive" was being taken to the extreme in their case. While they reflected on the news, Adrian appeared once again, coming up the path from the tents. "But we've just got word that a party of three will be coming tomorrow, so don't worry," Jane promised. "You'll have someone else to talk to besides us," she said with a laugh.

"Oh, no," Richard said, the news allowing him to be diplomatic about things, "We don't mind at all either way, do we?"

"No, of course not," Toshika said. "I don't need a crowd." Richard looked at her as she gazed out over the river and the wilderness beyond. She noticed Richard's attention. "It's beautiful, isn't it?" she asked him.

With their drinks finished, Richard and Toshika waited for their hosts to proceed as planned. "Shall I show you to your tent, then?" Tom asked them, rising and brushing a large insect from his arm.

"Yes," Richard said as he stood up and offered Toshika his hand.

"See you in an hour," Monica said, standing and placing her hands on her hips, obviously eager to return to whatever duties awaited her.

Tom led Richard and Toshika down the path, pointing out the swimming pool as they passed by it. "Use it any time you want," he told them, "as long as it's still daylight. Nighttime swimming isn't a good idea. You've noticed I'm sure that there are no fences here," he said, pausing for their response.

"Yes," Toshika said, "What happens if animals come into the camp? What do we do?"

"Well, first of all, you aren't to go beyond the grounds here to your tents or back from your tents to the main house without one of us. If you're at your tent and you need to come up, just hit the drum outside your tent. I'll show you when we get there. Now, we rarely have animals on the grounds, but when we do, as soon as any one of us sees them, we'll move them off. If you see any large animal or anything potentially dangerous, or anything that makes you uncomfortable, let us know. And if you see them near your tent, just beat the drum and we'll come. But really, this almost never happens," Tom told them reassuringly. "These animals out here are completely wild and they don't want to have anything to do with us. In two years I've only seen it happen once: one time a baboon strayed into the camp. We saw it and clapped our hands and that was that. Nothing, really."

The trail led from the edge of the sculpted grounds past the small pool and on to the tents that stood in a neat row not far from the river's edge. The tents were less than a hundred feet from one another, but dense vegetation between them afforded the guests a sense of privacy. They stood on flat platforms made of wood that sat atop what could only be described as a cement basement, buried in the ground halfway so as to hold the tents a few feet off the ground, and comprising a shower and toilet and a double sink. The tents themselves were really just tents. Large canvas affairs just like the one Richard's family had camped in when he was a boy, only bigger, with two beds, two night tables, and one chest against the wall opposite the beds. A balcony overlooked the river below, which they had been told was normally dry at this time. Unusually heavy rains had caused it to swell some weeks before, resulting in what was now more or less a narrow lake outside the tents as the water slowly dried up and sank into the earth. They were told they were lucky because the water attracted regular visits from a wide range of animals that they would be able to observe safely and comfortably from their balcony.

As the three of them stepped up onto the platform and into the tent, Richard saw something right away that he did not like. "There are two beds," he said. "When I made the reservation I said I only needed one double bed."

"Well, all our rooms have two double beds." Tom said. "That's not bad, is it?"

Richard apologized, noticing now that the beds were indeed large enough for two. Tom left them alone and reminded them that tea would be served in about forty-five minutes. Richard joined Toshika on the balcony and looked out over the still green water of the river below. "See anything?" he asked.

"No. I can imagine them though," Toshika said, "Look at it. It's just like in a movie. I can just see an elephant wading across, or a hippo floating along, eyes and nose poking out of the water, ears wiggling, or a lion coming down to drink.

Can't you see it?" she asked Richard, obviously thrilled with just being there.

Richard nodded and put his arm around her, holding her close to him as they stood looking out over the green wilderness. "This is going to be great," he told her.

They were glad the Land Rover moved slowly over the uneven terrain, their stomachs full from the tea that had turned out to be an opulent feast fit for twice as many people. Now on their first safari, they were eager to find out just how close they would come to experiencing nature in her finest and purest state. Adrian drove while Tholo sat on a special seat that had been attached directly to the hood of the car all the way in the front allowing his feet to rest on the front bumper and giving him a clear view of the ground in front of them. They moved along slowly, mainly in first and second gear, with Tholo watching always for tracks, freshly broken branches, and other animal signs. They had driven along the unpaved road at this cautious pace for perhaps a quarter of an hour before Tholo signaled Adrian to stop, then back up, then turn off of the dirt road and into the bush. There they moved along in first gear very slowly, crunching over everything in their path, going uphill and down, over rocks, through sand and water as Tholo guided Adrian.

Suddenly, Tholo called for a halt. He sat looking up ahead over bushes and through the grass and trees all around them. Neither Richard nor Toshika could see anything. Their breath slowed, and their pulses quickened as they waited and watched, their gaze shifting from the terrain around them to Tholo, who sat looking straight ahead, as still as the air around them. Tholo turned and spoke very quietly to Adrian.

"What did he say?" Toshika whispered to Richard, who answered with a shake of his head. Adrian turned to them.

"We have some lions ahead," he whispered. "In the riverbed. We'll go in slowly. When we see them, I'll shut off the engine so that they're not bothered. Now again, you can talk, you can take pictures, but keep your voices down and under no circumstances are you to stand up in the Land Rover or make any kind of quick movements, okay?"

389

Richard and Toshika nodded, with Adrian's warning making it difficult for either of them to express much enthusiasm as they peered forward anxiously, wondering what awaited them. The Land Rover began to creep forward, rolling about fifty feet before coming to the edge of a dry riverbed forty feet wide. They rolled down the gentle slope several feet into the bed. Right there, not more than thirty feet away to their left were two lions, male and female, lying on their stomachs near the opposite side of the bed in the shade of the bush that bordered it, with their heads up and tongues out. The male turned to look at the intruder, then easily swung his head back again, apparently unconcerned that their solitude had been broken. As Richard and Toshika drew in their breath at the sight, Adrian shut off the engine, leaving only the sound of the two cats breathing, the male's eyes nearly closed as his tail flicked once, then again.

"Wow. They're so big!" Toshika said. Adrian turned to them and spoke casually, keeping one eye on the beasts.

"They come here to the river to cool off. They lie down and rub themselves into the sand a bit."

Without taking his eyes off the lions, Richard asked Adrian why they were not alarmed at the sight of them in their vehicle. "Is it because they've seen enough of these trucks and people that they've gotten used to it?"

"They are used to it to some extent I'm sure," Adrian answered, his hand resting on the rifle that lay in a rack in front of him on the dashboard. "But they are still completely wild animals. The thing is, they look at us in the Land Rover and they just see an animal bigger than they are. They aren't afraid of us, but they don't want to give us any trouble either. Now if I were to stand up, maybe breaking the image of this big animal that he thinks we are, showing him that I was a human, I could be in trouble. We all could be in trouble."

"So they can't recognize that there are people sitting in this thing?" Toshika asked him.

"No, I don't think so. Not quite so easily as that, anyway. Not as animals not part of this Land Rover."

"So, are we lucky to have found these lions? I mean, in three days, would we have seen lions every day?"

"I think we always have to consider ourselves lucky to have found these animals, but no. In three days, we will most likely have seen all of the big five, or at least three of them, I would say." Adrian did not like to promise anything to his guests who, because they were paying so much money and had traveled sometimes from halfway around the world to be there, could sometimes be very disappointed and upset if they did not see everything they had been told about.

"What are the 'big five'?" Toshika asked him.

"The big five are the most dangerous animals on the continent: the lion, elephant, water buffalo, rhino and the leopard."

"What about the hippos?" Toshika asked him, "Aren't they also dangerous?"

"Yes, hippos can be very dangerous. First of all, they're massive animals, and their mouths are big enough to nearly cut a man in two. You definitely don't want to get between a hippo and her water."

"But water buffaloes?" Richard asked, "Aren't they just cows?"

Adrian laughed and looked quickly over his shoulder to check the lions before answering. "Aren't bulls just cows?" he asked. "The buffs are actually the most dangerous of the big five."

"Really?" Richard asked.

"Yes. You see, they are the only animals that won't do a mock charge. All the other animals will warn you when they're not happy with whatever it is that you're doing. They'll give you a chance to get the hell out of their sight before they attack you. But the buffs won't. You won't know you've done something wrong 'till it's too late."

They sat quietly for several minutes as Richard and Toshika thought about what Adrian had said. Toshika took several pictures of the animals, which had not moved an inch since they had arrived.

"What happens if you can't start the car again?" Richard asked Adrian, who turned and smiled.

"It's never happened," he said, willing to leave it at that. "But if it did, and we had a large dangerous animal this close, as close as they are now, I'd radio to see if there was anyone nearby who could pick us up. If not, I'd radio Tom or one of the girls and they would have to drive out and get us." Richard and Toshika looked at each other and raised their eyebrows, encouraged by Adrian's casual attitude but slightly unnerved all the same at the thought. "You know," Adrian began, "We have so few incidents out here, and we hear of so few from other outfits in the area – we all keep in touch with each other – that you really don't have to be worried. Statistically, what we're doing is very safe."

When he was satisfied that they had accepted his explanation he asked them if they would like to move on. They agreed. As the engine turned over and fired up, Adrian shot a glance back at Richard and smiled before he very slowly pulled away, driving forward across the bed and up the other side. Richard and Toshika watched the lions until they were gone from sight and instantly wondered if they had just experienced what would be the highlight of their trip. Soon they were back on a dirt road and Adrian brought the Land Rover up to a very low cruising speed.

"Shall we try for an elephant?" Adrian called to them over his shoulder.

Richard and Toshika grinned at each other. "Yes!" they cried.

Richard watched Toshika as she smiled in the sunlight, with the wind in her hair and the pure pleasure of a child in her eyes. My beauty, he thought. It was one of those moments in a person's life when they ask themselves if they will remember that single, shining instant as long as they live. As Toshika noticed his glance and smiled, then made a face at him playfully, so beautifully, Richard promised himself that he would.

At dinner that evening, sitting outside at a single long table a stone's throw from the smoldering coals that had started out an hour before as a roaring bonfire, Richard and Toshika silently basked in the African evening. They had just finished a dessert that neither of them could believe had been prepared out there in the middle of such rough country when a strong wind began to pick up. There was talk of rain at the table amongst the rangers, and of how strange the weather had been that year. Tom had just remarked that he did not think it would rain after all when the floodlights of the lodge suddenly ceased to shine. Despite the uselessness of doing so, everyone looked up on impulse. The rangers groaned in unison.

"Okay," Adrian said, getting up from the table. "I'll get the lanterns," he said as the others waited.

"Generator went out," Tom explained. "We'll get it back up in a minute when Adrian brings the lanterns." No sooner had he made the comment when Adrian arrived and set two kerosene lanterns on the table, lighting them quickly. The light was more than enough and both Adrian and Tom excused themselves to attend to the generator. While they were gone, insects began landing on the table, attracted to the light, one bigger than the next.

"My God," Richard declared, "they're like little airplanes."

"Oh well," Adrian said as he and Tom returned and joined the others at the table. "Can't get her started. Have to work on it tomorrow."

"That's okay," Richard said, "We've got ourselves some entertainment now." He flicked one of the larger creatures from the table with his finger before realizing that, sitting with four rangers, his behavior might have seemed especially uncivilized. "Oh, I hope that wasn't an endangered species," he joked uneasily. As the others laughed, a ripping sound that Richard and Toshika knew only from television rolled through the camp, silencing everyone. Richard and Toshika immediately eyed the rangers, waiting for a confirmation of what they knew they had heard.

"Well, that's a big one," Tom said to Adrian before flashing a smile at his guests. "Lion. Not far away."

Richard looked at Toshika. "How far would you say, Tom?" he asked.

"Oh, a stone's throw. Fifty yards."

Toshika looked out into the overwhelming darkness that began where the light from the lanterns left off, suddenly feeling very vulnerable. "What's it doing?" she asked.

"Probably looking for someone," Jane suggested before laughing and waving her hand in apology. "I mean, not a person, of course, but another lion. A mate, perhaps. Don't worry, they never come into the camp." They all sat quietly, each waiting to see if there would be another call. When it came, it was just as loud, but issued from somewhere else this time. Toshika eyed Richard and smiled courageously. He knew what that meant. With the wind gusting even more heavily, Richard stood and stuffed his hands into his pockets.

"Well, if it's all right I think we'll head back to our tent. Call it a night," he said, watching relief spread over Toshika's face.

"Sure, hang on just a minute," Tom said, disappearing into the main house momentarily before returning with a flashlight to escort them. They said their good-nights and were on their way. Tom entered the tent first and lit the lantern that hung from a pole on the balcony, hanging it on a hook near the roof of the tent inside before leaving.

"Remember," he said after saying good-night and zipping down the netting on their tent. "If you need anything, just beat the drum."

After brushing their teeth Richard and Toshika talked for a short time in bed before turning off the lantern and waiting for sleep to come.

It proved to be a long wait. Lying in the midst of this otherworldly place in a box made of canvas and plastic where animals the size of automobiles roamed freely found them listening to every sound, guessing which noise was that of the lion pushing past the bush, having picked up their scent, or that of a deadly snake looking for a chink in their canvas armor, or of a hippopotamus crunching through the underbrush on its way to do battle with this solid-looking threat to its watery home. Neither of them spoke, knowing that this would only make sleep more elusive.

Richard found himself at one point – whether it was hours or only minutes later he could not be sure any more – looking through the netting, over the balcony, into the night sky above the river, as the water below glimmered. The stars shone brightly, forming a ceiling over the sleeping world, and although he could not see it, the intensity of the light all around them told him that the moon must also be out there, sharing a little of the sun's light with them.

The water in the river below stirred, followed by the pig-like grunting of a hippo. Against that ceiling of sky, Richard watched as shifting points of light fashioned themselves into sharp-horned rhinoceroses, lions with gaping jaws, kudus with their powerful shoulders and magical horns, and elephants with swooping tusks. Will I ever sleep? The dreadful thought of having to face the day after a sleepless night had long ago detached itself from him, floating out and away into the night as he watched his world at work, and told himself again and again that this was Africa, that he was in Africa. Home of humanity, wellspring of the soul.

Although he did eventually fall into a deep, empty sleep, Richard awoke suddenly in the predawn blackness. The moon had deserted them. He turned his head to be sure he was not dreaming and was immediately struck by an odd feeling of relief, as if his sleep had been so deep that it had threatened to engulf him forever. A thrill simply to be alive spread through him. What warranted such gratefulness? It was not as if he had just escaped the jaws of death, or emerged unscathed from a train wreck. He was saved only from sleep.

The thought stayed with him. Why should it be odd to be thankful to be alive? Wasn't life special, after all? Of course it was, he wanted to say. Of course my life is special to me, but how can it be when I don't even know what I'm trying to do with it? He lay with darkness all around him, afraid that it was all that would be left when time ran out.

He saw a breath of light appearing faintly in the room. He turned to the balcony. The sun was nearing. Through the African bush, and over the water below, it came. He rose quietly, opened the bug netting of their tent and stepped onto the balcony. He lifted a chair and brought it to him, rather than drag it and risk waking Toshika. Soon it would be morning. He had accepted Tom's invitation at dinner to do an early morning walk in the bush, just the two of them. With that on his mind, he knew he would not be able to sleep any more anyway. Setting himself down in the chair, he wondered how long it had been since he had watched the sun rise.

He sat, frozen before the spectacle, as the bush began to warm under the sun's glow. The light grew more intense until a fire broke out behind the trees and the first bolt of pure sunlight split the indigo sky. He squinted and looked at Toshika. It was a shame to be missing such a marvel. But he let her sleep. He turned and watched the unfolding. It was wonderful to be alive.

33

The day was full of sun. Hot and dry but with a generous breeze. Richard and Tom set out from the camp directly, just the two of them and Tom's rifle, intending to make a small loop that would bring them back in less than an hour. Richard had been full of enthusiasm for this walk the night before, feeling ready to experience the new world that much closer, on its own terms, no longer a spectator but joining his surroundings fully, if only briefly. But as he muddled through the morning's routine, getting dressed, having some coffee and a bite to eat before a proper breakfast had been laid out, he could not take his mind off of the vision he had had before. He was eager to tell Toshika everything, but was sure that he would not be able to put her there. To bring it to life for her. He even had half a mind to just keep it all to himself, but was sure that he could not. As he and Tom tramped along on a dusty but barely visible trail, the fog in his head cleared, being washed away by the reality of the present. Soon, his clumsy attention was transformed into a growing sense of alarm just after they had put the camp out of sight. He pressed on, following close to Tom as an icy fear began to grip him. Anything could be out there, all the animals they had seen and then some: a lone lioness, waiting in the tall grass, fascinated as Tom and Richard trundled by, her muscles itching to set her in an accurate trajectory to take down one of these strange beasts. Or a rhinoceros, with its poor eyesight, frightened by their sudden appearance. Or a leopard, staring down from the trees over their heads, its tail flicking mechanically as it decided. Tom had the gun; Richard had only Tom. How quickly could Tom react to protect them against the sudden rush of a predator? The memory of daybreak seemed to taunt him.

Everything will be all right.

But as they walked on, the tall grass stood magically still. The breeze was haunting. Where are they? Which one will it be?

All at once he was struck by the feeling that his life was hanging by the slimmest of threads, causing his step to slow as he rethought the wisdom of what he was doing. But as he watched Tom moving farther away from him, Tom who carried with him their only means of protection, he began walking once again, his eyes shifting constantly over the terrain in front of and behind them, his sensory impressions having intensified markedly after being called upon to bring him safely back home. How would it be, he thought, to live as so many of our ancestors had, not too long ago, and how some still lived in places like this? Where normal life, one with as much justice if not more than any other, meant that every day could be one's last? One's triumphs, failures, and loves must be so much more meaningful in such a life. What new thoughts would be pulled from one's existence? What awareness, what knowledge would such people possess that would simply escape us in our modern world? He continued on in a kind of trance, resisting over and over the impulse to ask to be taken back to safety as the peace with this new experience that he had hoped would come remained only a hope.

Although they moved along silently and kept a sharp eye out, Richard and Tom saw nothing but a few birds. Suddenly, Tom stopped and turned, sending a wave of fear through Richard. "That's about far enough," he said, then looked at Richard apologetically. "Not much out here today, Richard."

"Oh well," Richard said, looking down into the dirt as a trail of mammoth ants made their way across the earth below, "that's okay."

"Maybe we'll see something on the way back," Tom offered, hopefully. Richard could only hope that he would be wrong. As they began their return, he tried to find again some of the comfort from his early morning experience, but it paled now compared to the moment when Tom had stopped and directed them back to camp. Watching the dust scatter under his boots, Richard was filled with doubt and told himself he would say nothing to Toshika of any of it.

Richard, Toshika, Tholo, and Adrian set off for the first run early after a sumptuous breakfast, and almost immediately found a pack of wild dogs, which they were apparently very lucky to have seen given that these animals were exceedingly rare on the continent. Only about two thousand, they were told, were in existence. They seemed like nothing African. Their size was like that of any number of dogs back home. They danced and played, nipped at each other, and rested in the morning's heat. Their big ears and skinny legs made them seem harmless – even comical. Richard and Toshika were surprised to hear Adrian explain that the wild dogs were the most efficient hunters in the bush, working in teams, running their prey down until they were too exhausted to move before they tore them to pieces. Toshika shuddered. Richard brought his arms back inside the Land Rover and looked at the rifle on the dashboard, trying to see if it were in fact locked into place with a key or if it could be swiftly removed if necessary.

They later found a herd of water buffalo at the edge of a large stand of dense greenery and shut off the engine, sitting in the open vehicle as the animals advanced on them slowly out of curiosity, their noses extended, sniffing at the air, completing the picture. In the afternoon they drove for some time without any major finds, but saw loads of zebras, kudus, antelopes, giraffes, waterbucks, with their bull's-eye hindquarters, as well as two hippopotami in a small lake. They even found more lions, and experienced the eerie solitude of sitting in the Land Rover in the middle of a broad, dry riverbed, grounded and stuck on a sandbar, unable to move forward or backward, with lions a hundred feet away, trying to beat the heat as they laid in the sand next to several large tufts of river grass. "Wait," Adrian had said, eyeing the lions before their wheels had begun to spin, "I can get us closer." Richard and Toshika felt like sitting ducks as they watched Adrian and Tholo dig the Land Rover out with tools they gingerly removed from a storage space at the rear of the truck. "Keep an eye out, now," Adrian had said to them once, and then again, as he and Tholo tried to balance strenuous bursts of activity with their shovels, with reassuring glances at their guests.

All in all it was a good day and left them with only the leopard to see from the list of the big five. Richard and Toshika returned to the camp invigorated and restless, eager to share a swim, some alcohol, and some sex on the balcony. Primitive urges gratified in primitive surroundings.

After showering, Richard beat the drum and was brought up to the lounge where he inquired about the new guests. They had not yet arrived. "Their flight must have been delayed," Tom said, sitting behind the bar reading a book on North African birds. "Tholo has been waiting for the call from the main camp. He'll go round them up as soon as we hear anything."

With the thrill of the day behind him, Richard started drinking in the lounge before dinner as he waited for Toshika to make herself ready. By the time they sat down for the champagne apéritif he had decided to treat everyone to, he had already finished four beers.

The drum beating from below set Tom in motion. Toshika finally appeared in her tropical weight attire and apprehended instantly and with pleasure the attention of the others. She noticed, in Richard's unusually enthusiastic welcome, the reason for his cheerful effervescence. Richard noticed her lingering gaze and smiling eyes and sidled up to her, smiling sheepishly while doing his best to be discrete. "I'm a little drunk," he whispered as he raised his glass to Tom and admitted once again his preference for viewing the wildlife from the safety of the car.

The minivan pulled up in the fading light of the evening and stopped just outside the door of the camp. Three people were helped out by the driver and welcomed by a young woman. She held out her hand to the one closest to her.

"You're the Miller party, right?"

400

"Right. Robert Miller," said the middle-aged man, smiling as he shook her hand vigorously and indicated the woman behind him. "This is my wife, Victoria."

"Pleased to meet you," the young woman said. She held her hand out to the man who had waited patiently while she greeted the others.

"We're not together, actually," he said, pointing at the Miller's with his chin.

"Oh, I'm sorry," the young woman said, looking down at her clipboard and studying the names in the calendar. "I must have been confused. I've got the Miller party as a party of three."

"No," the man said, obviously wishing to get beyond irrelevant details. "Hello," he said, shaking the woman's hand briefly. "I'm David."

"We're so pleased to see you," she told them all as she led them into the reception area just inside the door. "I'm sorry about the plane. Usually they don't have any sort of trouble." The three new guests signed in promptly and then sat in low, comfortable chairs, pouring over photo albums filled with snapshots of the local wildlife, until a man stood at the doorway and waited to be noticed.

"Oh, here he is. Your driver is here," the young woman called to them, coming out from behind the desk and following them all outside. The man led them to his Land Rover and waited while the guests said good-bye to the young woman.

"Hello," he told them as he gestured for them to be seated in the bench just behind his seat. "My name is Tholo."

The dinner that evening was a more lively affair than it had been the night before, with everyone a bit better acquainted, and with more stories to tell from the bush.

"The camp called," Adrian said as he returned from the main house to his place at the table. "The new guests have finally arrived. Tholo is leaving in a minute or two to come back with them."

"Well, they haven't much of the evening left," Jane said, pushing at her kudu steak and eyeing Toshika's nipples through the sheer cotton blouse she wore to the table, her disapproving intuitions fighting with her longing for a similar freedom. After all, she told herself, I'm young. I won't look this way forever.

Richard did not hear Adrian's announcement. He sat at the far end of the table staring into his wine glass, a kind of shame eating at him from the morning's walk with Tom that had shown him how easy it was to believe one knows what is coming, to believe one knows what one is doing, only to be proven so very wrong. He knew it was nothing to be ashamed of, and imagined that he could not have been the first guest to have been humbled by the bush, but still he hounded himself.

"Tom," he said, finally admitting defeat and not caring that everyone present would now know of his predicament. "I have to tell you something."

"Shoot."

"The walk we took this morning. I have to admit that it wasn't like I thought it would be."

Tom twisted in his chair. Another unhappy client. "I know how you feel, Richard, but we just can't guarantee that the animals will be there. That's what you get when you're dealing with a real environment."

Richard had to smile at the irony of Tom's comment. "No. You don't understand. I'm actually *glad* we didn't see anything."

"Oh, are you still torturing yourself with that?" Toshika asked Richard, recalling his explanation of the outing while she had made herself ready for breakfast that morning. She had been surprised at how it had affected him, and moved by his sense of appreciation for her that she assumed had been instilled by the walk, as he kept trying to hold on to her while he recounted his experience.

"Ah, I see. Made you uncomfortable, did it?" Tom asked.

"That's putting it very mildly, Tom."

"Well, that's normal. It takes a while to get used to."

Despite Tom's empathy, Richard's atonement was not yet complete. "I tell you," he continued, speaking slowly as he was brought back to the event, "I was so scared out there. I felt like I had a bull's eye on me the whole time. Like a sniper had me in his sights."

"Yeah," Tom said, laughing. "You grow eyes in the back of your head. I know the feeling. But you know what they say: fear is healthy." No one spoke as the noise of the insects rose all around them. Then Tom cleared his throat. "I hope you're not sore at me for taking you out there, Richard,"

Richard shot him a surprised look. "No! Don't be silly. Of course not. I wanted to go, and I'm glad I did. It was definitely a learning experience."

Toshika raised her glass. "Here's to learning."

When everyone had had enough, and the cooks had been thanked and commended, the others stood up as Richard and Toshika bid them good-night. Following Tom's flashlight beam, Toshika helped Richard against his protests back to the tent and watched him fall onto the bed near the door, the drink pulling him towards a heavy slumber. Tom wished Toshika a good night's sleep before going back out into the darkness and zipping shut the door of the tent. Toshika looked at Richard and began to get ready for bed. By the time she had gathered her bedclothes, he was asleep.

Adrian, Tom, Jane and Monica sat together at the table, waiting for the new guests. They had not finished their wine when they heard the engine of the Land Rover, followed by the crunching of stones under the tires as Tholo pulled up and stopped nearby.

"Well, here we go," Tom said as he got up and walked with the others to the waiting car. "Hopefully they aren't upset about the delay."

"Yeah," Jane agreed, "Hope they aren't drunk as well." The four of them met the three weary travelers and offered them a drink, which none of them accepted. They all simply wanted to freshen up, relax a bit, and then get some sleep.

"That's fine," Adrian reassured them, "there's been plenty of alcohol flowing tonight already." Then, his voice nearly a whisper, "Half of the other guests have just passed out and had to be carried to their rooms!"

As the new guests laughed uncertainly, Jane rolled her eyes and slapped Adrian playfully on the shoulder. "There are only two other guests," she told the others. "Sorry to ruin your story, Adrian." Jane and Monica said good-night as

Adrian and Tom switched on their flashlights and showed the guests to their tents.

"Here's where our other guests are, in the first tent," Tom said, sending a beam of light quickly down the fork in the trail, just missing Richard and Toshika's tent as he and the others passed by. "Your tents are just a stone's throw further. But don't worry, you aren't close enough to bother each other." They continued carefully along the narrow trail while Victoria Miller asked if there really were no fences around the camp. Tom was ready for her, responding to the familiar question without a hint of boredom or irritation.

Having brushed their teeth, with Richard nearly taking a tumble down the steps into the bathroom below the tent, the two of them lay in bed quietly, each feeling the pull of sleep. The stars and moon shone across them, bathing them in their steely blue beams. The insects roared, never ceasing to amaze them. Such tiny things. The hippo snorted now and then in the river nearby whose lifeless body remained silent unless disturbed. As he threw open his eyes once more, fighting off sleep in the face of this still very curious world they were in, Richard spoke into the peak of the tent overhead.

"Toshika, what does love mean to you?" As the words escaped him he was surprised at himself. Where had that come from? And what to do about it now? He was about to attempt a cover-up, to tell her to just forget it, when she surprised him with her answer.

"Love," she said, leaving the word hanging. Her voice was small, her mind crowded with sleep. "Freedom."

Richard knew he had heard right, but could not believe his ears as he lay there on the bed next to the woman that he wanted to know still more about. The woman who never failed to amaze and surprise him. The woman that he loved, more, he knew, than anything else his life had to offer him. *Freedom!* The word rang in his ears. A smile crossed his face and he turned towards Toshika, gazing at her profile against the moonlight. He was about to rise up and kiss her. Then the question formed itself in his mind and he turned again to stare at the canopy above them.

404

"Toshika, do you feel free?"

At first, her silence threatened to send him crashing into misery. He felt his heart beating. Felt the weight on his chest as his breath became harder to draw in. And then the depth and regularity of Toshika's breathing fell over him, and he turned to see her lying there, mouth slightly open, smiling, he thought, as she fell deeper and deeper into sleep. He smiled, relieved. The question was still there, but he told himself he knew the answer, and he believed it. He turned on his side, away from her. Laying there he noticed that they had forgotten to zip the tent door closed. As quietly as he could manage, he rose and crossed the floor, fumbled with the zipper, and returned to bed. Just then he heard voices. Propping himself up on his elbow, he looked across the floor toward the trail. Through a small window on the front wall of the tent he could just make out the sweep of a flashlight beam. Footsteps, and Tom's voice, came and went. Nothing to worry about. He turned again, this time facing Toshika, and fell asleep watching her.

34

He reemerged gradually. The familiarity of the buzzing and ticking of the insects outside made him wonder if he had not dragged them with him from his sleep. As he acknowledged the impulse to open his eyes, he felt the pain in his head, an aching drone from deep inside. Another hangover. He opened his mouth, his tongue dry and stuck, and wondered how he could have done that to himself again. He opened his eyes and looked to his right, to Toshika's bed, the early morning light just beginning to show. As little as it was, the light was painful, forcing him to shut his eyes again. Just then he heard her cough once. "Oh, Toshika," he said, the images from a dream all but gone. "I had such a terrible dream. Are you all right?"

There was no answer. He raised his head and squinted in the dimness. Then he noticed his hands. They lay on top of his belly, tied together. He raised them up to see what it was that bound them: two large zip-ties, snug but not tight, encircled his wrists, one looped inside the other. "What the hell?" He looked again to his right. Toshika was not in her bed. He sat bolt upright with wide eyes, and saw them. Toshika sat on a chair near the door tying her boots, dressed and ready to go. Behind her stood David Norton, a large knife in his hand, its tip just inches from her neck. Richard got to his feet and then froze, as David reminded him with his eyes that he held Toshika's life in his hands.

"Good morning, Richard," David said mechanically, sounding like a doctor coming to have a chat with a worried patient.

At the sight of him, Richard stared blankly at Toshika who sat staring at nothing, avoiding his gaze. He looked at David again with hatred in his eyes. "You son of a bitch!"

David responded with equal violence as he brought the knife up into the air, sweeping it and pointing it, like a gun, directly at Richard, as his eyes opened wide. "Don't make another sound unless you want her dead," David said quietly. "Don't fuck with me now, Peel, I mean it." Richard stared at him open-mouthed, terrified for Toshika's safety. He wondered how it was that David was there in South Africa, how it was that he had found them. His eyes fell to the floor where he stared, dumbly.

"Come here, slowly." David told him. Richard stepped into the middle of the room and stopped as David raised the knife, pointing the tip of the blade at him again. David told Toshika to get up and unzip the door of the tent. She did so quietly, and then stood just inside the door, waiting for his next command. "Go outside and wait," he told Toshika. "You," he said, jabbing the knife in Richard's direction, "come here." Richard went to him and stood near the door looking out at Toshika. David took him by the arm and pressed the tip of the knife into his back between his ribs, forcing him out the door and onto the platform. As the sun rose, spilling light onto the camp, all was quiet except for the swishing sound of a stiff wind through the bush all around them. David pushed Richard in front of him and motioned for Toshika to come to him. As she did, he seized her by her ponytail and brought the tip of the knife to her throat. "See what I got here, Richard? Okay. Don't be stupid. We're going to walk to the Jeep, slowly. Don't either of you make a sound, got it? You first, Richard." They went up the pathway through the trees towards the main pathway. As they passed by the pool and the lounge, not a soul was seen. Moments later, they stood next to the camp's open Land Rover. "Toshika, get behind the wheel. Richard, you're going to sit next to her," David said, the tip of the knife escorting Richard into the car as he climbed up, and sat just behind them. He handed Toshika a key. "Turn the key until the steering wheel lock releases, then coast down the hill."

Toshika turned the key in the ignition and took the car out of gear. It immediately began to roll forward. She steered it past the sign of the lodge and down the hill, the dirt road stretching straight out before them. They were picking up speed quickly. "The brakes don't work," Toshika said with fear in her voice as they rolled over the first large lump in the road, sending a shudder through the heavy vehicle that forced all of them to grab onto something.

"Just keep it straight!" David commanded. "They'll work when you start the engine. We're almost at the bottom." One or two more heavy thumps hit them before they rolled on quietly, slowing steadily as the road flattened out. "When we stop rolling, start the engine," David said. Toshika did as she was told. The Land Rover was not as difficult to drive as she had expected. She found first gear, and then second, where she remained.

Richard worked at his hands, moving them against the plastic strips that held them fast, trying to find a weakness. He tried pure force when they hit rough spots in the road, but as simple as they looked, the strips were more than a match for him. With his fingers he could grab the locking tabs of the strips, but could not force them open or force the strips back through them. Soon he gave up, and stared blankly at the bush ahead. "Where are we going?" he asked, still looking straight ahead.

"Nowhere," came the reply. "Just drive," David called to Toshika.

Richard looked at her as she drove, her face long, but expressionless. He wanted to reach out to her, but with his hands tied together he could not do it without being seen. He looked ahead out over the landscape, not recognizing any of it. All was perfectly still as the day began, the heat of the sun already powerful, warming the side of his face. It was going to be another beautiful day. "Nowhere?" Richard cried, suddenly feeling a familiar anger with himself at their situation.

"This ain't your show any more, Peel, you got that? It's mine now." David's voice was angry when he spoke, but Richard could hear something more than just anger. There was frustration and pain underneath that anger. Would he be able to use this emotion to save himself, Richard thought, or was David more dangerous now than a man who was only angry?

David sat up straight, eyeing a fork in the road ahead. He told Toshika to slow down, and then to take the left fork as they came upon it. As they turned, the road ahead became less and less noticeable as it disappeared into the bush.

"Where should I go?" Toshika asked.

"Straight on, just straight on." They drove for a moment in silence before David began again to speak. "I'm in no mood to wait for the next game. This whole thing is over between you two." David looked at Toshika and frowned.

Richard did not understand. He stared at Toshika for an answer, but she had set her jaw and simply drove, refusing to look at or speak to him. "What are you talking about?" he asked David, turning sideways to look at him. He was surprised then to see how close David sat to them. Then he noticed the rifle across David Norton's lap. How he managed to get ahold of it, he could only guess. With the rifle in his possession, David Norton was in complete control.

From his elevated bench he looked down at Richard, his face twisted in contempt, looking as though he were about to spit on him. "Just what is it that you don't understand, boy?" David yelled. "Are you stupid on top of being a lucky son of a bitch?" His eyes narrowed as he searched Richard's face, burning into him, unloading his anger. Just when Richard thought he would shout at him again, David's eyes softened. "Holy Jesus! You don't know what this is about, do you?" he cried. "Hans never told you about the bet, did he?" Richard stared at him blankly. "Did he!" David hollered. He sat up and slapped the back of the seat next to him, a smile on his face that soon turned to laughter. "Toshika!" he cried. "Your boyfriend doesn't know who you are!"

Richard looked at Toshika open-mouthed and feeling completely lost at sea beside two strangers he thought he knew. Toshika looked at him, an expression of surprise on her face. "Didn't Hans tell you about me? About the bet?" she asked him. He said nothing. David laughed heartily, slapping his knee before putting his hand on Richard's head and tossing his hair around the way one does with a child. Toshika wiped her eyes and then laughed bitterly, shaking her head in disbelief. "No wonder," she said to herself.

"Well that really *tickles* me," David cried, almost feeling sorry for Richard. This stupid boy. "You thought this whole time that she just *liked* you! Oh my God." Suddenly David realized that he might not have any trouble at all stealing Toshika away from Richard once he knew the truth. He laughed again, happy to have life made simpler for himself at the last minute like this. He wondered why he had not seen it in Richard before. It certainly explained his behavior at the game.

"Listen Richard, and listen good," David began, as Richard stared straight ahead and steeled himself for whatever was to come. Toshika looked at David pleadingly for an instant before realizing that there was no stopping now. "Do you remember that little black chip that you had at the game? That chip should have had a big golden 'T' painted on it, because that chip was Toshika. That's right, my boy. Whoever won the chip won Toshika. You inherited that chip from Hans, who had won it for the first time and had been holding it for several games and refused to use it, even when he was losing. That's how it became yours. That's how *she* became yours. Do you get it? She gambled her body for the *thrill*. It excites her! Come on, Richard, you know her, running around, taking off her clothes every chance she gets."

"Stop it!" Toshika yelled. David just laughed, as his words echoed throughout Richard's hollow being, trying to find a resting place. The sunny, wrinkled landscape Richard saw as they rolled along did not care about his troubles. The sun would rise, shed its warmth, and set. It neither loved him nor hated him. That was simply how things were.

He was not sure if he saw right at first. He strained to see in the early morning light. Yes, there they were, a pride of lions up ahead on a small hilltop. The face of one of them was clear. Numerous patches of brown fur appeared amongst the bush and trees. It was impossible to know how many of them there were. Mechanically, he raised his arm, his finger pointing at them up ahead. Moments later Toshika saw them too. "Shit!" she cried, bringing the vehicle to a stop just fifty feet from them. "Lions!"

David looked ahead and saw them with a start. There must have been six or more of them in front of the car to the left. "Hey! I'll be damned!" he said. "Look at that." He watched them from his perch for a moment, absorbing their alien beauty. He looked at Richard, who simply stared at the lions as if he had not heard a word of anything David had said.

"We've seen plenty of it," Toshika said, wondering if she should shut the engine off.

"Well, Richard, I'm sure you won't mind now if I return home with hot pants here, now that the cat is out of the bag."

Toshika turned her head sharply and looked David in the eye. "Who says I'm going with *you*?" The intensity of David's gaze frightened her for an instant, forcing her to turn around again. She looked at a proud female lion up ahead as she stood up and looked in their direction, the grass waving to her in the breeze as two of her cubs rolled playfully at her feet, out of sight. "I'm finished with the game, anyway."

That was the last straw for David. The audacity of Toshika's declaration struck him like a foul stench, forcing him to consider how unjust it was. After all, he had been reasonable, hadn't he? He had given them time, had made it clear that they should do themselves a favor and return to play out the game. He had given them every chance. But this was too much, after all he had been through. Too much.

"Finished with the game?" he asked, barely able to contain himself. Richard winced at the sheer volume of his speech, watching carefully the reaction of the lions. The lioness, still watching them, closed her mouth and flicked her tail. "Who the fuck do you think you're *talking* to, Miss 'Hey I've got an idea, let's kill Hans?' " David bellowed at Toshika.

"That's not true!" she yelled.

Richard looked at Toshika, her hands gripping the wheel, looking cornered. He shook his head slowly. He saw Hans again at the St. Francis, saw how his face lit up when he saw Toshika. It could not be true. He knew her better than that.

"Are you crazy?" Toshika asked David, this time returning the anger that had been showered on her.

"No, I'm not crazy, *you* are!" he cried. "You just *blew* it! You just blew the whole freaking thing out of the water!" David looked at Richard, feeling an avalanche thundering through him as he made up his mind. "Yeah, that's right, Richard. Here's your *Toshika*."

"Stop!" Toshika cried, tears streaming down her face. "Richard, I made a stupid joke once but I swear to you I didn't have anything to do with Hans' murder. That's just crazy. I would never want to see him dead. Especially not for a stupid game!"

"Not for the poker game, for *your* game!" David cried. He turned to Richard. "Hans kept Toshika out of the game for a year! Not that he was enjoying her the way the rest of us were, of course."

"Of *course* not" Toshika said to him, "He was *gay*, you idiot!"

"Oh yeah, that's what *I* used to think too. But there's *another* reason. He never told you about that. Neither did your mother, did she?"

"What?" Toshika asked him. "My mother?"

"Yeah," David said, "He kept his *promise* to her, didn't he?" He looked at Richard and continued. "He didn't approve of her part in the game, a part that came along long after he had started the game years ago. But of course he couldn't tell Toshika what to *do*. *Nobody* tells Toshika what to do, right baby?" he spat. He remembered the knife in his hand and brought it swiftly to the back of her neck. "Isn't that right? When it came to giving back the chip, you wouldn't support me. After all the complaining I had to listen to from you, you *abandoned* me!"

"So it was you? *You* killed Hans?" Richard asked, keeping his eye on David, fighting his impulses to act in the presence of both the gun and the lions.

David shook his head. "No," he said. "It wasn't like that."

"Sure it wasn't," Toshika said. Richard looked at her, but it was not her face he saw. He had never seen her with such a look of hatred before.

"You think I'm a *killer*?" David stood up and looked down at Toshika. "Is *that* what you think of me?" He reached down and took hold of Toshika's hair and pulled until she sat upright as far as she could.

"Oww! What did you mean?" Toshika asked him, her voice breaking. "What did you mean about my mother?" But David ignored her. He was hysterical. He held Toshika's hair in one hand and brought his nose to it, taking in the softness that had brought him to such extremes. Feeling Richard's stare, he turned to him.

"And why did I get so involved?" he asked Richard, pointing to his chest and tapping a spot there with the tip of the knife. "You know why. You of all people know why." Richard was shocked as David's gaze fell, his chin quivering.

"You can't just *force* someone to love you," Richard told him. "That's not the way it works."

David looked at him then, and for a moment Richard thought that it might be the end. That the whole scene might be brought to a close now. David brought a hand to his face and rubbed gently, at first in a slow circle, then more vigorously. "Oh, God! I haven't had enough *sleep*," he said to no one, as his composure slipped further. "Turn off the car," he told Toshika, releasing her hair. He rubbed his eyes and looked into the sky, breathing deeply against his fatigue. And then the memory hit him. Why then, at that moment, he didn't know. He saw her, Margie Clarkson, at the bar in San Francisco. He saw her face again. But now, he felt no anger. He did not feel the pain of failure. The humiliation. The hopelessness he had felt so many times before. Instead, he saw the whole episode as proof. If he could be worthy of her, there were surely many other women he could be with. He began trying to ascertain what it was about that event that had made it a success. What was the trick? The evening's events flashed through his mind in an instant. A moment later, he thought he knew the answer to his question.

He looked down at Toshika. He saw the fear in her eyes and felt words getting caught in his throat as he gestured to her not to be afraid. He looked at the knife in his hand and dropped it on the seat as though it had just bit him. He closed his eyes and smiled again, and before he knew it he was laughing. He looked at Toshika and Richard and shook his head. "I'm sorry, really. I'm... forget it. Forget about the whole thing." He stepped up behind the back of the seat and onto the back edge of the Land Rover, holding his arms aloft. "I can do this!" he cried. He jumped up and down and laughed.

Toshika turned and looked to where the lions had been, and looked at Richard. She could see it in his face. The same thought.

"No!" Richard cried, resisting the urge to stand up and shout at David. "Stop it! The lions!"

Toshika turned again and took a hold of David Norton's shorts just above the knee, pulling. "David!" she cried.

414

Richard heard the rapid thudding of feet on the earth coming from behind him and froze, his eyes drawing closed as a bolt of fear tore through him. David Norton did not see the lioness coming. None of them did. She was protecting her young. She did not kill out of hunger, or hatred, but out of fear for her dear ones. She acted as any mother or father would. She emerged from the bush like an arrow, her eyes locked onto her target as they had been hundreds of times before, as she moved with precision and purpose. She leapt easily above the height of the vehicle and took the offender down with her, swiftly, almost silently, ending the disturbance and ensuring the safety of her cubs.

Richard and Toshika could not help but watch the lion clamp her jaws around David Norton's neck as he struggled on the ground, the lioness on top of him. Suddenly another lioness, and then another behind that one arrived on the scene, each taking hold of part of the prize in their powerful jaws. In just seconds, it was over. David lay lifeless, face down, his neck at an impossible angle. Richard noticed that there was surprisingly little blood, making it all seem less real.

Toshika gasped and fell backwards, collapsing into the footwell of the passenger seat. Richard reached behind the seat to where David Norton had been and lifted the rifle from the floor of the truck. Struggling with the heavy gun, his hands still linked together, he managed to fire once into the air. The noise was devastatingly loud and seemed to threaten all of existence. The lions were jolted into action and scattered, stopping only when they were at a safe distance and turning to look back, tails flicking in the dry heat of the morning. Richard put the rifle down. Toshika sat cowering in the footwell, her hands over her eyes as she attempted to flee inside herself. Richard picked up David's knife and managed to cut one of the bands from his wrist. He got the Land Rover moving and did not look back. He drove mechanically through the bush, trying to point them in the direction of the camp, only remotely hearing the sound of the crunching engine or the squeaking of the suspension over the buzz in his mind. As the Land Rover rocked and groaned, rounding up over the edge of a dry riverbed, he glanced at

Toshika. At the sight of her he felt his heart fly up, oblivious to the doubt he now felt.

Finally he saw the road ahead that would bring them back to the camp. He turned the Land Rover to meet it, driving directly towards the sun. He looked at Toshika as she sat on the floor of the car, her shocked expression almost too much for him to bear. He reached out to her. Finally seeing his hand, she took it and got up onto the seat beside him. Putting her arms around him she began to weep. He stopped the truck and held on to her. "Toshika, I'm so sorry about Hans."

Soon they continued on. Up ahead Richard saw the camp on the horizon. A police truck was parked outside. The rangers stood amongst police officers. Someone scanned the bush with binoculars. A hand went up, then pointed in the direction of the oncoming Land Rover. Was it Tom? At that distance, Richard could not be sure. He held up his hand to them, a signal that it was all over.

www.ingramcontent.com/pod-product-compliance
Lightning Source LLC
Chambersburg PA
CBHW051514250626
47156CB00001B/92